About the author

Orna O'Reilly grew up in Ireland and practiced interior design for many years, both at home and abroad. She moved to Italy in 2013 to begin writing full time. Her award-winning blog, *Orna O'Reilly: Travelling Italy*, was begun while she was living close to Venice, from where she drew inspiration for her first work of fiction, *The Blonde in The Gondola*. Orna has been a contributing writer for magazines for several years and is now enjoying life among the olive groves of Puglia, in south eastern Italy, with her husband, Tom.

You can follow Orna's blog on www.ornaoreilly.com

Facebook: https://www.facebook.com/orna.oreilly

Twitter: https://twitter.com/OrnaOR

THE BLONDE IN THE GONDOLA

Orna O'Reilly

THE BLONDE IN THE GONDOLA

Vanguard Press

VANGUARD PAPERBACK

A CIP catalogue record for this title is
available from the British Library.

ISBN 9781784656478

*Vanguard Press is an imprint of
Pegasus Elliot MacKenzie Publishers Ltd.*
www.pegasuspublishers.com

First Published in 2019

**Vanguard Press
Sheraton House Castle Park
Cambridge England**
Printed & Bound in Great Britain

Dedication

For Tom

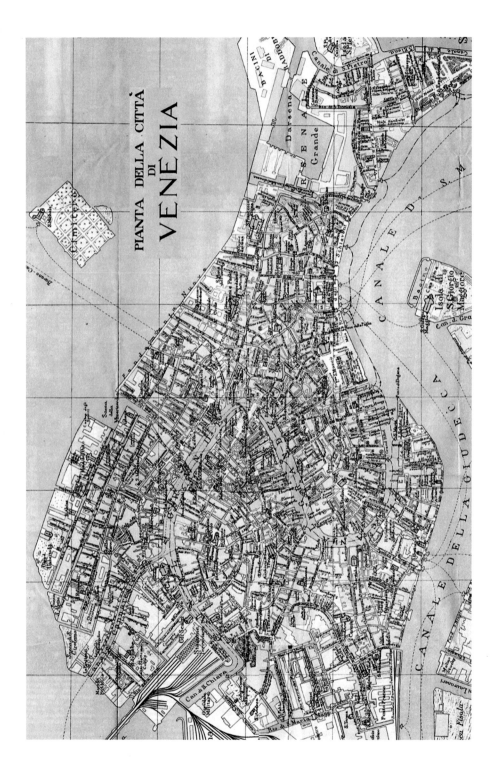

PIANTA · DELLA · CITTÀ
DI
VENEZIA

Prologue

Her flight to Venice would be boarding in an hour. Olivia carried her espresso to one of the tables beside the window and watched the dawn breaking over Dublin Airport. She was pensive, aware of how life-changing this journey would be. As she looked out at the distinctive shamrocks on the tails of the Aer Lingus fleet parked at the departure gates, many attached to the huge, modern building by air-bridges, she thought about Steve and wondered where he was now. It was a misty November morning and Dublin looked grey and cold. A few icy drops spattered against the window as she tossed back her coffee. But Ireland was home, she told herself. She would be back.

Around her, everyone seemed to be enjoying the idea of an early-morning departure. A few tables away, a hen party was gearing up for a few days abroad, with the bride-to-be wearing a small veil over her pink sweater and track-suit bottoms. All the giggling girls, with bobbing pink pompoms on satin hairbands, were already downing cider or beer while screaming with raucous laughter and apparently oblivious to the fact that it was barely 6am. Olivia looked at them and idly wondered how long it had been since she had been able to relax and enjoy herself like that.

At another table a middle-aged couple, huddled together in expensive-looking cashmere coats, were silently sipping large brandies. Perhaps they were nervous fliers, she mused, or out of their time zone. Elsewhere, a group of loud young men gulped pints of Guinness and eyed the girls. A holiday atmosphere prevailed, but not for Olivia, who touched her briefcase for reassurance as she pushed back her chair and headed for the departure gate.

She was moving to Venice. This was her opportunity to begin again, and she was grasping it with both hands.

CHAPTER ONE

The old fisherman tried to ease the pain in his back. The waters of the Venetian Lagoon were showing the first glimmer of light as the sun rose. He could almost taste that first cup of coffee that Luigi would prepare just as soon as he pulled in his catch and brought it ashore. Impatiently, he shuffled his arthritic frame over to the side of the boat. At first, he thought the swirling tendrils were seaweed. Just below the surface things looked different somehow, but he was unsure; his eyes weren't what they used to be. He tugged on the nets, but they seemed heavier than usual. He craned his neck to take a closer look to see what he had caught.

The shock of what he saw made him fall backwards into the boat, hurting his shoulder. He pulled himself upright again with difficulty and peered carefully over the side. He had not been mistaken. Long blonde hair was floating on the dark waters of the lagoon, and what made matters worse was the fact that it was attached to a body.

EIGHTEEN MONTHS PREVIOUSLY
OLIVIA

Before the disasters began to mount up, people described Olivia Farrell-Lynskey as good looking. Stunning, in fact. But they also said she was conceited and difficult; a woman used to getting her own way, no matter whose toes she stepped on. Undoubtedly ambitious; a beautiful and wilful woman indeed: she stepped on plenty as she strode through the first easy part of her life, which was to come crashing down so abruptly.

On this mild morning in May, unaware of how her life was about to spiral out of control, Olivia rolled over in bed and opened her eyes. The soft sound of the shower running in the en suite was soothing and she listened to her husband going through his morning ritual, the shower being turned off and Steve's tuneless humming as he began to shave.

'Morning, Liv,' he greeted her briskly, emerging from the bathroom, a white towel around his elegant waist; dark, wet hair standing on end. She admired his tanned and toned torso through half-open eyes. Their home gym was obviously working; now, if he could only give up those awful cigars, she thought lazily

'Morning, Steve.' She stretched luxuriantly on the white linen sheets, nestling among the mountain of feather pillows. She was tired after her thirty-fifth birthday celebration the previous night at Dublin's most expensive and prestigious restaurant.

Sounds of slamming drawers and cupboard doors accompanied an imperious demand. 'My yellow silk tie and matching handkerchief?' A brief pause and more crashing noises.

'I'll expect you home on Friday, then?' she added, indifferent to his early-morning moodiness 'We're expected at the Finns for dinner. Please try not to be too late. You know how much Penelope hates it.'

'That woman is a piece of work,' snarled Steve, emerging briefly into the bedroom, almost dressed this time, his tie mid-knot and his collar standing on end. His blue eyes were cold; a familiar look after eleven years of marriage. 'I'll be back as early as possible. I'm not letting that woman dictate my business hours.' He strode back into the dressing room, flinging the words over his shoulder. 'And I don't care if you tell her what I said.'

Olivia sighed deeply and studied her immaculately manicured nails. Perhaps she should have gone for a deeper shade of purple polish. 'Tell John to start the car,' came the commanding voice from the dressing room. 'It'll be cold after last night's rain. I want to feel warm this morning.'

Olivia picked up the phone which connected with the kitchen.

'Claire. Please ask John to prepare Mr Lynskey's car. He'll be leaving in about ten minutes. Tell him to warm the seat. Thanks. Yes, muesli, please, in bed. A late start today.' Claire's wonderful homemade Bircher muesli was made to the original Swiss recipe and just the way Olivia liked it.

Steve strolled into the bedroom, his straight black hair neatly combed, and the yellow silk tie and handkerchief combination looked well with his dark grey suit and snowy shirt. At 6ft 4in, he was a handsome man, and he knew it. He shot back one immaculate shirt-cuff and glanced at the gold Rolex, his pride and joy, presented to him by the yacht club in recognition of his many years of unpaid fund-raising work on their behalf.

'Got to go. Can't be late. We have a 9.30 slot out of Dublin to get us to Madrid. See you on Friday.' He leaned over the bed and gave Olivia a quick kiss on the forehead. She snuggled down once more. Steve's high-flying career largely funded their lavish lifestyle, so she was well able to tolerate these brisk dashes to the airport and endless shouting on his mobile.

Aware that he was still standing by the bed, she looked up and caught a strange expression on his face. Sadness? Guilt? She could not be sure.

'Steve?' But he was gone. Just the smell of his cologne lingered, and she lay back again, drowsy and relaxed, but slightly puzzled about her husband's expression as he left.

A gentle tap on the door was followed by her breakfast tray, being carried by Claire, which was carefully placed on the bed beside Olivia.

'Would you like me to run a bath for you, Mrs Lynskey?' she asked in her gentle Galway accent, bustling into the bathroom to pick up Steve's carelessly discarded towels and doing a quick tidy-up.

Olivia poured herself a cup of strong, black coffee.

Relaxing against her pillows, Olivia listened to the sound of water splashing into her tub and thought about the day ahead. Considerations as to whether she should wear her hair up or down for the photo-shoot idled through her mind. She was pretty sure she'd look great whatever way she wore it. Claire let herself out of the room quietly, carrying Steve's towels downstairs to the laundry room.

It was unusual to find Olivia in her bedroom at this hour and she revelled in the peace of her Georgian home, set in the leafy suburbs of south Dublin. She looked out through the window; being May, the garden was looking good. The manicured lawn displayed a satisfying balance of light and dark green stripes, about which she regularly obsessed. The flower borders were neat, with yellow roses making a sunny splash and the tall bank of daisies were all staring hopefully in the direction of the sun. Cardistown House had been an excellent purchase, and the property was an ongoing project into which she and Steve had lavished their attention.

Still glowing from her bath, she wrapped her cream silk robe around her and sank onto the deep, comfortable window seat, studying the garden spread before her. Yes, Jim, the gardener and handyman, had been a great find. Whatever would they do without him? The little wooden trellised arbour at the far end of the lawn looked inviting; summer evenings had often seen her there with her book, cosily seated on her favourite soft linen cushions. Maybe this weekend… She moved her gaze to the magazines fanned out on the window seat and noted their covers with satisfaction.

"Olivia Farrell-Lynskey, interior designer to the stars," blazed *Celebrity* magazine. "Farrell-Lynskey does it again!" shouted the cover of *Star Homes*. The undisputed number one interior designer in Ireland. A big fish in a small pond, she thought, smiling to herself and patting her blonde hair happily. That latest nightclub design project had got her lots of publicity, and that was what she needed to keep her business at the top of the pile.

Her Italian mother, in true Italian style, as far as Olivia was concerned, had reluctantly given up asking Olivia when she was going to provide her with grandchildren. She and Steve had postponed their family plans until their finances were secure enough, and then they just never quite got around to exploring the concept of parenthood. They enjoyed the life they had made together and, to be quite honest, she struggled with the idea of Steve and herself as being really suitable for such a role.

Apart from Cardistown House, they spent quite a bit of time on their smart yacht, currently moored a few kilometres away in Dun Laoghaire Harbour, where Steve liked to spend Sundays "messing about", as Olivia referred to his ongoing hobby of maintaining his boat and having a few beers with his boating pals. Hanging on to this lifestyle required a lot of dedication, to such a degree that they both felt — without ever actually mentioning it — that having children would require far too many sacrifices. She was aware that some of their friends looked on them as being selfish, but she cared nothing for their opinions. It was her life, and she would live it exactly as she pleased.

Her peace was suddenly shattered when her mobile phone began to ring.

'Fiona? I asked you to field all calls this morning.' She had been relishing her brief period of solitude.

'Sorry, Olivia.' Fiona's voice was calm. She was well used to the ways of her demanding boss and her calmness was, in fact, her best attribute as PA to "*interior designer to the stars*". '*High Design* magazine wants to organise a photo-shoot with you at home. They want to know today. What shall I tell them?'

'Really, Fiona, you know very well that this is what I've been after for weeks. Just ask them when they want me to do it.'

Fiona was silent for a moment.

'Is there something else, Fi?' Her tone became more conciliatory. 'You don't sound too cheery right now.'

'Well…' Fiona demurred. 'That contract for Hotel Newtown has been cancelled this morning; they just rang and said they wouldn't be signing the contract. And Anne Jenkins rang in just now to say she won't be going ahead, either.'

'What? I thought both those jobs were in the bag.'

'Hotel Newtown says their accountant won't allow them to get their renovation done until next year, and Anne Jenkins said she wants to wait a few months. I can't explain it, other than that the newspapers and radio are full of predictions of an impending recession. It's doom and gloom out there.'

'Oh, for heaven's sake! Who pays attention to the ridiculous carry-on of the media? I'll deal with this when I get in later.'

She hung up without waiting for a response and flung the phone on the bed. Her suit carrier was already hanging in readiness for the evening's shoot in Hotel Orologio.

In the mirror Olivia checked herself for flaws and found none. She admired her long shapely legs, still lightly tanned from her last visit to San Remo in Italy and selected a pair of tan leather ankle boots with medium heels, just in case the house she was to visit was in any disrepair. Her perfect olive skin and luminous sea-green eyes — a legacy, along with her voluptuous figure, from her Italian mother — stared back from the mirror, which, together with her mane of thick blonde hair, gave her an exotic beauty of which she was entirely aware.

Everything was perfect. But that was only Wednesday.

CHAPTER TWO
JANE

It was a beautiful day in Venice. The early-morning sun sparkled on the waters of the lagoon, as Jane and Sofia prepared for their annual summer visit to the family villa in the Euganean Hills, just an hour's drive south of the famous old city. The Hills were far enough away from the summer heat and influx of tourists which invade Venice in July and August, yet close enough to be able to pop back for the odd social visit, should the occasion arise. Sofia finished cramming her clothing into her big leather suitcase and pulled the lid down, sitting on it to try to close it. Without success. Maria, their housekeeper, bustled in and wrestled it closed, tut-tutting as she struggled with the old-fashioned locks.

'My goodness, Sofia!' she exclaimed, as she tried to lift it. 'What have you got in there? An anvil?' She laughed, her bosom heaving with merriment.

'Books!' giggled Sofia. 'Lots of books for the summer.' She grinned, showing off new braces on her front teeth. 'I have the entire five-book *Twilight Saga* with me, and I just want to sit on the terrace in The Hills and read and read for two whole months.'

She dashed into her pink and blue bathroom to collect her sponge-bag and crammed it into her hand luggage. This bathroom, with its blue floor tiles and blue and pink diamond-shaped wall tiles, had been a creation of her mother's, right down to the pink sanitary-ware. Well aware that it looked dated, Jane had, nevertheless, tried to recreate the bathroom of her teenage years in England for her daughter; but, in the huge Venetian palazzo, it looked very out of place. Regardless of the dictates of bathroom fashion, Sofia loved it. It was her second favourite room in the palazzo after her bedroom, which was also pink and ultra-feminine.

Helping Maria to drag her heavy suitcase out of her bedroom and down the corridor, across the priceless, original terrazzo floor of the huge living area that made up most of the *piano nobile*, or main floor of the palazzo, she called out to her mother.

'Mum! I'm ready to go!'

Contessa Jane di Falco raised her head from her journal and put down her pen, sighing deeply. She should be looking forward to this trip to Galzignano Terme with her beloved daughter, but the truth was she was anxious to see Niccolo. He had been in Ireland for more than two weeks, and she wondered when he planned to return from his supposed business trip. Once again, she wondered if he had taken a mistress, as was the custom with so many Italian men of their acquaintance. Or perhaps his annoying sister was pressing him to stay. But in her heart of hearts, she knew his long absence and recent lack of communication were indications that their marriage had lost its original closeness.

The gardens at Villa di Falco were his pride and joy, and this was where he always retreated when he wanted to be alone to tend to his precious garden. Perhaps he would arrive while she and Sofia were there, and they could talk.

Yes, she had been drinking too much. Yes, Niccolo had been angry with her when she fell asleep on her bed during their last dinner party before the guests had left; she had just planned to close her eyes for a few minutes after a visit to the bathroom. No, she hadn't gone to seek help, as he had insisted before he left. No, she hadn't been to see the doctor about her insomnia, preferring to self-medicate, so to speak, with a few tots of grappa before bedtime, which left her feeling less than energetic in the mornings. Yes, her father, Lord Remington, was an alcoholic, who liked to access his private stash of alcohol and binge drink himself into a comatose state whenever her step-mother was out of the house for more than a few hours. Yes, she knew it was a hereditary condition, and yes, she knew she was ruining her health.

But loneliness did odd things to people, and she knew she wasn't strong-willed. Niccolo was gone most of the time, designing fabulous

Italianate gardens all over the world. He felt her place was here in Venice in the ivory tower that consisted of his palazzo on the Grand Canal. She knew her position appeared perfect to outsiders. But she missed the closeness that she and Niccolo had once shared. When had things begun to go wrong? She couldn't pinpoint the exact moment.

Her son Max, from her first marriage to Geoffrey, which had been acted out in the leafy countryside of Sussex south of London, would be coming over to join her and Sofia in Galzignano next week. That was something to look forward to for sure. It was a pity he didn't have a better relationship with Niccolo, his step-father. Perhaps that was why her husband was in no hurry to return. Two weeks of Max's company was something he wouldn't relish and never had. Max had been ten years old when Jane had married Niccolo; an age when he was already feeling protective of his mother and saw Niccolo as a rival for her affection. Jane would have imagined that fifteen years would have been more than enough time for the two men in her life to establish a friendly relationship, but so far it had not happened, with Max constantly surly in the presence of Niccolo, and Niccolo abrasively defensive whenever Max was around.

Jane, or Lady Jane as she was known in England as the daughter of an earl, was a blonde, beautiful forty-three-year-old woman. Some would consider her fairly colourless, perhaps translucent, with her pale, and lightly freckled skin and almost invisible eyebrows. Naturally slender and small-boned, she gave the appearance of being tall and willowy, though Niccolo towered over her at more than 6ft.

She looked at the photos on the shelf over her desk. Niccolo, Max and Sofia; her family smiled back at her from their frames. She needed to see them smiling at her now.

As though in answer, Sofia's smiling face appeared around the door.

'Mum!' She peered quizzically at Jane. 'Are you coming? I thought you asked Marco to be here at 11.00am? It's five to already.' She added: 'My bag is already out beside the lift. I'm ready to roll!'

With that, she erupted from behind the door. 'Ta-da!' She threw her arms in the air. Jane couldn't help but smile. Sofia was wearing her bright pink "Ciao Bella" T-shirt over a pair of outrageously colourful floral leggings and her favourite Converse canvas sneakers.

'Look at you!' Jane exclaimed delightedly, her pensive mood suddenly evaporating. She rose from her desk and greeted her daughter with a hug. 'Let's get this show on the road.'

As she rose to leave her study high over the Grand Canal, where the gondolas flitted past below on the shining water, she paused for a moment uncertainly, then opened a cupboard to remove a small bottle of grappa, which she placed carefully in her capacious shoulder bag.

At that decisive moment, Jane was unaware that she had made what was to prove one of the greatest mistakes of her life, which would have consequences of which she could never have dreamed. She called 'Coming, darling!' as she took a last look around and headed for the entrance hall.

Sofia hurried ahead to the little wooden lift which daily transported its occupants down from the first-floor *piano nobile* of their palazzo, to where their boat was moored. Maria dragged and lifted the suitcases into the wrought-iron luggage rack in the lift and waved them goodbye, giving a special hug to Sofia. Marco, their boatman, was waiting to escort them down the final flight of stone steps, where they emerged into the gloom of the lower floor. He carried their suitcases through the tall studded doors onto a wooden jetty, to the gleaming boat which bobbed up and down on the pale green water of the Grand Canal.

Marco gave both of them his hand and helped them on board. Sofia cupped her hand over her eyes as the boat cast off, and she looked up at the façade of their palazzo. At that moment, one of the tall windows on the *piano nobile* opened and Maria stepped out onto the terrace to wave goodbye again, her small figure in its blue uniform framed by the ornate, bottle-ended glass of the tall window behind her.

The boatman wove through the busy waterway, skilfully avoiding gondolas packed with camera-wielding tourists, on the way to Tronchetto, where they began to unload their luggage from the motor launch. He heaped the suitcases onto a trolley and wheeled it to the nearby car-park, into the lift and up to the fifth floor, where Jane's trusty vintage Austin Healy sports-car was parked. Removing the dust cover, Jane looked at her old car with affection: not often driven these days, but red, shining and ready to go; she loved that old car. In fact, she had taken it to vintage-car rallies all over Europe for a few years before she had met and married Niccolo. Now, living in Venice meant that she rarely drove, but went everywhere by boat and on foot, like all Venetians. But she always relished the opportunity to get behind the wheel.

Marco helped Jane and Sofia to stow their suitcases in the smallish boot and behind the seats. Finally, he waved goodbye and stood watching for a moment, before strolling back into the hot summer sun, his mind now fully focused on the next task at hand: that vitally important matter of meeting some friends for a coffee.

Jane turned over the ignition and the car roared to life. She had put the hood down so they could feel the early summer breezes as they travelled to their villa in the rich countryside of the Euganean Hills, or Colli Euganei as it was called in Italian. The car was responsive and a joy to drive. What a sweet feeling it was to be behind the wheel again! As they headed out over the long bridge from the island of Venice to the Italian mainland, Sofia turned around to see the city recede behind them and looked out over the lagoon. Full of little boats and the occasional vaporetto, and dotted with tall wooden pylons, it was a glistening hive, bathed in the golden morning light. Sofia took what was to be her last, lingering look at the city of her birth.

'We'll be at the villa well before lunch.' Jane chatted as she drove. 'You can get started on all those books this afternoon. Won't that be bliss, darling?' She admired her daughter's pale beauty and her long blonde hair, which sailed behind her in the sunshine like a golden flag.

Sofia paused. 'When is Max coming to stay?' she asked her mother, her handsome half-brother never far from her mind.

'Next week.' As Jane joined the busy A4 Venice-Milan autostrada, she added, 'He's hoping to get away from London for a couple of weeks. It'll be great to see him.'

Suddenly, distracted slightly, she noticed the sign for her exit towards Bologna coming up and began to veer to the right. A truck honked warningly, and she tried to see it in her rear-view mirror, but Sofia's suitcase was blocking her view.

'And Papa?' Sofia fiddled with the buttons of her denim jacket and tried to look nonchalant. 'Will he come; do you think?'

'Oh, darling!' exclaimed Jane. 'Not now!' She turned towards her daughter uncertainly. 'I hope he turns up. You know that. We'll have to see... He's just so busy at the moment.'

In that split second between life and death, Jane reached out to clasp Sofia's hand reassuringly as the impact tore through them. Screaming, agony and confusion. She felt the little hand abruptly wrenched from hers and her beloved daughter was gone.

***

Two days later, Jane opened her eyes. Everything was a white, shining haze. A blurred face appeared above her.

'She's awake. Call the doctor immediately.'

Jumbled recollections assailed her. Sofia!

'Sofia. Sofia! Where is she?' Jane's voice was a whisper, but the face above hers suddenly stilled and a firm hand grasped her shoulder.

'The doctor is coming now. He'll answer all your questions.' The nurse's white cap seemed to shimmer as Jane tried to focus on the face above hers. 'Try to relax.'

'My daughter!' whispered Jane, her voice gaining strength, pushed on by a rising feeling of hysteria. 'Is Sofia all right? Please tell me!'

'Doctor!' exclaimed the nurse to another presence in the room. 'The Contessa is asking for her daughter. Sofia.' The nurse's voice dropped almost to a whisper as she mentioned the girl's name.

The doctor's face came into view. A slightly chubby face with warm brown eyes studied her carefully.

'Contessa,' he said gently, 'I'm going to give you something to make you relax now. Your husband, the conte, will be here shortly.'

'But Sofia!' Jane's voice was beginning to rise towards hysteria as she felt the tiny pricking sensation in her arm, followed by a feeling of warmth. 'My daughter...' She trailed off and lapsed into a drugged sleep.

The doctor looked at the nurse. Both their faces showed the strain of the past couple of difficult days. 'Let me know if she shows any sign of waking up before the conte arrives.'

Jane slept deeply for more than three hours and began to moan softly in her semi-conscious state. Eventually, her eyes opened again to see the dark, handsome features of her husband looking down at her.

'Nico,' she moaned. 'Nico. Tell me about Sofia. Please. Is she all right? Was she hurt? I think we were in an accident. I can't remember anything much at all... Is Sofia all right...?' Her words trailed off as she saw the look on her husband's face.

The conte took one of her hands in both of his and perched on the side of the bed. His hair was tousled, and his shirt was creased. His deep blue eyes were red-rimmed and shimmered with unshed tears.

'Sofia is no longer with us, Jane.' The words were spoken sadly, with a shakiness in his voice that made him sound unfamiliar to her. 'She lost consciousness instantly and, I have been assured, would have known nothing. No pain.'

Jane felt the shock ricochet through her body, taking her breath away. She felt completely numb.

'Your injuries are minor, my dear. Apart from your concussion, you have a broken collar-bone and some cuts and bruises.' Niccolo's voice sounded empty to Jane, almost disinterested. 'You'll be up and around in a few days.'

'Where is Sofia? I need to see her.' Suddenly, Jane felt an urgent need to check that her daughter was indeed dead. 'Are they sure it's her? Have they checked?' Hysteria was threatening to overtake her. 'Niccolo,' she sobbed. 'Have you seen her? Is it really our precious baby? Is she really gone?'

'I'm sorry, Jane. But yes. It's our little girl. There's no doubt whatsoever. I was with her when she passed." He drew in a sharp breath and Jane thought he was going to cry. But he turned two very bright blue eyes towards her; eyes full of tragedy and, Jane felt with an icy feeling in her gut, held more than a mere hint of accusation.

But what was without a doubt, was that her beloved daughter was dead.

CHAPTER THREE
OLIVIA

Olivia gunned her sports Merc through the leafy south Dublin side streets on her way to visit her new client. She had checked that all her equipment was on board: 10-metre measuring tape; colour swatches; laptop and camera. Ready for action.

She thought briefly about Steve. He'd be in Madrid by now, she estimated, in his gleaming private jet. A true Celtic Tiger acquisition. What a success he had made of his finance business! Right now, he was contemplating the purchase of a fabulous villa near San Remo, their favourite holiday destination, that prestigious piece of Mediterranean coastline in northern Italy close to the French border, and this was to be the cherry on the top of Olivia's very large and elaborately iced cake.

'Best climate in Europe,' she opined out loud, as she shifted down into third gear in order to navigate a sharp bend.

Olivia thought ahead to her new client. As usual, being a residential project, she would be dealing with a woman, Francesca Butler. From the tone of the enquiry that had arrived in her inbox the previous week, it seemed that a complete refurbishment of a country Georgian home was on the cards. Olivia loved commissions for luxury interior design projects. They were the high earners: all those designer fabrics, wall-coverings and furniture with high profit-margins were the things that kept her business afloat.

Well-heeled housewives clamoured for her attention, being aware that she had had a great deal of exposure to the homes of the rich and famous. Not only that, but she had the qualifications and imagination to recreate these fabulous homes for them, the housewives of Dublin's leafy suburbs. A lucrative business indeed!

Commercial work was far less profitable for the amount of time you had to spend, though it was usually more high-profile, so well worth the effort if the project was large enough.

She checked her sat-nav. Or rather, paid attention to the dulcet, but firm, tones of the sat-nav lady, who instructed her to turn right after two hundred metres. This she did, and found herself turning into a long driveway, whose electric gates were already open in readiness for her visit.

The house was lovely. 'Mellow,' said Olivia to herself, as she brought the car to a crunching halt on the gravel outside the front door. Virginia creeper grew over the wide front façade and drooped over the rich red Georgian door, which was flanked by two tall and beautifully proportioned windows on either side.

Before Olivia had time to ring the bell, the door opened and a tall, dark woman with striking violet eyes, whom Olivia guessed to be in her early forties, stood there smiling a greeting. Clad in what, Olivia calculated immediately, was a well-known Italian designer's skirt and blouse, she pulled the door open fully.

'Good morning,' she said, with an indefinable accent giving richness to her voice. 'I'm Francesca. You must be Olivia. Welcome to my home. Please come in.'

'Francesca!' Olivia exclaimed in surprise. 'I hadn't realised... hadn't known it was you.'

The elegant lady laughed softly.

'Ah, yes. We were never really introduced, though we have met several times at the Italian Institute. What was that last event we attended? Can you remember?'

'I think it must have been the Italian Poetry Evening back in February.' Olivia was recollecting the last time she had been there. How she had enjoyed these entertaining events here in Dublin; the women smartly dressed and many chatting in Italian, in which Olivia was completely fluent, as Italian was the language of her mother and spoken at home a great deal during her childhood.

Francesca's hand was cool and soft as she took Olivia's affectionately and drew her into the large, bright entrance hall. An air of opulence rested on the interior of the house. As exotic as the owner's accent, Olivia thought, doing her usual mental assessment.

Francesca led the way to a large sitting room with two windows looking out over the front driveway, where Olivia's gleaming black Merc was parked. A third window with a view of an immaculate tennis court faced the door. Olivia settled herself elegantly in a buttermilk-coloured linen-upholstered armchair close to the end window and surveyed the room for first impressions.

The room was beautifully proportioned, with egg and dart cornicing, plus an ornate ceiling rose, from which hung an enormous chandelier.

'Murano. Hand-blown glass.' Olivia immediately recognised it as being exotically Venetian. 'Straight from the island of Murano in the Venetian Lagoon,' she mused, admiring it in all its splendour.

A huge antique Persian carpet adorned the floor, around which glossy oak floorboards were visible. The fireplace was typically Georgian, in white marble, and looked original. Over the mantelpiece hung a fabulous gilded mirror of perfect proportions, while chintz curtains with a pale-yellow background, scattered with flowers, hung elegantly to the floor on the three tall windows. "Obviously fully aware of their own beauty," thought Olivia.

'Tea? Coffee?' enquired Francesca, standing graciously in the middle of the room.

'Just water, thank you.' Olivia preferred to drink water during the day, as tea alone made her feel queasy and she felt that coffee gave her bad breath, or "coffee-mouth", as she called it privately.

Some considerable amount of money and expertise had already gone into these lavish furnishings and she couldn't see why she had been called in the first place. She was mulling over this anomaly when Francesca placed a cut-glass tumbler on the table beside her, half full of sparkling water with a slice of lemon. She then sank gracefully into the large sofa opposite her. She crossed one elegantly clad knee over the other and sat back.

'I believe you are one of Ireland's top interior designers?' she said, with enquiry in her voice.

Olivia creased her face into her famous cat-like smile and sat back with her glass of fizz, ready to receive the adulation she felt was her right and due. 'So, I'm told,' she commented, suddenly feeling relaxed as she leaned back into her chintz cushion. This was her comfort zone, after all. 'But it's hard work,' she added, trying to inject a tone of humility into her voice.

'In Italy,' announced Francesca, 'we have wonderful designers, too. But they are there, and I am here in Dublin.' She smiled. 'And so are you,' she added.

Looking away briefly, she seemed to be mulling over her words.

'But,' she continued, 'I'm married to an Irishman and have been here for more than twenty years. He's an architect. Paul Butler. I believe you've worked with him on a couple of projects?'

Olivia knew Paul Butler's work well and had recently worked with him on the new Hotel Orologio. 'Indeed, I have!' she exclaimed. 'He's absolutely wonderful,' she added with enthusiasm, as indeed he was one of the top Irish architects practising in Ireland at that moment. 'In fact, I'll possibly see him this very evening at the photo-shoot there,' she added.

'Well, perhaps being married to an Irishman makes me at least partly Irish by now!' Francesca laughed quietly. 'Do you like my home?' she enquired. 'I have seen some of your work and I hope that you can help me with my project.'

Olivia gestured around the lovely room and, for once, was lost for words.

She managed. 'It depends on what you require me to help you with exactly,' she said in a muted voice, quite unlike her usual brisk tone; somehow Francesca's composure and the general air of elegance in her home had slightly intimidated her, and that was an unusual reaction. Normally, when Olivia arrived at a house where the owner required her services, it was pretty obvious, from the moment they opened the front door with that familiar frazzled look, and perhaps an old bicycle in the hall, that she was greatly needed. She just didn't get that feeling this time. Francesca's composure unsettled her in an indefinable way. Plus, her husband was a well-known architect. "Class," she thought. "This woman has class."'

'I'll take you to see the project I have in mind. And then you can let me know what you think.' Francesca got to her feet as though she had suddenly resolved some inner doubt.

Olivia joined her at the door to the room and Francesca gestured to her to follow as she led her down the hall to a sturdy door leading into the kitchen.

What a beautiful room, thought Olivia, admiring the cosy, though high-tech, kitchen with its huge Aga, long oak refectory table and windows looking over a walled garden, which appeared filled with fruit and vegetables in an immaculate array. "My garden isn't a patch on this," thought Olivia suddenly, and she looked at Francesca with new respect. A small woman in a blue housecoat and white apron looked up from a chopping board in front of one of the windows. She was round and dark, with more than a hint of a moustache on her upper lip, noted Olivia.

'This is Monica, our Italian cook,' volunteered Francesca, while Monica gestured a friendly greeting by brandishing the sharp, gleaming knife, which, until then, had been fully employed chopping vegetables.

'Ciao!' said Olivia, slightly absent-mindedly. "Where on earth are we going to?" she thought, as she followed Francesca out the back door and down a short flight of granite steps onto a broad gravel path bordered by an expanse of lawn on one side and the back of the house on the other.

Just before they reached the wrought-iron gate of the walled garden, Francesca changed direction and headed under a small arch. They stepped into a cobbled courtyard surrounded by old stables and carriage-houses. Francesca stopped dead and looked around, then waved both hands in an expansive gesture.

'This is your project, if you want it.' She smiled at Olivia, who was looking around in surprise. 'A stable-yard conversion. I want to add independent accommodation here for a family member. Are you interested?'

Olivia could only nod as she approached the first carriage-house and looked in. Obviously, it hadn't been used in the past twenty years, and the walls consisted of exposed stonework. Heavy oak beams spanned the width, supporting a slate roof in surprisingly good condition. The interior was dry, and the slightly spicy smell of horses and their feed lingered. A tiny scuffle announced the presence of mice, which was only to be expected in such a building. The six adjoining stables were in a similar condition, with their cobbled floors and metalwork which would have supported bales of hay and feed. The stable doors were still in place, though sagging on their old, metal hinges.

Olivia could feel a tiny bubble of pure excitement begin to well up inside her. A dream job, she thought. This could become fabulous, luxury accommodation with the right designs and finishes. Leaping ahead, she thought she would need to give the structural work to a good builder, and she knew just the one: Brendan, her long-time associate, would be the ideal person to undertake such a renovation.

'Of course, Paul has already drawn up the plans and all permissions have just been received,' added Francesca. 'Now he's prepared to bow out and turn the project over to us.' She looked at Olivia. 'I hope you will work with me on this. It should be fascinating.'

Olivia picked her way through the old stables and made some mental assessments. It was perfect for a conversion, she thought. They could get a large sitting/dining room and country kitchen installed on the ground floor, with French doors leading out into the walled garden. And there was easily room for three bedrooms upstairs, all with large en suites, if her experienced eye was to be believed. Which it invariably was. The old stable-yard in front would make a wonderful cobbled parking area with lots of pots, and the old cistern in the centre could be turned into a fountain... Her brain was virtually whirring as she looked around. She couldn't wait to see the plans.

She turned enthusiastically to Francesca. 'How many people will be living here?' she enquired.

Francesca didn't answer immediately. Then she responded thoughtfully, 'I'm not sure. Perhaps just one person for now.' She looked away. Olivia saw her guarded response and decided not to pry.

'I can get my team up here in the next few days to have a look around and we can come back to you with some preliminary designs shortly,' she suggested. 'If you could let me have a copy of Paul's plans, we could then discuss the needs of whoever will be living here. Perhaps you could jot down some notes and a rough outline of your proposed budget in the meantime?'

29

As Francesca and Olivia wandered back towards the house, they both chatted animatedly about the possibilities for the stable block, and by the time Olivia returned to her car, she was feeling better than she had done since Fiona's dire pronouncements that morning regarding the state of the economy. While people like Francesca were still prepared to spend large sums of money on such projects, she could ride out whatever economic storms that might lie ahead.

She slid into her shiny car and fastened her seatbelt, turning on the ignition and hearing the powerful engine purr to life. As she crunched over the gravel drive and headed towards the tall wrought-iron gates that were opening to let her out, she checked her lipstick in the mirror on the back of the sun-visor. Momentarily distracted, she almost ran headlong into a large, silver Range Rover that had just swung into the driveway in front of her. She jammed on her brakes and swerved slightly to the right, toppling an urn containing some sort of exotic shrub. The Range Rover swept past her, apparently oblivious of the incident with the urn, as Olivia ground her teeth in anger, wrenching open her car door and jumping out onto the gravel.

'Oh, damn!' she shouted, surveying the large dent in the front wing of her precious car. She turned around to see who had been driving the Range Rover so flamboyantly and saw that it had just parked outside the front of the house. A tall, well-built man was emerging from its smart leather interior, his black wavy hair tousled, and his sports jacket creased. He barely glanced in her direction.

Olivia marched across the deep gravel as elegantly as the heels of her stylish ankle-boots would allow, while smouldering hotly, and stopped in front of him as he pulled himself up to his full height. He was at least as tall as Steve, she noted absently as she looked up to find herself confronted by the most violet eyes she had ever seen. Not only were they violet, but they were fringed by the darkest, thickest lashes possible… 'Umm… my car!' she found herself stuttering helplessly.

The tall, violet-eyed stranger looked at her in bewilderment, as though he had just noticed her for the first time, then turned distractedly away and hurried up the broad steps towards the front door, which was in the process of being opened by Francesca. Olivia could see her reaching for the dark stranger with outstretched arms, drawing him into an embrace. She noticed that he kept his arms by his sides, with fists clenched, as though, at that moment, the last thing he wanted was to be hugged.

'Oh! Olivia!' she exclaimed in surprise, turning her head and assessing the situation quickly as she kissed the man on each cheek in the Italian custom and gestured to him to enter the house. Only then did she turn to face her. 'I see you've damaged your car. Are you all right?'

'I'm fine,' answered Olivia, stifling the angry tirade she was about to let loose on the violet-eyed stranger. She, too, had made her own speedy assessment and could see that this man was close to Francesca and that any aggression on her part right now could well jeopardise the prospects of her new project. She swallowed hard and waved her hand casually as though she was swatting a fly. 'No real damage done. Just a small dent. Sorry about the urn!' Then she turned on her heel and made her way back to her lovely car, which did not now look quite as smart as it had done earlier.

Reversing smartly away from the urn and spraying up gravel as she accelerated through the gates and down the road towards her office and sanctuary, Olivia tried to regain her upbeat mood from just half an hour earlier.

"Who was that dreadfully rude man?" she mused. Why did he ignore the situation? Why did he not say even one word to her? Olivia was unaccustomed to being ignored by men, especially one as handsome as the tall, dark stranger she had just encountered.

CHAPTER FOUR
OLIVIA

Glossy: her hair, lips and complexion. She had let her thick blonde hair down for the evening and her pendant earrings glistened as she, once again, admired her reflection in the long gilt mirror in her dressing room. Her Italian heritage showed clearly in her olive skin tone, which tanned easily, black brows and hour-glass figure. She stepped back and checked her appearance, doing a twirl in her slim-fitting black dress. The red detail on the heel of her high black shoes spoke volumes about how expensively turned out she was.

Olivia slid open the tall walnut door of her, naturally, bespoke wardrobe and reached inside. She selected, after a few minutes of pondering, a black, pleated coat, quite dressy, which she arranged carefully over her arm. She picked up her black lambskin Chanel shoulder bag and slipped the classic gold and black chain over her elegant shoulder. With one backward glance towards the mirror, she swung out of the dressing room and headed for the stairs.

'Claire!' she called, as she reached the hall.

The kitchen door opened, and Claire's enquiring face appeared. She looked tired, but alert and ready for action; it was obvious she was wondering "What now?"

'Mr Lynskey hasn't arrived home yet. He's late for dinner and I can't get hold of him. I'm heading to the Finns myself and he can catch up later.'

"Whenever that might be," she thought to herself and sighed resignedly, aware of Steve's antipathy towards Penelope Finn. He perceived her as bossy and as having encouraged her husband James to live an utterly louche lifestyle which consisted largely of hunting, shooting and drinking too much. In his book, these were leisure activities and did not qualify as a productive way of life. Yet, these were originally Steve's friends, as he had been "best pals" with James Finn since their schooldays, and they saw each other regularly.

She had been expecting him to be unenthusiastic about this particular evening and knew that he had, perhaps, even stopped off for a fortifying whiskey at the Coachman's Inn, near the airport, with his flying "buddies".

Olivia had long held the view that being married to a high-flying financier was no picnic, though she couldn't complain about the lifestyle Steve provided, so she kept her opinions to herself.

Claire hurried to the door and opened it for Olivia, who was sashaying elegantly down the hall, swinging her car keys on the end of one perfectly manicured finger. That purple nail polish was quite something, she thought, as she watched her employer head off down the steps. Olivia was aware that Claire envied her: a handsome husband, a fabulous home, a successful business, good looks... As far as outward appearances went, there was nothing she lacked in the eyes of her house-keeper. Or in her own, for that matter.

Grimacing at the sight of the fresh dent on her car, Olivia eased herself into the sleek Merc and gunned the accelerator, crunching over the gravel and heading down the driveway. The feel of the steering wheel in her hands and the smell of leather from the seats were heady. The throaty purr of the engine was music to her ears. She loved to drive fast, and this car certainly delivered the goods.

The electric gates swung open as she approached, and within a few minutes she was heading down the Stillorgan dual-carriageway towards the M50 to the strains of Vivaldi's *Four Seasons*.

Turning off towards Ashbourne on the N2, her mind returned to the problems she had been facing this week; it had been a difficult few days. Losing clients had been an unheard-of phenomenon up to this point, but it seemed as though most of them had suddenly decided to postpone their projects until the following year; recession permitting, of course.

Olivia's normally solid income seemed to be in jeopardy for the moment and she found the idea completely incomprehensible. Thank heavens for Steve's backing. She was unsure that she could keep her business afloat, without his help, for more than about six or seven months if things carried on the way they appeared to be shaping; but that was impossible, she told herself for the hundredth time that week. It was just a temporary glitch caused by the media fanning the flames by introducing the idea of a recession. Completely ridiculous, she thought. After all, weren't things booming in Ireland?

Just thinking about this week's photo-shoot at Hotel Orologio gave her a buzz. It had gone without a hitch, though she had been surprised that neither the architect nor the mysterious Italian owner had been present. She thought that someone may have mentioned a family death, but she was enjoying being the centre of attention too much to care.

Olivia had organised, with more alacrity than usual, to send her team to Francesca's home within the next few days to measure and photograph the stable block to prepare for the conversion. She was not prepared to let such a big fish slip away. She just could not afford to. Francesca had suddenly departed for Italy to attend a family funeral, and they would only be able to have their first really productive meeting on her return.

She approached the tall gates of the Finns' enormous Georgian pile just outside the quaint village of Slane in County Meath. The gates stood open and she drove straight up the long-gravelled avenue, overhung with chestnut trees. Horses pricked up their ears and stopped chewing, momentarily, to watch her progress, their mouths in mid-munch, their horse-faces showing surprise to see her. She could see blades of grass sticking out of the sides of their mouths, as they followed her progress with stolid equine curiosity from behind their post-and-rail fencing. Mainly hunters, they were out in the fields — at grass — for the summer months; time to have a little holiday and to get a little bit fat, relaxing in the daisy- and buttercup-strewn meadows.

James and Penelope Finn were standing at the top of the flight of steps to their slightly battered and dog-scratched front door when Olivia alighted from her car and crunched across the gravelled area in her high-heeled shoes.

'Olivia, darling!' Penelope's high, fluting voice with its upper-class tones floated down to Olivia.

'Hi, Penelope! James!' Olivia arrived at the top of the steps to be enveloped in Penelope's ample, floral-scented embrace. 'Steve's not home yet. I'm sure he'll come here directly from the airport. He's been in Madrid for the past few days. Late home as usual.'

This was not strictly true. Steve was usually meticulously punctual, as his life was dictated to him by arrival and departure slots at Dublin Airport. Except when it came to undesirable social occasions, when he occasionally went AWOL. But he hadn't phoned this afternoon to let her know his exact ETA, and she couldn't reach him on his mobile. Still, he was bound to arrive soon, as the Finns' home was not much more than half an hour from the airport, full of apologies and excuses, no doubt. On the other hand, the lure of a pint at the Coachman's Inn may well have proven irresistible, in order to fortify himself for his dreaded evening with the Finns, so Olivia made no further comment.

Though it was not yet dark outside, light from the expensive chandelier glinted as Olivia entered the drawing room. Three people were already seated on the chintz sofas with large pre-dinner drinks in their hands, reliving the season's most exciting fox-hunts and discussing the taking in of foxhound pups for the summer; a practice that entailed babysitting a couple of naughty, untrained puppies for the hunt kennels, which earned you lots of "brownie points" and plenty of damage to your flower beds. Olivia shuddered at the thought. She just didn't get this "hunting malarkey", as she referred to it to Steve in private. But these hunting folk made good clients, so she kept her views to herself. After all, sourcing antique crystal chandeliers from Venice and Oriental rugs from the East for the hunting-shooting-fishing brigade was a lucrative side-line.

She wished Steve would arrive and had a feeling that she was being looked at strangely this evening. Perhaps it was her imagination, but there was an uncomfortable air about the other guests, and Penelope kept looking anxiously at James.

Already assembled were Bill Burton, the perennial "spare" man and confirmed bachelor, and Richard and Cynthia Callan on the sofa opposite.

She greeted Bill, who was always invited if a single woman was to be included in this evening's quota of eight people around the table. This must mean that Diana Burke was to be joining them. Olivia groaned inwardly;

she couldn't stand Diana, previously a famous fashion model, now an extremely rich widow, who hung onto all the men's words admiringly. The fact that she was stunningly beautiful was no help; all the women were wary of her around their husbands and saw her as predatory with a carefully contrived helplessness, though Olivia doubted that Diana had a helpless bone in her body.

'And you, Olivia,' responded Bill, patting the sofa beside him, indicating that Olivia should sit there, enveloped in his warm, tweedy aura, until Diana should deign to arrive. At that point, Olivia would, undoubtedly, have to give up her place next to Bill. 'Looking gorgeous as always.' His laugh was as warm and smoky as his personal scent. Bill was renowned for his vast consumption of cheroots and Jameson whiskey.

She stifled a grin. Bill was a well-known bachelor with a tried and tested formula for flattering most females who fell within his radar. He was also legendary for his exaggerated tales of derring-do on the hunting field, and the thought of him actually sailing over the sort of fences he described with such enthusiasm beggared belief. Still, you never knew with these hunting types; once their blood was up there was no stopping them.

These post-hunt tales normally originated in whatever pub was handiest when the hunting folk slowly walked their tired, muddy horses back to the horse boxes at the end of a day spent careering across fields and cantering up and down muddy lanes. The hunting fraternity always spent an hour or so after the meet engaged in discussion of the day's cross-country adventures; their tired horses would already have been rugged up and munching their hay-nets in the horse boxes, their steam rising in the cold evening air, to the background sounds of raucous laughter that normally accompanied the consumption of hot port and handfuls of peanuts.

The other couple were seasoned hunting folk, too, though Cynthia — 'Call me Cyn!' — had lost her nerve after the birth of her third baby and preferred to follow the hunt these days with a car-load of children in tow. Richard — affectionately known as Dickie — already looked the worse for wear, and the evening had barely begun. Sporting a bandage on top of his head — 'You should have seen the branch afterwards!' — his florid face became even redder as he threw back his head and chuckled. 'Out on the tractor. Forgot to duck!' He took another deep draught of sherry, emptying his glass, and looked around anxiously to check if his hosts had noticed that he needed a refill.

"Call me Cyn" looked at him disdainfully, as usual. How they had managed to have three children together, with another one obviously on the way, defied logic. They rowed constantly and their bickering had been the background music to so many of these dinner parties that Olivia had lost count. That, coupled with Dickie's penchant for dozing off and snoring at the dinner table after his second or third glass of port, made them potentially annoying dinner guests. But they were so charming and entertaining — before Dickie fell asleep, that is — that they were well worth the effort, and everyone adored them.

'What on earth is keeping Diana?' Penelope swept into the room with Olivia's gin and tonic, ice clinking, on a small silver tray. 'Here you are, Olivia. Two slices of lemon. Any communication from Steve yet?' She looked over at Dickie and made a move to top up his glass.

Without waiting for replies or comments, after giving Dickie a generous top-up, Penelope sank into a large chintz armchair and took a long swallow of her vodka-tonic. James came in then with an enormous glass of red wine clasped in his large, farmer's hand and sat down opposite.

'I've just tried to phone Diana on her mobile, but it's switched off, or she's out of reach.' He glanced at Penelope uneasily. 'So, I phoned her home phone and left a message reminding her about our dinner party in case she's forgotten. We may have to go in without them.'

Olivia sensed the tension in the air and wondered if she was imagining it.

CHAPTER FIVE
JANE

Returning from the hospital had been a terrible ordeal for Jane. It was already getting dark when Marco had helped her from the motor launch and Maria came to meet her on the private jetty below the palazzo, taking her right arm gently, as her left one was still in a sling.

'Please bring the contessa's bags, Marco,' she addressed the boatman. 'But just wait until we are upstairs.' She pressed the bell to summon the lift. She was still holding Jane's arm when they emerged from the lift upstairs.

Jane could hear subdued voices issuing from the dining room and recognised her sister-in-law's voice. Francesca and her husband Paul must have arrived for Sofia's funeral.

'I'd like to go straight to bed, Maria,' she said, ignoring the open dining room door and moving quickly towards the sanctuary of her bedroom. She could not bear to see the look on their faces if she entered the room.

Undressing quickly, she slid into bed, lying gratefully back on the mound of pillows covered with crisp, white pillowcases. She sighed with relief at being back in her own bed.

Maria brought her some chamomile tea and toast on a tray, which she had placed beside her on the bedside locker, looking worriedly at her.

'Can I do anything for you, Contessa?'

Jane shook her head. Then, remembering her impeccable manners, she murmured a quiet 'Thank you, Maria. That will be all.' And Maria let herself out of the room, now dimly lit by only a bedside lamp, illuminating the grief-stricken occupant of the bed.

Jane reached for her bag and extracted the tranquillisers given to her when she was discharged from the hospital, taking one with her tea. Lying back on her pillows, she wished for death to come and claim her, but there was no escaping the harsh reality which faced her: her daughter was dead, and her husband blamed her for it.

A sleepless night followed; how could she sleep when she was burying her beautiful Sofia the next morning? She longed to pad down the corridor to her daughter's bedroom but could not bring herself to do so. Her own room was warm and slightly stuffy, but she could not bear the idea of turning on the air conditioner. So, she tossed and turned, dozing fitfully towards morning.

OLIVIA

'Cook's beginning to send up smoke signals from the kitchen.' James chuckled at his own sense of humour, as he saw it. 'She's made her "surprise starter", and you know how that can go flat if we leave it… and the roast is already out of the oven.' He fidgeted with his wristwatch and suddenly looked surprisingly uneasy for what was, after all, just a friendly dinner party.

Their cook, Mary, was well known in hunting circles for her cooking, and her "surprise starter" was famous at these predictable dinner parties, where there really were absolutely no surprises at all, with the same crowd always in attendance, varying only in number, depending on whether it was hunting season or not, and pretty identical menus. As regards the "surprise starter", Olivia suspected that this mysterious soufflé had some strong, canned French onion soup undertones. But she could be wrong!

'Sit there beside James,' Penelope instructed Olivia, as they entered the dining room. 'We'll leave the two places in the middle on either side for Steve and Diana when they show up. Strange they're not here yet…,' she added, thoughtfully, trailing off at the end of what she had been beginning to say and looking nervously at James.

Olivia caught the look that flashed between her hosts and wondered what was going on. Why did her host and hostess look so ill at ease? She decided.

'Just give me a moment,' she murmured to Penelope. 'I'm going to try Steve again, and if he still doesn't pick up, I'll ring Dublin Airport and see if they have his ETA. It's most unlike him not to have phoned by now.'

She got up and swiftly left the dining room and stood in the large front hall while she fumbled for her mobile phone, dropping it in her haste.

'Here, Olivia.' Penelope came up behind her, proffering a portable telephone. 'Don't worry. Use this. The mobile signal isn't great from here.'

Olivia gratefully took the proffered phone and dialled Steve's number as her hostess hovered; her curiosity obvious.

'The telephone you have dialled is either switched off or out of range,' the computer-generated Irish accent informed her.

Now angry as well as frustrated, she dialled the private arrivals section at the airport; a number she knew by heart. When it was promptly answered, she gave the registration number and details of Steve's Gulfstream. She waited while they checked.

Her heart suddenly beat painfully when she heard the terse statement: 'Sorry, Mrs Lynskey. Mr Lynskey's Gulfstream is not listed here. And there's no note of a flight plan, either. Sorry,' he added.

Olivia persevered, though her instinct told her something was terribly wrong. 'Are you absolutely certain? He left on Monday for Madrid.'

The operator paused, as though trying to decide what to say.

'I think the plane's parked on the far tarmac. If it's Mr Lynskey's Gulfstream I'm looking at... well... it's been there all week.'

'No!' Olivia was experiencing the first feelings of shock 'That's impossible. Do you think someone there could check it out for me? Here's my number.' She reeled off her mobile number and gave them Penelope's home number, too, just to be on the safe side. 'Please phone me back. This is a very worrying development. I can't imagine...' Now it was Olivia's turn to trail off as she turned to Penelope in despair.

She hung up and handed over the phone with a resigned sigh.

'What on earth is going on? When's Steve due to land? And what did you ask them to check at the control tower?'

'Never mind. There's obviously some mistake. They say that Steve hasn't filed a flight plan and they think his plane has been at the airport all week. They're checking and they'll get back to me.' She made a visible effort to pull herself together and linked her arm through Penelope's. 'Now, let's go and eat the "surprise starter" before Mary has a fit.'

Penelope laughed, but it sounded hollow to Olivia's ears.

As they entered the dining room, James looked up and gave his wife a meaningful stare. 'Well?' he demanded. 'When can we expect the whizz-kid to arrive?'

'I'm waiting for the airport to phone back to confirm. Obviously, a mix-up.' Olivia gratefully picked up her spoon and attacked the starter. "Yuk!" she thought, but tonight she was glad of the diversion as they all tucked in to the oniony soufflé.

A few minutes later the phone rang, and Penelope bounded out to the hall to answer it. It wasn't the airport; it was Diana's brother Mark.

She re-entered the room looking grim. 'That was Mark, Diana's brother; you know, the accountant,' she began. 'He just arrived unexpectedly and wanted to check if I knew where she was; he thought she might be here. Apparently, her car is parked in the driveway and she's not there. He knew she had planned to come here this evening.' She paused for dramatic effect. 'He also told me that he found a note on the fridge for the cleaning lady saying she would be away for at least two weeks.' Her face reddened. 'She didn't say where she was going.'

With that, Olivia's mobile went off in her bag. She pulled it out, jumping to her feet at the same time. 'Olivia Lynskey here,' she said nervously, while she listened to the air traffic controller on the other end. 'Are you serious? Oh my God!'

'I'm so sorry, everyone. But I have to go.' Olivia was just barely hanging onto her composure.

You could have heard a pin drop as the significance of the furtively exchanged glances suddenly became clear to Olivia. She felt her stomach clench in sudden pain as the truth hit home.

She looked at the two empty chairs, reserved for the no-show couple, Steve and Diana. Well, they'd have to wait indefinitely, as it appeared that neither of them was going to show up any time soon. Then she saw the faces of her friends as they gazed at her with a mixture of concern and, yes, she could see it, pure elation at the thought of being in the eye of the storm which would certainly be caused by this major scandal, unfolding for their titillation in their very own dining room in County Meath.

A huge wave of emotion hit Olivia, followed by a feeling of humiliation so strong it was like a physical blow; like nothing she had ever experienced before in her life.

'Steve's having an affair with Diana?' It was more a statement than a question, and it was met with silence. 'You all knew? Well, they say the wife's always the last person to find out.'

She got up and fled from the room.

CHAPTER SIX
JANE

Next morning, the morning of Sofia's funeral, Jane stood in front of her full-length mirror surveying the shell of the woman she had been until the previous week. Her cheeks were deathly pale, emphasised by her black dress and the sling she wore over her shoulder to support her broken collarbone. She prepared to leave the palazzo with Niccolo, who had not spoken to her since she had returned from hospital the previous evening, and her son Max, who had arrived in Venice a few days previously. Francesca and Paul would be accompanying them, too.

Now they waited for her, dressed in black, in the large salon on the *piano nobile*, overlooking the Grand Canal, where the occasional excited shout from the myriad tourist population wafted up through the open windows, seemingly changing the mood from minute to minute. Maria's husband, Gianni, walked quietly around with a tray bearing snacks, in case anyone had missed breakfast.

Niccolo's face was grim and, though tanned from so much time spent outdoors, had an unhealthy pallor: evidence of several sleepless nights in a row as he waited for the final farewell to his precious, beautiful daughter.

Jane's son Max hurried to her side, his angular frame and worried expression reflecting his anxiety at her bowed head. He put his arm protectively around her shoulders.

'How are you holding up, Mother?' he asked. 'Would you like me to get you something... a glass of water, perhaps? You look very pale.'

She smiled gratefully at him.

'Max. I'll be fine,' she reassured him gently, and looked past him at her husband standing at the window, looking out over the Grand Canal.

Niccolo turned and appeared to stare at his wife for a long moment, his face grave, even stern, as he examined her closely.

'You're ready then,' he spoke at last, his voice raspy and gruff, as though he had not spoken for a long time, though Jane knew that he had been crying; she had heard his muffled sobs in the night, from his bedroom next door to hers. He had stayed away from her and her bedroom after she had returned wearily from the hospital and gone straight to her room.

Niccolo's sister, Francesca, and her architect husband Paul rose from the sofa where they had been sitting quietly. They had arrived from Dublin the previous day and Jane saw sympathy on their faces as they came to greet her. She had always found Francesca slightly aloof and treated her warily. That she had loved Sofia was not in doubt, however, and she obviously adored Niccolo, who spent a great deal of his time at their beautiful Dublin home.

They brushed cheeks in greeting.

'We're here to support you. Both of you.' Francesca looked searchingly at Jane. 'Jane, I'm so sorry for your loss.'

Jane struggled to find words for her sister-in-law, but was silent, head bent, nodding her head mutely in response, afraid she would burst into tears at the words of kindness.

She and Max descended with Maria in the tiny lift, leaving the others to follow when it had creaked back up again. There was no way that six adults could have fitted inside at the same time.

Jane emerged onto the wooden jetty and looked up and down the Grand Canal. It was an unseasonably cool and breezy day, and clouds scudded across the sun. Small waves broke against the pylons underneath her feet. She shivered. "How can I get through today?" she asked herself.

Maria stood back as Marco, the boatman, hurried forward and helped Jane solicitously into the motor launch which was moored against their private jetty. Max, Francesca and Niccolo followed her into the narrow cabin. Paul stood on the outer deck, as he loved to do, watching the hustle and bustle of the Venetian canals. They bobbed gently in the wake created by the many boats that plied up and down the Grand Canal. Tourists eyed them curiously from the passing vaporetti, and they must have looked conspicuous, this obviously prosperous group of people exiting a private palazzo dressed formally in black and entering a particularly smart motor launch.

Marco made sure they were settled in the cabin and, going up to the controls next to Paul, eased his way out into the busy waterway, passing quickly under the long wooden Accademia Bridge and past the ornate façade of Santa Maria della Salute. Passing Punta della Dogna, he expertly guided his craft into the Giudecca Canal and finally pulled to a stop on fondamenta della Zattere so that Niccolo, Jane and Max could alight and make their way to the church of Santa Maria del Rosario, otherwise known as I Gesuati, where the funeral Mass was being held.

A large crowd of darkly dressed people fell silent on the steps of the church as they approached. A crowd of schoolgirls, Sofia's school-friends, lined the entrance. Most were in tears, sobbing uncontrollably at this drama which affected them all deeply. Fourteen-year-old girls, beautiful fourteen-year-old girls to be exact, did not die just like that. It was a very frightening concept for these youngsters as it brought them face to face with their own mortality at a tender and impressionable age. They were all deeply shaken by the tragedy and it showed in their reaction to seeing Sofia's family ascending the steps. The dam waters broke, and they were virtually all in tears as Niccolo and Jane walked slowly past.

Jane felt as though her heart would break as she walked up the aisle and recognised familiar faces among the standing mourners. The church was very full. Jane had never seen so many people there. Sofia's white coffin was standing on a trolley at the head of the aisle in front of the main altar. Jane's heart beat so loudly she was sure everybody could hear it. She, Niccolo and Max took their seats in the front row, followed by Francesca and Paul. As they sat beside the coffin in silence, Jane heard the sounds of the congregation settling down behind her. Some coughing. The occasional sob. Funereal sounds. The service began.

The eulogies were simple and kind. Memories of Sofia from her friends, and then Niccolo mounted the altar and spoke movingly about his beautiful daughter. Jane looked up at him with his handsome face and tired eyes and knew that every woman in the church, young and old, wanted to comfort him. He was that sort of man. Little did they know the real Niccolo: withdrawn and cold. He had visited her on only one occasion while she had been in hospital, on that first day after Sofia had died. It felt as though their marriage had died, too, along with their daughter, and Jane knew that he blamed her for the accident. She wasn't sure she didn't blame herself either, but her recollections of that day were hazy. And she didn't really want to think of it anyway. There was time enough for that when all this was over. Memories of Sofia flooded her mind and the tears fell.

After the Mass, Sofia's coffin was lowered carefully into the funeral launch, while Jane boarded the di Falco boat, with Marco being extra solicitous. His soft brown eyes searched hers for indications of how he might be able to help her. But she was mute and unable to communicate with him or anybody else. She sat in the launch with her head bowed, her thin arms folded on her lap, while Niccolo and the others stood on the fondamenta, shaking hands with acquaintances and accepting their condolences. She felt she couldn't face her old friends and Niccolo's many relatives; after all, there was still a large cloud hanging over her regarding the circumstances of the accident, and many of the congregation looked at her with unease.

Several mourners boarded their private motor launches and specially hired taxis for the short journey to the island of San Michele, where the di Falco family had their own crypt. And so, Sofia made her last trip up the Grand Canal, passing the palazzo where she had grown from a pretty blonde baby into a graceful fourteen-year-old with all the promise in the world. Passing through the district of Cannaregio and out into the open sea, heading for the cemetery island of San Michele, Jane felt as though she were living in a dream; or, more likely, a nightmare. Niccolo sat silently on the opposite seat, his eyes fixed on the funeral launch in front of them, oblivious to the busy canals and the old bridges under which they passed. Max sat beside her on the narrow seat and held her hand in his. His eyes were red-rimmed from crying, but he did his best to put on a brave face for his mother.

Walking behind their daughter's coffin and seeing it placed in the old di Falco crypt was heart-breaking. Made doubly so for Jane as she desperately needed Niccolo's support at this time, but that had been withdrawn, and she had no-one to hold her and tell her that everything would be all right. She craved a comforting shoulder on which to lay her weary head. Max was her son and too young to understand how deeply she was suffering. Nobody wants to be a burden to their offspring, but suspicion hung in the air of peaceful San Michele. They had read about it in the papers, after all: she was being investigated for the accident which caused her daughter's death.

How Jane missed her mother. She thought of her less and less these days, but right now she could have done with her reassuring presence. But her mother was gone, dead before her time, only two years previously. Too young, in her early seventies, the result of many years of chain-smoking, drinking and neglecting her health in general. Depression had haunted her.

Jane's father, Lord Remington, had been an intimidating presence in their lives, who had demanded — and achieved — rigid discipline in the home. Jane had loathed him and had moved away with her new husband at a young age. Her mother had not been so lucky and had turned to alcohol and anti-depressants. Now she was gone, and Jane longed for her presence in a way she had not done since she was a child.

Contact with her father was limited to phone calls on birthdays and at Christmas, and to the occasional visit by her to their palatial home in Gloucester. Even now, though he was almost eighty years old, he managed to retain his formidable air, and Jane could not shake the feeling that, no matter what she did, it was never enough to gain his approval.

Max, her son by her early first marriage, had taken his two weeks in Italy as planned, but under very different circumstances than first envisaged. An idyllic summer in Venice and the Euganean Hills had been replaced by a visit shrouded in tragedy, and he was in shock, too. Jane looked anxiously at his bowed head beside her as they watched the interment of their beloved Sofia. She tried to stifle the small sob that escaped her throat and felt Max slide his arm around her waist. Her son. She must put him first from now on and wished he lived in Italy and was not studying in London. Perhaps he would come out to live later on, she thought idly, but knew that he would not. He was English, spoke very little Italian, and his life and future were definitely going to be played out on English soil.

Perhaps she should move back to England: the thought flashed across her mind. Then she looked over at Niccolo and her heart swelled. No, she could never leave him, not now. They just needed time to recover from this terrible blow to their lives. But she loved him more than ever and wished he could open up to her and that they could be close again. She longed to hold him and help him to deal with all this pain, but it was not an option. His emotions were not to be shared with her, his wife, in their hour of mutual need and anguish. She felt the first real stirring of resentment.

CHAPTER SEVEN
OLIVIA

The call from the bank came early the following morning. Olivia had spent the night sleepless and alone in her emperor-sized bed. She had undressed in a daze: removing her make-up, applying moisturiser, brushing her teeth; this nightly routine calmed her slightly, and by the time she slipped into her silk pyjamas and lay down between the cool, white sheets, her threatening hysteria had diminished somewhat. But she certainly did not sleep.

Steve's empty pillow was reflected by the moonlight that glimmered through the white muslin curtains. She had not pulled the heavy drapes. She wanted to think. What on earth was going on? Where was Steve? And was Diana Burke with him? These were questions urgently needing answers, and the sooner it was morning and she could begin to try to piece things together, the sooner she would like it.

She rose at 6am and sat on her window seat, looking out over her immaculate garden. Today would be an important one; make or break, she knew it in her bones. She felt a sense of calm resignation. She just needed to sit still and wait for whatever was going to happen.

By 8am, still quietly calm, she was dressed in an elegant navy pencil skirt and white shirt, with her hair in a tidy knot at the back of her head. She glanced at her gold Ebel wrist-watch — a birthday present from Steve; was that only last year? Time appeared to have stood still. She went downstairs and tried the door to Steve's study. It swung open to reveal his large desk and computer, positioned in the bay of one of the tall Georgian windows, looking out over the gardens.

She crossed the room and sat down on Steve's leather swivel chair. First of all, she swung it to face the immaculate gardens. What a mellow view! Then, resignedly, she turned it to face the computer and switched it on. It lit up and asked her for the password. She had no clue what it could be. She tried a few names and dates to no avail, then left it alone while she began to go through the drawers and cupboards underneath. Nothing of interest, as far as she could see.

Something prompted her to lift the blotter. Two sheets of paper had either been placed there or had slid underneath. One was, of all things, a hand-written list of Trivial Pursuit questions. Steve was obsessed with the game and had even been known to take the box of questions into the bath with him, so keen was he to try to memorise as many questions and answers as possible. This had been a game that he constantly played with Diana. Whenever they had a dinner party, he and Diana would repair to a corner of the sitting room and play it together, laughing conspiratorially. He was possibly asking her Trivial Pursuit questions over the phone and left this 'cheat-sheet' under his blotter. Who knew?

She picked up the other piece of paper. Pinned to the top was a photograph of a sprawling one-storey house. She looked at it closely. No, it was not familiar. It looked Spanish or Portuguese in style, all white stucco and red terracotta roof tiles. "Africa project" was written in Steve's untidy handwriting underneath. She wondered what it could mean

The phone rang suddenly, jolting Olivia into a state of red alert. Could it be Steve?

'Olivia Lynskey,' she announced into the receiver.

A man spoke. 'Ah! Mrs Lynskey. This is Bank of Ireland here.' Olivia felt an icy tendril touch her heart. 'Is Mr Lynskey available?'

'I'm sorry,' she replied hesitantly. 'Mr Lynskey is away at the moment. Can I help you?'

'I see. When will he be back? Can we get hold of him?' The questions from the bank were fast and furious, giving her no time to think. 'It's urgent we speak to him immediately.'

'I'm sorry,' replied Olivia, her hand clasping the telephone feeling slick with sudden perspiration. 'I don't know where he is, nor when he'll be back.'

The man from the bank found this difficult to believe and spent the next five minutes emphasising the fact that Mr Lynskey must, absolutely must, contact them immediately. The man left a name and number and Olivia promised she would pass on the message as soon as possible.

Olivia hung up and immediately dialled Steve's long-term personal assistant Carmel, who answered on the first ring.

'Carmel!' Olivia had difficulty keeping the anxiety and fear out of her voice. 'Do you know where Steve is? I hate asking you, but he didn't return last night, and the Gulfstream is still parked at Dublin Airport.'

There was a moment's silence at the other end of the phone while Carmel evaluated her words.

She said carefully, 'Olivia. I have absolutely no idea where Steve is. I'm truly concerned. He was supposed to be in Madrid for a meeting on Monday but didn't show up. Nobody knows where he is. I have been trying to track him down all week, with no success. The hotel says he never even checked in.'

'Why didn't you let me know?' Olivia was having a hard time keeping her voice modulated, while she wanted to scream at Carmel. Why hadn't that stupid woman let her know before now? She had told Steve many, many times that Carmel was a waste of space, but he paid no heed. Said she was "loyal and discreet", whatever that meant.

'I didn't want to worry you needlessly,' said Carmel primly. 'I kept thinking he'd be back from wherever he had gone by yesterday. After all, it's not the first time he hasn't been where he was supposed to be...' She sighed theatrically. 'But it seems I was wrong, and I think we should perhaps let the police know he's actually missing. Let them track him down.'

Taking a deep breath, Olivia asked her, 'Do you know anything about a friend of ours by the name of Diana Burke?' She trod heavily on the word "friend". She found this very difficult to ask and hoped she wasn't raising an unnecessary new scenario. But her gut instinct told her that the two disappearances were interlinked.

This time, the silence from the other end of the phone seemed endless. Finally, Carmel spoke.

'Oh, Olivia. I'm sorry. I know the wife is always the last person to know, but yes. I'm pretty sure Steve has been seeing Diana for the past year.' Carmel hesitated a moment, then carried on, 'I saw her boarding the Gulfstream a few months ago in Dublin when I had to rush some documents to the airport for Steve to sign. They were heading to Paris together at the time.' She continued carefully. 'And, well, um, one evening a couple of months back, I rang Steve when he was away staying in a London hotel and the receptionist told me that Mr and Mrs Lynskey had just stepped out for a walk. I knew you were at home and I guessed he must have had a female friend with him. Sorry.'

Olivia felt an icy calm descend and braced herself and asked the next important question on her list. 'The bank is urgently trying to get hold of Steve. What's going on? Maybe it's time we had a talk.'

'Okay. Yes, you're right. Do you want me to call over? I can be there in an hour.' Carmel sounded almost relieved, like a sinner being released from the confessional.

Olivia hung up and stared at the telephone. This was getting worse and worse. Steve and Diana. Steve and the bank. The Gulfstream parked at Dublin Airport. Steve missing. Diana missing. Who could she turn to? Nobody at all, she figured correctly.

But still, she picked up the phone again and dialled that familiar number.

'Mamma?' she held the phone tightly against her burning cheek. 'Are you there?'

ONE MONTH LATER

From the night of Steve's disappearance, Olivia realised that, without Steve's capital to prop up her business to see her through the pending financial recession in Ireland, she would not be able to survive for long. Her carefully nurtured interior design business was vulnerable, being so closely tied to the property market. The fact that so many others were probably in the same boat did nothing to comfort her. She felt very alone.

First of all, Olivia thought she could work from home. But the bank manager put a damper on that idea, as he pointed out that she would be unable to afford to maintain Cardistown House without Steve's income. She knew that the house would have to go when he told her the extent of his accumulated debts and the terrifying fact that their mortgage repayments hadn't been paid for almost a year.

She needed to move out within the next few months and find herself less expensive accommodation, even contemplating her parents' offer of her old room in her childhood home until she was back on her feet. She had advised Fiona and the rest of her design team to look for other positions as soon as possible. It broke her heart to have to give her loyal staff one month's notice. Claire and John were devastated, as they had looked on their gatehouse cottage as home. How she would be able to look after the enormous house on her own until she moved out, she had no idea. But she would have to manage somehow.

Lease repayments on the Gulfstream had also been unpaid for many months. The business was being closed down completely, as, without Steve, it just did not exist anymore. His shocked employees were to be made redundant, and most of them were claiming redundancy payments that Olivia was sure could not be committed to.

The police called to see her. Had she any idea where Steve could have gone? Had Diana Burke gone with him? Olivia was unable to answer either of these important questions but was pretty sure that Diana was in this mad adventure up to her elegant neck. Her family had no clue where she was, only that she had contacted her brother and confirmed that she would be out of contact for a while as she was in Africa with a friend. They informed the police that Diana had, apparently, flown to Lisbon that Monday morning and was, apparently, flying to West Africa on TAP, the Portuguese national carrier. Her sister had found an itinerary in Diana's bedside locker when she went looking for clues as to where she might have gone.

Other than that, they had no information, but had promised to contact the police if they heard anything from her.

Could Steve be in West Africa? If so, he would be impossible to trace. Perhaps that was the general idea. Extradition treaties were thin on the ground between Africa and Europe.

In the meantime, she looked upon her pending project with Francesca Butler as a lifeline, temporary though it would be. Work was due to commence on the revamped stable block in six weeks' time. Up until then, she had been trying to concentrate on making sure that all the interior layouts, colour schemes and fabric samples were being efficiently organised; not easy under her present circumstances.

Francesca had been in Italy for much of the previous three weeks and was due back in Ireland shortly. Apparently, a family member had died, though Olivia had not seen her since and knew no further details. She was looking forward to Francesca's return so that they could up-date on all the design schemes which Olivia had prepared with difficulty, as her normal design team had been disbanded and were only helping her on a *pro bono* basis.

Her phone rang.

'Olivia Lynskey,' she announced herself slightly nervously, as these days she never knew which creditor would phone to demand information as to Steve's whereabouts.

'Olivia! This is Francesca Butler.' The soft Italian accent brought her back to the gorgeous house in south county Dublin.

Olivia was delighted and relieved to hear her voice.

'Oh, Francesca!' She sounded tremulous; she knew. The stress had really got to her recently. Her self-confidence was at an all-time low. 'I've been looking forward to hearing from you. Are you home?'

'Yes, I'm home, Olivia. And I know about your problems,' said Francesca kindly. 'I read about your husband in the papers. I don't want to put any pressure on you after the past few terrible weeks, but I know you said you would work on the designs for the stable block. I would understand completely if you said that you had not been able to work effectively with all this hassle going on in the background.'

'All's ready and awaiting your approval, Francesca.' Olivia realised that these were probably the first positive words she had uttered in over three weeks and suddenly felt her spirits lift.

'Can you call to see me?'

'Well… yes. I could call over later today, if that suits you?' Olivia was eager to see her. 'Say 4pm?'

'Perfect,' said Francesca warmly. 'I'll see you then.'

Olivia hung up. She was aware of the first frisson of vigour she had felt since Steve's disappearance. She dashed into the kitchen and put together a quick sandwich of whole-wheat brown bread with cheddar cheese and a dab of Marmite, washed down with a cup of strong "builder's tea". As she sat at the breakfast bar in her beautiful cream-painted kitchen, she admired the Waterford crystal chandelier over the island and the gleaming quartz counter tops.

"Whoever buys this house from the bank will be doing well," she thought sadly. How could she bear to be parted from this home on which she had lavished such care and attention? Everything had been carefully chosen and was of the highest quality. How could this be happening to her?

Pulling herself together, she climbed the stairs to her bedroom, where she headed to her wardrobe to find something suitable to wear. Her navy suit with the white shirt and the navy pumps, she thought. Stylish, but sensible.

As she entered the dressing room she had shared with Steve, she felt a sudden wave of nostalgia sweep over her. There was his collection of silk ties and matching handkerchiefs, his pride and joy. His handmade shoes and tailored suits. What was she supposed to do with everything? Keep them in case he returned? She could hardly throw everything out. Or could she? If he had absconded with Diana Burke and left her with a huge financial mess, she could certainly throw everything out; perhaps a bonfire?

As usual these days, rage quickly overtook her feelings of sentiment for her husband and she dressed quickly, before striding purposefully from her bedroom suite, picking up her light summer trench-coat as she left. On second thoughts, maybe a bonfire was a good idea.

She would survive; she was a fighter.

CHAPTER EIGHT
JANE

The soft white muslin curtain moved lazily in the afternoon breeze. Her blonde hair fanned out and gave her — to anybody who might have bothered to look — an interesting halo.

Jane watched the dust motes dancing in the light and, sighing deeply, she closed her eyes, resting her head against the pale lemony velvet cushion.

Contessa Jane di Falco was reclining on a large bamboo chair in her study in Venice. She looked considerably older than her years. Her face was pale; grief had a way of getting under your skin.

How she hated this palazzo! She knew that people would give all they possessed to trade places with her. Married to a Conte and living in one of the premier palazzi on the Grand Canal in Venice seemed like an enviable position to be in.

Jane eyed the drinks cabinet longingly, though she knew it was empty. She stretched her legs restlessly. No more alcohol for her. Ever. The day she had returned from hospital, Niccolo had arrived with an empty cardboard box and unceremoniously emptied all her precious bottles of grappa and brandy into it, marching out the front door. She had rarely seen him since.

The Polizia from Venice Questura had been visiting fairly regularly to go over and over her statement about the day of the accident. Had she been drinking? Had she taken drugs? Was her car properly maintained? So many questions, and so few answers. Her emergency bottle of grappa had been found in her handbag at the scene of the accident, accompanied by a couple of blister packs of diazepam. Why did she have a bottle of grappa in her handbag? How many tranquillisers had she taken? They pressed their queries relentlessly over and over again. How she wished she had refrained from taking that bottle of grappa with her!

Her car was classed as vintage and spent most of its time parked in Tronchetto. She knew, or thought she knew, that all had been in order that fateful day, though perhaps her reactions had been slow due to the fact that she had been drinking heavily the previous evening and had taken a couple of sleeping pills. Well, she'd had a lot on her mind, what with Niccolo's absence.

What saved her from being arrested and charged with dangerous driving, or for driving under the influence of alcohol, was that her blood-alcohol tests had been clear. However, the same tests picked up the diazepam and, as a result, they felt they had some idea of her mental state, which they considered food for thought. Now they all awaited the result of the analysis of her car. Had the steering been faulty? Or was it driver error due to the diazepam? Jane was terrified.

Niccolo continued to look at her with suspicion combined with something that looked frighteningly like distain. Coldness emanated from his every pore, or so it seemed. He was obviously grieving deeply, and dark shadows were etched beneath his eyes.

OLIVIA

Arriving at Francesca's home, Olivia was once more struck by the calm elegance that greeted her. She parked her car on the gravel driveway and mounted the steps, remembering the previous visit when the tall, unpleasant stranger had caused her to dent her beautiful car on a flower pot. The indignity of it! Despite everything, she still smouldered with anger at the thought of his complete indifference to her and to her accident; caused by him.

"That beautiful car will have to go, too, I suppose," she mused unhappily, not yet knowing quite how far she had still to fall financially.

The front door opened before Olivia had reached the top step. Francesca was dressed in black from head to toe and her expression was solemn. Her eyes looked tired and bloodshot. Could she have been crying, Olivia wondered?

'Olivia!' Francesca greeted her warmly. Standing, backlit by the lighting in her exquisite hallway, Francesca reached to give Olivia the customary Italian two-kiss greeting. Left cheek to left cheek, followed by right cheek to right cheek. 'Come!' She ushered her into the sitting room and rang for tea.

Olivia sat on the same sofa as previously and looked around. The room was as pristine and sophisticated as she remembered. Was it really a matter of a few short weeks since she had been here last? So much had happened, it seemed like a lifetime ago. Monica brought a large wooden tray for afternoon tea, resplendent with a white linen cloth, silver teapot, jug and sugar bowl and pale, floral bone china cups and saucers. She placed everything carefully on the walnut coffee table. A plate of tiny, white-bread sandwiches with their crusts cut off, filled with delicate slices of cucumber, plus another of chocolate biscuits, completed the beautifully presented afternoon tea. Olivia gazed admiringly at the vintage cups and saucers.

'How gorgeous,' she said. 'I absolutely love that antique tea set.'

'Yes. I love it, too,' agreed Francesca. 'It belonged to my mother-in-law. She passed away last year, and I had always coveted these cups and saucers. So, I brought them home with me when we were packing up her belongings.'

They sipped their tea companionably. Olivia waited. Finally, Francesca put down her cup and spoke.

'I must tell you that I have had a terrible family bereavement, on the very day you were last here, to be exact.' She paused to let the significance of this statement to filter through Olivia's thought processes.

'Oh! I'm sorry…,' she began in response. Francesca cut across her and said:

'My niece was killed in a car accident in Italy. I have just returned from Venice.' She paused, then went on, 'While I was there, I stayed in my family palazzo and it is not a happy place. I have suggested to my family in Italy that you should be retained to oversee its renovation.' Francesca said all this without taking a breath. As if she wanted to say it out loud, or get it off her chest, Olivia thought.

Francesca sat back against the chintz cushions and seemed to struggle to compose herself. Olivia thought quickly.

'Tell me more, Francesca,' she pried gently, sensing the other woman had retired into herself and was revisiting the difficulties of the past few weeks. 'What would it entail?' She tried to smother a burgeoning feeling of excitement and then felt guilty at her lack of sensitivity in the face of such obvious tragedy.

Francesca seemed to shake herself out of her sad thoughts and said, 'The palazzo is full of reminders of my niece's life and, besides, it is in urgent need of an upgrade.' She continued, 'You would travel to Venice and stay there for the duration of the project. It would take about six months, not counting all the preliminary designs, which can be done by you here in Dublin. Obviously, accommodation would be included. If you undertake this project, you will be well rewarded financially.'

Olivia sat forward. 'How exactly would it work, Francesca? I have never worked outside Ireland before, and you already mentioned the wonderful Italian designers…' She trailed off, mystified, as the full weight of Francesca's words hit her.

'You would be given a list of trusted contractors with whom to work and discreet suppliers to use. It would take you away from Ireland for a while…' She looked at Olivia meaningfully and continued, 'A new environment. A new start. What do you think?'

'But why me?' was all Olivia could think of to say. Her thoughts soared. 'Why not a local, Venetian, interior designer who knows their way around?'

'I knew you'd ask me that, and it is something that has occupied my mind a great deal for the past few weeks.' She sat forward; her eyes now keen. 'First of all, you speak fluent Italian.'

Olivia nodded her golden head in agreement and thanked her lucky stars that her mother always spoke to her in her native tongue.

Francesca smiled sadly. 'The tragedy of my niece has been open to huge media scrutiny, and we don't want to use someone local. The palazzo must be renovated as soon as possible. It has become dated and is too full of sad memories. My brother has asked me to take over this project on his behalf; he doesn't want to return there until all renovations have been completed. A new start, so to speak, for all of us,' she added, and gazed out the window with a faraway look in her violet eyes.

Francesca made a visible effort to shake herself back to the present and said in a firm voice, 'Now is the time to do this work, but there cannot be too much local involvement. By the way,' she added, 'my brother owns Hotel Orologio, the hotel you designed, and he likes your work. He knows you have been contracted to restore the stable-yard here and agrees with me that this project should be offered to you.'

This surprised Olivia. She had never met the owner of Orologio, though she had worked on the project for more than a year. She knew it was owned by a mysterious Italian nobleman, but — to the best of her knowledge — he had not appeared during any of Olivia's many site visits.

'Can you tell me why the media is interested in the death of your niece?' Olivia ventured. 'Or is that too personal a question?'

'My niece was killed on an autostrada in the car of my sister-in-law under circumstances which are currently being investigated,' replied Francesca. Olivia could tell that that was all she was going to hear on the subject and decided to let it drop. She would find out more as she went along. She had begun to feel a buzz of real excitement.

Francesca continued, 'The stable block should be completed within six months, I think. Then we can begin to plan your move to Venice, if you are interested in taking up this project?'

Olivia could hardly contain herself.

'I'll do it!' she exclaimed, no longer able to contain her excitement at this proffered lifeline. 'I'll go to Venice!'

JANE

After Sofia's funeral, Niccolo appeared to withdraw into himself. Jane wanted to hear him talk about this terrible tragedy, but he never mentioned Sofia. She wanted to be able to share their terrible loss together, not separately. She needed him. They would sit at the breakfast table in mute silence, after which he would stand up, fold his newspaper, kiss her briefly on the forehead and leave the palazzo, only returning in the late afternoon.

She assumed that most of these days were spent at their country villa in the Euganean Hills, about an hour's drive away. The gardens there were a full-time job, and he looked tanned and fit from all the time spent out-of-doors. Looking at him, she could barely suppress her longing for him to hold and comfort her, which confused her, as these feelings were mixed with resentment for his coldness.

One bright, sunny Venetian morning, he delayed his departure and remained seated after he had folded his newspaper. He looked at her pensively.

'I want you to pack up the palazzo and move with me to the villa.'

Jane was startled.

He continued, 'Francesca has hired an interior designer to renew this home of ours' — he indicated their surroundings — 'I think that's an excellent idea. This place looks in dire need of modernisation.'

'Francesca!' exclaimed Jane angrily. 'What has your insufferable sister got to do with this? It's my home, not hers,' she fumed.

'Francesca grew up here and is part of this family. And don't you forget it. She sees how things are and everyone can see that you pay no attention to how the place looks. This palazzo looks dreadful. She had my permission to proceed and the interior designer we have chosen is excellent.'

'Some Venetian who'll have a field day with gilded mirrors and plenty of gossip, I'm sure,' she responded tartly.

'No,' he countered. 'Francesca was anxious to avoid the inevitable stories and rumours that would fly around Venice's tight-knit design and architectural community. She and I are keen to avoid speculation about Sofia's death while this investigation is ongoing. No. This interior designer is Irish.'

'Irish!' Jane sneered. 'What do the Irish know about designing a palazzo in Venice? For heaven's sake! There are other possibilities, surely.'

'Ms Farrell-Lynskey has worked with Paul in Dublin and was involved in the designs of Hotel Orologio. She speaks fluent Italian and is extremely well thought of in Ireland. She is, according to Francesca, a capable woman of great style and experience.'

'Nico…' She looked at him pleadingly. 'I could look after the interior design here myself. I thought you liked it the way it is at the moment.' She glanced around the huge room, thinking she did not want some ghastly Irishwoman organising her home.

'No, Jane. I've made up my mind. We're moving to the villa until the palazzo is completely refurbished. And that's the end of it. If you want some input into the colour schemes, well, I'm sure Ms Lynskey would be happy to run things by you as the project progresses. She hopes to begin in about six to eight months and will stay at Casa Antica for the duration of the work.'

Jane knew when she was beaten.

'Sofia's bedroom…' She trailed off.

'Will remain untouched,' Niccolo finished the sentence for her. 'I don't want it changed in any way. Not yet, anyway. Not yet.'

He stood up and paused behind her chair.

'I'm going to be in Ireland working for the next few months. I'll come and go, but I will base myself at Hotel Orologio for a while. I will be working with Paul on a project there for the next while. But I'd like to see you safely ensconced at Villa di Falco before I leave. Can you decide? Please?'

Jane remained silent. She knew, deep down, that an important part of her marriage to Niccolo had died along with Sofia, quite apart from the fact that she knew that he had not felt any passion for her for the past couple of years. She wanted this marriage, but at what cost to her sanity? She felt for the reassuring packet of tranquillisers in her pocket.

OLIVIA

The telephone rang shrilly in the early morning. Olivia fumbled around on the bedside locker and looked at the time, 5am. What sort of time was this for anyone to be phoning her? She had reluctantly moved in with her parents on a temporary basis as her house had just been sold. She hoped they had not been disturbed.

'Yes? Olivia here.' She was almost whispering. Her father was a very light sleeper and irritable when disturbed. It was difficult enough to have found herself back at her parents' home in the hills outside Dublin, without waking them at an ungodly hour.

'Olivia? It's Steve.'

Steve's familiar voice jolted her fully awake. She sat bolt upright, clutching the phone to her ear.

'Steve! Where are you? It's been months without a word.' Agitation sounded in her voice.

'Olivia. I'm sorry I took off like that. I'm sorry every day.' He sounded hoarse, as though he had been chain-smoking his favourite miniature cigars, as usual. He broke off and cleared his throat. 'I just wanted to hear your voice and to check in on you to see if you're okay.'

Her instinct was to switch off her phone and throw it across the room. Maybe even smash it against the wall. All thoughts of her light-sleeping father in the next room had completely vanished. She shivered.

Her voice was now measured. 'You phone me NOW after six months of silence and expect me to believe you care about how I am? For goodness sake, Steve! You left me with a mountain of debt. You obviously know I had to leave our home, sell your precious yacht and, as for that aeroplane leasing company... well, you must know they came down on me like a ton of bricks. It's been a nightmare.'

'Oh, God, Olivia. I never intended it to be so hard on you. I was overtaken by events, financial disasters and miscalculations. And then the Recession.' His voice had developed a new tone, one Olivia remembered as the slightly whiny voice he used when he was feeling sorry for himself.

'And you humiliated me.' Her voice rose. 'You left with Diana Burke. I believe she comes and goes from West Africa regularly. Where are you? What's going on?'

'Diana and I have a small villa here on the coast. Portuguese style. Look, Olivia, there are too many questions I have to answer to be able to do it over the phone. I'll try to see you soon. I'm sorry.'

With that, Olivia found herself listening to silence. The phone was dead. He had hung up. She flung the phone on the bed, but not before checking caller ID; but no, it was "Unknown Number", and no way to call back.

There was a tap on her bedroom door. She opened it and saw her mother standing on the landing in her night-gown. Making shushing signals not to wake her husband, she slipped into the room and they sat together on the bed. It was like old times, thought Olivia. Her mother took both her hands in hers.

'I heard your phone, *carissima*.' She looked at her daughter enquiringly.

'Mamma. It was Steve. He's in Africa with Diana Burke. Just what we suspected.'

Suddenly, she burst into tears. All the months of stress and pent-up emotion caused the dam to break and she wailed and sobbed in her mother's arms for the first time since she was about five years old and had fallen from her bicycle.

CHAPTER NINE
OLIVIA

It was a cold, windy morning and the rain lashed against Olivia's windshield as she swung her car up the driveway at Francesca's home. The site meeting was scheduled for 9am, and she was just in time as she drove around to the back, where the archway into the stable-yard was located.

Half way down the avenue, a large silver Range Rover blocked her way. She looked around and could not see any sign of the driver. The vehicle looked as though it had been abandoned in the middle of the laneway and had a small metal trailer attached to the back, which was parked at a slight angle. She beeped her horn and waited, peering out through her windshield into the driving rain.

After about five minutes, and several extra beeps of the Mercedes' horn, Olivia decided she would have to walk the rest of the way. Fuming with anger, she donned her woollen cap over her hair and pulled the hood of her waterproof jacket over the top. Gloves on and the folder containing her designs under her arm, she stepped out into the angry winter weather, abandoning her car where it stood.

Dashing around to the boot, she retrieved her hard hat and high-visibility jacket. All regulation wear on building sites throughout the country.

She marched up to the side window of the Range Rover and peered in. Then stopped in her tracks. She was sure she had seen this silver vehicle before. Could it possibly be the same one that was being driven by the tall, dark man who had caused her to dent her beautiful car? She wondered at the casualness of it all.

Squelching through the mud, she entered the stable-yard through its ancient arch, feeling like a drowned rat. The site visit had begun, and Brendan was there with the electricians and plumbers, discussing the timetable for first fix. A portable cabin had been brought on site a few weeks previously and was situated at the rear of the stable-yard. She entered, dripping rainwater on to the linoleum floor.

Looking around, she welcomed the sight of a gas heater, which sputtered in the corner. A large table had been erected in the middle of the floor and was currently covered in plans. A kettle stood on a side table with a small electric ring, several tea-stained mugs, a giant box of tea bags, some sugar and a bottle of milk. A few copies of a well-known tabloid newspaper, featuring ample, semi-clad ladies on its third page, were lying around, and plastic sandwich boxes containing lunch for the workers were stacked on the corner of the battered table. Half a dozen metal chairs with plastic seats were dotted around the room, now occupied by men in high-visibility jackets, metal-tipped boots and hard hats.

They looked up as Olivia entered and angrily threw her hood back, showering drops everywhere.

'Whose is the Range Rover blocking the laneway?' she demanded angrily. 'How can I get my car into the yard with that vehicle in the way?' She briskly removed her woollen hat and ran her fingers through her hair, shaking it out and looking challengingly at the men sitting around.

Brendan was quick to reply. 'It's probably that landscape guy. Nick, I think his name is.'

'And where is this Nick person?'

'Not sure. I think he was dropping off some pieces of pergola. He may have gone in to have a coffee with Mrs Butler. They seem to know each other pretty well.' Brendan's normally cheery face looked worried at the thought of a confrontation. He well knew Olivia's lack of patience after many years working with her.

Olivia spun around and began to exit the site office, when she stopped in her tracks. She couldn't barge in on Francesca. If what she remembered from her last encounter with this Nick person was accurate, he was a close friend, and she was anxious not to jeopardise her relationship with Francesca in any way at all. After all, the contract for her job in Venice had yet to be completed. No, she would bide her time. If Nick was the same annoying person who obviously had no consideration for other people's convenience or feelings, and he was going to be doing the landscaping here, she would have many opportunities to plot her revenge.

She turned to Brendan and the other men in the cabin and said sweetly, 'Have you a chair for me? Oh, the yellow one! Thank you.'

Brendan looked visibly relieved and hurried to push a chair up beside the table, where she placed her hard hat and parked her briefcase on the floor where she could access it readily.

And there she sat, small, feminine and elegant, surrounded by these large, burly men in muddy, steel-capped boots who listened to her with respect, eyes friendly under their hard hats.

Returning to her vehicle an hour later, she was peeved to see that the Range Rover was still blocking the driveway. As she returned her hard hat and high-visibility jacket to the boot, she looked up just in time to see the tall, dark man stride through the rain towards her. He was wearing a waterproof jacket with the hood up and green wellington boots.

'You'll have to reverse,' he called to her in a commanding voice. 'I can't reverse on this narrow laneway with a trailer on the back.' With that, he got behind the wheel and turned over the engine.

Olivia was incandescent with rage. But she kept silent, sat into her car, started the engine and began to reverse down the laneway. She could see that he could not possibly turn his car or manoeuvre in such a tight space, so she held her tongue. The rain scudded down, and visibility was difficult, but she managed to back as far as the turning circle in front of the house, whereby the man she now thought of as Nick swept past, the trailer bouncing behind him, spraying gravel in her direction. Car and trailer disappeared through the tall gateway and she sat behind her wheel, angrily wishing for his downfall.

And so, the stable-yard conversion continued over the next six months. It was a wonderful project; very satisfying, and the results were truly fabulous. Designed and decorated in a fitting country style, with chintz-covered sofas and airy, floral curtains, the painted woodwork looked great. Olivia was proud of her design work, and justifiably so. Francesca was equally delighted, and Olivia knew that the proposed project on the palazzo in Venice was now hers for the taking.

All had gone smoothly, with the exception of the occasional run-in with Nick, the landscape gardener, who acted like he owned the place, so annoying and intrusive did Olivia find him. He was often to be seen strolling around the stable-yard with Francesca, who looked as though she could not see enough of him, so Olivia kept her mouth shut and made no comment. But chances for revenge were not to be found easily, so she kept aloof and ignored him completely, which was her way of doling out punishment. Whenever she arrived on site to find him filling pots with roses and geraniums, or digging holes to plant laurel, she stuck her nose in the air disdainfully and marched past.

Summer ended and so did the stable-yard project. Francesca threw a little party for the builders and Olivia to "wet the roof" of what she referred to as The Mews. Greeting everyone with a glass of Prosecco, she looked relaxed and cheerful. Her old self, Olivia thought. Her husband, Paul, who had done the architectural designs for The Mews, was by her side to shake the hands of all the builders and craftsmen who had participated in the job.

Olivia wandered around, admiring her handiwork, with a glass of Prosecco in her hand. She had taken a great deal of trouble with her appearance and the men with whom she had worked for the past six months cast shy, admiring glances in her direction, being transfixed by the change in her from hard hat and jeans to high-heeled shoes and a clinging silk dress.

She fully expected to see Nick arrive and, knowing she looked stunning, was looking forward greatly to ignoring him for the evening. Smiling inwardly and expectantly, she found herself watching the door for his entrance. When he didn't show up after the first hour, Olivia was surprised to find herself disappointed. After another half an hour, she realised he was not going to appear and decided to go home. Tomorrow was another day, and she had Venice to look forward to in just a few weeks.

Next morning dawned on the final day of her involvement in The Mews project, as she called it. Arriving at 9am for her meeting with Francesca to go through the final "snag list" — or notation of any small items that might need attention now that the builders and decorators had finished — she drove through the newly refurbished arch and swung her car around the new fountain in the centre of the old stable-yard. Perfectly laid cobbles welcomed her underfoot as she made her way to the front door.

She looked around to admire the courtyard, which had been in ruins before she began work, and gave a satisfied smile. The "snag list" would be non-existent, she promised herself that.

Monica opened the door for her. She was clearing up the debris after the previous night's "roof wetting" and gave her a warm Italian greeting, '*Buongiorno, cara!*', bustling through to the kitchen with a tray laden with glasses.

Olivia looked through to the back of the mews to where French doors led to a small courtyard. She noticed that there were gardeners finishing up out there and decided to have a look. Perhaps Nick was around. She smoothed her hair, took a quick look in the gilded Venetian mirror that hung over the fireplace and stepped outside.

It was a sunny day, with white puffy clouds floating overhead in the usual westerly breeze. She breathed in deeply, happy because the job had gone so well, she had money in her bank account again and she was about to move to Venice in a few weeks. She spotted a familiar figure hunched over a colourful border of hydrangeas and began to stroll casually in that direction.

Suddenly, she saw stars. Literally, she almost knocked herself out. The culprit was a rake that had been left standing against a wheelbarrow. She had stepped on the prongs and it had sprung forward, in true comic-book style, giving her a firm, though harmless, smack on the forehead. She gave a loud yelp and clutched her head in both hands. Looking through her fingers, she saw Nick standing in front of her.

'What a stupid place to leave a rake!' she shouted angrily. 'That's the sort of thing that happens to cartoon characters. How could you leave it there?'

'Are you okay?' he asked. But she could see that he was merely being polite and noticed that he was having great difficulty keeping a straight face. He looked as though he was stifling a laugh and she realised that she had never seen him smile before.

'No thanks to you!' she snapped, as she turned on her heel and strode back to the house, her face flushed with embarrassment and anger in equal measures. "That man again!" she muttered ferociously to herself, suddenly feeling vulnerable and surprisingly close to tears.

CHAPTER TEN
OLIVIA

Olivia looked down from the aeroplane at the Alps unfolding underneath the wings. How beautiful, she thought, examining the network of roads and, seemingly, tiny houses clustered around the lake shores. Being November, the snows had arrived, and the high peaks were sporting a considerable frosting. She thought they looked like chocolate mousse with a generous dusting of icing sugar on top. Then the plains of northern Italy began to unfold with their glorious patchwork of pastures and red-roofed houses lying warmly bathed in the morning sunlight. She felt the beginnings of excitement stirring inside her.

She thought about the past year and a half and about how she had done everything possible to try to find Steve. According to the private detective she had hired at the beginning, the trail had gone cold in Libreville, Gabon. Unable to afford to spend much money on fruitlessly searching for her errant husband, she had chosen to concentrate on holding what was left of her business together, helped greatly by her project as designer for Francesca Butler's stable-yard conversion.

Her self-respect had returned somewhat, and she attributed this, largely, to the fact that she had managed to keep her life on track despite all the setbacks. Her parents had rallied round, too, but did not really know how to cope with this new situation. Her father appeared to think that Olivia had done something to drive Steve away and was quick to criticise her way of life, lack of children and general lifestyle as being the causes for the breakdown of her marriage.

Lucia, her mother, was supportive and loving, but to mention one single word of criticism against her husband was anathema to her very upbringing and lengthy marriage. She was always there in the background as a loving wife and mother, without ever coming forward with an assertive idea of her own.

Olivia used to think that her mother was a product of her generation but had changed her mind over the past few years when, as a businesswoman, she met many women also in their mid- to late-sixties who were dynamic and forward-thinking. It was just Lucia's way, she thought. Always there for her, but only up to the point when her opinions might differ from John's, and then there was a brick wall of loyalty to her husband to surmount.

She sighed with frustration and realised that they had crossed the Alps and were approaching Venice. She felt a buzz of excitement. The conical peaks of the Euganean Hills peeked at her over the light haze that was a more-or-less constant winter fixture over the Po River Delta as the plane began its descent into Venice. She gasped in delight at the sight of the ancient city on her right-hand side as they flew low over the Venetian Lagoon. Then they were on the ground and the crew was telling the passengers not to unbuckle their seatbelts and to keep their mobile phones off; instructions that everyone on board seemed to be deliberately flouting.

The doors were opened and the friendly Irish hostesses in their green uniforms gave her, and all the other passengers, a cheery send-off. As Olivia stepped from the aeroplane, she felt the warm Italian sunshine brush her cheeks and was soothed. That blue sky! The queue for passport control was slow, but the friendly officials gave everybody a smiling 'Buongiorno!', which more than made up for the delay. Her bags arrived onto the carousel fairly quickly, then she walked briskly past the Customs officials and stepped out into the arrival's hall at Venice International Airport.

"OLIVIA LYNSKEY". The small, dark man holding the notice waved back at her as she indicated that she was the woman he was there to meet. Identifying himself as Marco, he expertly guided her and her bags through the throng of excited holidaymakers, out of the sliding doors and across the covered walkway to the large black Audi that was parked by the kerb. The boot closed on her bags and the car doors softly closed, before they glided away from the airport building and followed the signs for Venezia. Before she knew it, the car was speeding across the long bridge that divided Venice from the mainland, pulling into a multi-storey car-park in Tronchetto and gliding up the ramps to the fifth storey.

Exiting the car-park with her bags and her escort, Olivia was charmed to see that the next vehicle she was entering was a smart wooden motor launch with lots of chrome trim. Marco helped her aboard and fired up the engine. So, he was a boatman too, she mused. The boat weaved its way down the Grand Canal. Marco pointed out various famous landmarks, such as the Rialto, as they headed down towards Ponte Accademia, the large wooden bridge which crosses the Grand Canal before it enters the basin in front of Piazza San Marco. Looking up at the crowds of tourists on Ponte Accademia, Olivia felt her head reel slightly. So many tourists, she thought, while looking in amazement at the Peggy Guggenheim Museum, wondering why it was only half the height of its neighbours.

Her dream-like trance ended then, as their boat took a sharp right down a narrow side canal and Marco expertly guided the launch under a small bridge, eventually nudging up against a dock on the right-hand side, where he jumped overboard and tied the motor launch to one of several wooden poles sticking out of the canal beside the dock. He took Olivia's hand as she climbed out onto the pavement and looked around.

Red brick and painted stucco-finished buildings looked down on her, mostly four storeys tall, all of which appeared to have the main living floor one flight up, with tall windows leading onto small balconies. She knew that this floor was called the *"piano nobile"* and was, indeed, the main living area in most Venetian homes, raised well above the high tide mark.

Unloading her bags, Marco pulled two of them down a narrow calle — or alleyway — to the front door of a tall, narrow house. It was painted a deep shade of terracotta and the letterbox was full to overflowing with leaflets and circulars, advertising its current status as vacant. A heavy metal barrier was affixed across the bottom half of the door.

'Che cos'è? What's that?' she exclaimed, never having seen such a contraption before.

'It's for Acqua Alta,' he informed her, taking a key, inserting it into a small lock and levering the heavy metal panel from its frame.

'For high tide!' she exclaimed. 'A flood barrier!' Olivia tried not to feel intimidated as she raised her chin and looked up at the high terracotta walls of her new home-to-be. Its dark green shutters, now closed, and the bedraggled wrought-iron flower containers proclaimed its emptiness. Was this to be her home for the duration of the interior design work on the palazzo? She turned to Marco.

'Is this my house?'

'Si!' Marco responded with enthusiasm, bringing out a bunch of keys and inserting one into the lock. 'It's called Casa Antica: old house. It belongs to the conte.'

The door opened and Marco waved his arm to indicate that she should enter. Olivia took a tentative step into the dark hallway.

A quick peek into a downstairs room whose door was on her right revealed a dark bedroom with a terrazzo floor and a heavily beamed ceiling. The room had been decorated simply. Painted white, with a single bed piled high with silk cushions of various vibrant colours. Marco pulled back the white linen curtains, opened the window and parted the shutters, letting in some sunlight. Olivia tentatively opened an adjoining door and found a shower room finished in terracotta and cream marble tiles, with old-fashioned Victorian style brass fittings in the shower.

Following Marco, Olivia climbed the stairs to the first floor with a feeling of dread. What was she doing here in this dark house in a strange city? Where had her excitement gone? She felt a clutch of fear in her chest. She felt vulnerable and very alone.

The wooden stairs arrived at an open-plan room that, she was relieved to see when Marco opened the windows and shutters, was cosy, well-lit and resplendent in her favourite terrazzo flooring: *pavimenti alla veneziana*. She looked out of one of the windows at the rear and saw that it overlooked a small courtyard where a clothes-drying rack displayed a startling array of colourful ladies' underwear. Her neighbour must be quite an amply developed lady, thought Olivia, smiling to herself.

Once Marco had opened all the shutters, the little house was transformed from a dark space into a light and comfortable home. A sofa upholstered in charcoal grey linen with red silk cushions looked comfortable next to a small inlaid chestnut table with four dining chairs upholstered in red and grey striped linen. Along one entire wall, a massive dark green and brass unit housed a hefty gas cooker, complete with hood, and a sink and worktop were adorned with a set of knives. The white walls throughout the tiny house gave it a feeling of spaciousness.

A further flight of stairs brought her up to her bedroom. Here the room was dominated by an enormous four-poster bed dressed in sumptuous white linen. The floor was carpeted in a pale lemon wool and Olivia began to feel that the house was actually quite cosy and certainly very prettily decorated. The adjoining bathroom was almost identical to the one downstairs, right down to the oversized shower fittings. She loved it all.

Marco's departure was preceded by a hand-over of a huge bunch of keys and an envelope containing instructions on how to use the air conditioning, heating, and notes on bin collections, which were rigorous in Venice, where rubbish was collected on trollies and trundled down the alleyways to special boats. Her head swam. Just then, her mobile rang. It was Francesca.

'My dear!' she exclaimed. 'Have you arrived safely? Are you in your dear little house yet?' Her voice was warm and enthusiastic.

'Francesca! How lovely to hear from you!' Seating herself on the grey linen sofa with the silk cushions, she was happy to hear a friendly voice. 'Yes, I have arrived. The house is very sweet, thank you. I haven't had an opportunity to take it all in yet.' Then she added, 'Marco has just left.'

'Oh, yes. Dear, sweet Marco,' enthused Francesca. 'He's been with our family for years and years. He's the one to ask if you need anything.'

The thought of getting back to work excited Olivia. She couldn't wait to get her teeth into this project. After so many months of uncertainty, career-wise, the idea of working again had a powerful effect on her and she suddenly felt rejuvenated.

She had spent the past few months studying drawings and photographs of Palazzo Berberio Falco and had drafted several possible plans for its renovation and redecoration, visiting Francesca on a weekly basis to run her ideas past her new employer. It appeared that her designs had met with the approval of Francesca's brother, the mysterious Conte di Falco, too. As far as Olivia could gather, he was now staying at his country retreat, somewhere near Venice.

By now, she felt she knew most aspects of the palazzo intimately but was eager to walk through the doors and see the great rooms for herself.

'Thank you, Francesca,' she said agreeably, all thoughts about the unfamiliarity of her new surroundings gone for the moment. 'I'll be ready.'

MARCELLO

Marcello Roselli stood at the stern of his gondola and surveyed the scene as he rowed through the Venetian canals. His persona was like a magnet for the female tourists. And he knew it.

Most of the gondoliers whose images stared broodingly from the glossy photographs of Venice were portrayed as dark and swarthy, with soulful brown eyes and romantic Mediterranean looks. But Marcello's hair was blond, tied back in a ponytail, and he could be guaranteed to catch the eye of many a female tourist out for a good time and longing for romance, hopefully in the form of a Venetian gondolier.

His broad shoulders were evident from the merest glance at his navy-and-white-striped gondolier's sweater, and his tight black trousers showed off his muscular physique to its best advantage as he crouched to row under a low bridge.

Various tattoos were partially visible on his forearms, the most obvious being a zodiacal Sagittarian symbol. A wooden bead bracelet on one tanned wrist was there to bring good luck, and so far, it had served him well, as his success with female tourists was legendary, even amongst the gondolieri of Venice; an achievement in itself.

This morning, three American girls dressed in smart Capri pants and bright T-shirts sat in his gondola, taking selfies.

Marcello eyed the girls with their perfect skin and teeth, in particular a leggy blonde with striking blue eyes, cast mainly in his direction. He began to sing his favourite barcarole "La Biondina in Gondoleta"; or, in English, "The Blonde in the Gondola". Translated into English, it goes like this:

"The other evening, I went rowing with a blonde in a gondola.

The poor girl was so happy that she fell sound asleep immediately.

As she slept in my arms, each time I woke her

The rocking of the boat sent her back to sleep again."

Sung in a reasonably good tenor, he was happy to note that the girls all looked suitably impressed and began to pay closer attention. He fingered his lucky wooden beads; he considered himself a true Romeo when he saw a girl he liked. He was a gondolier, after all, and every bit as romantic as they had imagined when they were planning their trip.

He was tempted to try out his seduction routine but needed to figure out how to get this particular girl on her own, preferably in the evening. He needed to cut her off from the pack. If that was impossible, he could always call on a couple of his gondolier colleagues to come along as partners for her two friends. His precious gondola could seat six people and his selected male pals enjoyed these bonus outings accompanying willing girls down the darkened canals by night.

At the end of the twenty-minute trip, Marcello skilfully guided his gondola into the narrow canal in Giglio and tied it tightly to the side. It needed to be firmly in position to encourage tourists to take those first tentative steps towards a romantic trip down the Venetian waterways. He began to help the girls from the gondola and noticed the blonde lingering.

Realising that this was going to be easier than he had hoped, he took her hand as he helped her onto the wooden jetty, too. He squeezed it gently.

'Are you busy tonight? Perhaps you and your friends would like a night-time trip? Or if you come alone, you'll be completely safe. I promise. Venice by night is very beautiful.'

'Oh!' An excited gasp. 'That would be amazing! Hey! Wait up!' she called after her friends, who were strolling towards the nearest bar for a lunchtime snack. They turned.

After consultation between them, they agreed that they would all meet that evening at seven o'clock.

'My name is Candice.' Her eyes took in every romantic inch of the gondolier.

'Marcello, at your service, Candice. See you this evening.'

As the girls strolled away, chatting animatedly, he took out his mobile phone to call his pals. Smiling to himself, he could already tell that he would have no difficulty in separating her from the pack later that evening.

Not one to waste a moment, as he put the phone away, he flashed his eyes at two approaching teenage girls and gave them what he thought was a sexy smile. They obviously found it sexy, too, as they blushed and giggled their way past his gondola, taking quick glances over their shoulders as they rounded the next corner.

But lunchtime called, and he decided to take a stroll and fuel up with a sandwich at one of the many bars in the area across the Accademia Bridge. A strikingly beautiful woman was sitting at the base of an ornate cistern in the piazza ahead of him. Her face was to the sun and her long blonde hair was in vivid contrast to the grey stone behind her. He felt no premonition that from that fateful moment onwards, life would never be the same again.

CHAPTER ELEVEN
OLIVIA

After chatting with Francesca, Olivia clicked her mobile off and threw it down on the sofa. She wanted to have a really good look around her new house, but first of all, she opened the fridge and found that it was completely empty. A cupboard revealed a packet of coffee, but nothing else. She would have to go shopping. But first, she suddenly decided that she wanted to go out to explore her surroundings. The house could wait.

Throwing on a jacket and inserting a map of Venice into the pocket of her shoulder bag, she closed the shutters carefully and exited the front door. She didn't know what to do with the flood barrier, so she slid it into the hallway. Surely there wouldn't be an Acqua Alta today! The canal at the end of the *calle* had looked pretty low. Not having a clue what to do, she decided to chance it. Locking the front door behind her, she headed off towards the end of the calle with a spring in her step.

Cautiously memorising where she was going — she had read that Venice was like a maze and that it was easy to get lost, even with a map — she crossed over a small footbridge and headed in the direction of the nearest large canal. A statue of the Virgin Mary was mounted on the wall of a nearby house, sporting a turquoise copper umbrella or sunshade.

"That statue can be my landmark! The Madonna with the Umbrella." Olivia noted it carefully.

Consulting her map, she understood that this large canal where she was heading was the wide Giudecca Canal, which divided the old city and the island of Giudecca.

Her stomach rumbled ominously, and she was reminded that she had had a very early start that morning with her flight from Dublin and had been too tense to eat breakfast. But she needed some supplies first. Walking along fondamenta Zattere, she was stunned to see a vast cruise ship edging its way slowly up the Giudecca Canal. Attached to a tug-boat and with another small vessel chugging along behind this colossus, she could see that the decks were lined with tourists, all flashing their cameras, staring out over the rooftops of the city, which was being dwarfed completely. As the voice of Luciano Pavarotti belted out Nessun Dorma from the upper decks high above, she could see what she understood to be the beautiful Palladian Redentore church, looking tiny as the ship headed up the canal.

At first, she could not see how such a slow-moving ship — no matter its size — could be causing the sort of damage the Venetians claimed it did. And then she saw it. Waves, left behind in the cruise-liner's wake, began to lap over the side of the Fondamenta. As she passed over a small footbridge beside the Zattere vaporetto stop, she could see what looked like mini tidal-waves heading down the side canal, with the result that the wake could be felt all the way down these small canals, too. She began to feel indignant on behalf of the Venetians, who complained so bitterly about this invasion of their space; and she had only been there a couple of hours!

Passing over another bridge and arriving at yet another vaporetto stop, she spotted a good-sized supermarket and popped inside. Wheeling a small orange trolley around, she bought pasta, coffee, wine, milk and the various essentials that she thought she could probably carry unaided back to her little house. But she needed to eat and decided to head back home.

Using her excellent sense of direction, she ducked down another alleyway on her way back, one she had not seen before. On the corner, an old building on stilts claimed her attention for a few minutes as she headed in the general direction of home. Amazed to see a gondola repair shop across the canal, she stopped to linger a few minutes and noticed several people standing around in the alleyway, eating what looked like delicious open sandwiches on white napkins and drinking wine from clear plastic cups.

Her curiosity aroused, she saw that she had arrived at what looked like a shop selling wines and spirits. The window was full of bottles of whiskey, vodka and liquors sporting star-shaped price tags. She peeped timidly inside and saw that it, in fact, sold what she was to discover later were *cicchetti*: deliciously small open sandwiches which were displayed under glass cases. She entered and looked around to see what other people were eating and drinking. Most had a glass of what looked like white wine and a small plate of *cicchetti* in their hands or balanced on the side counters and shelves provided. Apparently, if you took it outside, you were given a plastic cup and a napkin, no plate.

The woman behind the counter was friendly.

'Could I have what they're having?' Olivia pointed at two well-dressed customers perched on bar stools, engaged in vigorous discussion, which seemed to involve many hand-signals, drinking what looked like white wine and eating delicious-looking open sandwiches. She could see some hard-boiled egg on top.

'Certo!' agreed the assistant, and she poured a small glass of white wine. 'Un ombra,' she added.

She then placed two overflowing *cicchetti* on a plate, with a napkin. As it was handed over the counter, Olivia paid what felt like a pittance after prices in Dublin, which were horrendous when it came to food.

Placing her plastic bag full of groceries at her feet, she bit into the first one. The egg was on top of a generous amount of black truffle mixed with a cream cheese that Olivia was pretty sure was robiola. The second one was salami and mozzarella. Beautifully prepared. She sipped her white wine and marvelled that she could eat all this for less than €5.00. As she emerged feeling replete and relaxed for the first time in months, the low November sun was warm on her face and she crossed a little bridge and strolled over to sit on the step at the base of a cistern, where she leaned back and closed her eyes for a few minutes.

Opening them, she realised she was not alone any more. A tall, blond man was standing looking at her quizzically. Dressed in a navy-and-white-striped sweater, with a black jacket thrown over his shoulder, he was obviously a gondolier. Unfamiliar with Venice, having just visited once when on honeymoon with Steve, she was not completely sure about this, but then she saw that he was carrying one of the trademark Panama hats with the navy ribbon, and she realised she was in the process of meeting her first gondolier.

'You are American perhaps?' he enquired politely in heavily accented English. 'Your first time in Venice?' Then he noticed the bag of groceries at her feet. 'You have rent an apartment?'

Olivia was flustered. Unaccustomed to being addressed by total strangers as she was, it seemed more acceptable somehow to be addressed by a real-life gondolier in Venice.

'Yes. No. Not exactly.' Switching immediately to Italian, she responded, 'I'm here to work for a while and have just arrived today.' Just saying this out loud made her feel a bit strange, and she suddenly felt overwhelmed and anxious to get away.

'You speak Italian!' He was overjoyed. 'Have you had a ride in a gondola yet?' He sat down beside her on the edge of the cistern.

'No. Not yet,' Olivia responded, remembering — particularly now that his handsome face was at eye-level — all the dire warnings about the price of a gondola ride and being aware that her funds were pretty limited until her first pay cheque in two weeks' time.

'Would you like me to take you out in my gondola later when it is less busy?' He looked pretty self-confident and Olivia felt slightly uneasy. It was a long time since she had been chatted up by a man; and such a handsome one at that. 'No charge. My way to welcome you to Venice.'

Olivia was sorely tempted to say yes, but she felt that good sense must prevail. Tomorrow was her first day of work at Palazzo Berberigo Falco, after all.

'No, thank you,' she said with real regret in her voice. 'Perhaps another time. I'm sure we'll bump into each other again. I'll be working near here for the next six months,' she added.

'What is your job?' The gondolier seemed to have accepted her rejection with equanimity.

'I'm an interior designer,' she replied, not sure how many details to give to this muscular stranger in the tight black trousers. 'I've been given the job of renovating one of the palazzi on the Grand Canal.'

His eyes lit up, obviously impressed by this news.

'If you change your mind, my name is Marcello and my gondola is moored not far from here in Santa Maria del' Giglio, just over on the far side of the Accademia Bridge. You can find me easily if you ask around.'

'I'm Olivia,' she responded. 'I'll remember your offer and maybe I'll take you up on it when I've settled in a bit.' She smiled at him warmly, as she couldn't help but like his looks and manner; she was truly enjoying the repartee and his polite chat-up lines.

She stood up, collecting her bags of groceries.

'Arrividerci!' she called over her shoulder as she made her way back towards Zattere and the fondamenta, which would take her back to her little house.

Marcello stood for a few minutes watching her departing back, clad in a snugly fitting jacket, her tight jeans showing her long, shapely legs, feet and calves encased in black suede knee-high boots. Her glorious golden hair was moving as she walked, effortlessly carrying her bags of shopping. He was thoughtful for a few minutes and then began to stroll back to his gondola at Giglio.

"Arrividerci bella!" he said to himself. "Ci vediamo. Until we meet again."

CHAPTER TWELVE
JANE

WILTSHIRE, ENGLAND. 1999

Jane wished she had brought a sun-hat. She felt as though her fine blonde hair was sticking to her head as she wandered down to the Palladian Bridge at Wilton House. The air was warm, and she brushed away the occasional fly that buzzed around her head. The bridge looked magnificent bathed in the afternoon sun, and she sat on a bench to admire it.

So lost in thought was she about her problems, that at first, she didn't notice the tall, dark man standing on the lawn a few metres away. Where had he come from? She looked at him for a moment, taken by his elegant figure and obvious air of self-confidence. He noticed her stare.

'You like the bridge?' he asked her in softly accented English. Maybe Italian? Most other English speakers didn't pronounce the word "bridge" with a double "E" in the middle, she thought.

He turned to face her. Large violet eyes, surrounded by thick black lashes, dominated his handsome features.

'I love it,' she responded. 'I've always been a great fan of Palladio. In fact, I think if I'd been born five hundred years ago, I'd have been a Palladio groupie.' She laughed. And he laughed, too. A clear burst of happy laughter on a warm summer's day in an English garden.

'You know, of course, that this was not designed by Palladio?' he enquired politely. 'Inigo Jones was the architect here; a great fan of our Andrea Palladio, by all accounts.'

'Yes, indeed!' she agreed. 'I've just been to the house for the first time and it's so beautiful. I'm still feeling overwhelmed.'

'Me, too. It's the nearest I can get to the wonderful architecture of my homeland, Italy.'

'Ah! So, you *are* Italian!' Jane was enthusiastic about her deductive powers when it came to be accented English, boasting that she could pinpoint an accent within fifty kilometres of its source. 'What are you doing in England? Are you on holiday?'

'I'm studying landscape design in London,' he responded. 'I came to see the gardens here at Wilton and thought I'd have a look at the house, too, while I was here. The Palladian link made it very appealing to me,' he added. 'Have you visited Italy?'

'A few times. With my, erm, ex-husband,' she added, looking down at her canvas espadrilles for inspiration, wanting to say something interesting about her links with that warm, beautiful country. 'I've been to Venice and to Rome a couple of times, but I suppose that's hardly an unusual thing to do.'

'I'm from Venice!' he announced suddenly. 'And my name is Niccolo di Falco.' He proffered his hand, which Jane shook. She felt a sudden shock at the electricity which passed between them as their gazes locked.

'Jane Maxwell. Pleased to meet you Niccolo,' she said in a soft voice. I'm visiting my aunt in Salisbury. But I live in London,' she added.

As they strolled back to their cars, Niccolo asked Jane for her phone number and promised to telephone soon. She watched him drive away.

"I wonder if I'll ever see that man again," she thought, hoping she would.

That night, Niccolo phoned.

'When will you be back in London?' he enquired, seeming pleased to hear she was due back the following day. 'Can we meet for dinner?'

'Yes,' she said in her calmest voice, hoping that her eagerness was not audible down the phone line. Not to mention her beating heart.

They arranged to meet at the busy Chelsea Brasserie, which was just around the corner from Jane's Sloane Street flat. "Not, perhaps, the most romantic place to dine," Jane thought, "but it is our first date and I know nothing about him."

That first evening together was memorable. The food, however, was quickly forgotten as they hurried back to Sloane Street directly after the potted shrimp starter, all thoughts of the main course forgotten, and headed without delay to Jane's four-poster bed, where they made love over and over again on her fine, white cotton bed-linen. She had never known such ecstasy. Such passion.

Lying together, propped up on Jane's down-filled pillows, they talked steadily into the small hours, broken only by intervals of love-making so intense that Jane thought she would die of pleasure.

'I'm just recently divorced,' she told him some time during their first night together. 'I had to leave Geoffrey. He was a violent alcoholic who hit me so hard when we were on holiday last year that he actually perforated my ear-drum.' She fell silent and stroked his chest with her fingertips, adding, 'He's given me so many black eyes I've lost count at this stage.'

Niccolo turned to her in horror. 'Your husband beat you?' he enquired incredulously. 'A little woman like you? What sort of man does that?'

'I was just nineteen when we married,' she said. 'The beating began about a year later, while I was expecting my son Max. He lives with his father now. Oh, and Maxwell is my maiden name. My son is Max Lewisham. I'm actually the Hon. Jane Maxwell. My father is Lord Remington, from Gloucester.'

'Why is your son not with you?' Niccolo asked incredulously. 'Surely the courts would not leave a young boy with a violent alcoholic.'

'Money buys a lot,' Jane responded non-committedly. 'I just see Max at holiday time. He's fourteen years old now and seems to enjoy his father's company. It's... tricky,' she added.

'What else did he do, this awful husband of yours? I've a feeling there's more.'

'Well, he was unfaithful to me on many occasions, but I think the worst thing was how he neglected me when I was expecting Max, and the fact that he went off on holiday for three weeks just after he was born, leaving me on my own in the middle of the countryside. I mean, I didn't even have any home help at that stage.'

During those first halcyon days of their relationship, Jane told Niccolo everything she could think of about her childhood in England, her friends and, particularly, about her short-lived marriage to Geoffrey. She didn't want to have any secrets from him. She even told him about her first boyfriend, Philip, with whom she went to the local Saturday-night dances, assuring him that this teenage relationship was entirely innocent.

She had been a virgin when she married Geoffrey at the age of nineteen. Her upbringing, being an only daughter, combined with having to deal with a strict, over-protective father, had exerted such an influence on her that she would have been too terrified of being found out or, the ultimate disgrace, becoming pregnant. This fear, instilled in her by her father, kept her chaste until the freedom brought about by her burgeoning friendship with Geoffrey — seen by her parents as a "suitable match" — made marriage seem like a good idea, if only to get away from home.

Talking together as they strolled through Hyde Park in London later that summer, Jane began to open up about her darkest secret, untold to anyone previously and unknown to all except her family doctor.

'Geoffrey was seen as a safe bet,' she explained. 'He came from a wealthy family and, being almost ten years older than me, appeared to be a man of the world; in my father's eyes, someone who would take care of me.'

'So, you married him,' Niccolo added.

'I did,' Jane agreed, 'and it was a disaster. I hate him now. I hate him for destroying my precious twenties. Almost all that decade was taken up with being beaten, cheated on and lied to constantly. I spent five years trying to escape and to get a divorce. By the time I had my longed-for freedom restored to me, I was almost thirty years old, with a ten-year-old son who now lives with his father.'

'It sounds so unfair. How did you lose custody of Max? Do you mind me asking?'

Jane tensed herself. It was the moment she had dreaded for so long. Could she trust Niccolo to cope with this long-hidden secret? She tried to sound calm. This was one subject she was afraid to discuss, terrified he would leave her when he knew the truth, but she wanted to be as honest as possible.

She cleared her throat nervously as she prepared to unburden herself.

'I don't want to make excuses for my past, but all that terrible stress with Geoffrey almost drove me crazy. I'm afraid I developed an unhealthy relationship with alcohol, tranquillisers and sleeping pills in my mid-twenties.' She paused, searching for the right words. 'I accidentally overdosed one night when Max was staying over at Geoffrey's. That finished off my one attempt at motherhood. Only for my house-keeper Mary, I might have died. She arrived early the next morning, found me unconscious and called an ambulance. I had the awful indignity of having my stomach pumped, and not a lot of sympathy from the medical staff, who thought I was an attention-seeker. But it really was an accident. It's easy to overdose on sleeping pills when you've had so much to drink you haven't a clue how many you've taken.'

'What happened then?' Niccolo asked her quietly.

'Well, I lost custody of Max. Plain and simple. Geoffrey took legal steps to have my son removed from my home and now it's just too late to fight for him. He's well settled and enjoying school. He appears to be perfectly happy and I see him regularly.'

Niccolo frowned. 'And how are you now? As regards the pills and all that?'

'Oh, I don't take pills any more, and just have the occasional glass of wine in the evenings. My life is completely different now,' she added, picking an imaginary piece of fluff from her sleeve. Any excuse to look down and not meet his eyes. She was ashamed and — she knew — not entirely truthful either

'I'd love to meet this Geoffrey person,' he growled. 'Did none of your family intervene? How could they let you go through all this without doing something? Why did nobody ever take a swing at him?'

He was so indignant, he walked over to a nearby bench and sat down heavily. A little old lady, who was sitting at the other end with her dog, eyed him warily. Apparently, not liking what she saw, she stood up and walked away, dragging her reluctant cocker spaniel along with her.

Jane sat down beside him and put her hand on his arm.

'Niccolo,' she began to try to explain. 'I told nobody. I was so young; I thought it must somehow be my fault. I was doing something wrong. I felt I must need punishment for whatever it was. It's hard to explain all these feelings, so many years after the event.' She patted her hot cheeks with a tissue. She could feel herself becoming heated. 'But when he perforated my ear-drum, I knew I couldn't take it for one minute longer. Then I went to my parents and told them about the awfulness that had been my marriage to Geoffrey. And do you know what my father said?'

Niccolo looked at her enquiringly, a sad look on his face.

'I can't imagine. But I hope it was supportive.'

'Hardly!' she exclaimed. 'He said, "What will our friends say?" She looked at Niccolo with sad, blue eyes. Jane could read compassion for her in the emotions clearly etched into his facial expression and wondered if she should have told him these stories at all. Should she have kept her own council? But she wanted him to know everything, and to be completely honest with this wonderful man, so she held her ground and said, 'I never forgave my father for his lack of support and understanding. And for never, ever addressing the issue with Geoffrey. We seldom communicate. Until this day there's been a chasm between us that I just can't describe.'

That night, feeling vulnerable after all she told him, she turned to him. 'I love you, Nico.'

No response. Niccolo turned his face towards the window, where the bedroom curtains idled in the night air.

It was the first time those words had been uttered between them over the few months they had been together; those first months, when their passion for one another seemed all-consuming and mutual, and she had felt the stirrings of feelings over which she felt she had no control. She realised she loved him and felt that she needed him to know.

Saying those words had caused her to feel as though she was stepping into outer space; into the unknown, especially as he had remained completely silent, causing her to experience a huge feeling of anxiety. She did not press the subject but decided to let it rest for a while.

That night, she watched his handsome face on her pillow as she lay beside him, wondering how to react to his silence. She was aware that he seemed unhappy at her revelation and felt that he would have been far more comfortable if she had said nothing at all about her feelings for him.

'You're very silent on the subject,' she heard herself saying, regretting the words even as she was uttering them. It sounded suspiciously like begging.

'What do you expect me to say?' he asked her calmly. 'Love is a big word. I don't know how I feel about you at this point.' He propped himself up on one elbow and looked down at her. 'Isn't what we have enough? We're friends who have great sex. We enjoy each other's company. We have lots in common. What more do you want? Why do you need to hear the "L" word anyway? What difference would it make?'

He lay back down on the pillow, obviously expecting no reaction from Jane. And he got none. She lay there with her heart pounding, while a physical weight — a sort of grief — pressed against her heart.

"I'll figure this out tomorrow," she thought to herself, remaining silent, feeling faintly humiliated. "Perhaps it's just too soon. I'll give him time."

But nothing changed. A year later, she was no wiser. Every now and again, when they had a disagreement, she would ask him if he loved her and he would become angry.

'What's the hurry?' he asked her angrily one night. 'I don't know how I feel about you. I don't know if I'll ever love you or anyone else. Maybe there's something wrong with me, but I'm not going to tell you I love you if I don't. At least in the way you want me to.' With that, the subject was closed; until the next time.

And Jane still hung in there, realising full well that if she pushed the subject of his feelings any harder, he would probably leave her. She was terrified of losing him.

"Is it possible to love someone too much?" she wondered. "Is this really what I want?"

Every time she thought of walking away, she realised that she needed him in her life, no matter how he felt about her. He was with her, and that was what mattered. At least, that's what she told herself, time after time.

Niccolo found affection very difficult. In the early days, Jane used to throw her arms around him for a hug. This was almost always rebuffed or barely tolerated. He would stand there with his hands down by his sides, giving the occasional sigh of frustration. He hated any intimacy outside of the actual act of sex, which he performed with great enthusiasm and expertise. Jane found this perplexing, and it made her long for the touch of his hands so keenly that she found herself instigating love-making on a regular basis. In other words, as long as she didn't spontaneously throw her arms around him when she felt a rush of warm feeling towards him, he seemed quite content to live without physical affection of any sort.

'You're so insecure. Why are you so insecure?'

She had asked him once more, after a bout of passionate love-making, if he loved her. The words had slipped out and she regretted the question. 'Because I'm in a one-sided relationship,' she responded, tears not far away.

'How do you figure that?' His voice had a dangerous edge. 'You must know that I care about you and enjoy your company. Who else do I spend all my time with? Who comes everywhere with me? Who sleeps in my bed at night?' He paused, and his voice softened. 'Don't I make you happy? I just don't know about the "L" word.' He still could not bring himself to use the word "love".

A few months later, Jane discovered she was pregnant. Knowing that she probably hadn't been as careful as she should have been in the taking of her birth-control pill, she was terrified of telling Niccolo. She expected outrage and accusations of manipulation. But he was surprisingly relaxed about the whole thing.

'We'll get married,' he announced, taking her calmly by the hand. And so, they did, just fifteen months after they first met.

Of course, Jane knew that Niccolo didn't love her the way she dreamed of. Perhaps he never would. But Jane felt that she loved him enough for both of them and kept her silence on the subject of the "L" word.

Then Sofia was born and Niccolo fell in love for the first time. His baby daughter completely captured his heart. She would run to him when he arrived home in the evenings and he would take her onto his lap to stroke her white-blonde head and kiss her tiny heart-shaped face. Jane would watch the two of them together and feel the conflicting emotions of envy and love clench inside, like a physical reaction. As Sofia grew into the beautiful teenager she had become, she and Niccolo shared a relationship that was close, warm and mutually exclusive. Jane lived just outside that magic circle, created whenever father and daughter were together.

And now Sofia was dead. Jane felt that it would have been much, much better if it were she who had died, as her life had become a living hell.

***

'They found a flask of grappa in your bag,' Niccolo informed her a few weeks after she arrived home from hospital. 'They're taking your alcohol and pill intake seriously. They're wondering how much you'd had to drink in the days leading up to the accident.' His voice was dispassionate and cold. 'They're wondering how impaired your reactions might have been.'

Jane felt an icy finger touch the back of her neck and felt real fear. How could he be so cold towards her? Did he not realise that they had both suffered the same loss and that she was also feeling deep pain and grief at the horrific death of their daughter?

'I had nothing to drink on the day of the accident,' she stated, hating the way her voice quavered with unshed tears and trying to hold them back, while feeling the first hit of moisture on her eyelids.

'They found drugs in your system,' he stated baldly. 'Valium was it, Jane?' His voice sharpened. Her tears fell.

'I was feeling stressed,' she blurted. 'I didn't know where you were or when you were coming back.'

'You're blaming *me*?' he shouted angrily and with mounting disbelief. 'You knew I was in Ireland staying with Francesca and opening Orologio. You knew I'd be back when I was ready.'

'You never called. I hadn't heard from you in days.' Her feelings of indignation were helping her to be a bit stronger on a subject which had caused her endless stress and many — too many — hours spent waiting for the telephone to ring, knowing that if she called him she would, inevitably, interrupt him in one of his lengthy meetings and bring about an angry response. Or worse, she would be accused of hounding him. She wanted to appear to be coolly accepting on the subject of his lack of communication in the weeks and months prior to Sofia's death.

'I was busy.' Niccolo was winding down now. His sudden rages were always followed by seeming resignation to whatever it was that had annoyed him in the first place.

He added, seemingly as an afterthought, 'The Carabinieri will want to talk to you some time over the next couple of days.'

CHAPTER THIRTEEN
OLIVIA

Getting out of bed on her first morning in Venice, Olivia looked around the darkened room with its heavy decoration and moved into the marble shower-room to prepare for the day ahead. She was excited and full of anticipation about the fact that the day had arrived: day one of her biggest adventure.

Dressing in tight black stretch pants, tucked into leather boots, and donning a camel-coloured cashmere turtleneck sweater, she ate a banana with some yoghurt that she had bought at the supermarket the previous day.

'Mmm!' she exclaimed aloud, as she tasted the delicious creamy yoghurt from the South Tyrol area of northern Italy. This Tyrolean yoghurt was going to be addictive, she thought, as she made a mental note to buy a few more tubs.

She turned her attention to the files spread out on the table in front of her. The photos of the palazzo showed a magnificent exterior fronting onto the south side of the Grand Canal, close to the Accademia Bridge, approximately a ten-minute walk from her little house near the fondamenta Zattere. The interior photographs were another matter altogether. They showed her that the palazzo needed drastic modernisation.

For a start, some of the wonderful Venetian terrazzo-style flooring, known as *pavimenti alla veneziana*, had been covered over by wood-patterned linoleum, and most of the furniture was either out of proportion to the rooms it occupied or was outdated, neither being antique nor modern, but of an era probably set somewhere in the sixties or seventies. She had been stunned when she saw the photographs first, having expected Venetian nobility to have decorated their priceless palazzo in a more luxurious style. I mean, she thought, ugly bamboo furniture on the *piano nobile*! What next?

But, above all, an air of sadness permeated the photographs. Perhaps because she was aware of the tragedy which had indirectly brought about her change of fortune, Olivia could not be unaffected by the appearance of neglect and disinterest which showed clearly through the eye of the lens that had taken these photographs. Here was a home which needed more than a decorative pick-me-up, she thought.

Packing her files into a briefcase, which doubled as a back-pack, she donned her purple down-filled coat, a black woollen hat and fur-lined gloves. Throwing a long wool and cashmere black and grey scarf around her shoulders in true Italian tradition, she hoisted the back-pack onto her shoulders and opened the front door of the house onto its little alleyway. It was a foggy morning, "a real pea-souper", she thought. Locking the door behind her, she walked towards the small canal, where she turned left and headed in the direction of the Accademia and her new adventure.

As this was her first visit to the palazzo, she carefully followed the instructions mapped out for her by Francesca before she left Dublin. Walking along Calle Chiesa, close to the Peggy Guggenheim Collection, which became Calle Sant' Agnese after a few minutes, she passed in front of the famous Gallerie dell 'Accademia. Crowds of tourists were already gathering at the base of the high, wooden bridge which spanned the Grand Canal at that point. Slipping down another narrow alleyway, she arrived at a tall gate and knew that this was the palazzo.

Pressing a big brass bell-push on the wall, she waited for a response. A woman's voice said, 'Si?', and Olivia spoke her name into a metal grille. The gate snapped open and she entered. A set of double doors greeted her, and when she approached them, a snapping sound announced that these had also been opened from upstairs. She entered a vast cavernous tunnel-like room. At the far end she could see the reflection of the waters of the Grand Canal casting flickering light onto the arched ceiling. Half way down, on the left-hand side, was a flight of wide, stone steps heading upwards into the gloom. Olivia made for these, a trifle tentatively. Two huge statues, held together with what looked like plastic tape, loomed out of the semi-darkness. She quickened her pace and headed up the staircase.

At the top, she was just in time to see a wooden door sliding open and a cheerful face peeping out of what Olivia now saw was a small lift.

'Buongiorno! Good morning!' said the woman. 'My name is Maria. Welcome to Palazzo Berberigo Falco.'

She extended a friendly hand, which Olivia shook gratefully, nerves forgotten.

Maria ushered her into the lift and Olivia looked around with curiosity. It appeared to be no more than a tiny wooden box, studded with warning signs about how the door must be firmly closed to prevent it stopping between floors and forbidding the transport of building materials or large electrical appliances within its tiny confines. Olivia struggled to imagine anybody even contemplating fitting a refrigerator or a wheelbarrow into such a small space and smiled amusedly to herself.

Creaking upwards, the lift finally stopped, and Maria opened the little door. Olivia stepped out onto the *piano nobile* of this great palazzo. Her beloved *pavimenti alla veneziana* greeted her warmly, she felt, as she walked forward into the enormous open space that comprised the living quarters of one of Venice's most noble families.

Drawn forward by invisible strings, she found herself gazing in wonderment at her surroundings. She had never imagined the grandeur and scale of the home she now entered. The photographs had merely emphasised the decorative problems to be dealt with but had not done justice to the magnificence of this five-hundred-year-old palazzo. Tall rose-pink marble columns supported an off-white beamed ceiling, the edges defined with expertly applied gilding. Floor to ceiling windows topped with decorative Venetian-style mouldings looked out over the roof-tops of Venice at one end of the great room and over the famous Grand Canal at the other. High chestnut doors with decorative panelling led to various ante rooms.

Maria began her guided tour. Olivia, taking out her camera and beginning to take some photographs to remind herself of pertinent details, noted that all the marble fireplaces had been bricked up throughout the palazzo.

'Fire regulations,' explained Maria, noticing Olivia's interest. 'There are no open fires permitted in Venice any more.'

Olivia already knew that fires in Venice were greatly feared and that regulations had been brought in to forbid the use of open fireplaces in the city. With houses so close together and the difficulty of erecting proper fire-fighting ladders in the narrow alleyways, fires were extremely dangerous. Apparently, there is not even a wood-burning pizza oven in the city of Venice, and the glass-blowing factories, with their ovens, are all safely located on the island of Murano.

Many of the rooms were draped with cream and gold silk curtain-type wall hangings that fell from ceiling to floor in neat pencil pleats. Over these hangings much of the cornicing incorporated lozenge-shaped mirrors, which Olivia found most unusual. Enormous two-tier Murano glass chandeliers hung in the sitting and dining rooms, and matching wall lights were positioned on either side of the defunct marble fireplaces.

Following Maria through one of the lofty chestnut doors into a narrow hallway, she entered the master bedroom. It was decorated in a feminine style, with a pink bed-throw at odds with the large blue and gold wallpapered panels on the walls of this huge room. Entering the en suite bathroom, she was intrigued to find that everything was of cream and gold marble; even the loo had a matching marble cistern and seat.

Progressing to the next bedroom, Olivia was mildly surprised to find it entirely masculine: from the Spartan single bed to the plain navy wrap-around headboard affixed to two of the walls in an L-shape, it proclaimed itself to be the bedroom of a lone male. She idly examined the books on the bedside table and found them to be books on garden design and horticulture. Had Francesca mentioned that her brother, the conte, had an interest in garden and landscape design? She thought not, as he was a hotel owner in Dublin, surely?

Moving on from this masculine domain, she tried to turn the handle of the next room on the corridor. It was locked.

'Maria!' she called. 'This room is locked. Do you have a key?'

Maria hurried towards her, key in hand.

'Sorry,' she apologised. 'That is Sofia's bedroom. It is always kept locked. It is not to be touched. But,' she added, 'you can have a look if you like.'

Olivia's curiosity immediately got the better of her. Despite feeling that she should keep out and mind her own business, she was intensely interested in seeing what Sofia's bedroom looked like. The girl's presence had not been evident in the apartment so far. In fact, it had felt fairly soulless and lacking in character. Would Sofia's room change her impression of the di Falcos's living conditions, she wondered.

Maria turned the key in the lock and the door swung open. Olivia stepped inside and stopped in her tracks.

'Goodness me!' she murmured. 'What the...?'

The bedroom was a pink and mauve teenagers' delight. So out of keeping with the rest of the palazzo as to draw an exclamation of astonishment from Olivia, who, accustomed to seeing other people's homes in all sorts of conditions, was still surprised to see such obvious evidence of a happy, normal teenage girl who obviously thrived independently of such an austere environment, grand as it undoubtedly was.

Moving to the pink-painted dressing table, she picked up a photo and examined it. A professionally taken photograph, it showed a pretty, blonde girl who smiled unselfconsciously. Behind her, with her hands placed formally on her shoulders — Olivia could almost hear the photographer calling "Smile!" — was, undoubtedly, her mother Jane. The enigmatic English woman she was due to meet at the weekend. She studied the two faces smiling their formal smiles. The woman's hair was blonde to the point of being almost white and she was ethereally pretty in a delicate way. The skin on her slim arms was white and her eyes were pale blue, fringed by light eyelashes.

'What a stunning photograph!' she exclaimed.

Maria, who had been just about to leave the room, stopped in her tracks and turned around.

'You have not yet met the contessa?' she asked politely, stepping forward hesitantly.

'At the weekend, I hope. She looks beautiful.'

'Yes. She is a beautiful lady, in every way,' agreed Maria. She looked away suddenly as if she felt that she had already said enough, while carefully locking the bedroom door behind her.

Olivia continued to survey the palazzo, noting the tasteless bamboo furniture in the study and the too-small dining room table in the dining area. The floor above was where Maria lived with her husband, Gianni. They both managed the palazzo and had been working there for several years. Marco, the boat-man and chauffeur, also lived on the top floor and it was not in need of redecoration, apparently, having been well maintained by the di Falcos's loyal staff over the years.

Returning to the living area, Maria handed Olivia a small envelope which contained a note. It was from Francesca and was a print-out of an email containing a list of instructions and a personal note.

Dear Olivia,

I hope you have had a good tour of the palazzo. You will see that it is sorely in need of redecorating with care. As we have already discussed, no structural work of any sort can be carried out as the palazzo is a listed building — along with most Venetian palazzi — and it is not worth the bureaucratic nightmare involved in trying to change anything other than the décor.

Maria has a list of sub-contractors for you with their telephone numbers, and also the details of what shops and factories you will need to use to purchase furniture, curtains and wallpaper. I have also noted the name of a good company who will restore the terrazzo flooring to its original condition. Plus, a good electrician and plumber.

Please try your best to keep to this list as I have personally interviewed these people and know that they will not betray any details of a personal nature that they may find on their visits to the palazzo.

When you have chosen the soft furnishings, please let Jane, the contessa, see your selection for approval. She is at the villa in the Euganean Hills and will remain there for the duration of the project. She awaits your visit at the weekend. Marco will drive you there.

Good luck with everything.

Francesca

Olivia placed the email in her briefcase and accepted the proffered list of sub-contractors that Maria now handed her, putting it with the email. No mention of the conte, she noted. He was, apparently, reluctant to become involved in any work on the palazzo. I wonder where he is, that mysterious count, she mused. She wondered why Francesca had not emailed her directly, but she thought it was probably her attempt at keeping Maria in the loop. Undoubtedly an invaluable ally for the future, she decided.

Planning to head back to her little house to study the list and contact the various suppliers, she bade Maria farewell and arranged to return in a few days, when she had had time to visit the various fabric and wallpaper outlets and to contact the contractors mentioned.

Shutting the wrought-iron gate behind her, she stepped into the narrow alleyway and headed towards the Accademia and the throngs of tourists. The fog had lifted, and it was a beautiful late morning in Venice. Olivia ducked down a side street behind the museum and, as though her brain had no control over her legs, found herself walking back towards the wine bar where she had had a *cicchetti* and an *ombra* the previous day.

Her eyes searched the piazza where she had sat against the cistern. It was empty except for a few tourists wandering around with their cameras. She entered the bar and ordered two *cicchetti* and an *ombra* of the local white wine, which was handed to her over the counter with a friendly smile. Taking her precious cargo outside, she leaned against the low wall along the canal to eat and drink. She balanced her paper plate and plastic beaker on the wall and nibbled a piece of soft white, crunchy-crusted bread, topped with baccalà mantecato — a local delicacy of creamy cod — while taking the occasional sip of refreshing white wine.

She felt a light touch on her shoulder and looked around. It was Marcello, the gondolier from yesterday, smiling down at her with a bright blue twinkle.

'Buongiorno!' He bowed towards her slightly as if to kiss her cheeks in the Italian fashion, then changed his mind. He obviously felt that such a greeting might be inappropriate in the eyes of an Irishwoman. But Olivia, being half Italian and feeling completely Italian right then, was happy to receive the two-kiss greeting and raised her left cheek in his direction. He was happy to oblige and pecked her left cheek carefully, followed by her right one. They smiled in greeting at one another.

'I have come to ask you if you would like to come with me in my gondola tonight,' he announced. 'If not tonight, then whatever night you wish.'

Marcello was apparently determined to entertain her in his gondola, and Olivia felt herself relenting slightly.

'Soon,' she promised. 'Maybe next week? I just completed my first morning's work at the palazzo and have no idea how the week is going to go. I have a feeling I'm going to be very busy. Sorry.'

'How about Monday after work?' he enquired. 'I could meet you right here at, say, seven o'clock.'

'Won't it be dark?' She glanced nervously at him. The last thing she wanted was to be seduced by anyone, and certainly not a gondolier, with their interestingly dubious reputations.

He noticed her discomfort and laughed.

'We do After Dark gondola trips all the time!' he exclaimed. 'They're fantastic. It's a great way to see Venice. I might even bring some friends along. I'm sure you'd like to meet some other Venetians. Even gondoliers,' he added. 'Oh, do bring your camera if it has a night-time setting. Going up the side canals underneath all those bridges after dark is a great photo-op.'

Olivia felt herself relaxing and agreed to meet him on the following Monday evening.

'Make sure you're wearing a warm coat, hat, gloves and a scarf,' he advised. 'After all, it's winter.'

Feeling relaxed and happy for the first time in months, Olivia headed back to her little house. She had telephone calls to make, though all the shops and suppliers on the list would probably be closed until half past three or later, being Italy, as she well knew.

A trip to Vicenza was high on her list, too. She had other, more personal matters to attend to. Being in Venice was a great bonus, as Vicenza had been the location of her mother's family home many years ago. She had always longed to visit that small, beautiful city, full of classic Palladian architecture. Perhaps she could go there by train some weekend soon to spend the day looking around.

CHAPTER FOURTEEN
OLIVIA

Saturday morning dawned cloudless and blue. Olivia prepared to leave for the Euganean Hills. Putting her hair up in a casual knot on top of her head, she donned a pair of smart black jeans and her cosy black lambskin boots. A black turtleneck sweater, scarf, gloves and her down-filled coat completed the ensemble and, right on time at 8.30am, Marco appeared at her front door.

Staggering slightly under the weight of several fabric sample books and catalogues, Marco muttered that he should have brought along a trolley to take them to the motor launch. Jane followed him, feeling slightly alarmed by his heavy breathing and reddening face.

Following him down the alleyway to the fondamenta, she saw that the smart di Falco launch was tied to a pole at the side of the narrow canal. Marco helped her to board, and she decided to stay up on deck to enjoy the bright, sunny winter morning, while he stored the fabrics in the cabin.

Gliding smoothly out onto the Grand Canal and turning left towards Tronchetto and the multi-storey car park, Olivia revelled in the sights and sounds of Venice in the early morning. Vaporetti churned up and down the canal, already laden with tourists photographing every single thing they saw. Gondolas drifted in and out of the traffic, apparently unaware of anything other than their customers' enjoyment of the most romantic city on the planet. Barges laden with boxes, bottles and building equipment charged past, their drivers chatting loudly on their *"cellulare"*.

She turned her face towards the sun and looked up at the palazzi as she passed. Shutters were open and here and there she spotted bed-linen airing on window-sills and people on their terraces enjoying their first cup of coffee in the morning sunlight. She loved it all. Venice was awake. Still alive and vibrant after hundreds of years.

Arriving at the car park, she climbed into a large SUV for the journey south- west to the Euganean Hills.

'How far away is Galzignano?' she enquired, once all the samples had been loaded into the boot. 'I'm looking forward to seeing their famous villa and gardens. I believe it's fabulous.'

'It's less than an hour away. We'll be there before you know it.'

Heading onto the motorway towards Bologna, Marco picked up speed, turning on a CD containing wonderful Italian music.

'Oh, that's fabulous!' she exclaimed. 'Who is that singing? Fantastic!'

'That's Zucchero. One of our most famous singers and composers. A great favourite of mine.'

Olivia made a mental note to get all the Zucchero music she could lay her hands on. Just the sort of music to relax and read to. "Perfect," she thought, her body moving gently to the beat of the music.

Turning off the autostrada at Termee Euganee, Olivia was struck by the sight of several high, conical hills covered with trees. The scenery was breath-taking, with vineyards and olive groves abundantly strewn over the landscape. Marco guided the car down several winding roads and after about ten minutes arrived at what appeared to be a public park with a sign at the entrance which read, "Parco di Falco", where groups of people were entering an arched gateway.

'Is the villa open to the public?' she queried, watching a large family with several children heading towards what appeared to be a ticket booth.

'Only the gardens. They are very famous around here and are a popular place to walk and bring the family at weekends. You should see the display of tulips in April! And the roses in May bring photographers from all over the world,' he added as proudly as if he were in charge of planting them himself.

A few minutes later, the car approached a set of tall wrought-iron gates supported by two large brick columns with urns on top. Bringing the car to a stop, Marco got out and went up to an intercom on one of the gate posts.

Some words were exchanged and as he climbed back into the driver's seat, the gates opened slowly, and he eased the car into the driveway.

Olivia gasped. A long, curved avenue lined with cypress trees gave way to the most magnificent gardens she had ever seen. Here and there, through the trees and neatly clipped hedges, she glimpsed fountains sending their sparkling water high into the air. On a small island in an ornamental lake she saw two black swans, and she was aware of order and symmetry and a great sense of peace and tranquillity.

As they rounded a final bend, a huge villa came into view. Pale pink in the morning sunshine, three storeys high, with several tall windows leading out onto small terraces, the main central building was flanked by two lower wings, forming a U shape. Enormous chimneys sat proudly on the roofs of the side wings.

Bringing the car to a gentle, scrunching halt close to the front door, Marco climbed from the front seat and helped her out onto the gravel with her briefcase, folder and several fabric and wallpaper sample books borrowed from one of the local suppliers for the weekend. A small, portly man dashed forward to help.

'This is Antonio. He and his wife, Paola, live and work here,' Marco informed her.

Within seconds, the front door opened, and a tall, blonde woman came forward to greet her. Jane and Olivia were finally face to face after all these months.

'Welcome to Villa di Falco,' Jane said, descending the short flight of steps and giving Olivia the customary two kisses of greeting. 'I'm Jane di Falco, and it's lovely to meet you at last.'

She spoke with a crisp, cut-glass English accent and was poised and graceful, though with a slightly nervous manner. Olivia immediately formed the opinion that she was highly strung and probably high-maintenance, too. Woman to woman, they eyed each other carefully, trying to assess the situation in which they found themselves. Jane's blue eyes looked searchingly into Olivia's green ones. It occurred to Olivia that Jane appeared to be looking for reassurance of some sort.

They walked towards the front door. Jane was quite a bit taller and of a lighter build than Olivia, though both were slim, beautiful women who could hold their own and attract admiring glances in any company.

Entering the cool hallway of the house, Jane and Olivia began to climb the vast curved staircase that wound its way towards the *'piano nobile'* or main floor. Jane led the way, followed by Olivia, while Marco and Antonio puffed along behind them under the weight of the samples and catalogues. Olivia carried her own bulging briefcase, as she never felt comfortable with clients unless it was with her.

Seating themselves in a large sitting room overlooking the garden, Jane called for coffee and Marco went to organise it with his great friend Paola, the cook and housekeeper who had been looking after Villa di Falco for many years. They heard his effusive greetings and knew he was settling himself down in the kitchen with a pastry or two to go with his coffee.

Olivia got up and opened her briefcase and began to set everything out on a side table, specially cleared for the occasion. As she bent to pick up a particularly beautiful book of floral silk fabric samples, she glanced out into the garden and saw a man crouching over what looked like some rose bushes, but it was difficult to tell for sure from upstairs. Scruffily dressed in a navy-blue gilet and sweater, with dishevelled dark hair, he looked vaguely familiar, and she assumed he was the gardener.

'Your gardens are absolutely magnificent.' She turned to Jane with a smile. 'I have never, ever seen anything quite like them before. Really fabulous.'

'My husband is a landscape architect. He designed all of it himself and takes a keen interest. He's out there now, I'm sure. He's always there, if he's not away designing other people's gardens.' A faint hint of bitterness had crept into the conversation, which made Olivia look at her more closely.

On hearing this new note in Jane's voice, Olivia decided that all was not well in the di Falco family. Fairly sure it had to do with Sofia's death, she knew that there was still some suspicion that Jane had either been drinking or on tranquillisers at the time of the accident, but she did not want to dwell on what could be idle gossip. She had, after all, been chosen to work on the palazzo because of her lack of involvement with this family, and her discretion was essential. She looked away.

The morning was spent poring over the fabric and wallpaper books, photographs, Olivia's sketches and comparing their ideas as to how to bring the palazzo back to life. Jane seemed quite animated after two hours of intense discussion and appeared to be quite surprised when Paola came to tell them that lunch was ready to serve.

Entering the dining room and taking their places opposite one another at the long table, Olivia noticed another place setting at the head of the table between them. Jane noticed her gaze.

'My husband will be joining us for lunch.' Then she added, 'If he can tear himself away from his precious roses.' She laughed lightly with embarrassment, as if suddenly remembering that Olivia was in her employ and not a friend.

At that moment, the dining room door opened, and the conte strolled in. Olivia almost fainted with surprise. It was Nick, her old enemy from Dublin. "Oh, my goodness!" she thought. "He must be Francesca's brother." She quaked inwardly. "I never suspected."

'Niccolo. This is Olivia Farrell-Lynskey,' announced Jane from across the table. 'Our interior designer from Dublin.'

'Yes. I'm pleased to finally meet you.' Niccolo's voice was deep, with the slightest hint of an Italian accent. He looked down at her piercingly with the enormous violet eyes that Olivia remembered so well from the day when he caused her to knock over the urn in Francesca's driveway in such an undignified fashion.

She gulped. 'I'm pleased to meet you, too.' She half rose from her chair to shake his proffered hand, dropping her white linen table napkin on the floor in her confusion. He bent to pick it up for her, handing it to her gently.

'Didn't you two manage to bump into one another at Francesca's in Dublin?' enquired Jane in a puzzled voice. 'You were both working on the stable block conversion at the same time. Surely you must have crossed paths?' She looked genuinely confused.

Olivia was, for once, entirely lost for words.

CHAPTER FIFTEEN
OLIVIA

'We weren't working together and never formally met, though I did notice Olivia on site from time to time.' He responded agreeably to his wife's question. 'I was working outside, and she and her team stayed indoors most of the time. With the Irish weather, I think they had the better deal.' He grimaced at the memory of the teeming rain and wind that seemed to assail him from all directions at once while working outdoors in Dublin, though there had been some lovely warm spells, too, which had made it all worthwhile. As they said in Ireland: four seasons in the one day! And the garden barely needed watering after all, not like here in Italy, where irrigation was required, he thought.

Olivia bristled with irritation at his relaxed manner. Who could forget the myriad annoyances caused by his presence at Francesca's house, and to be embarrassed now by the discovery that he was, in fact, her new employer! She looked coldly at him, her green eyes flashing. Was he chuckling at the memory of her accident with the rake?

'It was a wonderful project,' she said in a cool voice. 'Francesca is a fabulous person and I loved working with her.'

Their first course arrived and Niccolo poured some deliciously cool white wine into her glass.

'Francesca is a dear sister,' he said, then added, 'Taste!'

She picked it up and took a sip. Yes, it was perfect.

'What is this wine?' she asked, trying to diffuse the situation and change the subject.

'That's a Moscato Secco,' he responded. 'This dry Moscato is local and organic. My favourite lunchtime tipple, in fact. The vineyard that produces this is only a few kilometres up the road. You must visit there some time.'

Olivia, being a polite person — especially to those who employed her — made all the correctly appreciative sounds and agreed to visit there as soon as possible. She loved the dry, fruity taste, too, and thought that buying a few bottles would be a lovely idea. Perhaps she could persuade Marco to show her the vineyard. Maybe it was on her way back to Venice. She would ask.

She stole a glance in Niccolo's direction and saw that he was looking at her strangely. His look was unfathomable and, as their eyes briefly met, she wondered at it.

Lunch progressed with Olivia beginning to relax and answering their many questions regarding her career and varied clients, being careful never to mention names. Being an interior designer had brought her into intimate contact with many well-known and influential people.

'When you're in and out of people's bedrooms on a daily basis, you'd be amazed at what you find out. And the confidences and secrets they betray are often pretty surreal. If there's a next life, I'm coming back as a marriage guidance counsellor!' She laughed, then stilled as she realised that Niccolo was looking at her intently.

'We'll have to be very careful what we reveal about ourselves, then.' He said this with a smile, though Olivia took it as a gentle warning and decided to be very careful herself.

She told them about her love for the works of the famous architect Palladio and of her great wish to see some of his old country villas, which he designed and built early in his career.

'I would so love to some of them over the next few months while I'm here and they're on my doorstep.' Her eyes shone.

Out of the blue, Niccolo said, 'By a strange coincidence, I will be visiting a newly restored villa on Monday to advise the owners on the layout of the grounds. One of Palladio's earliest. It's near the city of Vicenza.' He hesitated a moment. 'Would you like to come along?'

The invitation was such a surprise to Olivia that she almost inhaled a mouthful of wine.

'I'd absolutely love to go. Thank you. If you don't mind the company.'

'Not at all,' he said, and his eyes twinkled.

JANE

Jane watched Niccolo in surprise. He was looking at Olivia with an expression on his face that she had never seen before. She could not figure out what it meant. His eyes were fixed on her face as though he wanted to touch her. Her heart felt as though a knife had been thrust through her ribcage. It was a physical pain.

Olivia seemed like a nice enough woman, she thought. Very good-looking in a voluptuous, big-breasted way. Her mane of golden hair shone, and her green eyes were luminous as she returned Niccolo's stare. Jane knew instinctively that this woman had the potential to cause problems, but she could not quite put a finger on what it was that made her feel uneasy. Though she could plainly see that, for some reason, Olivia was slightly hostile towards him, she knew that Niccolo could be charming and he would win her over sooner or later, if he chose to do so.

Or was the Irishwoman's display of faint hostility just an act? She needed to find out.

She focused on her lunch, but barely tasted the home-made bigoli — the local pasta — with duck sauce that Paola had lovingly prepared that morning. She looked longingly at the bottle of Moscato Secco that Niccolo was now proffering at Olivia's glass. She knew she should not be drinking.

Then she heard the invitation from Niccolo to Olivia. "He's taking her to Vicenza," she thought venomously. "He never brings me anywhere," she seethed, "and he knows that I'm a fan of Palladio, too. Doesn't he remember how we met?"

'I'll have a glass, too, Nico,' she said, pretending not to notice the way he froze when he heard her request. She had promised to stop drinking, but surely just one glass would hurt nobody. And she felt she needed to bolster her self-confidence if Niccolo's way of looking at Olivia was to be taken seriously.

He filled her glass to the half-way mark and placed the bottle on the table, well out of her reach, looking at her anxiously.

'Saluté!' she said, lifting her glass towards Olivia. 'Here's to the successful interior design of Palazzo Berberigo Falco. I think your design scheme is quite clever and should work well.' And she raised her glass silently to herself as she resolved to be present at as many site meetings as possible. She needed to keep her eyes open and to ensure that Niccolo had as few dealings with this woman as was humanly possible. But bringing her to one of his precious villas, that was really a step too far.

Lamb chops followed, accompanied by tiny roast potatoes and string beans. The remainder of the white wine was removed and replaced by a bottle of the local Cabernet. Deep ruby red and strong.

'Irish lamb!' Jane stretched her arm out and helped herself to a fresh glass of wine, ignoring Niccolo's silent plea, and addressing Olivia, 'Paola managed to get some yesterday in Torreglia in your honour. I hope you like it.'

'It's lovely, thank you,' said Olivia, her knife cutting into the lamb, which was as tender as butter. 'You obviously have a wonderful cook. These are perfectly done.'

Jane was tired of hearing Olivia's stories "about me, me, me...," she thought bitterly, particularly as Niccolo seemed to be interested in everything she said, and she wished lunch would end so she could escape.

Dessert was a light, fresh *pannacotta* with raspberry coulis poured over the top, red and glistening. Jane barely touched hers, topping up her wine instead, before Paola could remove the bottle. She was beginning to feel slightly tipsy, but so much better than she had half an hour earlier.

'Let's have coffee in the sitting room,' she suggested, and rose from the table. Olivia followed suit and Niccolo jumped to his feet with alacrity, helping her to push back her chair. Jane watched this performance and wished she could run and hide. Her insides ached as she watched her husband lavish his attention on this other woman.

'I'll pick you up at Vicenza railway station on Monday morning.' She heard Niccolo confirming with Olivia as he helped to put her sample books together and bring them downstairs. 'There's a train that gets in at just before 9am.' Jane's blood ran cold with dread.

After they had loaded up the SUV and Marco and Olivia had driven away, Niccolo rounded on Jane.

'How could you have drunk all that wine when you promised you had given up drinking completely?' he demanded. 'What's got into you? Is this what I can expect every time we have to entertain a guest?

'A guest?' She spat the words at him. 'She's our interior designer, employed by you and Francesca without my approval. Now you're taking her out and about on Monday. How could you?' she stormed. 'Did you have a fling with her in Dublin? Is that it?'

'What?' he retorted incredulously. 'A fling? With Olivia? Are you completely mad? I only spoke to her properly for the first time today.'

'You expect me to believe that? You worked with her for six months in Ireland.'

'She was working on the interior of the stable-block conversion while I was putting the landscaping together. Don't exaggerate. Our paths rarely crossed.'

'Why did she look less than happy to run into you today?' Jane was beginning to wonder what was going on. 'She looked as though she'd seen a ghost when you arrived for lunch.'

Niccolo laughed wryly.

'I'm not sure she knew who I was until today. I think she thought I was a gardener who worked for Francesca. We had a couple of minor run-ins on site, to be honest. But nothing serious,' he added. 'She's a wonderful designer — you should have seen what she managed to do with Orologio — and I was keen to have her work with you in Venice. I thought you and she would get along brilliantly.' His voice dropped. 'But you, Jane, I can't believe that you would make up a stupid reason like jealousy as an excuse to hit the bottle again.'

'Jealousy!' Jane cried. 'You never look at me the way you were looking at her; and, as for inviting her to meet you in Vicenza! Don't blame me for being upset. I'm sorry I had the wine, I know I shouldn't have, but I really and truly needed a glass or two. I'm quite stressed. If only I were sure about your feelings for me, I wouldn't feel so insecure. Especially since Sofia...' She trailed off and gulped back a sob. 'Don't you love me at all, Niccolo?'

'I care about you, Jane. You know that.' His eyes shifted to stare unseeingly at, apparently, a red velvet chair in the far corner of the room. 'Don't press me. It's too soon.' The words faded away as he walked swiftly out of the room.

She knew he would go straight back to his precious roses. They were his real loves, after all.

OLIVIA

Olivia's thoughts were confused as they began to pull away from the villa. She still felt quite indignant about Niccolo's apparent subterfuge as to his identity. However, she was aware, well aware, that she found something about him that was dangerously attractive.

She thought about his extraordinary violet eyes and handsome face, then mentally shook herself.

"Don't get mixed up with him on a personal basis," she told herself firmly. "First of all, he's a client, and business and pleasure do not mix. Secondly, he's married and probably very vulnerable after his daughter's death. Go to Vicenza and enjoy your visit to a Palladian villa but be careful!"

She turned to Marco.

'Marco. This vineyard where the conte buys his wine, where is it? Is it far from here?'

'Would you like me to bring you there? It will be open again after lunch. It's just a couple of kilometres from here.'

'Oh, fabulous!' She just managed to stop herself from clapping her hands like a child. Lunch had been very stressful and confusing, and she was looking forward to some light relief after all the drama.

Driving from Galzignano, Marco pointed the car firmly uphill. The road wound its way steeply through a thickly wooded landscape, with vertiginous drops towards the valley floor which Olivia was able to see between gaps in the trees. A multitude of cyclists, all dressed in colourful cycling gear, rode the hills in front of them, their taut rear ends high in the air as they stood on their pedals to climb the steep gradient.

Suddenly, they crested the hill and the entire Faedo valley fell away beneath them. It was breathtakingly beautiful. Vineyards and olive groves spread out below as far as the eye could see.

'It's so beautiful here,' she breathed. 'Quite perfect and idyllic,' she added, looking at the spectacular scenery in front of her.

Suddenly, Marco turned sharply left and Olivia noticed the sign with "Villa Fiorita" beside a set of gate posts as they drove down a winding olive tree-lined avenue towards the winery.

Getting out of the car, she looked around and marvelled at the position of the vineyard, with its vines stretching downhill as far as the eye could see, in arrow-straight lines. Dark, twisted and leafless now, being November, she could only begin to imagine how fantastic everything would look in summer when all was green and verdant.

Following Marco towards a building with a deep veranda in front and barrels doubling as tables dotted around, he pushed open the door and they entered the dim interior. Warm wine-laden smells greeted them as they stepped to the counter, where bottles were set out in a row with several tasting glasses. A wood-burning stove in the corner emitted a cosy heat.

From a back room a small dark lady erupted.

'Marco!' she laughed happily, and came forward to kiss him; apparently, they were old friends. She turned to Olivia. 'My name is Rita. Lovely to meet you. And welcome to Villa Fiorita. I like to think it was named after me, but no, sadly! It's named after the wildflowers that grow here in spring.' She laughed again, this cheerful lady from the Euganean Hills who now bustled her way behind the counter. 'What would you like to sample?'

She pushed a glass towards Olivia.

Olivia looked at all the bottles ranged before her and chose an organic cabernet/merlot blend to sip. 'Delicious!' was her verdict, and so began an hour of merriment and wine-tasting with the jolly Rita. By the end of the hour, Olivia had purchased a dozen bottles of wine and made a new friend. They parted, promising to meet again soon, and Marco loaded her spoils into the boot of the car.

'Wait!' Rita was rushing towards them with a bottle of olive oil. 'A gift! Come back soon!' And with that, they turned and headed back downhill towards Venice.

CHAPTER SIXTEEN
OLIVIA

Bright and early on Monday morning, Olivia was stepping onto the train at the railway station in Venice. As it crossed the long bridge to the mainland, she looked back at the receding skyline of the old, mellow city on the water. Small fishing boats dotted the lagoon and she watched them pulling in their nets, seemingly unaware of the train swishing by above their heads.

Passing through the busy station in Padua, many people got on and off. These appeared to mainly consist of university students, from what Olivia could see. She was aware that both Venice and Padua were home to large university complexes, and these bright young Italians seemed to be bursting with energy and enthusiasm as they filed through the carriage where she was sitting.

Exiting the station in Vicenza, she looked around. Several white taxis were lined up in a row, and opposite her was what looked like open parkland. It was an attractive sight, and she would have loved to go and explore, but at that very moment a white Range Rover pulled up beside her and, seeing it was Niccolo at the wheel, she climbed aboard.

She felt very self-conscious in his company, just the two of them for the first time, and tried to keep up a conversation about the palazzo and how much she was looking forward to beginning work on it that week. He seemed to be in a quiet mood, so after a while she stopped talking and admired the countryside.

They were driving along what seemed to be a valley floor with a large escarpment on her right, which he told her were the Berici Hills. The countryside was very flat, and the arrow-straight roads were lined with canals for irrigation. It appeared to be a very fertile area, with several crops growing between the waterways, mainly maize, from what she could make out.

Along one of these narrow roads, Niccolo began to indicate left and swung the car between two tall brick pillars and up a rutted driveway to the front of a large grey villa with the traditional arched entrance, windows on either side and small granary windows overhead. She felt a buzz of excitement.

Exploring the villa alone, as Niccolo had gone outside with the owner to discuss the grounds, she wandered through the rooms, marvelling at the beautiful lines of the architecture, the colourful frescoes overhead and the original tile and terrazzo flooring underfoot. It was hard to imagine that this villa was more than five hundred years old and that so many of its original features were still in excellent condition.

As they exited the villa an hour later, Olivia felt elated. She wanted to see more villas and promised herself that this would just be the beginning of her tour of Palladian and Venetian villas over the next few months.

Niccolo seemed in a good humour, too, and suggested they stop for lunch in Vicenza before she returned to Venice. They parked in an underground car park and walked up to the street, which was cobbled and surrounded by mellow brick buildings.

'What a beautiful place!' she exclaimed in delight at this small jewel of an Italian city. 'My mother's family came from here, but they are all gone now.'

'That's interesting. Where did they live?'

'I don't know exactly. But I think they had an apartment close to the city centre. Mum rarely speaks about her roots, but I know my grandmother spent her last days in a nursing home on Monte Berico.'

They chatted amiably as they strolled into the main piazza, where she could marvel again at yet more Palladian masterpieces in the form of the enormous basilica and mayoral offices, a popular place to get married against this magnificent backdrop, creating photo albums of great beauty. A statue of her hero Andrea Palladio surveyed the scene from his high pedestal in the piazza, and Olivia looked up at him in fascinated awe.

Down a side street, they arrived at the Duomo, and Niccolo guided her into a small restaurant close by. The owner showed them to a table in the corner and they sat down, having given their coats to a waiter who was hovering respectfully in the background.

'May I order for you?' he asked politely. 'I'm sure you would like to try some typical local dishes.'

Her *bacalà alla vicentina* was delicious. Milky codfish on top of soft, white polenta, the favoured maize meal staple of the Veneto, was accompanied by a perfectly chilled bottle of crisp Vespaiolo from a vineyard in the hills of nearby Breganze.

Somewhere during their lunch, Olivia noticed that Niccolo had turned his violet eyes in her direction and he began to gently interrogate her.

What about her husband? Had she had word yet of his whereabouts? He told her that he knew about her many problems with her marriage and her business woes from the Irish newspapers and wondered how she was managing now. She answered his gently probing questions as honestly as she could.

Had she a man in her life? Did she mind being alone? She answered in the negative to both of these questions, though she confessed she was still coming to terms with living alone.

Then he began to speak about his daughter. He told Olivia how close they had been and how distraught he was that he had been away in Ireland when she was killed. He blamed himself for not having been there and for leaving her to travel to their country villa with Jane. He did not say much more, just that he thought he would never recover from the pain and loss. Then he had to stop speaking about Sofia, as she could see that he was struggling with his composure.

Pulling up outside the railway station, Olivia alighted from the Range Rover, thanking him for a lovely day.

'Maybe we'll do it again some time.' He smiled warmly at her and she could feel herself begin to melt. When Niccolo was charming, he was very, very charming, she thought.

EVENING

The sun was just setting over Venice when Olivia made her way to Marcello's docking place in Giglio. She was looking forward to the diversion, still feeling slightly dazed by her day out with Niccolo.

Up one set of steps and down another, Olivia crossed several bridges on the way. She found them intriguing. Some were wrought iron, most were made from brick, and the famous Accademia was made from wood. Along the paved streets she marched. Dressed in casual jeans, plus a sweater, scarf and warm jacket, she enjoyed the clear and cold evening. December was only just around the corner, she reminded herself. The moon was already high, and she was conscious of the gentle lapping of the dark water against the sides of the canals as she made her way to her rendezvous. Walking past cafes, bars and pizzerias, with their lights flooding onto the pavement and emitting tantalising aromas and friendly chatter, it appeared everyone was out for an evening *passeggiata* with their friends and, of course, for an aperitivo.

As she crested her final bridge, she spotted Marcello sitting beside the canal chatting with another gondolier. They were both dressed in the traditional striped sweaters but wore warm black jackets over them to guard against the chill of this winter's night. He looked up and waved when he saw her on the bridge.

Arriving at his side, he introduced her to his friend, Gino, and took her hand to help her across Gino's gondola onto his own, which was moored on the outside. The gondola was black and glossy, with plenty of gilded ornamentation and lengths of red and gold silk rope. He held her hand until he had carefully guided her to a throne-like chair with a gold-trimmed red velvet cushion.

Undoing the ropes which bound his gondola to Gino's, Marcello picked up his oar and began to row them down the canal, ducking his head as they passed under the first of many bridges. He began to sing his song, which suddenly seemed entirely appropriate.

'The other evening, I went rowing with a blonde in a gondola.

The poor girl was so happy that she fell sound asleep immediately.

As she slept in my arms, each time I woke her the rocking of the boat sent her back to sleep again.'

He had quite a nice tenor voice, and the melody was quite operatic, Olivia thought.

'What is the song called?'

'The Blonde in the Gondola,' he replied, and then, suggestively, 'Maybe it's you!'

'Oh, I don't think so! I'm wide awake, honestly!'

They both laughed at the very idea and progressed through the gloom of the late winter's evening in Venice. The lapping of the water against the sides of the gondola and the tap of the oar as Marcello steered them expertly down the dark canals, past bars and restaurants full of lively chatter and tourists walking alongside, had her marvelling at the beauty of the place.

Nudging their way up a small side canal, Marcello put down his oar, threw the rope around a wooden pylon and sat down beside her. She was aware of his closeness as his thigh was pressed against hers.

"Uh, oh!" thought Olivia. "What now? Is he going to make a pass at me?" Despite her reservations, she felt a frisson of pleasure at his touch. She had not been touched by a man since the day that Steve had left more than eighteen months previously, so her awareness was heightened by the strangeness of it all. He slid his arm around her in an apparently practised move.

'Are you warm enough? Here, let me put this rug around you.' And he placed a cosy plaid rug across her shoulders. She shivered, but it was really more from a strange excitement than from the cold.

Marcello seemed to recognise the fact that she was nervous. The lights from the canal-side played on his handsome face and he placed his hand gently on her cheek. She left it there and decided to relax and enjoy the moment.

'You are very beautiful. Do you have a husband? I have never asked you this. Tell me, is there a man in your life?'

Olivia shook her head mutely. 'There's nobody. I'm alone. My husband left me for another woman last year.' She stopped herself, aware that she had told him far too much.

He kissed her lightly on the mouth. It was just a brush of his lips, but she withdrew immediately as though she had been stung. She was unsure why she had reacted this way. After all, everything was perfect. What could be better? A handsome man in a gondola after dark in Venice, of all places. What was wrong with her?

'Maybe we should be heading back?' she ventured. 'I've had a fabulous evening. Thank you so much, Marcello.'

He looked nonplussed. It was obvious that he had expected her to fall straight into his arms. She had no doubt that he took his pleasure with many of the female tourists who fell for his charismatic charms. She could not explain her reservations, but it was all just too much too soon. She was just not ready for romance, and it had been many years since she had had any man's arms around her, other than her husband's.

'I'll take you home,' he announced, sounding slightly offended. Climbing back onto his perch at the back of the gondola, he picked up his oar and cast off, deftly steering the gondola out of the dark side canal where they were moored, heading back towards the brightly lit Grand Canal and his docking station in Giglio.

Olivia realised that he was very quiet on the return journey and berated herself for her tactlessness. Her first friend in Venice, and she had treated him with coldness. How was she going to put this right? 'Maybe we could do this again some time?' She turned her green eyes towards him and watched him catch his breath. 'I'm under such a lot of pressure with my work at the moment, but perhaps we could even meet for lunch when you're free?'

She knew she was feeling emboldened by her romantic surroundings and, to be honest, her deep loneliness. This was something she found difficult to admit, even to herself. She had been pretty starved for company over the past eighteen months as her friends had drifted off one by one and her clients, on whom she relied for company on a daily basis, fell by the wayside as their finances hit rock bottom.

'That would be great,' replied Marcello, his dignity and self-confidence apparently somewhat restored. 'I will find you opposite the gondola factory at lunchtime during the week?'

The little gondola factory — or *squero* — was Olivia's favourite sight at her now regular lunchtime haunt. She loved to watch the men working away on the upturned gondolas beside the slipway. The little factory was built of deep red brick and had a tall chimney to one side. It looked as though an entire family lived there, but she could not be sure. She longed to visit and hoped to persuade Marcello to arrange this at some time in the future. She just could not stand it if she had offended him and lost her new Venetian friend.

'Sounds good to me,' she laughed happily. Their friendship would continue, but she wondered at the strange expression on his face and the way his eyes glittered when he spoke. She looked away hurriedly and turned her gaze to the beauties of Venice, seeing Palazzo Berberigo di Falco slip by on her right-hand side as they approached the Accademia Bridge and glided underneath.

CHAPTER SEVENTEEN
OLIVIA

Olivia was surprised when she arrived at the palazzo the next morning to see Jane there looking around and chatting to Maria.

'Good morning, Olivia,' she said in her crisp upper-class English accent. 'I've just popped in to have a look around. I've been going through your designs and I wanted to be sure I understood everything perfectly before we proceed to order the fabrics and furniture you've proposed.'

'That's excellent. Shall we start out here in the main living area?' Olivia waved her hand around the pillared room with its faded grandeur and reached into her briefcase for the small sample boards she had brought with her for reference.

Three hours were spent, interspersed with cups of excellent coffee from Maria, going through everything in the palazzo, from fabrics to furniture to wallpaper to paint colours. Every detail was confirmed, and Olivia promised to get the quotations from the suppliers to her before the end of the week.

It was a great deal of work, but she could have done it in her sleep at this stage, after so many years as a hands-on interior designer and project manager. The only unknown factor was working with the Italian design industry, as she knew none of the suppliers or craftsmen and had had no time to build up a working relationship with any of them; a vital part of her normal day-to-day working life, she thought.

These Italian craftsmen, however, all seemed highly professional, though she had some doubts about Francesca's choice of kitchen supplier. The enormous gentleman who owned the company and showed her the samples seemed far too relaxed for Olivia's liking. He also liked to have his own way with the finished design; in fact, he was fairly dismissive of her carefully drawn plans. Unfortunately, he was one of those professionals who hates being told what to do. Especially by a small Irishwoman, Olivia realised. She could see some battles ahead that she would have to win.

'Would you like to join me for lunch?' The invitation from Jane took Olivia by surprise. 'There's a darling little restaurant just off Piazza Barnaba where we can eat fresh fish and enjoy a glass of their excellent house wine. Do join me.'

Pleased that her employer appeared to be making friendly overtures, she accepted the invitation, and they left the palazzo for a five-minute walk through the piazza and down a narrow side street, where the small, busy restaurant looked cosy and inviting on this winter's day. Its windows were slightly steamed up and, as they opened the door, they were greeted by a variety of mouth-watering smells. Olivia was hungry, and a seafood platter was exactly what she wanted.

Inside, it was indeed inviting and was busy with many lunchtime diners. Olivia noticed that they all seemed to be Italians on their lunch break and women lunching together. The owner came rushing up to greet Jane.

'Contessa!' His warm brown eyes scanned her face and he pecked her on both cheeks in greeting. 'It has been so long. How are you?'

'I'm well, Roberto. How are you?' Jane began to unwind her scarf and open the buttons on her coat. 'This is my Irish friend Olivia.'

'A pleasure!' Roberto shook her hand, then led them to a small table in the corner, where he recommended a platter of *fritto misto* to share. Jane added half a litre of the house white wine to the order and he bustled off to the kitchen.

Settling themselves into their cosy corner, having hung their coats on an old wooden coat-stand, they set about relaxing for the first time that day. Their morning together had been busy, and they had not had any time for discussion over and above how the fabric and wallpaper choices they had made were going to look on a room-by-room basis.

A basket of warm bread was placed on the table between them. Wrapped in a white napkin, the smell of freshly baked bread reminded Olivia that it had been several hours since she had eaten her fruit and yoghurt that morning. She reached for a piece and began to break it immediately, tasting the warm bread, soft and snowy white with a crisp crust.

Jane reached for the jug of wine and poured both of them a generous glassful.

'Cheers.' She raised her glass. 'Here's to working with a "Designer to the Stars".'

Olivia wondered if she was imagining it, or was Jane being sarcastic? As she noticed Jane virtually throwing back her glass of wine, she had an instinct that this cosy lunch might not be as cosy as she had hoped.

JANE

Jane put down her glass and tried to damp down the sudden feeling of animosity that overcame her whenever she remembered how Niccolo had looked at Olivia when they met on Saturday. Its defied belief that they had not met in Dublin, and Jane wanted to get to the bottom of this burning question. And the surprise invitation to Vicenza. Had that been pre-planned?

She had felt so hyper this morning before her meeting with Olivia that she had taken a Valium before she left Villa di Falco with Antonio, Paola's husband, in the driver's seat.

She wondered how the day in Vicenza had gone, but Niccolo had avoided the subject completely the night before at dinner. Her curiosity was aroused.

Was there something going on here that she should know about? She would find out before this lunch was over. She helped herself to another glass of wine and looked at Olivia eating bread and obviously enjoying every bite. All those carbs! How did she stay so slim? Well, she would not be slim for long at this rate. Then see how Nico would like her. Her eyes narrowed spitefully.

Their platter of grilled mixed fish arrived, providing a welcome diversion.

Jane put a few pieces of octopus, calamari and a couple of scallops on her plate. Olivia followed suit, picking up her fork to take a bite.

'Delicious,' she pronounced, obviously delighted to have an excuse to change the subject, Jane thought. Well, as far as she was concerned, Olivia had questions to answer before she would be let off the hook. She prepared herself to attack.

'So, how was it? Working in Dublin with Francesca.' Jane thought she would kick off the conversation with the easy questions first.

'Francesca was wonderful to work with. We had a great time putting The Mews together.'

Olivia looked demure and a little uneasy. Jane felt a moment of triumph. She was definitely not going to let this little fish off the hook without providing some answers. Nobody, certainly not little miss "Designer to the Stars" Farrell-Lynskey, was going to seduce her husband and escape lightly.

Emboldened by two glasses of wine on an empty stomach, she decided to bypass all the other polite lead-in questions she had had in mind and get straight to the point.

'I find it very difficult to believe you had no contact with Nico while you were working on The Mews. You worked together for six months, for Heaven's sake.' She took another gulp of wine and hailed the waiter. 'Another half-litre, please.'

She noticed the shock in Olivia's eyes and assumed that the question had rattled her, not imagining for a moment that the shock might have anything to do with the fact that half a carafe of wine had already been consumed. She could see that Olivia was choosing her words with care.

'I never spoke with the conte before Saturday,' she said quietly. 'However, I did come into contact with him a few times over the months we were working on the Mews, but I had no idea who he was. He kept himself to himself and our roles were completely different, with no real need for communication except through Francesca.'

'Ha!' she barked a sarcastic laugh. 'A likely story. Do you really expect me to believe that?' Jane's voice rose and the two women at the next table stilled to listen, all conversation forgotten, as this was obviously far more interesting than their discussion about how ridiculous their friend Fiorina looked with her hair newly dyed red.

'It's the truth!' The women at the next table craned to hear her muted voice and wished they could ask her to speak up.

Jane laughed in disbelief and refilled her glass. 'And what about your trip to Vicenza? My husband certainly seems to know you well enough to invite you along on a visit to one of his precious clients.' At the word 'husband', the eavesdroppers leaned closer. 'I found out that he was the one who recommended you for the job at both Francesca's home and here. I don't believe a word of what you're saying, and I want to know why you're lying. Do you think I'm a fool?' Shrill now.

Olivia remained silent. She was incredulous. Why, when she was in Ireland, she had not even got on with Niccolo! Had he really recommended her?

'You're here because you're having an affair with Nico. I know it. I just know it.'

A bottle of olive oil was suddenly overturned with a crash at the next table. Jane barely noticed it, nor registered that the waiter was rushing over to the two ladies to see what had happened.

Jane went in for the kill. 'Why else did he not hire a Venetian designer to do the work? Goodness knows, there are enough of them!'

She sat back in her chair, finally feeling satisfied that she had brought this obvious truth to the surface. She saw that Olivia looked pale and saw guilt written all over her elegant features. It was a shame she could not fire her on the spot, but that would have made things even more complicated with the family. Even through the haze of wine on an empty stomach, she had the wit to know that.

'Jane...' Olivia trailed off. 'I don't know what to say to make you believe me, but the first proper conversation I had with the conte was on Saturday at Villa di Falco over lunch. What you are saying is just not true. In fact, I didn't even think he liked me.'

Jane looked at Olivia's distress with distain. She was a contessa, after all, and married to Nico, her wealthy Count, whom she would never let go. She was going to fight this ghastly Irishwoman with all the ammunition she could muster and, when this project came to an end, Olivia would be dispatched back to Ireland. She would see to that. She had already lost so much. Sofia... not Nico, too... She reached for the wine.

Having left most of the *fritto misto* untouched, Jane and Olivia left the restaurant. The two women at the next table were sorry to see them go as they sipped their *caffè coretto*, espresso with a shot of grappa, to keep out the cold. For medicinal purposes, they assured themselves.

Walking back to the palazzo through Piazza San Barnaba once more, they were both silent, locked in their own thoughts, both equally anxious about the turn their lunchtime outing had taken. Olivia wondered if it had been a deliberate set-up; she suspected it had been. Jane was worried that Olivia, if she was indeed having an affair with Nico, would tell him about it. They had their heads lowered slightly against the winter chill when a friendly voice cut through their thoughts.

'Olivia!'

They both looked up at the same time. Marcello's handsome face and lithe figure came into view. He was smiling and came over to greet them.

'Ah! Marcello!' Olivia did not know where to place herself. She knew instinctively that Jane would not approve of her interior designer fraternising with gondoliers. 'I'd like you to meet the Contessa di Falco, my client.'

Formal greetings were undertaken as Jane and Marcello quickly shook hands. Jane was stunned at being introduced to a gondolier, and more than a little bit curious.

'I have heard many things about you, Contessa, and I am sorry about the loss of your daughter last year.'

Jane looked as though he had slapped her. 'Thank you,' she responded curtly. "What nerve!" she thought, and said, 'Come, Olivia. I need to get back. Antonio is waiting to take me back to Galzignano. My husband will be missing me.' She gazed at Olivia and Marcello; her blue eyes expressionless.

She turned on her heel and made a hurried goodbye. She heard Olivia following her and saying 'Must go' to the gondolier.

'See you later?' she heard him say to Olivia and turned back for a moment just in time to see him looking longingly at the Irishwoman. Then the two women disappeared around the corner into another narrow alleyway.

Marcello stood there for a moment with a thoughtful expression on his face.

***

At home in Galzignano and in the comfortable surroundings of her bedroom, Jane wondered about the gondolier. Was this significant? Olivia had seemed quite uncomfortable when they met.

She thought about Marcello and his blond good looks. Not all gondoliers were actually handsome, though they certainly seemed to attract the ladies, no matter what they looked like. She could not see the attraction herself. Before today, that was.

"I think he fancies little miss perfect," she mused to herself. "I wonder. He's actually quite gorgeous."

CHAPTER EIGHTEEN
OLIVIA

Back in her little house that evening, Olivia was feeling deeply uneasy about her disastrous lunchtime with Jane. How could the woman be so insecure? There she was, a Contessa with a palazzo on the Grand Canal in Venice, a magnificent villa in the beautiful Euganean Hills, a life of leisure and a handsome son in London who, from all accounts, adored her. That she had lost her daughter in appalling circumstances the previous year was certainly a life-altering tragedy, but Olivia felt that that did not excuse this vicious attack.

Olivia would have given everything to have such security again. It seemed an age since she had lived a life of luxury with her wealthy husband and lavish lifestyle, her magnificent home in Dublin, a yacht, luxury holidays every year, a designer wardrobe filled with clothes with eye-watering price tags, a successful interior design business and plenty of staff to make her life easy. Now she was dependent on whatever client she could get to keep her business going; she considered this work for Francesca a windfall of huge proportions. If she could put enough money aside from both The Mews project and this one, she could keep going indefinitely if she was careful. Hopefully, the recession in Ireland would turn around soon and life would resume its normal pace.

She remembered the auction, when she had sold off all her treasured possessions and the meagre personal items she had managed to salvage, which were now in storage at her parents' home in Dublin.

She could not afford to lose this job. Her very survival depended on it. She would make a point of avoiding Niccolo, as much as possible, from now on. Jane had her eye on her, and Olivia knew that this was just far too important to be able to take a relaxed attitude in the face of such jealous anger as she had witnessed today. In fact, Jane posed a great danger.

Her phone chirped in her bag. She rummaged quickly for it and brought it out to see who it was. Please don't let it be Jane, she thought. It was Marcello.

'Hi, Marcello.' She answered the phone on the fourth ring.

'Come with me for an aperitivo? I'm just around the corner by the Accademia.' His voice was soft, and Olivia was desperate to see a friendly face after today's disaster. 'I could come to your home if I knew where it was,' he added, mischievously perhaps, she thought.

Thinking that a visit to her little house by a romantically inclined gondolier was probably not a great idea, she responded quickly. 'That's not necessary. I'll meet you at the foot of the bridge in, say, about twenty minutes?'

Quickly dashing to the bathroom, she had a quick shower, a spritz of perfume and touched up her make-up, releasing her lustrous blonde hair from its knot at the nape of her neck so that it fell loose around her bare shoulders. Donning a pair of denim jeans and one of her signature-look cashmere turtleneck sweaters, this time in a more feminine pale pink, throwing on her down-filled coat, hat, scarf and gloves, she hurried out the door.

Darkness had fallen over the city and most of the tourists had gone to ground. She passed lively bars along the sides of the canals, full of light and laughter, doorways crammed with people having a cigarette outside, a drink in their other hand. Rounding the final corner, she saw Marcello standing at the foot of the wooden Accademia Bridge, chatting to another gondolier. He turned to her as she approached.

'Giuseppe! This is my friend Olivia,' he announced.

Giuseppe shook her hand and looked at her appraisingly. She was becoming accustomed to the interested glances of the handsome Italian men at this stage and paid very little attention.

'Have a good evening,' said Giuseppe with a knowing look at Marcello. Olivia caught the glance and wondered if Giuseppe thought there was something between her and her gondolier friend. 'Buona serata! Have a good evening!' He loped down a side alleyway in the direction of Zattere, waving over his shoulder.

'Let's walk a bit first,' suggested Marcello, as he tucked Olivia's hand companionably into the crook of his elbow. She let it rest there. It was good to be in peaceful company after her lunchtime experience.

They climbed the Accademia Bridge, pausing on the top to admire the Grand Canal, dodging couples taking selfies, and leant on the railings to gaze in awe at the view of Santa Maria della Salute, the gigantic church that overlooks the Venice Lagoon.

Strolling through the evening crowds, Marcello suggested they stop at a little bar tucked away in the corner of Piazza Santo Stefano. Walking inside its dark interior, they chose a table alongside a banquette, lit only by a wavering candle. Olivia slid onto the banquette and Marcello sat on the chair opposite. Ordering two Aperol spritz, he asked her if she had tasted this aperitivo before. She had to confess that no, she had no idea what it was, and when she saw the waiter bring the tall glasses full of an orange-coloured liquid with ice, slices of orange and a black plastic straw sticking out of the top of the glass, she was positively gleeful.

'I've seen these orange drinks before, but I had no clue what they were,' she exclaimed. 'I've been dying to try one. What's in it exactly?'

While the waiter unloaded his tray of nuts, olives and little savoury biscuits onto their table, he explained that it was a combination of Aperol, an alcoholic drink invented in the Veneto, prosecco and a splash of soda water. She took a sip of the herbal-tasting, refreshing drink and pronounced it 'Wonderful!'

Marcello was pleased. They raised their glasses, clinked them together and said in unison, 'Saluté!'

Normally, Olivia was not much of a drinker. Years of self-discipline, having been married to a control-freak like Steve, who would have been furious if she had shown even the smallest hint of alcohol-induced behaviour, she had abstemiousness down to a fine art by this time. But tonight, was different. She was feeling anxious and lonely, with nobody to turn to. Marcello was the only friendly face in town, as far as she was concerned.

'Would you like another?' he asked, and she looked in amazement at her empty glass. Where had it gone? She must have knocked it back without thinking about it. To be honest, she liked the Aperol spritz a lot, and it didn't taste greatly of alcohol. So, she agreed, and two more orange drinks appeared on their table pronto.

She was suddenly aware that Marcello had left his chair and joined her on the banquette. She could feel the heat of his black-clad thigh pressed against hers. Suddenly, it did not seem very important, and she enjoyed the closeness for a few minutes. Then she moved away slightly and hoped that he would take the hint. She was not interested in a flirtation but was happy to have his friendship.

She knew, however, deep down, that most men were not good at maintaining a platonic relationship, especially with a beautiful woman. But for now, she hoped that this would be the outcome. She was disinterested in involvement, especially as she knew that she would be returning to Dublin in a few months. Instinct also told her that she was in the presence of a practised Romeo.

He slid his arm around her shoulders, along the back of the banquette. She allowed it to remain there, for the moment.

'Tell me more about the life of a gondolier.' She was genuinely curious. 'Where, for example, do you live? Here in Venice, I assume.'

'Oh, no!' he replied, his smile ironic. 'It is difficult for us to be able to afford to live in Venice. The price of an apartment here is far more than we can afford. So many outsiders have bought properties here that there are only about fifty-five thousand real Venetians living here in the city now.'

Olivia was surprised. The city was so busy. She said so.

'It's mainly tourists and expats,' he told her. 'I live over on the island of Giudecca in a small apartment with my parents, and many of us have homes out in Maestre, coming to and from work by train to Venice on working days. If they live out there, they can have a garden and more space for the same money as an apartment on Giudecca, but there's very little hope of ever affording a property here in Venice itself.'

'How about the romantic image of the gondoliers? Is it true that they have a lot of luck with the lady tourists?' She laughed a little but was interested to hear his response.

'We gondoliers are romantic people.' She felt his thumb softly stroking the back of her neck and froze. 'And like all young men, we are always hoping for romance. I think, though, you will be surprised to hear that many gondoliers are married to foreign ladies, particularly to Americans.'

Olivia's eyes widened.

'Many of them come here with romantic expectations,' he continued. 'I have some friends who have married rich American girls and travel regularly to the US.'

With Marcello caressing her neck with ever more deliberate strokes, Olivia felt a long-forgotten warmth spreading throughout her body. She realised that she was enjoying the physical contact and tried to pull herself together, remembering, with difficulty, that she was supposed to be an aloof interior designer from Ireland.

What would the "hunting, shooting, fishing" crowd in County Meath think if they could see her now? She grinned at the thought. Mistaking her smile for pleasure, Marcello felt even further emboldened, and moved even closer on the banquette.

She could feel his breath on her neck as he whispered, 'You are a dangerous woman.'

'Oh, I don't think so.' Her voice was husky. 'Let's walk a bit more.' She gently removed his hand and moved down the banquette to retrieve her coat from the coat stand. Turning to look at him, she noticed that he looked flushed and slightly peeved, even disgruntled.

Feeling sorry for her abruptness, she gave him a warm smile.

'Thank you so much, Marcello, for such a lovely evening and for introducing me to Aperol spritz!'

After a long moment, he appeared to cheer up and jumped to his feet, heading over to the bar to settle the bill. 'You're welcome, Olivia,' he replied over his shoulder. 'Andiamo! Let's go!'

Strolling back towards the Accademia Bridge, Olivia wrestled with the problem of how to dissuade him from walking her back to Casa Antica. She was deeply conscious of his hand on her back as he guided her through the evening crowds clustered on either side of the Grand Canal as they crossed over. Reaching the foot of the bridge, she turned to him.

'Thanks, Marcello. I'll be fine from here. It's just a five-minute walk, and there are plenty of people around.'

'But it's dark! And anyway, I'd like to walk you home. I'm curious to see where you live.'

'Honestly, that's not necessary.'

His face fell.

'You don't want me to see where you live, do you?' More a statement than a question, as he stroked her upper arm gently. 'It's okay. I'm your friend. I'm no threat, but if you are more comfortable keeping me at arm's length, then that's fine. Really.' He suddenly sounded cold and decidedly petulant.

He stepped back slightly, releasing her arm. She felt the absence of his hand for a moment.

Olivia felt unaccountably guilty.

'Well, okay, then. But just to the door and no further.' She tried not to sound like an immature teenager as she made her pronouncement, but she needed to digest this evening alone.

'It's a deal! Okay, which way, then?'

He took her hand and tucked it into the crook of his elbow. And so, linking arms like two old friends, they strolled down the alleyways, over a little bridge. past the, allegedly, haunted house that overlooked a little piazza, over another steep bridge and down along the side of a quiet canal, its dark waters reflecting the moonlight. A turn to the right down a short calle and there they were outside her new home.

'This is it.' She rummaged in her bag for her keys, produced them and inserted the key in the lock.

'Where's your flood barrier?' he asked. 'Acqua Alta is due this week. You need to have one installed.'

Olivia looked at him stupidly. 'Oh, yes. Since it was removed when I got here, I stowed it in the downstairs bedroom. I didn't know what to do with it, nor when to use it. The water in the canal is nowhere near the top of the paving.'

'Ah, but Venice has high tides regularly, particularly during winter, and every house around here has to have a flood barrier installed at this time of year. You don't want the house to flood. Here, let me install it for you.'

He stepped into the dark hall and opened the only door on the ground floor, looking inside and retrieving the heavy metal flood barrier. He slipped it into two brackets already fixed to the sides of the door and asked her for the key. Examining the bunch of keys in her hand, she located the correct key and he locked it into place.

'There you are!' He stood back to admire his handiwork. 'Keep an eye on the Internet. The flood warnings will be posted online. And listen for sirens, too,' he added.

'Sirens?' Olivia's voice reflected her alarm.

'You'll hear different sirens to warn you if it's going to be particularly high. There's lots of information online. You need to study it.'

'Thank you so much for your help.' She began to edge into the hallway and put her hand on the door. He stopped her.

'Don't I even get a nightcap?' he asked, putting his hand gently on her shoulder. 'I promise I won't bite. You're quite safe with me.' His thumb stroked the side of her neck.

She pulled herself together with difficulty.

'Not this time. But perhaps on another occasion.' If there is another occasion, she thought to herself, removing herself out of arm's reach and beginning to close the door. He stood on the other side of the low flood barrier, looking slightly forlorn.

'I'll be in touch.' He backed into the alleyway as she gently shut the door on the dark night.

In the shadows, something stirred. A leaf crunched. Marcello stopped to listen, but all was silent. He strode back to the busy alleyways with a slight swagger. Eyes followed him until he disappeared.

JANE

'Where is the conte this evening?' Jane quizzed Paola as she entered the dining room at Villa di Falco. She had noticed that the table was set for one and was displeased.

'He said he would be late, Contessa. He asked me to go ahead and not to expect him for dinner.' Paola sounded apologetic, though obviously this event was entirely out of her control. She wondered why she had to be the one to pass on this news and why the conte could not have told his wife himself. But then, the contessa had been lying in bed all afternoon since she returned from Venice, obviously the worse for wear. She pursed her lips. 'I think he didn't want to disturb you, Contessa. You were sleeping this afternoon.'

Jane was annoyed. She had thought that Niccolo was in the greenhouse potting some of his precious roses, or whatever it is that one does in a greenhouse. If she had known he was planning on going someplace, she would probably have angled a way to have gone with him. She so rarely went anywhere these days and she found their country villa boring. She preferred Venice, where she had friends and where the shops were so wonderful. Who wanted to sit out in the country anyway with nothing to do? An afternoon snooze was an excellent idea, to her way of thinking, especially after a couple of glasses of wine at lunch earlier.

Sitting there alone as Paola bustled about preparing her dinner, Jane gazed unseeingly down the length of the table. She felt as though everything had fallen apart since Sofia died; as if she had no further purpose in life. She had given birth twice, and now with Sofia gone and Max so busy in London that she rarely saw him, she was bored and lonely and looked forward to seeing him at Christmas.

Nico was still withdrawn and never spoke with her about their young daughter who had been snatched from them so suddenly just one and a half years ago. He had taken to sleeping in a separate bedroom and she had long ago given up trying to persuade him to come back to the room where they had lain in the same bed together for the previous fifteen years. Maybe she was depressed, she thought. Perhaps they were both depressed, she mused.

As Paola put a plate with some sliced melon and prosciutto crudo in front of her, with a small basket of soft white bread with a crisp crust, Jane made up her mind.

'Paola. Please bring a bottle of our Merlot. I think I would like some wine this evening.'

If Paola felt uneasy about this request, she did not show it. She knew the conte's edict about wine for the contessa. He felt that she reacted badly to alcohol on top of the anti-depressants she was taking on a daily basis and had forbidden her to drink for the time being, especially as the investigation into Sofia's death was still ongoing. But it was not her place to comment, so she went to retrieve a bottle from the cellar and opened it, sniffing the cork to check that it was good.

Paola remembered the recent Saturday when that blonde bombshell of an interior designer had come to lunch. What a row the conte and contessa had had after that! The contessa had seemed to take a dislike to the Irishwoman and made her feelings known in no uncertain terms. Paola did not like to eavesdrop, but she could not help overhearing all the shouting after she had left the room.

Mind you, Paola had liked her. Very good-looking in a slightly Italian way, being so voluptuous and not too tall. And her Italian, with hints of the Veneto and Ireland in her accent, was perfect. She thought the contessa looked too angular and pale beside this vibrant creature. Especially now, when she appeared to have lost interest in her looks and barely went outside the door. It was so sad really, and she still ached inside when she thought of poor Sofia. How she had loved that child!

Bringing the bottle to the table, she poured a glass of the berry red-coloured wine into Jane's glass.

Jane brought the glass to her lips and took a large mouthful without even stopping to savour its wonderful bouquet. Paola looked at her nervously.

'Ring for your main course when you're ready, Contessa.' She backed away from the table and left the room. There was going to be trouble when the conte found out that wine had been consumed at dinner. She imagined she could hear the shouting already. Sitting at the kitchen table, she picked up her daily crossword and tried to relax.

Jane pushed her plate away. She was not hungry at all and was only interested in having some wine. She wondered where Niccolo was this evening. They had had breakfast together and he had made no mention of any plans to go out today. She stared at nothing and took another large mouthful of wine.

She thought about the palazzo. She had not enjoyed her lunch with Olivia. In fact, she was consumed by jealous thoughts about her. She wondered about the gondolier. He had seemed quite taken with the little Irish interior designer. All the men appeared to be intrigued by this woman. Perhaps it was time to pay another surprise visit to Venice. Yes. She would go tomorrow.

CHAPTER NINETEEN
OLIVIA

Olivia opened her bedroom shutters and peered out. Fog! Impenetrable fog. She could see nothing except the grey mist that hung like a curtain outside her window. Pulling on her warm velvet robe, a relic of her moneyed past, she slipped downstairs, filled the kettle with water and switched it on.

She could never function before she had her first mug of Lyons Green Label tea, which she had brought with her from Ireland. She had been told that strong Irish tea was difficult to come by in Italy, and she was taking no chances with her favourite beverage.

Bringing the kettle to a rolling boil, she splashed some of the boiling water into her mug to warm it first, threw in a tea bag, poured on the boiling water. Stirred it for a minute; then, removing the bag, she reached for a bottle of milk and poured some into the tea. After quickly stirring it again, she raised it to her lips and took her first sip of the day.

'Mmm… that's good!' She perched on the tall stool at the breakfast bar and opened her laptop. The dining table was covered in files, wallpaper and fabric samples, along with colour swatches and fabric samples. Her new home had become an office. She realised that entertaining was out of the question at the moment. She had nowhere to put all this stuff.

Online, she perused the news both in Ireland and abroad. Nothing in particular caught her attention and, finishing her tea, she headed to the shower to get ready for the day ahead.

Today she was meeting with the contractor who would be restoring the beautiful floors. This was an important task, as *pavimenti alla veneziana* required a great deal of skill. She was looking forward to her day and felt that things were moving along at a healthy pace. She had already interviewed most of the sub-contractors and was experiencing a real feeling of achievement.

Locking up her house and making sure that the flood barrier was fixed in place, she walked briskly along narrow alleyways and through little squares on her way to Palazzo di Falco. The fog was very thick, so thick that she had to keep a close eye on where she was going and was afraid of getting lost. At last she arrived at the Accademia Bridge and, keeping it on her right, dipped once more into the maze that was the set of streets on her way to the palazzo. It all looked very different in the fog and the narrow alleyways were almost empty except for the occasional Venetian hurrying to work or for a coffee.

Maria buzzed the gate and Olivia mounted the wide marble stairs, past the statues bound in tape, and stepped into the tiny lift, which would take her to the living quarters in the palazzo. It creaked upwards and Olivia admired its solidity and rich wood trim.

Stepping out into the enormous *piano nobile*, Olivia started. The Conte himself was getting to his feet and approaching her with a set of drawings in his hand.

'Good morning, Olivia.' He paused briefly and raised an eyebrow.

'Good morning, Conte,' she responded, and wondered what on earth he was doing there. According to Francesca, he had barely set foot in the palazzo since Sofia had died and had planned to stay away while the work was ongoing. She was glad she was looking smart in her high leather boots and tight black pants, her hair neatly fashioned into a thick blonde plait at the back of her neck.

'I don't want to interfere, Olivia, but I have been studying the plans and colour scheme and would like to have some small input. After all...' He paused. 'This palazzo has been in my family for hundreds of years and I have a responsibility to make sure that everything is perfect.'

Olivia swallowed her annoyance. Of course, he had every right to be here, but she had gone through every single detail with both Francesca in Ireland and with Jane here in Venice and felt that she could be trusted to ensure that every detail was meticulously looked after. As she had already confirmed most of the work with the sub-contractors, it would be extremely inconvenient if he should change anything at this point. She tried to remain calm and not to show her impatience.

'Of course, Conte.' She drew herself up to her full 5ft 3in and looked him in the eye. 'In what way can I reassure you?'

He replied by pulling out a chair from the table and gesturing her to sit down, while he resumed his place beside her. Spreading the plans in front of both of them, he asked her to explain everything. In detail.

As she listened to his questions, Olivia realised that he was very well aware of every facet of the work required to put the palazzo back on track. She became so engrossed in her explanations and descriptions that it took her a few seconds before she realised that Niccolo was looking back over his shoulder with an expression of irritation on his face. She turned around.

'Jane!' he said. 'What are you doing here?'

'I might ask the same of you,' came the angry response, as Jane strode forward and stood in front of them. Niccolo stood up abruptly and faced her. 'Where were you last night? Here?'

'No. I came home last night — I looked in on you — you were sound asleep. Dead to the world. Or should I say, "out cold"?' His voice was steely, and Olivia noticed that his hands were clenched by his side. He was obviously furious with Jane for some reason. He continued, 'I decided to come up here this morning. I want to be more involved in the work on my family palazzo. So here I am, discussing the plans with Olivia.'

Jane flinched at the use of Olivia's first name. Nico had been very formal the day she had come to lunch at Villa di Falco. As was his normal habit, he rarely addressed anyone by their first name unless he knew them well.

Suddenly realising that she needed to maintain a dignified air in front of her interior designer in order to keep the peace with Niccolo — she planned to keep her husband, after all — she stepped back.

Changing tack, she adopted the cajoling voice that Niccolo had learned to dread. She continued, 'Oh, Nico! I have been so enjoying this project, helping Olivia with everything, that I felt I just had to come again today, so I got Antonio to take me to the station at Monselice this morning and came up by train.'

She began to unbutton her expensive grey wool coat and unwound the scarf from around her neck.

Niccolo looked surprised. Jane continued, 'And what do you think of our progress? Olivia and I have been working together to make your family home beautiful. We want his opinion, don't we?' She turned to Olivia, smiling at her as though they were old friends.

'Umm...' Olivia was lost for words. She thought about their last encounter and realised that Jane was playing some kind of game. A dangerous game.

'I like it,' pronounced Niccolo. 'I never knew you had such talent, Jane. Usually you are completely disinterested in this sort of thing. After all,' he added, his mouth twisting bitterly, 'it was you who allowed it to deteriorate so badly in the first place.'

Jane's normally white face flushed ominously. 'Well, I am interested in it now. And I have been working hard to have it exactly the way you want it.' Her voice quavered slightly. 'I want things to be perfect again. This is our home, Nico.' She swallowed and put an elegant hand to her forehead. 'Sorry, I have a bit of a headache this morning.'

Niccolo said nothing, but Olivia noticed his eyes were glinting dangerously.

She looked up as Maria entered the room and announced the arrival of the flooring consultant.

'Bring him in, Maria,' said Jane, her cut-glass tones brooking no discussion.

A slightly-built gentleman in his mid-forties, wearing a neat navy suit, white shirt, silk tie, gorgeous black shoes and carrying a briefcase entered the room. Niccolo stepped forward, smiling, and clasped the man's hand.

'Giuseppe! How wonderful to see you!'

Giuseppe looked pleased and smiled widely. 'Conte di Falco,' he responded. 'The pleasure is mine.'

Introductions were made all round. Olivia thought he looked like a nice man. "Well turned out," she thought to herself. "Always a good sign."

'Sit down, man,' said Niccolo, waving at one of the bamboo chairs. 'Are you the contractor who'll be restoring the floors?'

Everyone sat around in a semi-circle on the uncomfortable armchairs and looked at Giuseppe expectantly.

'Yes, indeed! At least, I hope so!' He crossed one elegant leg over the other and appeared to relax, though how this was possible on such a hard chair under the gaze of the conte, Olivia was unsure.

'Olivia!' Niccolo addressed her expansively. 'This gentleman was responsible for the floors at Villa di Falco. Why, he even did the floors in your house, too! Casa Antica,' he added for Giuseppe's benefit.

Giuseppe preened himself happily and straightened his already incredibly straight tie.

'I have an excellent team,' he offered, looking at Olivia. 'We always do our very best. Our craft is traditional — an old family business — and we pride ourselves on our work. I, myself, have been working at fashioning *pavimenti alla veneziana* since I was a boy at my father's knee. Nothing is too much trouble. You must just tell me what you want, and we will do it!'

As she responded to this serious little man with words of encouragement while he continued his business spiel, Olivia looked up and caught Niccolo staring at her intently. Their eyes met for a long few seconds and she hurriedly looked away, afraid that Jane had noticed this brief exchange, which Olivia filed away mentally, to explore later.

Niccolo appeared to be on familiar terms with Giuseppe, and Olivia saw a warmth in him that she had never seen before, nor ever really expected to see. She watched him with interest.

'How is your family? Silvia and the bambini — three, I think, last count?' he enquired enthusiastically.

'They're all well, thank you, Conte. Elena is already at college.'

After a friendly chat about Giuseppe's family, Olivia felt she could now get to the point of his visit and tactfully guided the conversation to the task at hand: the restoration of the floors at the palazzo.

Niccolo took the hint and beckoned to Jane, who appeared to be in a dream-like state and had not contributed to the conversation in any way.

'Come, Jane.' The conte stood up and went over to her. 'Let's get going. I'll let Marco know and he can take us to Tronchetto. I'll drive you back.'

Olivia felt herself relax a little, but still felt uncomfortable after Jane's strange visit and Niccolo's intense presence.

JANE

'What are you playing at, Jane?' Niccolo's eyes were fixed on the autostrada as the exit to Terme Euganee approached. 'You had absolutely no reason whatsoever to visit the palazzo this morning.'

He had been silent for most of the drive, apart from berating the dangerous drivers who loved to tailgate, then zoom past with inches to spare.

'Look at that idiot!' was the constant refrain, as he guided his Range Rover towards Villa di Falco. He waited until they were within five minutes of home to address Jane directly.

'Why are you meddling in Olivia's work? I know you wanted to have some say in approving the colour schemes for the various rooms, but to drop in like that unannounced…' He trailed off, probably realising that he had been guilty of doing exactly the same thing that very morning.

Picking up on his train of thought, Jane jumped right in with the expected question.

'And was she expecting you?' she enquired, a sharp edge to her voice. 'I suppose little miss perfect interior designer was delighted by your visit.'

Niccolo swallowed the harsh words he felt were bubbling to the surface.

'No, Jane. Olivia was not expecting me, just like she was obviously not expecting you, either.' He spoke calmly. 'I was very keen to see how things were going. It's important to me. I don't want any surprises when it's finished. The entire visit was on the spur of the moment.'

Jane was silent. He added, 'It looks as though things are going smoothly. And I think you need to stay away from the palazzo unless Olivia calls to ask you for your opinion. But, as far as I am aware, schemes for all the rooms are now complete and she is currently interviewing all the sub-contractors. So, stay away. Please.'

Jane furtively opened her handbag and slid her hand inside. She knew Niccolo was angry. Thank goodness she had some diazepam in the inner zipped pocket. Niccolo would freak out if he knew she was taking one every time she felt stressed, and that was all too often. She really did not care. Turning to appear as though she was looking out the window, she slipped one between her lips, letting it dissolve on her tongue. She then put her head back and closed her eyes, waiting for the familiar warm feeling of the drug to invade her system and bring relief.

As the car crunched up the long gravel drive, Jane opened her eyes and looked at Niccolo. She could see that he felt something close to peace as he looked out at his beloved gardens. She knew that this was where he really wanted to be. And she also knew, deep down, that he would be happier without her. He had loved Sofia dearly, but without their daughter's presence in their lives, she was convinced that he wanted nothing more to do with her.

She sighed. Niccolo looked at her enquiringly.

'You should go and lie down straight away.' He pulled the car up to the front door, got out and strode around to the passenger door. Opening it, he helped her from the car.

"Whoa!" she thought. "How many of those did I have?" Her knees buckled slightly and Niccolo held her firmly by the elbow.

'Have you been drinking, Jane?' he enquired sternly.

Jane answered truthfully. 'No, Nico. I haven't touched a drop today.'

'Last night?' He looked at her with a penetrating stare in his violet eyes.

'Last night was last night. You didn't come home.'

'Yes. I did come home. Just not early. As I told you, I had a late appointment.'

'Where?' she demanded. 'Were you in Venice?'

'This conversation is over.' He escorted her firmly through the front door and up the stairs to the upper floor. 'Now go and have a lie down. Paola will attend to you. I'll call her.'

Once Paola had entered Jane's room, he donned his favourite gardening attire, consisting of ancient denim jeans, a navy sweater and gilet. Sliding his feet into a pair of wellington boots, he returned to doing what he loved most: tending to the gardens at Villa di Falco. He whistled for his little Jack Russell terrier, Oscar, who was the only one who could tell how troubled his master's thoughts were as he entered the huge greenhouse.

CHAPTER TWENTY
OLIVIA

As the days turned into weeks, Olivia began to gradually explore the wonders of Venice; otherwise known as *La Serenissima*. She realised she had a unique opportunity to become familiar with a magical place where most people visited for a day or two as tourists. She knew that she was incredibly lucky to have all this beauty and culture on her doorstep.

Her daily routine varied little. Arriving at the palazzo just after 7.30am, she was ready for the arrival of the workers at eight. She would then ensure that all work was progressing satisfactorily and either sit at the dining room table and update her notes or else visit the outlets and factories that were making up the furnishings, to check on progress.

As is normal in Italian culture, lunch is an important ritual. Having previously only worked in Ireland, as far as Olivia was concerned, lunchtime consisted of a half hour break. She was accustomed to the on-site contractors taking this break at noon, when they would sit around on the floor or in their vans, depending on the weather and the stage of the build. There they would sit, reading that day's tabloid while eating sandwiches from their Tupperware containers and having a strong dark brown mug of tea from a flask. "Builders' tea," she said to herself, and bemoaned the fact that the tea available in Italy was so weak to her Irish palate.

But in Italy things were markedly different. The workers would leave at noon, returning two hours later and working through until 6pm. She was aware that in most parts of Italy, *pausa pranza* began at one o'clock, with employees returning at four. She found that, working within the building industry, things were actually quite reasonable, once she became accustomed to it. And it gave her two hours every day to explore the city and to have her lunch in a variety of places, which was a huge bonus.

Olivia soon identified her favourite walk. She would cross over the Accademia Bridge and head in the direction of St Mark's Square via Campo Santo Stefano. Passing by the Doges' Palace and over the tourist-packed little bridge where the curious gathered to take photographs of the famous Bridge of Sighs, she would continue along Riva Degli Schiavoni towards the mellow old church of San Pietro di Castello, where she would sit on a bench under the trees and eat her sandwich in peace and tranquillity, surrounded by history. On her way back along fondamenta Santa Anna, she would often purchase some fresh fruit and vegetables from a boat moored on the canal. "The real Venice," she thought. "How I love it!"

These lunchtime and weekend walks were what she considered to be her "quiet time", when she wanted to speak to nobody and mull over her thoughts, which were becoming more confused by the day.

JANE

Darkness fell over the dining room at Villa di Falco. Paola bustled in to arrange the table for dinner, lighting two large candles in silver candlesticks. A delicious scent of cooking wafted behind her as she closed the curtains and looked around the room, checking that the large fire was banked up with logs and giving off a good heat. The room felt warm and intimate. She hoped that this evening would be calm and peaceful, not like many of the previous occasions over the past few months since the conte and contessa had moved here while the palazzo in Venice was being refurbished.

Paola pursed her lips disapprovingly. Imagine bringing an Irish interior designer to do up the palazzo! Rich people squandered their money on fripperies, she thought, as she bustled back to her kitchen.

Niccolo pulled out Jane's chair and saw her comfortably seated. She was very quiet this evening. He looked at her closely.

'How are you feeling, my dear? Better, I hope?' he asked solicitously, seating himself at the head of the table and picking up his white linen table napkin.

143

Jane looked at him directly; her pale blue eyes looked tired and she had, perhaps, been crying. Maybe not. He could not be sure.

'I'm fine, Nico,' she answered after a moment's pause. 'Thank you for asking.'

They busied themselves with some antipasti in the form of small white polenta slices with fragrant porcini mushrooms on top. It was one of Niccolo's favourite dishes, and Jane was glad that Paola had made it for him tonight. She was tired of all the fighting and discord in the house these days.

'I thought you were planning to go to Ireland for a while?' she queried. 'Didn't you say you were working on a project with Paul over the next few months?'

'Yes indeed, my dear. I will be heading for Dublin next week but will be over and back. I want to keep an eye on the palazzo, while there is so much work going on.' He forked up some of the polenta with gusto and savoured the taste for a moment. 'Paola has done a wonderful job with this antipasto.' Paola smiled happily as she bustled to top up his wine glass. None for the contessa this evening, she observed.

Jane watched the golden liquid splashing into Niccolo's glass. Just one would hardly do any harm, she thought.

'Paola. Pour some for me, too, please.' She indicated her glass.

Niccolo looked at her disapprovingly. 'I thought you weren't going to drink any more. You know it's a bad idea.'

'Just one teeny weeny little glass, Nico.' He hated when she put on her baby voice. It made him cringe. He could see that Paola did not enjoy it much either, or she hesitated.

'Paola!' Jane's voice was sharp. 'Pour!'

Jane was on her third glass, half way through their grilled sea bass, when she forgot she was trying to be peaceful with Niccolo this evening. She was still brooding about Olivia. She was sure she had noticed Niccolo looking admiringly at her cleavage. She could not stop thinking about how different his expression was when he looked at the Irishwoman than when he looked at her. Full of respect and admiration for Olivia and nothing but disdain for her; she was more and more convinced as she threw back her third glass and went into attack mode.

144

'You like Olivia, don't you, Nico?' I'll just mention her, she thought, to see what reaction I get.

'I barely know her, Jane. But she seems to be a competent and likeable person, yes.' He sipped from his glass and tried not to tense up when he saw her reaching for the empty bottle.

She rang her little bell. 'Another bottle, Paola,' she said imperiously.

'Are you sure, Jane?' Niccolo's voice had become wary. 'You've already had quite a bit to drink. Maybe not the best idea?'

'Don't nag, darling. But do tell me how you managed not to meet Olivia when you were both working on Francesca's precious Mews project. I find it unbelievable, really. Come on! Tell me!' Now she had adopted a wheedling voice and Niccolo bristled inwardly.

'I've told you over and over that I saw Olivia a few times on site, but we never spoke. She was working inside, and I was doing the landscaping, outside. What exactly is your problem?'

'I saw you ogling her cleavage. You fancy her, don't you?' There, she had finally said it. 'She's very beautiful and clever, and you want her. Come on, Nico, admit it. And anyway,' she added maliciously, for good measure, 'her husband is in Venice right now.'

'What's this about Olivia's husband? How do you know he's in Venice?'

'He phoned today, asking for her address.' She looked pleadingly at him.

'And I suppose you just gave it to him?'

'Yes, I did. He's her husband, after all. And he needs to see how she's behaving with that gondolier chap. Quite the little tart, your Irish designer!'

Niccolo finally cracked. That last remark was, for him, the final straw. He was livid.

'You do know, Jane, that you are killing this marriage? Stone dead,' he added for emphasis. 'You make no effort whatsoever to pull yourself together. I'm reaching the end of my patience. And I refuse to discuss Olivia any further. She has nothing to do with our problems. Our marriage is dying and I'm having serious thoughts about the best way to deal with that undeniable fact.'

Then he added, 'Maybe we need to think about a permanent solution.'

'Oh, Nico!' Jane was truly alarmed. Niccolo had never spoken these words to her before. 'If I thought you loved me, everything would be different. I'm so lonely.' She burst into loud sobs.

Paola had been entering the dining room with a fresh bottle of wine but backed out again hastily when she heard Jane crying.

But Niccolo was now unstoppable. Something had given way and he had plenty to say.

'Jane,' he began, 'I must be honest with you. Before we lost our beautiful daughter, I was planning to take some time out of our marriage. Things were already terrible between us. Your drinking and pill-popping had become intolerable.'

'But I was depressed because you were hardly ever around!' she exclaimed. Her voice sharpened. 'Your precious garden gets more attention than I do.'

'I was around enough to know that our marriage was a disaster.' His voice had risen dangerously. 'You have scarcely any friends, just a few hangers-on who like hobnobbing with a contessa, no hobbies worth talking about. Unless, of course, shopping counts.' His voice was withering. 'Why, you barely even read. You spend your time either watching rubbishy soap operas or moping around the palazzo while it deteriorates and crumbles around you. Being there with you was intolerable. Do you hear me, completely intolerable! What happened to the interesting woman I married?'

He had raised his voice; something he rarely, if ever, did. Jane remained silent. Her mind was slowly trying to process this thunderbolt. Surely Nico could not be serious. He would never leave her. Or would he? She longed for another glass of wine. Where was Paola with the new bottle, for heaven's sake?

'When we first got married and when Sofia was a baby, you were full of life. You loved moving to Venice and were full of plans for the future. But you went back to your drink and pills as the years wore on and I couldn't see why.'

Now she was frightened, and she could feel the weight of tears forming and her throat felt tight. She needed to remain composed, but that was now impossible. It was all just too much to bear.

'Oh, Nico!' She was sobbing now. 'You know how much I love you. But I get so depressed and I don't know why. You've tried to get help for me, I appreciate that, but nothing works. I'm too scared to go back again to that psychiatrist in Vicenza. Terrified he'll want to put me away and give me electric shock treatment or something horrific. You must know how scared I am.'

'But, Jane, what has that got to do with the fact that you are so dreadfully jealous?' he continued more quietly. 'Jealous of the garden, jealous of my life away from you, my work and, even now, the interior designer working on the palazzo. You are making an utter nuisance of yourself. I can't imagine what she must think of you. Can't you at least just try to pull yourself together?'

With that, he suddenly stood up, grabbing his chair before it fell over backwards, righting it and storming towards the door.

'Good night, Jane. We'll talk again when you're sober.' He looked back at her. 'If that's ever a possibility.'

The door slammed behind him.

***

Jane heard his bedroom door close quietly at about 2am. She was sleepless, lying in her four-poster bed alone. How long had it been since Niccolo had come to her in the night? Not for about two years, she figured. Perhaps she should try to seduce him, she thought. Maybe a visit to that lovely lingerie shop in Este was what she should do tomorrow. Yes, she decided, she would get Antonio to drive her there in the morning.

She would go to his room at night in a silky negligee and slide into bed beside him. Imagining his hands on her body like before, she nuzzled deeper into her pillows. She should have done this ages ago and not waited for him to take the initiative like he used to do with such skill and enthusiasm.

She would go to the beauty parlour in Este tomorrow and have a manicure, a pedicure and a frangipani wrap, which entailed a great deal of pampering and a massage, which would leave her skin smooth and fragrant, ready for Nico's touch. And she would visit the hairdresser, too. Perhaps a whole new look might work! She smiled to herself in the dark.

Dreaming of how she would keep Niccolo interested in their marriage, and of all the loving ahead, she drifted off to sleep. Her mind was filled with aroused images of lying sensuously in her husband's arms once more.

CHAPTER TWENTY-ONE
OLIVIA

Walking briskly on her way to the palazzo in the early morning, briefcase in hand, Olivia spotted a familiar figure ahead at the newspaper kiosk, lounging against the counter, chatting to the owner.

'Marcello!' she called, and he stood up straight and strolled in her direction. "My goodness," she said to herself, "he does look quite gorgeous! That physique!" She smiled at her boldness and went to greet him like the old friend he was beginning to become — at least in her new Venetian life.

'Olivia!' His face lit up and he strode briskly towards her. 'I was hoping to catch you on your way past, so I can persuade you to come with me for another aperitivo this evening.'

'Oh, Marcello!' She was surprised how disappointed she was to have to tell him, 'I have to work late this evening. I have meetings with sub-contractors quite late when their working day is over. They cannot meet me during working hours.'

He looked crestfallen.

'I could meet you after you have finished your meetings and we could have a pizza or something?' he asked hopefully, ever optimistic.

'No, Marcello. Not this evening. I'll be far too tired to do anything other than hurry home to bed. I will grab a quick bite in a bar when I have a chance later on. Perhaps tomorrow? Though I'm not sure what time I'll finish up. I'm extremely busy at the moment.'

Looking at his petulant expression, she added, 'I'm in Venice to work, you know. Not to run around with gondolieri!' She laughed.

'Okay, then.' He arranged his facial features into the most charming and seductive expression he could muster. 'I will phone you tomorrow in the late afternoon and perhaps you will come for another moonlight gondola ride?' His eyes gleamed. 'I think that would be the perfect way to relax. I'll sing for you, about the Blonde in the Gondola.' He put his hand on her upper arm and rubbed it gently.

Looking up, she was horrified to see Niccolo standing just a few feet away, staring at her in disbelief. Then he hurried off and was quickly swallowed up by the crowds that swarmed around the base of the Accademia Bridge. Her discomfort was acute.

'I need to go now, Marcello.' Perhaps she sounded slightly sharp, as he stepped backwards quickly and, giving a little bow, strolled off.

Olivia watched him as he disappeared into the gaggle of tourists queuing for the Accademia museum. Tall and well built, in his navy jacket and tight black trousers, with his long blond hair and confident demeanour, he cut an attractive figure, as evidenced by the flirtatious stares he was generating among the ladies in the queue. And he had called her a dangerous woman! As far as she was concerned, he was the dangerous one.

She thought of Niccolo. His appearance from nowhere, when she was talking to Marcello, had taken her by surprise. She remembered how the gondolier had been stroking her arm and doing his best to work his considerable charm on her at that moment.

She cringed inwardly, then thought, "Why should I care about what Niccolo thinks, anyway? It's got nothing to do with him."

And she continued on her way to the palazzo and her first meeting with the company who would be making up the curtains.

JANE

A sunny day in the Euganean Hills and Christmas was on the horizon. When Jane arrived in the lovely market town of Este, she noticed that the festive lights were strung all around the narrow streets and piazza.

Antonio dropped her off at the side of the street opposite the castle and promised to return when she phoned. Strolling down the cobbled street towards the square, Jane turned right and walked under the long shady portico to the lingerie shop of her choice.

Trying on a short, see-through silk negligee trimmed with lace, she admired how it skimmed her slim figure and accented her breasts. "Yes," she thought, "resist that, Nico, if you can."

Entering a nearby perfume shop, she purchased a new Gucci perfume. "A new smell, too." She decided that a complete change was on the cards.

The beauty parlour came next, and she gave herself over to three hours of beauty treatments, enjoying the pampering and the feeling on her skin. Niccolo was going to have quite a night of it, she thought, if she had anything to do with it. "Why didn't I do this before now?" she mused, as she succumbed to the sensual feel of the masseuse's hands rubbing frangipani oil into her thighs.

Arriving at the hairdresser's salon in a winding, cobbled Este street, with its back tucked up against the medieval town walls, she instructed them to give her a fuller style than normal. More like Olivia's, she realised, as she picked out her favourite hairstyle from hundreds that were offered by Fernando, her favourite hairdresser.

Emerging into the early afternoon sunlight and feeling a little bit peckish, she decided to go into one of the local bars that line the huge piazza and have a tramezzino. Well, one could hardly have a sandwich without a glass of wine. She called the waiter over and placed her order.

Relaxing in the cool winter sunshine in the piazza in Este, gazing up at the castle walls that overlook the pretty town, sipping her glass of wine and nibbling a tramezzino, her parcels at her feet, her hair and nails perfect and her body glowing after her massage, she felt an unaccustomed sense of well-being. "All will be well," she told herself. She had to believe that Niccolo still loved her, in his own way, admittedly, and would never leave her.

OLIVIA

It had been a long day. Olivia was pretty wiped out when she finally said good night to the last sub-contractor as he left the palazzo and headed home.

She entered the palazzo's lofty kitchen and opened her laptop on the long table in order to update her notes while her thoughts were still fresh, and she reached into her briefcase for the sandwich she had bought earlier and had had no time to eat. She opened the fridge and found a three-pack of Peroni. Nothing else. "Oh well," she told herself that one beer would not hurt. Searching in the kitchen drawers, she finally found an opener and popped the lid off the bottle.

Looking around, she could find no glasses, as pretty well everything had been removed. She knew that Maria, Gianni and Marco were upstairs in the staff quarters, but she had no intention of disturbing them for something as trivial as a beer glass. Tipping her head back, she took a cool, refreshing swig from the bottle. While it was still to her lips, she heard a small sound and her eyes locked onto Niccolo's. He was standing in the entrance foyer, staring at her with curiosity.

She jumped guiltily and put the bottle down, feeling self-conscious.

'Oh, my goodness, you startled me!' she exclaimed.

Wordlessly, he approached her. He was looking haggard, his huge violet eyes red-rimmed with exhaustion. Silently, he stood in front of her.

'My goodness, Conte!' she exclaimed. 'You look ill. What's the matter? Can I get you something?' Remembering that there were only two beers in the fridge, she added, 'A beer, perhaps?'

He hesitated. 'Okay then. I need to sit down. Sorry.' He virtually collapsed onto one of the dining chairs and rested his elbows on the table.

She noticed that he had a small suitcase with him, which he had placed on the floor. He saw her studying it as she popped open his bottle of beer.

'I'm planning on staying here for a few nights. I thought you'd have gone home by now. I didn't mean to disturb you.'

'Really?' Olivia was incredulous. 'But the bedrooms have all been dismantled and there's nowhere suitable for you to sleep. I thought you would have known that.'

'Don't worry about me.' He waved his hand towards the corridor, where the stairs to the servants' quarters began. 'I spoke to Maria earlier and she has prepared a small bed for me upstairs. There are four bedrooms there and two are vacant. It's no problem. Only until I head off to Ireland for Christmas.'

He took the proffered beer from Olivia and downed a long draught.

Olivia was astounded. "Has he left Jane?" she wondered. Out loud she ventured, 'But why?', sitting down again at the table in front of her laptop. Her sandwich was untouched and lay beside it.

'Eat,' he commanded. 'You probably haven't eaten for hours.'

She agreed and opened the cellophane. The scent of truffles wafted towards her. Her favourite sandwich combo: black truffles and Robbiola cheese. She took a large bite, realising she was starving.

Niccolo cleared his throat. 'I couldn't help seeing you with that gondolier this morning near the Accademia.' He paused, as if not quite knowing what to say next. 'I recognise him, though I don't know his name.'

'Marcello,' she answered, and stopped. She realised she had no clue what to say next.

'I've often seen him around the city with various young, mainly American and Scandinavian girls on his arm. He appears to be quite the ladies' man.'

Olivia smiled. She could not help being amused, as Marcello was very definitely a man who fancied himself as a latter-day Romeo, who worked the crowd with all his tried and tested techniques. She had no doubt that the only reason he was still calling her and begging her to go out with him was because she had not succumbed to his manly charms.

Niccolo noticed her smile and misconstrued it completely.

'I must say, I'm surprised at your friendship with a gigolo like this Marcello person. I had thought you would have had more sense. And decorum,' he added disapprovingly.

Olivia was stung

'Excuse me!' she retorted angrily. Her voice was sharper than she meant it to be, and she made the effort to appear calm, though her thoughts were in turmoil. This was her employer, after all, and she was conscious how much she needed to keep this job. But she was also very tired. 'He was kind to me when I arrived first and knew nobody. We're just friends, nothing else.'

But Niccolo was not finished.

'I understand that your husband may be in Venice.' This was a bombshell. 'Don't tell me you don't know.'

He sat back in his chair and waited for her response. Olivia was aghast.

'What?' she exclaimed. 'I had no idea.' She thought for a moment and added, 'How do you know?'

'Jane told me,' he admitted. 'Apparently, he telephoned looking for your address.'

Tears stung her eyes and her throat felt as though it was being squeezed. She blinked hard and reached into her handbag for a tissue.

'I haven't seen Steve for eighteen months; actually, nineteen now. I thought he was in Africa.'

'I'm sorry.' She was surprised to hear him apologise. How was he to know the truth?

'I should go,' she said, getting to her feet once more.

To her surprise, he held her wrist firmly. 'Sit down, Olivia. I'm not at my best today. We all have our problems, I promise you.'

She sat back down and took a sip of her bottle of beer. It was warm and flat. She rewrapped her virtually untouched sandwich and put it back in her briefcase for later.

'I should be going,' she repeated. She put the beer bottle down again and began to put her files together decisively. 'I have an early start in the morning.'

Niccolo sat in complete silence. He looked as though he was in pain, she thought. He finally broke the uneasy silence.

'Then I'll see you out,' he said, rising to his feet. Olivia took that as a signal that she could get up, too, and she reached for her coat, which was draped over the back of her chair.

He took the coat from her and held it so that she could slip her arms inside. She was aware of his brooding presence behind her as she buttoned it up and wrapped her scarf around her neck. His hands remained on her shoulders as she turned around in time to see the expression on his face. Desire. Unmistakable desire.

Olivia almost fled from the palazzo and hurried back to Casa Antica, barely noticing her surroundings. Once inside her cosy home, she began to breathe normally again. "I must have been imagining things," she thought, as she walked slowly up the stairs, thinking about Steve. Could he really be here in Venice?

JANE

Jane's alarm woke her at 3am. She rolled over in her enormous bed and became wide awake almost immediately. This was it, she thought. Her plan to seduce her husband was about to materialise.

Niccolo had not returned for dinner the previous evening, but that was nothing new. He rarely went to bed until late, so she thought that three o'clock was probably the best time to catch him asleep and off guard.

Giving herself a spritz of a sensual, floral Gucci perfume, she checked herself carefully in the mirror. She liked what she saw and smiled her sexiest smile. Slipping on a silk robe, she sallied forth.

His bedroom door was just a few metres away from hers. She tried the handle and the door opened soundlessly. She slipped inside, closing it carefully behind her. The robe slipped to the floor and her new silk negligee and freshly styled blonde hair shone slightly in the faint moonlight that came from behind the damask curtains. She approached the massive bed and pulled back a corner of the sheet, sliding underneath.

Her hand felt for Niccolo. Nothing. She turned on the bedside lamp. Its warm light revealed that she was alone. She looked around. The bed was unslept in. Darting out of bed and opening one of the closet doors where she knew he kept his overnight bag; she was shocked to find that it was missing.

Niccolo had carried out his threat. He had left her.

She climbed back into his bed and put her head on his pillow. Perhaps if she slept on his pillow and dreamed of him, he would sense it and come home to her. She began to sob.

Tears fell on her new silk nightie and her carefully applied eye make-up ran down her pale cheeks and onto his empty pillow.

OLIVIA

Olivia tossed and turned in her crisp white linen sheets in Casa Antica. Her thoughts were in turmoil.

She thought about Steve and wondered if he was, in fact, in Venice, or if this had been some fabrication of Jane's, for some unfathomable reason.

She thought about Marcello and about how easy it would be just to give in to his desires and have a good time while she was in Venice. After all, she would only be here for a few short months. She expected to be heading back to Dublin before Easter. She had never been any good at flirting with men; and having been, as she thought, happily married, she had had no reason to test her skills with the opposite sex. It would be fun and romantic to enjoy the company of this handsome gondolier in every sense.

But mainly she thought about Niccolo. A married man. Absolutely taboo. Why did he confuse her so totally? She thought that they were enemies, after all the nonsense in Dublin. But here he was, showing up and looking at her with naked desire on his face this very evening.

She did not know what to think and went to sleep dreaming of hands caressing her body. But whose hands? She had no idea who she dreamt was touching her so intimately.

Olivia awoke, hot with longing for she knew not what.

CHAPTER TWENTY-TWO
JANE

After tossing and turning in Niccolo's bed for a few short hours, Jane lay back among his sheets and tried to get her thoughts in order. Where was he? Why had he taken his overnight bag? She would quiz Paola and Antonio. Then she would decide. She was not going to give up so easily. Niccolo was her husband, and she was going to get him back.

With new resolve, she returned to her bedroom and, after showering, went down to breakfast.

'Paola!' she called imperiously. 'Please tell Antonio I want to catch the early train to Venice from Monselice. I'll be downstairs in twenty minutes.'

'I'm going to find out what's really going on in Venice,' she muttered.

***

The Regionale train pulled into Santa Lucia station in Venice and Jane joined the throng of tourists and workers dragging bags along the platform towards the exit. She had not appraised Marco of her arrival, and nobody, other than Paola and Antonio, knew that she was here.

She set off on foot. Having lived in Venice for more than sixteen years, she knew her way around the narrow alleyways of the city without having to ever reference a map. How different from her early days here! She had been pregnant with Sofia and, on her daily walks, got lost regularly. But Venice was a city for walkers, and she always found her way to where she was going without too much difficulty. Wandering down the many dead ends and having to retrace her steps was, to her, part of the great charm of this unique city.

Arriving at Campo San Stefano, she wandered towards a side canal where there were several gondolas tied up, with the gondoliers hanging around touting for business among the hordes of tourists. This part of Venice was always pretty busy, she thought. And it was only December. How she dreaded the hot crowded months of July and August, when they always decamped for the Euganean Hills.

Walking up to the nearest gondolier, she asked him bluntly, 'Do you know a gondolier called Marcello?'

She knew his designated spot was around here somewhere. Had she not seen him coming from this direction when he and Olivia met like old friends?

'Marcello?' quizzed the gondolier. 'There are a few gondoliers called Marcello. Do you have a surname?' He was polite and had large brown eyes, which kept flitting over her shoulder, anxious not to miss a paying client.

'No surname. No. But he is tall, with long blond hair and blue eyes.' She remembered how handsome she had thought him. 'Very good-looking,' she added.

'Ah!' The man's eyes lit up with comprehension. 'Yes. I think the Marcello you want has his berth over near Santa Maria del Giglio. Behind the Gritti Palace Hotel. Just head down that calle.' He pointed.

'Thank you!' Jane was already moving in that direction.

The gondolier eyed Jane's retreating figure with a knowing look.

OLIVIA

Olivia returned to the palazzo just before two o'clock, in time to see how the work was progressing. Most of the internal walls were now being stripped of fabric, wallpaper and paint, ready to present a clean sheet for her decorating skills. She was pleased with progress and even more pleased that she had not encountered Niccolo that morning, though she knew he must be in the vicinity. Perhaps he was staying out of her way. She hoped so.

As she walked briskly down the corridor to check on progress, she noticed that the door to Sofia's room was slightly ajar. She pushed it open quietly and looked in.

Niccolo was lying stretched out on the pink and white bed, fast asleep. She began to back out.

'Stay!' the voice from the bed commanded. 'Shut the door. I don't want any of the builders to come in.'

'You left it ajar,' she said, almost accusingly. 'I didn't mean to intrude.'

Niccolo sat up and swung his legs over the side of the bed. He looked at her. His hair was unkempt, and he looked utterly miserable.

Olivia caught her breath. Compassion was not something she wanted to feel for this powerful Conte. He was her boss, paying her salary and basically calling the shots. How could she keep her distance from him if he allowed her to see how vulnerable he obviously was?

'I know you know that this was my daughter's bedroom. My only child,' he added.

Olivia was unsure as to how to handle this situation, so took refuge in a few platitudes.

'I'm so sorry, Conte,' she began. 'It must be very difficult for you and the contessa to come to terms with the death of your daughter.' She kept her voice neutral, remembering his outpouring over lunch in Vicenza.

But he was on an emotional roller-coaster. Something had obviously upset him, and his mood was bleak. 'She didn't need to die.' He did not elaborate further, leaning heavily on the back of Sofia's pink velvet armchair and seemingly trying to gather his composure.

Olivia kept her counsel; but finally, after a full minute of silence, she said, 'I really don't know what to say, Conte.' She looked up at his handsome, grief-stricken face. His lips were twisted into a grimace and he was looking at the photograph of Sofia and Jane. That happy photo taken on a sunny day just a couple of years ago.

Olivia felt something give inside her. She reached out and put her hand over his, where it rested on the pink fabric. It was an un-thought-out gesture

159

and whose unforeseen consequences she would have to live with for the foreseeable future.

'What's all this, then?' A sharp voice with a clear, cut-glass accent, broke into Olivia and Niccolo's silent reverie. 'What's going on?'

Olivia was struck dumb. Niccolo stared at Jane, who was standing in the doorway, looking accusingly at both of them. They jumped apart guiltily.

Niccolo recovered his composure almost immediately.

'I might ask the same question, Jane.' His voice was stern. 'I'm here to see what's going on with my palazzo. Why are you here?'

'You didn't come home last night. I came looking for you.' Suddenly, Jane sounded plaintive. 'Where are you staying?'

'Jane. I am not going to discuss our differences in front of our interior designer. We will talk later on. But suffice it to say I'm staying here. Upstairs in the servants' quarters, to be exact.'

'The servants' quarters!' Jane's voice rose an octave. 'You're joking. Up there with Maria, Gianni and Marco? I wonder what they think of that!'

With that, Jane pivoted on the heel of her expensive suede boot and stalked out. Niccolo followed. Olivia stayed exactly where she was. She looked at her hand that had covered his so recently and could almost feel it burn.

JANE

'I saw her!' Jane shrieked. 'She was holding your hand!' Jane was truly upset. She could feel herself beginning to hyperventilate. She needed to take her medication. Where was her handbag? She had to have something to keep her calm. She felt hot and flushed.

'No, Jane. She offered comfort when she found me in Sofia's room and could see that I was grieving.' He kept his voice as cool as possible. He never shouted at Jane when he saw that she was genuinely angry and upset. But a note of sarcasm had entered his voice. 'It's called compassion, in case you didn't know.'

'What about someone showing compassion to me?' Her voice became even more shrill. 'I lost a daughter, too, you know. This cannot be all about you, Nico. I'm grieving, too. We never talk anymore.' Her voice broke and she began to sob. Her heart felt as though it was going to break. This was all becoming too much. "Pull yourself together!" she screamed silently to herself. "This the side of you that Nico despises."

But Jane was at the end of her tether. Nico had been away last night without warning, and now she had found him in Sofia's bedroom, of all places, being consoled by that Irish bimbo, as she always referred to Olivia in her head. It was intolerable. She cried harder. Then she went quiet. Nothing was to be gained by an outburst. She had to keep her eye on her game-plan.

Wiping her eyes with determination, she turned and picked up her handbag, preparing to leave the palazzo, saying goodbye to nobody. The workers, having heard the outburst, kept their eyes averted diplomatically and continued with their task. She gave them all a withering stare as she passed by, heading for the lift.

She had an appointment for an aperitivo, after all, with a gondolier. She had concocted a plan and now, after finding them together, her resolve had hardened into a lump in her chest. She raised her head and let her long blonde hair drift behind her as she walked.

OLIVIA

'I'm sorry if I made things worse.'

Olivia was seated at the kitchen table, going through her work schedule, when Niccolo pulled up a chair beside her and sat down.

'Don't even think of it,' he responded. 'You have nothing to feel guilty about. It was entirely my own fault.' He stared at her and she quickly lowered her eyes.

'Are you happy here in Venice?' he asked suddenly. 'Is there anything I can do to make your stay easier? It must be difficult being here without friends and family.'

161

'I'm fine, thank you,' she said, puzzled about the turn the conversation had taken. 'I go for lots of walks and am learning about the city. It's fascinating,' she added.

'Well, you're here at the best time of the year. No queuing. No hordes everywhere. It's almost quiet away from the tourist trail around the Rialto Bridge and St Mark's Square.'

Olivia kept her eyes on the computer screen. Anything to avoid looking at those long black lashes that surrounded that penetrating violet stare. She felt warm and uncomfortably self-conscious under that gaze and wished he would leave and let her get on with her work.

As if he had read her mind, he said, 'I should let you get on with your work. I know you're very busy. What happened this afternoon was not your fault. I should have told Jane that I was going to be here, but things have been strained and, to be honest, I didn't think she'd notice that I was gone last night. We rarely spend time together these days.'

He got up and left the room while she continued with her work, her mind elsewhere. Confused thoughts flew around her brain.

An hour later, just as she was contemplating a visit to the supermarket on the way home, the door opened and Niccolo entered, a bottle of Prosecco in one hand and a bag of cashew nuts in the other.

'Aperitivo time,' he announced. 'I need to make it up to you. Today was very embarrassing for you and I don't want to risk losing my Irish interior designer now, do I?'

He produced a small key and proceeded to open an ancient cupboard that had somehow remained beautiful and unscathed during the renovation process and produced two glasses and a small bowl for the cashews. Popping open the Prosecco, he filled the glasses and, handing one to Olivia, he sat down at the table beside her.

She smiled, despite the thoughts that were whirling in her head. An aperitivo with this aloof conte. How intriguing! She felt herself begin to relax as the first bubbles hit the back of her throat. Prosecco with a conte! What next? Laughter filled her throat and her eyes sparkled.

'That Prosecco seems to have cheered you up anyway,' said Niccolo, smiling gently at her, his eyes taking in everything about her. She sparkled like a glass of Prosecco, too.

CHAPTER TWENTY-THREE
JANE

They sat close together in a discreet table in an out-of-the-way *baccaro* near the Rialto market. Apparently, the legendary lover Casanova had frequented this dark wine bar back in the day. Jane liked to think that it had not changed since then, with its dark oak flooring, quaint windows and general old-fashioned décor. The aperitivi were great here, too. She pointed to a big platter of *polpettine* and the waiter put a few of the spicy meatballs on her plate. They ordered a half-litre of the house red — a mellow Merlot — and retired to their corner table.

'You're a friend of Olivia's?' enquired Jane, picking up a little meatball and taking a nibble. She nodded approvingly and put the rest of the delicious snack into her mouth. She had missed lunch and was hungry. The wine was good, too. She poured herself a second glass and began to relax.

This innocuous question was merely her opening salvo, as she wanted to approach this gondolier in a calm and calculated way. She needed to find out how the land lay first, before she went any further.

Marcello had seemed perfectly happy to meet with her when she spoke to him earlier. He remembered her being with Olivia, and from the introduction he knew she was a contessa. Who turned down aperitivi with a contessa, after all? Not this gondolier, with his eye on the future, for sure.

'I know Olivia, yes.' He was as noncommittal as Jane was. 'I have met her several times since she arrived in Venice.'

'Do you like her?' Yes, Jane knew that that was a loaded question, but she was keen to know what was going on. She tried not to show her anxiety.

'I did like her. I suppose I do still like her. What's not to like about Olivia? She's a very beautiful, sexy woman. Why do you ask?'

Jane could see that he was wondering where this conversation was going. 'Has she said anything about any men in her life?' she enquired, adding hastily, 'Apart from you, of course.'

'I have no knowledge of Olivia's circumstances, as far as men are concerned. She told me she was separated. Apparently, her husband ran off with another woman. I think that's what she told me.' He lifted his broad shoulders in a theatrical shrug, showing her the palms of his hands in a typically Italian gesture.

'Are you in a relationship with her?' Jane decided to cut to the chase. He seemed to be more forthcoming now; it must be the wine, she thought.

'I'm not sure if I get your meaning, Contessa.' He leaned towards Jane, adding, in a slightly suggestive tone, 'There are many different kinds of relationship.'

'Have you slept with her, then?' There, she had said it.

If Marcello was shocked, he hid it well.

'No. Olivia has made it pretty plain that she is not interested in a relationship. At this point,' he added carefully.

'Do you think that may change in the near future?' Jane was becoming enthusiastic now. She smiled encouragingly at Marcello, who was regaining his air of confidence.

'With these things, it is always a matter of time. She is lonely and I am her only friend here in Venice, as far as I know. I'm sure she is attracted to me. I'm waiting for her, and I think she will be worth the wait. In fact, I'm sure of it.' He thought of touching Olivia's voluptuous body and felt a thrill of anticipatory excitement. But he would not be touching her tonight. He had other plans. Blonde Swedish plans, to be accurate. Well, when it was offered on a plate… He broke off his reverie when he realised that Jane was looking at him intently and was speaking again.

'I will need proof of it, when you finally succeed,' she stated baldly.

'What!' exclaimed Marcello. 'How can I give you proof of such a thing?'

'I'm sure you know how to take a photograph.' She was now in full flow. 'I will make it well worth your while. Just name your price.'

OLIVIA

Olivia looked at the empty bottle of Prosecco in amazement. "Did we really drink an entire bottle of wine?" she thought. She looked over at Niccolo. He was leaning back in his chair, looking more relaxed than she had seen him before.

He met her gaze and smiled lazily.

'What are you doing for supper?' he asked carefully. It was obvious he was on unfamiliar ground. 'We all have to eat, after all.'

Olivia hesitated.

'I would love to have supper with you, but I am afraid that Jane is very, very angry with both of us and I am conscious that I am here working for you. You're my client,' she added.

'You don't want to mix business with pleasure.' He looked at her thoughtfully. 'And I must admit, I don't want to antagonise Jane any further, either.'

'It might be better if I left,' she admitted reluctantly, sliding her glass away, inwardly hoping he would find some way to make her change her mind. What was coming over her? She had decided long ago that she found him difficult and arrogant. Now she found him devastatingly attractive.

However, she needed to think this entire thing through alone. She could feel that Niccolo was attracted to her. His wonderful eyes were on her, and occasionally she noticed that, when he thought she was not looking, they roamed over her body, as though undressing her mentally.

'For this evening,' she said calmly, though she felt far from calm, 'I need to go back to Casa Antica and do some work. I have a busy day tomorrow.' She began to gather her things together and slip them into her briefcase. She closed her laptop and slid it into its case, standing up.

'Whoa!' She put her hand on the table to steady herself. 'That Prosecco!'

He put his arm out to steady her, and then he was holding her against him. Olivia was startled, but suddenly it felt completely natural to be standing in the kitchen of this enormous palazzo with her head resting against his chest while his arms encircled her. She placed her hands lightly on his waist and could feel his warmth.

He held her close to him and stroked her hair for what felt like a short moment, a heart-stopping moment, then he released her gently and looked into her eyes. For one giddying moment she thought he was going to kiss her. But suddenly he released her.

'This is dangerous,' he breathed. 'I apologise, Olivia. I don't know what came over me.' His hands were clenched by his sides. 'It won't happen again. I'm sorry.'

With that, Niccolo turned on his heel and stalked out of the room, his back rigid.

JANE

Jane's proposition hung in the air in that dimly lit wine-bar in a narrow alleyway near the Rialto Market.

That was the moment when Marcello should have risen to his feet and walked away. This woman was dangerous. But no. He stayed where he was and topped up their wine glasses, passing the point of no return.

'What sort of price are we talking about?' he asked animatedly. 'This will really cost you; maybe thousands.'

He was taking a chance here, but what the contessa was proposing was undoubtedly illegal. He continued, 'What will you do to protect me? I would not want such a business proposition to ever become public.'

'I will make sure that your name is never mentioned. The photos can be printed out and given to me. Your name will never be made public. You have my word.'

Marcello thought for a moment. He was dubious about taking the word of someone as devious as this contessa, but the idea of making some money was too tempting. He was hooked.

Jane had not finished, however. Far from it.

As the evening progressed, Marcello was becoming noticeably keener on the idea of being paid to seduce a beautiful, voluptuous woman. Jane noted his change of heart and smiled with satisfaction. "Greed and lust," she thought. "Two great human failings so easy to take advantage of."

'In the meantime, her husband has just arrived in Venice and I gave him her address. I expect he will be calling on her at any moment.' She sounded excited at the prospect.

'Perhaps I should go over to her home this evening,' he mused, all thoughts of the Swedish blonde temporarily eradicated. The lure of making some extra cash was too attractive. 'If I get some photos of her with her husband, maybe that would be enough?'

Jane looked down at her glass of red wine and nibbled more polpettine. "Gosh, these are good!" she thought.

'No. That would definitely not be enough,' she added with an icy smile. 'I need you to get up close and personal. Otherwise forget about it. But if you can get some photos of her with her husband, that would definitely help. Presuming she agrees to let him in. After all, he had to phone me for the address. He didn't even have that much information.' Jane was becoming desperate. She had to persuade him to do this for her. Nico had to be kept away from this slut.

Marcello looked puzzled. She continued, sounding deliberately composed.

'As you say, he left her for another woman. He may not get the greeting he's probably hoping for. She may refuse to see him. But you never know.'

'I'll go over there straight away and check out the situation.' He began to push back his chair and looked at her enquiringly. 'What about a down payment?' he suddenly asked, emboldened by Jane's excitement.

'Also,' she continued, holding up her hand imperiously to indicate she would not brook interruption, 'I want to see how she spends her evenings. Who knows what a ghastly little tart like that gets up to? Watch her house, too. I will pay you well.'

Jane looked at his flushed face and at the brightness in his blue eyes. She could tell he was excited by his assignment. She noticed, really for the first time, how extraordinarily handsome he was, in a body-builder sort of way. But she supposed that many women were attracted to that sort of thing. Personally, she preferred men who had a more sophisticated presence, like her Nico. Her heart ached for him. She would do anything to have him back. Anything.

'A down payment tomorrow night and the balance when I have proof in the form of photographs.' Jane was in her element, though it was quite scary, too. Marcello could plainly see that she was a woman teetering on the edge of sanity.

Marcello decided to be a bit more honest.

'I have to admit that Olivia has been fairly resistant until now, though I am sure that will change in time. How long do I have?'

He looked puzzled, as though, as far as he was concerned, a resistant female was an unusual occurrence.

'As soon as possible,' she laughed.

OLIVIA

Fog blanketed Venice. It had thickened dramatically as Olivia made her return journey home to Casa Antica. Darkness was falling over the city as she moved slowly along the now-familiar route of dark alleyways, lined this evening with seemingly eerie street lights. Her thoughts of the interlude with Niccolo were tormenting her as she pulled her jacket more tightly around her shoulders. She crossed a little bridge and down the alleyway that passed the iron gates of the famous Peggy Guggenheim Collection, entering a small piazza which looked entirely different in the thick fog. The small patch of grass in the middle was barely visible, but she could hear the old pump dripping water onto the ancient stones which surrounded the base.

Suddenly, she felt as though an icy finger had touched her spine and she whirled around. Overlooking the piazza was a tall, deserted house, its windows, with their torn curtains, gaping soundlessly at her through the fog. She had read about this palazzo which was, apparently, haunted and had scoffed dismissively when she had read about it at first. Now that she could see it looming through the fog, she could imagine why most Venetians agreed that the ghosts of the many people who had lived there were still present and inhabited its darkest corners.

Something moved in the shadows behind her.

Picking up speed, she rounded the final corner, anxious to return to the warmth of her little Casa Antica. Pulling the keys from her bag and fumbling for the lock, she screamed when a hand closed around her upper arm.

CHAPTER TWENTY-FOUR
JANE

On the spur of the moment, Jane reached for her capacious handbag and felt around in the inner pocket, finding the comforting feel of the card of pills that, she felt, kept her from the brink of mental and emotional disaster. Triumphantly, she pulled them out and held them aloft.

'The very thing!' she exclaimed in excitement. A few of these tranquillisers will knock her for six. At the very least they'll relax her. Take the edge off miss interior design,' she added bitterly, her intense dislike for Olivia showing clearly. 'But on second thoughts…' She returned the pills to her handbag and mused, 'I want these photos to have her looking as though she is enjoying herself. Not out cold.'

Marcello was confused. He had never had to drug anyone before, as most of the women he cast his piercing blue eyes on came to him willingly. He had also, if the truth be told, begun to find the idea of persevering with Olivia quite annoying and a stain on his manhood. This was new territory indeed for the romantic gondolier.

'I have the very thing at home,' Jane announced triumphantly. 'I'll put them in the envelope with your down-payment.'

Marcello was now uneasy, but slightly excited by the idea of the hunt. His burning cheeks were evidence of his agitation.

'What are they? How many can I safely give her?' he enquired tentatively. 'How long do they last?'

'Oh, one or two will be perfectly safe and effective.' She could not wait to get her hands on these photos. She would ruin Olivia. Niccolo would never, as far as she knew, have a relationship with anyone he perceived as a loose woman. He had always been a faithful husband, until that Irish witch came along, she thought.

They stood up and parted company at the door of the *baccaro*.

'Tomorrow night, as arranged. And good luck.' Jane emphasised the words in her clipped accent as she hurried down the dark alleyway towards the bright lights of the Rialto, to catch a water taxi back to the station and home.

OLIVIA

'Olivia. It's me, Steve.' His voice was hoarse, not much more than a whisper.

The hand on her arm in the dark had left her shocked, and she was speechless as she opened the door and let him in. Her legs wobbled as she climbed the stairs. He followed behind her.

Looking at him for the first time in eighteen months, she was shocked at the change in his appearance. She pulled herself together.

'Sit down.' She indicated one of the chairs at the dining table. 'What's going on? Why are you here?'

'Do you have any whiskey?' he asked, his voice still hoarse.

'No, Steve. What's wrong with your voice?'

'Some wine?'

Getting reluctantly to her feet, Olivia opened the fridge and withdrew a bottle of Moscato Secco from the Euganean Hills. Her favourite. She opened it while he sat in silence. She studied him.

Always tall, he was now gaunt, with slightly hunched shoulders and his once neatly-cut dark hair was almost completely grey, long and unkempt. It seemed as though his immaculate dressing was a thing of the past. She recognised the battered jacket as one she had packed for him to take with when he left their home for the last time all those months ago. It seemed like a lifetime.

Handing him a large glass of wine and taking another for herself, she sat down again and faced him squarely.

'Right. Steve. What's going on? Get to the point, please. Why are you here?'

She wanted him to speak. She needed to hear why he had left her with so many problems and doubly humiliated her by leaving with another woman. She had so many unanswered questions.

'I have cancer,' he suddenly stated, his voice rasping. 'Lung cancer. I have a tumour the size of an orange, according to the doctors.'

Overwhelmed by the suddenness and the baldness of the statement, Olivia fought for breath. She could not speak for shock and sat looking at him in horror.

'I have six months, maximum. I won't see next summer, unless there's a miracle cure out there. My voice has already gone. That's the worst bit. I can't even speak on the telephone now. And if I'm in a crowd and I can't be heard, I have a little amplifier that I carry around with me.'

Reaching into his pocket, he produced a small black box with a wire and a microphone. She looked at it in amazement.

He gulped down another mouthful of Moscato and continued.

'If I get through this, I'll contact you. Otherwise, you won't be hearing from me again.'

'But...' Olivia tried to form the words of horror that seemed to choke her.

'Diana will be looking after me.' He looked down at the glass of wine and would not meet her eyes. 'She has generously rented an apartment for me in Dublin and will come and go from County Meath. I'll be close to the hospital for treatment.' Then a note of bravado crept into his voice. 'I'm being admitted in three days and I intend to have my final cigar and a large whiskey before I sign myself in.' He gave his signatory wry smile that had, in another life altogether, caused Olivia to melt.

She let him talk on — not much more than a rasping whisper — without interruption.

He added, 'There's a grand pub just across the road from the hospital and I'll have one for the road. I'll even raise a toast to you, my wife. Almost widow.' Another wry smile turned to a grimace. 'When I come out, I'll move into Diana's apartment and attend the hospital for pain relief and whatever treatment they see fit to give me. She has even organised a Filipino guy to look after me every day, though I've told her I'll be fine.'

Olivia finally found her voice. 'How do you feel about all this, Steve?'

He shrugged. 'I've been abusing my health since I left for Africa and I was always a heavy smoker, virtually chain-smoking my miniature cigars. For crying out loud, I acted as though I was immortal! This was always on the cards. I still find it hard to come to terms with, but please don't phone or email me. Diana would have a fit.' He whispered, 'Even after I left with her, she still feels insecure about you and is constantly worried that I might love you still.'

Olivia looked down at her glass. 'And do you?'

He paused briefly to think about this question; it seemed as if it was something he had not considered previously.

'I don't actually know if I've ever really loved anyone, though with you I came close. I'm being honest now. You were the most beautiful and desirable woman I had ever met, back when we were really not much more than kids. Now I see you in the same light; very beautiful and desirable.' His voice cracked completely as he went to cover her hand with his. She drew it away quickly. 'I couldn't believe my luck when you fell for me, and I know that you've been faithful to me for all these years. I'm well aware I didn't deserve a wife like you and that I'm a stupid ass.' He tried in vain to reach for her hand once more.

'And Diana? How do you feel about her?'

'Well, I hate to tell you, but feel I must, that I had an affair with Diana when she was just eighteen years old. We were immature and broke up, then we both got married to different people. I married you and Diana married Richard, whom you will remember was an ultra-rich hotelier more than thirty years older than she was. But after Richard died, Diana and I got back together, and she began to pressure me to leave you.'

Olivia recoiled in shock.

'But Richard died more than five years ago! Have you been seeing her for all this time behind my back?'

Steve had the grace to look shamefaced.

'Yes, Olivia. I'm afraid so. As you know well, Diana is a gorgeous, sexy, rich woman. And she's devoted to me. Exactly what I need at the moment. Especially the rich bit, to be honest.' He smiled like a naughty boy caught with his hand in the biscuit tin. 'I can't understand what she sees in me, but she's young and quite impressionable. She believes everything I tell her. I remember how she was bowled over by my private jet and all the trappings before she inherited all that money from Richard, and she has always been convinced that I just needed a break in order to make a big comeback in the world of business. She's completely devastated by this news.'

Olivia tried to hide her shock at these revelations and wondered how she had had no suspicions. They must have been very careful, she thought. But she needed to be brave now. For both their sakes.

'I'm glad you have someone to care for you. Someone who can actually afford to look after you, as you just admitted. Because I couldn't possibly be of any use to you right now. So, it's really just as well you have her.'

'I actually believe she loves me.' He had the grace to look slightly ashamed.

Olivia could not believe she was speaking to Steve like this, as if he was just an old friend who had popped by for a glass of wine and not the husband who had walked out on her with another woman, leaving her financially crippled. You never knew, did you? Life was strange.

'Diana has been supporting me since I left. Until now, she kept telling me that it was an investment in the long term and was hopeful that I could soon return to Ireland or be free to start a new business wherever I wanted.' He tried to sound self-confident, but the whine in his voice gave him away. 'I'd been hoping for a job as a freelance financial consultant, maybe even in South Africa. In the meantime, she financed our little Portuguese villa on a West African beach, surrounded by coconut palm trees.' He closed his eyes for a moment, remembering; then looked directly at her. 'Honestly, Liv, it was idyllic there, like paradise really. Or a dream. But that's over now and the villa is on the market. I won't be going back.'

He stood up abruptly.

'Goodbye, Olivia,' he said in his new hoarse voice, and she moved into his arms for a brief hug. Her heart should be breaking, but she felt strangely detached. She felt how thin he had become and was overcome by deep sorrow.

As he picked up his trench coat and put it on, she noticed that his Rolex was missing. She pointed this out. Steve never went anyplace without his most treasured possession.

'I pawned it in Dublin a couple of days ago and used some of the cash to come over to see you.' He hesitated. 'Diana pays for everything, but she would never have paid for that.'

A thought suddenly struck her.

'By the way, Steve, I believe you phoned my employers to find out my address. I was very surprised that they told you. It's supposed to be private information.'

'Oh, it was easy. I phoned the di Falco residence in Galzignano and spoke to the contessa. Very English upper-class. She told me exactly where you were staying and didn't seem to be aware that your whereabouts was supposed to be confidential. Especially when I told her I was your husband.'

So it was that easy to find her. Jane must have been delighted to think that her husband had returned. She felt a stab of anxiety.

CHAPTER TWENTY-FIVE
OLIVIA

A feeling of sadness overwhelmed her. Steve was her husband, no matter what had happened. He was the only man she had ever been with. They had been so young when they met, and he was her first lover.

'Where are you staying?'

'Oh, at a B&B out in Maestre. I've got to get the train back there shortly and then I fly back to Dublin tomorrow from Treviso.'

Descending the stairs together slowly, Olivia in the lead to open the door, she looked back at Steve and saw true pain and grief in his expression. She suddenly gave way emotionally, having had her feelings bottled up for so long and enmeshed with feelings of anger, humiliation and helplessness. As they stepped outside into the foggy calle, they looked at one another and she fell into his arms, overcome by sadness.

'Oh, Steve!' She hugged his thin body tightly. 'I loved you so much, you know that. And I'll be thinking about you and sending positive thoughts your way. I'll be hoping that one day the phone will ring, and it will be you, with your voice back again, telling me you're on the mend.' Even as she said these words, she knew in her heart that she would never see her husband again and had, somehow, forgiven him.

'Olivia.' He held her close and stroked her hair gently. She could see that his eyes were wet. 'I'm so sorry for everything. You were the best wife a man could have asked for. When you fall in love again, I hope you do a bit better than you did with me.'

They said goodbye at the doorway of Casa Antica. It was a poignant moment, and Olivia was greatly confused and upset by the entire interlude.

As he walked away, shoulders hunched, she quietly closed the door and climbed the two flights of stairs to her bed and to sleep.

Outside, in the dark, foggy alleyway, something stirred.

***

Her phone rang early in the morning as she headed for the palazzo. It was Marcello.

'Hey,' Olivia said warmly. She was happy to hear a friendly voice, especially after all of last night's turmoil. First, Niccolo's warmth, followed by his abrupt withdrawal. Then her encounter with Steve. It was all too much. She actually wished it were Saturday, so she could take the day off. But no, she would have to wait two more days for that pleasure.

'Hey,' he responded, encouraged by her tone. 'On your way to work?'

'Yes, indeed. Just rushing along. I have loads to do today.'

'Are you free this weekend?' he enquired. 'How about another night-time ride in my gondola?' He kept his voice as neutral and friendly as he could, but Olivia could tell he was keen to see her. He, in fact, sounded overly keen. After the way she had rebuffed him previously, she had wondered if she would ever see him again. And, as she had witnessed, there were plenty of gorgeous blondes, other than her, to keep him company on lonely evenings.

Olivia hesitated, but only for a moment.

'Okay,' she agreed. 'I'll be free on Saturday. Does that work for you?'

'Absolutely!' Marcello sounded delighted. She could hear lots of noise and screams of excited female laughter in the background, so she was sure he was at work. 'Eight o'clock?'

'See you then. Usual spot.'

He hung up and went about his day with anticipation and just a little nervousness keeping him unusually preoccupied. He would have to be incredibly careful. Olivia was working with Conte di Falco, a rich and powerful man who could ruin Marcello if his part in Jane's little plot ever came out. He would have to tread warily.

JANE

Jane paced up and down the lengthy terrazzo floor of the *piano nobile* at her home in Galzignano. It was a mild December day and the double doors onto the terrace were overlooked by the thickly forested hills which surrounded the villa. The gardens looked elegant, even though they lacked colour at this time of year.

"All this beauty," she thought. "Am I handling this the right way? Or am I doing something I am going to regret for the rest of my life?"

She continued her agitated pacing and tried to think things through in a logical way. Difficult for her to do, she knew, while so nervous and desperate. Had she gone too far?

"If Nico finds out what I've done, I'm finished," she mused "But if I don't do something to keep him away from Olivia, I'm done for anyway. At least this way I have some chance of keeping things on track. Keeping my husband, hopefully."

How was she so sure that Olivia was a threat? She knew Nico so well and was well aware of how he reacted to most women. He was always respectful, though eternally disinterested in even her most glamorous friends and acquaintances. Almost disdainful, to be accurate. His reaction to Olivia was different. So entirely different that she was immediately suspicious, even at that first lunch. It was mainly to do with how he looked at her. A mixture of admiration and something she could not quite put a finger on. Was it lust? Maybe, she thought. Respect? Definitely. He seemed to be in awe of her. And then he had taken her to see a Palladian villa. She wondered what had happened that day.

Would Niccolo divorce her? She did not know the answer to that, but she thought it could well be in the affirmative. According to what he had implied the other night, he had been considering it even before Sofia died. She was pretty convinced that the only reason he had stayed with her was because he could not leave her with her sadness, which had in turn meant even more mental and emotional problems, after the accident.

She felt a clutch of fear. What about the Polizia? Would they arrest her for manslaughter or dangerous driving? She thought not, but they were certainly taking their time to make up their minds. It had been more than a year and a half since the accident.

Thank heavens she had not had a sip from her bottle of grappa that morning. But her driving skills were definitely rusty, and she had taken a heavy sleeping pill the night before, so her reactions were probably not perfect. What had possessed her to take such a chance, when she knew she had to drive the following day? It was all Nico's fault, she thought, that she had to take such strong pills. If he weren't away all the time and so withdrawn when he was at home.

She thought about those innocuous-looking green pills. They were strictly for emergencies, but that night she had been desperate. These pills made her feel euphoric for a while and always gave her a great sleep. She had obtained them from a South African friend who always took them when she attended raves in the Johannesburg mine dumps; a well-known party spot for young people who wanted a hallucinatory experience. So, it was really a harmless party drug, she supposed.

She told herself she had been a little bit preoccupied at the time of the accident. She buried her guilt under a veneer of accusation: why had Niccolo been away? If she had been happier all would have been well. As far as she was concerned, Sofia's death was on his conscience entirely.

OLIVIA

As she sat on her favourite bench beside the old church of San Pietro di Castello, eating a prosciutto and cheese sandwich, while sipping fizzy water straight from the bottle, Olivia thought about what was happening in her life.

First of all, she felt a sadness about leaving her past life behind. Steve had turned everything upside down pursuing his own selfish agenda and, much as she hated the thought of him with terminal cancer, she felt the need to quell feelings of anger towards him that occasionally bubbled to the surface. She would have to try to deal with this, and only time would heal these still-open wounds.

Secondly, leaving Ireland and her beloved mother and her small circle of friends had been difficult, but now that she was removed from her normal milieu, she missed the things she had thought of as indispensable less and less. She knew that, only one year ago, she would not have believed how easy it was to put one's previous life in the rear-view mirror and pursue a new one.

Then there was her new life — was it a real life, or just an interlude? She was unsure. Niccolo, the rich, powerful Conte, had a definite hold on her imagination and she seemed to veer between loathing him and feeling a strange thrill of excitement when he was around. His life was complicated; he had lost his daughter the previous year, a life-altering event and he was married to a jealous, depressed and potentially toxic wife. She needed to stay out of his orbit as much as possible, as he was dangerously attractive, but completely out of bounds for her, despite their brief moments of closeness recently.

She thought about Marcello. Dear Marcello. She pictured his distress whenever she rebuffed his advances and wondered why he bothered with her at all. He was handsome and attentive and appeared to come without complications. An uncomplicated fling with a gondolier while in Venice would be pleasurable, of that she was sure. So why was she so reluctant? Perhaps it was a combination of her natural reserve and the fact that she had never been with another man other than her husband, which she knew was fairly unusual in this day and age. But it was what it was.

And Steve. Poor Steve. His life had turned on its head in no uncertain terms. How far could one fall; he had been at the pinnacle of his success, or so she had thought. Now his business had failed dramatically, he had hidden out in Africa waiting for the dust to settle with his mistress, Diana, for more than a year. Then disaster had claimed him, and terminal cancer was the outcome.

She walked back in the direction of the palazzo. She had stayed away a little bit longer than usual, but the men were efficient, knew what they were doing, and Maria or Gianni would have let them in after their lunch break.

It was a sunny winter's day. A perfect day for walking. As she approached the bridge at Giglio, she looked down. There was Marcello's gondola; he was in the process of helping some young American or Scandinavian girls –– they were tall and blonde — ashore. Just as Olivia was about to announce her presence on the bridge above, she saw Marcello take the prettiest of the girls to one side to talk to her. Olivia could see the girl was blatantly flirting with him and his eyes were fixed on her ample breasts. She could see all that plainly from where she stood. The blonde was obviously delighted by all the attention from the handsome gondolier and she saw him stroke her arm with his thumb. Gently up and down, with a blatantly seductive look on his handsome face. He then took a card from his inside pocket and handed it to the girl, who tucked it into her own pocket and strolled off, glancing back over her shoulder with a suggestive smile. She heard him call, 'See you later, beautiful.'

Olivia skulked away, hurt at this betrayal. But she soon realised that if she was not with Marcello, she had only herself to blame. How many times had she rebuffed him anyway? He had hundreds of beautiful girls hanging on his every word on a daily basis. She should not be naïve. But she was slightly offended all the same, and this gave her pause for thought.

CHAPTER TWENTY-SIX
JANE

Needing to draw cash for Marcello, Jane decided to walk to the local ATM in Galzignano. Readying herself in a warm coat, boots and gloves, she set off on foot. Galzignano was a small, prosperous town consisting mainly of one wide street. On either side were most of the shops one could need for day-to-day basic living. She manoeuvred her way past a shop whose ladders, buckets and garden tools were sitting out on the pavement. Crossing the street outside the pharmacy and heading towards the bank, she met some people she knew, mainly older *signore*, ladies in fur coats, out with their shopping bags on wheels, who greeted her with a degree of deference, which gave her a sense of self-affirmation. She was a person of substance, after all.

'Contessa! Buongiorno! Good day!' She stopped to speak with one or two that she knew relatively well, then continued on her way.

Reaching the ATM, she put her card in the slot and put in her pin. She was unaccustomed to drawing cash and hoped this was not going to be a tedious procedure. Checking her pin number on a card in her purse, she inserted the number with an elegant finger, topped with an immaculately manicured long red fingernail. Luckily, it was all very straightforward, and the required cash was disgorged from the machine, completing its journey from the bowels of the bank and ending up in her large handbag. She felt a thrill of anticipation. Marcello had better not let her down!

OLIVIA

Olivia showered early that morning and applied almond-scented body cream; she loved that the Italians really knew how to make these wonderful creams. Massaging it into her breasts, she realised that she was longing to be touched intimately, but it had to be by someone she cared about. As she spritzed herself with J'Adore, this thought became stronger and she was aware that, all of a sudden, she missed being with a man. But not just the first man who came along, she told herself firmly.

She was overcome by the sudden realisation that what she needed was to save herself for the right man, wherever and whoever he might be. Her thoughts were jumbled, with too many conflicting emotions right now. She knew she was vulnerable at this point in time and needed to be careful not to allow herself to get carried away on a tide of passion.

Olivia boarded the vaporetto to take her to the island of Murano. This was her first visit, and she was anticipating the day ahead. There had been Acqua Alta warnings online, but everything seemed fine and, as far as she knew, Murano would not be affected, and she should be back in the city of Venice after the tide had receded.

Her visit to Murano was in pursuit of three new chandeliers for the palazzo. She had received the name of the glass factory from Francesca and was looking forward to seeing the glass-blowing demonstration she had been promised when she made the appointment.

Having enjoyed a brisk half-hour walk from Casa Antica to Fondamenta Nuove, past the remarkably beautiful building which housed the main hospital, she boarded vaporetto number 4.2 to the island. She stood out on deck, trying to dodge the large back-packs worn by so many tourists, who carelessly ignored the large signs telling them to put their bags on the floor, as they swung this way and that, taking photos of everything in sight.

Finding a safe corner, she noticed the graveyard island of San Michele. The vaporetto stopped there for a moment and two elderly ladies, carrying flowers, alighted without a break in their intense conversation. She considered getting off and following them, as she was curious about this little island surrounded by high red-brick walls, over which loomed many towering cypress trees.

It appeared to be an island steeped in quiet atmosphere. She decided to visit there on her way back later that day.

Approaching Murano, she was aware of several red-brick chimney stacks looking neat and orderly, with many bridges over a wide canal.

The island was busy, and Olivia wended her way among the disembarking passengers, who were being solicited to visit various establishments with the lure of a glass-blowing demonstration, followed, undoubtedly, by some high-pressure sales in its adjoining showroom. She had been warned about this by Francesca and she gave them all a wide berth. On the other hand, she mused, if she were in Venice for only a day or two, she might be tempted to go to one of these tourist-oriented establishments just for the experience. It was one way, after all, to see these gorgeous glass items being manufactured.

Checking the address on her phone, she found her way quite easily, over a bridge, past pretty shops selling glass jewellery and ornaments, and arrived on time, entering a large showroom of glass shelves showing off colourful glass decanters, goblets, vases, dishes and objet d'art. The ceiling was ablaze with lighting of all shapes, sizes and colours. There were traditional Murano-glass chandeliers, plain and brightly coloured, plus plenty of less conventional fittings.

Approaching her was a gentleman, immaculately attired in a dark blue suit, blindingly white shirt, blue silk tie and expensive-looking brown brogues. Introductions over, Signor Morelli guided her into a large industrial area at the back of the showroom, where a man in a leather apron and goggles was working away with a red-hot piece of molten glass on the end of a metal rod. She watched fascinated as this was moulded into a colourful vase over the space of about fifteen minutes. Aware that Signor Morelli was waiting for her to enter his office, she tore her eyes away from the glass blower and followed him. Sitting down, she discussed the sizes, shapes and style of the three large chandeliers she needed to order.

Standing up at the end of their meeting, business completed, they shook hands and she departed with his promises to have designs and a quotation ready for her shortly ringing in her ears. Thanking him, she strolled down the fondamenta, looking into the shop windows as she dawdled along, absorbing the sights and sounds of this pretty island.

Admiring the Murano-glass jewellery in a shop window, Olivia spotted a pendant on a silver chain that looked appealing, so she entered the small shop, where the owner sat behind her counter, listening to the radio. Olivia ended up buying a red and silver glass pendant for her mother, which she would give to Niccolo to bring to Ireland when he went, as he had promised to visit her parents and give them an update on how she was. She knew her mother was concerned and would be grateful for the visit.

Lunch was a tramezzino in a small bar on a side canal which was full of old men playing cards and laughing a great deal. It was not a tourist hangout; that much was for sure. They barely looked up from their game when she found a corner table to eat her sandwich and drink a glass of white house wine. She felt like treating herself today.

Back on the vaporetto, Olivia decided to alight at San Michele. She was the only person to get off the water bus, and she stepped off the floating wooden jetty and entered the graveyard. The little island was quiet and peaceful. She noticed a supply of small green watering cans hanging on a metal rack, obviously for use by family members and friends who came to tend the graves.

Her first impression was of the long straight avenues lined with tall cypress trees. Thousands of little white crosses and marble headstones stood in neat rows. Off to one side were high walls with crypts set into them, completely covered with flowers in attached receptacles; a sign of all the love and care that went into the respect with which Italians look after their dead. Still more of the Venetian dead were housed in small mausoleums. Some of these mausoleums looked as though they had been sadly neglected for a long time, but she soon noticed that one of them was particularly immaculate, with bouquets of fresh flowers in small urns behind a glass door.

She read the inscription of "Di Falco" on the exterior and knew that this was where Sofia was entombed. A wave of compassion for Niccolo came over her. Though she was, obviously, very sorry for Jane's loss, too, it did not compare to the sorrow she felt whenever she thought of the poignant scene in his daughter's bedroom recently.

Hearing a twig snap behind her, she whirled around. It was Niccolo, and he was carrying a bunch of pink roses. Their eyes met and their gaze held for a long moment. He stepped towards her.

'It's you,' he said, his voice not much more than a whisper. 'Why are you here?'

'I wanted to pay my respects to your daughter and to try to get a feeling for where she lies.' Suddenly, she added, 'I hope you don't mind.'

'No, Olivia.' He came closer until his face was no more than a few inches from hers. 'I think it's very thoughtful of you.'

Stepping towards the mausoleum, he produced a large iron key and opened the door. Once inside, he placed the flowers in a small receptacle. As he stood there with his head bowed, Oliva watched in silence, careful not to disturb his thoughts.

Her feelings suddenly overflowed with an emotion she could scarcely admit to. She was falling in love with Niccolo di Falco, the Venetian Conte. She knew he was married, however happily or unhappily was none of her business, but she could not help this new feeling and knew that her compassion for him was not misplaced. This was a deeply unhappy man on many levels, and she wanted to hold him in her arms and comfort him in a way she had never done for a man before.

Niccolo and Olivia left the island of San Michele together. The towering cypress trees grew smaller in the distance and they alighted from the vaporetto at San Zaccaria, beside St Mark's Square.

She was surprised to see that the tide was creeping higher, and Olivia wondered how high her very first Acqua Alta was going to be. Platforms had been erected down the centre of the square, and most people were using them to get about. Others were wearing high rubber boots and appeared to be enjoying what they considered a phenomenon, but which was actually a natural occurrence in this part of the Venetian Lagoon.

She was fascinated to see that the usual queue of tourists waiting to enter the Basilica were on a special platform that ended at the door, and they were all standing a few feet above the water, which was still quite low.

Strolling companionably through the excited crowds who thronged the square, despite the rising tide, they mounted a platform and walked past the expensive designer shops, their feet sounding hollow on the wooden boards, as they headed towards the Accademia Bridge. The sun was setting when they crossed from San Marco to Dorsoduro, and though they had seen and admired it many, many times before, they could not help stopping at the highest point to once more marvel at the sight of the huge church of Santa Maria della Salute, guarding the entrance to the Grand Canal.

She looked up at him as he gazed at the view and saw a glitter in his eyes. Maybe a tear, she thought. He took her hand and tucked it under his arm. She stiffened slightly and hoped that none of the workers or staff at the palazzo would choose that moment to cross the canal. Holding onto the conte's arm was not normal employer/client behaviour.

Descending the bridge together, she made to bid him goodbye at the bottom, as she was to turn left to Casa Antica, while the palazzo was to the right. He held onto her hand.

'I'll see you home,' he insisted. 'With this rising water and darkness falling, I want to make sure you're safe.' He looked down at her with an unreadable expression on his face. Was it desire? Olivia was unsure of how to behave or react to this new situation. She was sure the thumping of her heart was audible to all.

The platform ended at Rio della Fornace and she needed to go down that fondamenta to get home. It was under water, and she was in normal boots. In fact, they were suede. What now, she wondered. She looked down the canal at the Madonna with the Umbrella and asked her advice. She was silent, though Olivia thought that maybe she shrugged her bronze shoulders.

'Two choices,' said Niccolo, breaking into her thoughts. 'I'm wearing my rubber boots, as you can see, so I'm either going to have to carry you, or we sit it out in a bar for a couple of hours until the waters recede.' He looked at her enquiringly and broke into one of his rare smiles. 'I think I should carry you.' He laughed at her stunned expression. 'It's so close. Two minutes, maximum.'

Before she had time to argue or discuss the other possibility, he had put one arm behind her knees and the other around her shoulders and lifted her up. She was small and light, and he carried her effortlessly.

As they splashed along the fondamenta, she looked up at him from where her head nestled against his shoulder. His jaw was set and determined.

She felt her heart beating in a most unusual way. Anticipation for she knew not what flowed through her body.

Rounding the final corner into the little alleyway where Casa Antica was situated, she fumbled for her keys, so when they got to the front door, she was able to lean over and open it. He stepped over the flood barrier into the little hallway.

That was when he should have put her down, turned around and left, but he did not and he stood still, looking down at her in his arms. Their eyes met and they both knew what was going to happen next. This was what she wanted, she realised.

Using his foot, Niccolo closed the front door firmly, then, taking the steps two at a time, he wordlessly mounted the stairs, both flights, until they entered her bedroom and lost themselves in their mutual passion.

Eyes watched from across the alleyway and saw the light go on through the slatted shutters of the upstairs bedroom. He checked his camera. Yes, indeed, some interesting photographs there, for sure.

CHAPTER TWENTY-SEVEN
JANE

Alighting from a water taxi close to Santa Maria del Giglio, Jane strolled into the Gritti Palace Hotel, where she entered the bar. She was well known here and liked its quiet, up-market atmosphere. The bar opened out onto a magnificent view of the Grand Canal and she sat at a table, looking out at the view. She felt tense about her coming meeting with Marcello and needed a glass or two of Prosecco to help her to relax.

Marcello's gondola was moored nearby, and they had arranged to meet at a small, out of the way bar, close by. Jane sipped her bubbly wine and nibbled a couple of peanuts.

She hoped this plan of hers would not backfire. A great deal was at stake, and she knew she was trusting Marcello with a difficult task. But he seemed fairly excited about the entire proposal, both the idea of making some money off the record and the idea of that money being given to him to take compromising photographs of a woman he so obviously desired. And who had obviously rejected him. His pride was badly dented. His revenge would be sweet, and she just hoped he would leave no trail of evidence that would lead back to her.

She fingered the package she had brought with her. "Roofies", the infamous "date rape" drug, were what her South African friend had called the pills she would be giving him to administer to Olivia. He needed to give her only one, as that should be enough to make her acquiescent to his advances and had the added bonus of erasing short-term memory for several hours. If anyone came knocking on his door afterwards, accusing him of sexual assault, he could claim that their little romp was consensual. She would have a hard time convincing anyone otherwise.

She had also brought the down-payment that she had withdrawn from her personal bank account in Galzignano.

If this works, she thought to herself, I will have Niccolo back and our lives can move on from the death of Sofia and his obvious infatuation with this man-eating Irishwoman, as that was how she viewed Olivia.

Noticing the time as she was half way through her second glass of Prosecco, she knocked it back and stood up quickly. Paying at the bar as she hurried past, she headed for her meeting with her gondolier.

Marcello was there waiting for her on the street. She passed him and went into the bar. He followed a minute later, having checked that there was nobody around that appeared to have recognised either of them.

Joining her at a small table at the back of the bar, he sat down beside her. She looked at him closely. He seemed fairly calm and ready for action. She opened her bag and began to speak, without going through any of the normal greetings.

'Here are the pills, though you will probably need only one. They're strong and will take effect within half an hour. You will then have several hours to take photos and do whatever it is you have been longing to do for the past couple of months.' She laughed, a sharp, cutting sound that annoyed Marcello.

'I'm ready,' he said, and, getting down to business, said coldly, 'Give me the pills. Do you have my down-payment with you?'

'Yes, I do.' She handed him a thick envelope. He looked around, but nobody in the almost-empty bar was paying the slightest attention.

He opened it and quickly checked the contents. Jane handed him the receipt from the ATM.

'Just put your initials there.' She instructed. Let's have no misunderstandings. This is a business transaction.'

Marcello scribbled his signature on the slip of paper and handed it back, whereby she slipped it into her purse.

'I can expect the balance on delivery of the photographs?' he enquired, putting the envelope and little packet of pills into a shoulder bag he was carrying.

'Of course. I will meet you here to pay the balance and receive the photos. Send me a text to let me know and I'll be here. Just text the word "DONE", and I will meet you the next evening.'

He nodded confirmation. Their Aperol spritzes arrived and they each took a long swallow.

'A perfect spritz,' commented Jane, beginning to relax slightly. 'Not too much soda water. Now, tell me something,' she began, as she was genuinely curious and perplexed. 'What is it about that Irishwoman that attracts the men like flies? She's small with big breasts, but no great looker, in my opinion.'

Marcello looked at Jane in surprise. He thought her beautiful, too, but in a completely different way to Olivia. He thought about it for a moment.

'She looks as though she needs protecting,' he said. 'She is very, very feminine. Yes,' he raised his hand to stop Jane from stating the obvious, 'I know she is probably a hard task-master where all those builders and sub-contractors are concerned, and she certainly doesn't suffer fools gladly, but she has a vulnerability about her that is very appealing.'

Jane could not stop herself from asking, 'What has she got that I don't?' It was a bald question, and as soon as she uttered it, she felt foolish. But she was curious. Why did Nico fancy Olivia so much? And Marcello was obviously in lust, too. She wanted an answer.

'Contessa...' Marcello kept his attitude formal. 'You are a very beautiful woman. Much more beautiful than Olivia.'

She was annoyed. She could see he was just trying to keep her happy. 'I have been told many times that I am beautiful, but do I not have her sex appeal? Is that it?' She was feeling braver now. 'Am I not sexy enough?'

He was silent for a moment, obviously weighing up his answer. He needed to keep her on-side: she was rich and a contessa. It would be excellent to have a Venetian contessa as a friend. If he played his cards right and did everything, she wanted him to do this time, perhaps there would be other services he could provide as time went on. Jane could plainly see these thoughts flitting across his handsome face.

'I'm going to have a cognac!' she announced. 'Enough Prosecco and Aperol, I want a real drink right now. Tell me, Marcello, do you find me attractive? I know you say I'm beautiful, but am I sexy, too?' She leaned closer to him and he could smell her perfume. He perked up and looked at her more closely.

'You are a dangerous woman,' he breathed. His tried and tested line usually worked a charm. His blue eyes narrowed as he took in the scene. Here was a beautiful woman, a contessa no less, needing assurance that she was desirable. What could be more tempting?

Jane's cognac arrived and she knocked it back in one go. She stood up. 'Let's go!' Walking to the bar, she paid and left. Marcello followed her outside.

'Walk me to the taxi stand down by the Gritti Palace,' she commanded. They set off at a leisurely pace.

'Don't you have to get home to Galzignano?' he enquired. 'Won't you be missed?'

'There's nobody at home to miss me, unless you count the servants.' She could not keep the bitterness out of her tone. 'Oh, look!' She stepped into a deep, darkened shop doorway and made as if to study the jewellery within. He followed her. She looked up at him, her blue eyes huge and her blonde hair shining in the reflected light from the street. 'Would you please kiss me? It's been so long since I've been kissed.' She came closer and stood directly in front of him, challengingly.

He lowered his head and their lips met. She wound her arms around his neck and embraced him passionately. He held her close, feeling her tall, slim body pressing against him.

'You surprise me,' he whispered into her hair. 'I thought you were cold and unemotional.' He held her tighter, becoming aroused.

Suddenly, she pushed him away. 'Not one of my better ideas,' she announced in her brittle cut-glass accent.

Jane could see he was offended, but she had felt a rush of desire for him that was, to her mind, wholly inappropriate. What on earth had come over her? Was she completely losing the plot? Kissing gondoliers in shop doorways like a common tart, she thought.

'I'll see myself to the taxi,' she announced, and said curtly, over her departing shoulder, 'I'm counting on you to do this job properly.'

Marcello just stood there, looking confused. 'I'll text as we planned,' he responded lamely.

But she was already gone.

OLIVIA

Waking up in her four-poster bed in Casa Antica, Olivia stretched among the white bed-linen and marvelled at the sight of Niccolo asleep beside her.

"He looks so beautiful," she thought to herself, admiring his long curling eyelashes, fine features and thick black hair on the pillow in the early morning light that filtered through the slatted blinds. He lay on his stomach with his head turned towards her and she was overcome with a need to touch him.

Running the palm of her hand lightly down his back, into the hollow at its base, she saw him open his eyes, slightly startled for a moment, and then he smiled and reached for her. Her happiness knew no bounds as she gave herself to him gladly.

Later, at breakfast, they sat close together at the breakfast bar, as trying to use the table, piled high with working folders and fabric swatches, was impossible. She told him, laughingly, she had not exactly been expecting company. They drank coffee and ate some fruit, revelling in their new-found love affair.

'I wish I didn't have to go to Dublin right now,' he said, taking one of her hands in his and kissing her fingers gently. 'But I've agreed to spend Christmas with Francesca and Paul.' He paused. 'I would like to stay to spend more time with you. But I'll be back in ten days and I promise you I'll make it up to you.' He rolled his eyes at her suggestively and she felt herself melt.

'That's okay, Nico. I'm very busy with the palazzo now and I'm just happy to spend the Christmas period relaxing.' She thought for a moment. 'What about Jane?'

'Oh, Jane. Well, Max is coming over from London in a few days to spend the holiday period with her, so she won't be alone, if that's what you're wondering. He's bringing his new girlfriend along. Undoubtedly yet another in a long list of Tabitha's, Sienna's, Poppies and Cressida's that populate his love life. In fact,' he added, 'I think her name *is* Cressida!' He laughed ironically.

Olivia realised immediately that Max was not one of Niccolo's favourite people but did not comment.

'Have you decided what you'll do for the Christmas holiday?' he enquired.

'No. Not yet. I'll decide nearer to the time. I thought I might like to head south by train with a pile of books and just relax in slightly warmer weather for a week or so. I like the thought of visiting Puglia. I believe it's beautiful?'

'It is indeed! That's a lovely idea. Perhaps I could meet up with you there. I have been meaning to visit some close friends who live near Brindisi for ages. It would be an excellent opportunity. Have you been there? It's very different to this part of Italy.'

They chatted about the possibility of Olivia visiting the old White City of Ostuni for a week. It was easy to get there by train, and if Niccolo could join her, well, that would be just fabulous. And the weather would surely be milder than in Venice. She began to feel excited by the prospect.

As Niccolo was about to head straight for the airport and his flight to Dublin, Olivia hugged him tightly and gave him the neatly wrapped present for her mother.

'Give mamma my love, and hurry back,' she whispered, as they kissed once more, entirely unaware of the disaster that was about to befall their newly found love affair.

CHAPTER TWENTY-EIGHT
OLIVIA

Olivia had a lot to come to terms with. She had fallen head over heels with Niccolo and knew that this could get her into a lot of trouble. Jane was vindictive, of that she was certain.

Steve was never coming back, and her marriage was over. This would be her last outing with Marcello; she certainly did not want to jeopardise her budding relationship with Niccolo, no matter how dangerous it was. She would say goodbye to Marcello tonight, over a last friendly drink. She did not want to give him false hope, but did not want to stand him up either, as he did not deserve that humiliation. It was a bit of a dilemma, she thought.

Little did she know how the next few hours were going to evolve.

She had mixed emotions about Marcello. On the one hand, he was obviously keen on her. On the other hand, he was a serial womaniser, from what she could see. But maybe he was just a harmless flirt in reality. She really did not know, but she hoped that their evening would go smoothly, as it would be their last.

Slipping down the dark alleyways, past bars with cigarette smokers huddled outside in the chill winter air, she saw Marcello ahead at the foot of the Accademia, as usual. His eyes lit up when he saw her and he greeted her with the traditional double kiss, one on each cheek. Real kisses, too, she noted, not just the usual cheek-to-cheek interaction. His lips were warm. He held both her hands in his and looked at her carefully. She tried to quell her uneasiness.

"Was this a mistake?" she wondered, little realising that it would prove to be one of her greatest mistakes ever.

'You look beautiful this evening.' His voice was slightly husky, and she could clearly see that he was ready to take their friendship to the next level. She felt nervous but managed to smile. Maybe this outing was indeed an error of judgement; but it was now too late to change her mind. She needed to keep this casual and then say goodbye.

Keep it light and friendly, she thought. 'Thank you, Marcello. It's good to see you,' she said.

They climbed the Accademia together and she linked his arm companionably. It was just a five-minute walk to where his gondola was moored, and they chatted about inconsequential matters as they strolled through the evening crowds. She told him about today's meeting with an electrician who had wanted to place the wires for the wall lights higher than she had specified.

'We argued for at least an hour before he would agree to work to my plan. He was convinced he knew better than I did,' she moaned. 'Why do men have to be so difficult?'

Having no answer to this perennial question posed so regularly by women, Marcello took her arm as she climbed across the gondola moored at the side of the canal and helped her onto his own black, shiny one tied to it on the outside, forming a floating platform.

'I love your perfume,' he breathed in her ear, and she felt the friction of the wooden beads he always wore on his wrist as he helped her to her red velvet seat, facing away from him, as he climbed up behind her on the stern of his gondola and, having untied the ropes, began to row.

He sang:
'The other evening, I went rowing with a blonde in a gondola.
The poor girl was so happy that she fell sound asleep immediately.
As she slept in my arms, each time I woke her
The rocking of the boat sent her back to sleep again.'

Olivia, reclining on her velvet love-seat, began to relax. She thought of Niccolo. How she would love to have him here beside her! The gondola glided along the dark canals, under damp, mossy bridges, past busy restaurants and pizzerias, into the night. In a darkened canal, Olivia knew not where, he pulled the gondola to a halt and tied it up. He looked down at her questioningly, then sat on the velvet seat beside her. Without preamble, he slid his arm around her shoulder and drew her to him.

'Do you like me, Olivia?' he enquired gently. 'I hope that you do, because I think you are one of the most beautiful women I have ever met, and I find you infinitely desirable.' He stroked the side of her face with his thumb. 'You must know how much I want you.'

Olivia was completely thrown by such a direct approach. 'No, Marcello!' she objected, wriggling from his embrace. 'Look, I like you,' she whispered. 'But…' The darkness had closed in around her and she felt that she should whisper. It was quiet and all she could hear was the lapping of the water against the bottom of the gondola. That, plus Marcello's quickened breathing. She smoothed her already well-groomed hair nervously and tried to sit up straight. But Marcello had other ideas, as she saw his face loom out of the darkness and felt his lips on hers. They were soft and warm. She froze. "No!" she thought. "This cannot be happening." But Marcello had other ideas; she could see that clearly.

JANE

At home in Galzignano, Jane paced up and down the *piano nobile*. She was in a state of nervous excitement. Much as she wanted to see her rival vanquished and shamed, she was terrified that somehow Niccolo would find out. If he did, it would all have been for nothing. Everything she held dear would come to an end. Her life would be over.

She reached for her pills.

OLIVIA

'Please!' she breathed softly. 'I don't think this is a good idea. Marcello…' He kissed her softly again and she felt his right-hand approach her breast. 'No. Please.'

'No?' His eyes glinted and teased her in the moonlight. 'I can see you want me as much as I want you,' he whispered in her ear, gently blowing on it and kissing her neck sensuously.

She moaned slightly with frustration. How was she going to get herself out of this predicament? He immediately interpreted her moan as one of acquiescence and he began to move his lips lower.

'Stop! Please, Marcello!'

He was startled and looked up at her in the gloom. 'Why should I stop, Olivia? I can see you're enjoying this every bit as much as I am.' His voice was self-confident and lazy. He was convinced she was his for the taking. 'You're hot and ready for me. Tell me I'm wrong.' A challenging note had entered his voice.

'I'd like you to take me home, please,' she implored, now fully alarmed. 'I'm sorry, really, but this was a bad idea.'

Marcello stared at her coldly. 'Very well.' His voice was louder than before. A spell had been broken and things would never be the same again.

Olivia accepted this fact as a certainty, but she had to be true to herself, and she only wanted to be with Niccolo. 'I'm really sorry,' she repeated. 'I need to go home now.'

Soundlessly, Marcello untied the gondola and turned it to face towards the Grand Canal once more.

As the gondola nudged silently into the dark, narrow canal that led to Casa Antica, he broke the heavy silence. 'At least let's share a glass of Prosecco before you go. To celebrate our friendship.'

His voice was persuasive and Olivia, feeling guilty about having rejected him so completely, heard herself say, 'Okay. That sounds good.' As he seemed offended and she had not meant to allow things to get to the point where she would make an enemy of her first Venetian friend, she thought a simple glass of Prosecco would be harmless enough.

Alighting nimbly onto the fondamenta and tying up his gondola to a mossy vertical post, he got back on board and got down on his hunkers. He had a cool-box under one of the seats and pulled it out. Lifting the lid, he put his hand inside and produced a bottle of Prosecco like a rabbit out of a hat. He also produced a thick fleecy rug and spread it on the floor of the gondola.

'A picnic!' He put his hand out to help her from her chair.

She was dubious about sitting on the floor of the gondola with him in the darkness but acquiesced out of a need not to offend him further. She wobbled a bit when she stood up, a mixture of nervousness and the movement of the gondola on the still oily waters. Sitting down on the rug, she leaned back and looked up. She realised suddenly that they were completely invisible to anyone who might pass by. She felt a slight frisson of alarm but hid it behind a beaming smile.

'A picnic in a gondola. What an unusual way to spend an evening!'

Marcello promptly produced two glasses, white paper napkins and a plastic container of olives. The scene was complete. He sat down beside her and began to tear the foil from the top of the bottle. She noticed it was wet and chilled to perfection. She began to relax.

Noticing that he had pulled out his camera, she asked him if he was planning on taking some photographs. He agreed that indeed he was and planned to take one of her as soon as she had a glass in her hand. He placed it beside him on the rug and proceeded to pour their glasses full of glorious fizz. "The taste of Italy," she thought. "On a night to remember." Olivia did not realise that this was indeed going to be a night to remember, but for all the wrong reasons.

"Marcello is happy just to be friends," she mused to herself. "I can now relax and absorb this new adventure."

He turned his back to her while he poured the wine, so she did not see the little green pill that was dropped into her glass. Nor did she notice him give her Prosecco a quick stir with a cocktail stick. He turned back to her and gave her the glass of spiked Prosecco he had carefully prepared. In the dark, under the starry Venetian sky, she could not see the slight tinge of colour in her glass.

Olivia raised her glass to Marcello.

'Here's to friendship!' Feeling nervous, she finished the glass of wine fairly quickly.

They clinked glasses companionably and, putting down his glass carefully, he picked up the camera.

'Cheese!' The camera flashed in the dark and she smiled happily as she raised her glass.

As he quickly topped up her glass, she caught him looking at her with a slightly uneasy expression on his face and tried to decipher it. They sat together on the fleecy rug and, leaning back, looked at the stars that sprinkled the night sky over Venice. She felt relaxed and happy.

Suddenly, she felt dizzy. She looked at Marcello and realised that she could see two of him, or so it seemed. He appeared to be about to kiss her. She felt disorientated and groaned slightly as she felt his hands on her.

'No!' she exclaimed feebly. 'Please, no!' she begged, as he laid her down on the rug.

She felt completely disoriented and confused as she felt him unbutton her jeans and pull up her jumper. She felt powerless to resist. She felt the winter chill on her breasts and realised that they were fully exposed to the elements. She saw the camera in one of his hands, while the other pulled at her clothing. His breathing was harsh in the quiet air as he determinedly slid his free hand behind her and quickly unfastened her bra.

She struggled vainly as he began to pull off her jeans. She managed one final protest before she became helpless, lying there in the bottom of the gondola, quite unable to move.

'No! Please don't do this!' she begged, trying to push him away. Her mind was registering what was happening, but she was powerless to resist. She felt his hot breath on her neck and his hands seemed to be all over her. She heard a ripping sound as her underwear was roughly removed.

She was in a type of trance and seemed to be experiencing an out-of-body experience, like a dream, as she began to float in a strangely pleasant way. She was vaguely aware of a feeling of sensuality as she drifted helplessly. The constant flashing of the camera added to the sense of unreality.

She was only semi-aware of what was happening to her for the next half hour or thereabouts as Marcello took charge of her body in its entirety. Then, wrapped in her coat, with her clothes in a plastic bag and his arm around her waist, he assisted her the short distance home to Casa Antica. Taking her keys from her bag, he unlocked the front door and helped her up the stairs to her bedroom, where he removed her coat once more and laid her on her bed.

The humiliations had not ended.

JANE

Her mobile phone bleeped. She picked it up.

'DONE!' Just one word. Jane felt elated.

CHAPTER TWENTY-NINE
OLIVIA

Waking late the next morning with a pounding headache, Olivia sat up in bed. She was naked. She looked around wildly. There were her clothes, folded neatly on a chair next to her bed, with her boots placed side by side underneath. She got out of bed, wobbling slightly and holding onto one of the bedposts for support. Her head swam. She looked at her clothes carefully. Everything appeared to be in order until she got to her underwear. Why were her panties torn? How had that occurred? She had no idea what to think.

What had happened? She had no recollection of anything after looking at the stars with Marcello.

Marcello! She gasped out loud. She reached for her phone, which was in her handbag at the foot of the bed.

'Buongiorno!' The melodious voice at the other end of the phone was a jolt.

'Marcello?' she enquired. 'What happened last night? I have no recollection.' She felt silly asking him, but what choice did she have, she asked herself.

'Olivia, my darling,' he said, his voice suggestive and treacly. 'I had to take you home and put you to bed. Surely you remember?' he laughed. 'You can't seriously say you don't remember!'

She collapsed back onto her pillows, stunned.

He continued, 'I hadn't expected you to drink so much. You acted as though you wanted to drink yourself into oblivion. Quite a surprise!' he added.

'But…' She trailed off. 'Marcello, I really don't remember anything. Please tell me what happened? How much did I have to drink?' She was far too mortified to ask him about the ripped panties at this point. 'And you're telling me you put me to bed?' she enquired incredulously. 'You took off all my clothes?'

'Oh, I just helped.' He laughed again. 'You're quite a little tigress when you've had too much to drink.'

Olivia felt herself redden to the roots of her blonde hair. She could think of nothing to say.

He admonished her. 'How can you not remember? You were quite drunk, to be sure, but it was great fun. Quite a night! Then he added, 'Now, I must go. I have a group of American tourists just boarding. Some pretty girls, too!' He laughed suggestively once more.

Olivia was numb with shock. She dashed to the bathroom and vomited strongly. She then climbed into the shower and stood under the hot water for what seemed like an age. Emerging from the shower, she examined herself carefully in the mirror. She looked normal, just like she had yesterday and the day before. And, on further examination, she was pretty sure that she had not made love with anybody the previous evening, despite Marcello's heavy hinting and the implications suggested by the fact that she had woken up naked in bed with no recollection of the night before.

A woman knows these things, she thought.

Returning to bed, she promised herself that she would try to figure things out later. But not just now. Now she needed to sleep.

JANE

'DONE!' Just four letters, but, hopefully, a solution to the thorny problem of the Irishwoman, Jane thought. She could not wait to meet Marcello to see the photographs. She would go to Venice today to meet him.

As she showered and prepared herself for the day ahead, she thought about Marcello. He was a dangerously attractive man in an unpolished sort of way, according to her own particular standards. She was accustomed to the air of sophistication that was part of the conte's demeanour, and the men in their social circle exuded refinement. But she was definitely attracted to Marcello. On the other hand, he was a gondolier and she was a contessa, far apart on the social scale, to her way of thinking. A dalliance was out of the question. She put her fingers to her lips. In her mind, they still burned where he had kissed her, and she was hungry for loving, longing to be caressed and made to feel that she was attractive.

The death of Sofia had been a terrible blow to her, and she was still grieving deeply. She knew very well that she would never fully recover from this unbelievably tragic event and realised that so many of her old friends had stopped calling, as it had become too difficult to be around her for long. She knew she was terrible company these days.

It was Niccolo's love she craved. Anything else would merely be a diversion.

She made an extra effort with her appearance. Her new hairstyle suited her and gave her a certain glamorous edge. She dressed carefully. Tomorrow she would be collecting Max at Venice Marco Polo airport, and if she were to meet with Marcello, it would have to be today.

Donning a figure-hugging black wool coat with a black and red silk scarf at her throat, she called for Antonio and the car. He was ready and waiting to drive her, first to Galzignano, where she would withdraw the balance of what was due to be paid to Marcello, and then to the train station at Battaglia Terme nearby, where she could catch the Regionale to Venice. Of course, she would not hand over such a large sum of money to the gondolier without seeing the photos first. She was not stupid!

Climbing into the Range Rover, she settled back in its leather seat. A quiver of anticipation shot through her as she thought of what lay ahead.

OLIVIA

Waking some time during the afternoon, Olivia still felt groggy.

"What happened last night?" she wondered. "I need to find out. But I still feel terrible."

She threw on a thick, white towelling robe and a pair of mules and descended the steep stairs that led from the bedroom to the living area.

Putting on the kettle, she thought longingly of a mug of strong tea. Just the routine performance of warming the cup and pouring the brown beverage, topping it up with milk, made her feel a bit better. She sat at the breakfast bar and tried to work things out as she sipped her tea.

'Okay. What's the last thing I remember?' she asked herself out loud.

'That glass of Prosecco with Marcello,' she replied to herself.

'Could it have been drugged?' she wondered and dismissed the idea out of hand. Why would Marcello want to drug her? He was her friend. At least she had thought so. She tried to figure it out. Yes, she had rebuffed his advances. Yes, he was peeved. But he seemed to have accepted the situation without argument.

She honestly did not believe him when he implied that they had made love. Or had he really suggested the possibility to upset her? She was sure her body would have shown some sign of untoward activity. There was nothing out of the ordinary to be seen or felt, apart from her torn underwear.

So, what was all this about, she wondered. Why would he imply that something had happened between them if it were untrue? She was greatly worried by this strange puzzle and decided to go to Giglio to see him at lunchtime the following day. She needed an explanation urgently.

Her phone rang. She snatched it up.

'Niccolo!' She was overjoyed. 'How are you? How is Dublin?'

'Olivia…' His voice was tender. 'I'm here at The Mews, thinking about you. This Irish home of mine reminds me of you no matter where I look. It's just heavenly.'

'I'm so happy you love it, Nico,' she whispered.

'I just got back from seeing your parents. Your mother was overjoyed to hear from you and was delighted with her Murano-glass pendant.'

'Oh, thank you, Niccolo. That was sweet of you.' She was pleased that her mother had met Niccolo.

'I miss you so much,' he breathed. 'I can't wait to see you again. Have you booked your accommodation in Puglia yet? You'll want a cosy hotel, and there's a very lovely place with a stupendous view of the Old Town of Ostuni. It's just a ten-minute stroll from the Centro Storico. I will book it and get us a Romantic Room; the one with the balcony and the view.' He gave her all the details and she noted them carefully. 'They know me well. I'll ring Francesco on reception. He'll look after things.'

'Wonderful, Niccolo!' She was speaking in barely more than a whisper, her thoughts flying ahead to a romantic week with this wonderful man.

He continued, 'Get the train to Ostuni and a taxi up to the hotel. We can celebrate the New Year there together.' He was obviously excited by the thought. 'I can't wait to see and hold you again. We'll ring in the New Year at a masseria just outside the town. The food and wines are stupendous. I'll book that, too.' He sounded so enthusiastic.

'A masseria?' she enquired. 'What's that?'

'Ah. A treat awaits! The masserie of Puglia are mainly old farmhouses, many with restaurants, who provide what they refer to as "farm to fork" dining, where everything is produced on site, usually including the wine and olive oil. Zero kilometres! You'll love it.' He sounded truly enthusiastic, and Olivia marvelled at this new side to Niccolo that she had not expected to find underneath his veneer of aloofness. 'There's one I particularly love that has a small ante-room for private dining, which I'll book.'

He added, 'I'm longing to hold you in my arms again.'

Olivia's body tingled in anticipation of her time alone with Niccolo. All thoughts of the previous night were temporarily wiped from her mind.

'Yes, Niccolo. I'm dying to see you, too.'

CHAPTER THIRTY
JANE

Arriving in Venice, Jane exited the railway station and stood for a moment at the top of the steps, taking in the view. Below her was spread the Grand Canal, with all its hustle and bustle. Water buses, taxis and gondolas all vied for space on the busy waters, while tourists thronged around the ticket booths, trying to figure out how to get to St Mark's Square and the Rialto; the top two most visited tourist areas in the city.

It would be Christmas in just a few days and festivity was in the air. She tried to regain the old excitement she used to feel when the holiday season came around. She remembered her last Christmas with Sofia. All she had wanted were books, books and more books. Plus, a new tennis racquet and a pair of high boots that Jane felt were far too grown-up. But Nico had insisted on buying them and, as a result of Sofia's wheedling, had brought her to one of the most expensive shoe-shops in Venice. She remembered how thrilled Sofia had been and the loving looks lavished on her by Nico when she paraded them around the palazzo on Christmas Day. Her throat clenched, remembering the happy scene as they gathered around their enormous Christmas tree. Good old days were, inevitably, remembered at this time of year by most people, she thought sadly.

Many of the shops were playing Christmas carols, and she felt unbearably nostalgic. A lump had formed in her throat, and she was afraid she might cry.

"Snap out of it, Jane," she admonished herself. "You have important business at hand today."

Entering the same little bar where she had met Marcello the last time, she found him at a table tucked away at the back. He was staring moodily at his mobile phone and had a large brown envelope in front of him on the table. Seeing this, Jane instantly cheered up. "Excellent!" she thought, sitting down at the other side and looking at him expectantly.

Marcello pushed the envelope towards her mutely. 'Two copies of all of them,' he confirmed.

She picked it up and opened it feverishly. She noticed that he was looking at her with something like disdain on his handsome face. She wondered at it.

But she really did not care about his facial expression when she began to look at the blown-up photos in her hands.

The first one showed Olivia with her arms around a tall, thin man outside Casa Antica. They were hugging, and Jane guessed that this was her missing husband Steve.

'Steve?' she enquired of Marcello, who was sitting there looking sulky.

'Yes. The husband,' he agreed; and, getting up, he went over to the bar to order an aperitivo, having waved the barman away earlier. 'Wine? Prosecco?' he enquired.

'Prosecco.' She barely registered her automatic response. What else would she drink at this time of day, for heaven's sake?

'Then there's this one. Another man.' Marcello pushed the next photograph, which clearly showed a man carrying Olivia over the threshold of Casa Antica.

Jane recoiled in shock. She had been right to have her suspicions.

'It's my husband!' she stated baldly, reaching for her handbag to seek refuge in the embrace of a tranquilliser.

Marcello was stunned. 'You mean this is the conte? Olivia is really having an affair with him?' He looked confused. Up until now, he had imagined that Olivia was probably innocent of the charge of being a home-wrecker by Jane. Now he was not so sure. There was the concrete evidence, after all. He tried to divert Jane by bringing out the photographs of Olivia in the gondola, lying on the fleecy rug.

Jane studied them carefully. The first was of Olivia with her jumper and bra pushed up to reveal her ample breasts. Jane inhaled sharply. She was a beautiful woman indeed, and she felt a stab of very real fear. That naked olive skin glowed under the camera flash, and Jane felt inadequate as she looked at the photos. She knew she could not compete physically with such a woman and realised that her only trump card was the fact that Nico was her husband. But he was obviously already having an affair with Olivia, and she was frightened to have seen evidence of this and also to see the woman's beauty on display.

As she studied the photos of Olivia in various poses, most of them explicitly nude, the initial feeling of fear disappeared, and she began to experience a strange sense of excitement and power. There she was on a fleece rug, and then again, tangled in the sheets of her four-poster bed in Casa Antica. To see her rival, as she now knew was the case and no longer imagined, in so many undignified positions was heady, to say the least.

'I have to ask you,' she started, slightly hesitantly. 'Did you actually have sex with her?' There it was. The dreaded question that she had almost been afraid to ask. If he had, the situation could be dangerous in the extreme for both of them if Olivia found any evidence to support the notion that she had been fully violated, should the truth come out. It was dangerous enough as it was.

He smiled sardonically. 'No,' he stated baldly. 'I did not have sex with her. And, Jane, I must tell you that that was the most difficult part of the entire evening.'

'Really? I'm almost afraid to ask why.' A malicious tone had crept into her voice.

'Olivia is a truly beautiful and infinitely desirable woman.' His voice was husky. 'But it would have been a terrible idea. I already feel bad enough about drugging her and taking photos of her in such compromising positions.'

Jane looked at him in surprise.

He added proudly, 'I am a Venetian, after all. My honour would have forbidden such a thing. It is not necessary for me to drug a woman in order to have sex with her.'

He was obviously becoming angry, and Jane said nothing. She replaced the photographs in the envelope and put them in her bag, withdrawing the bulky envelope she had there and handing it to him.

'Count it,' she demanded, but he told her it was unnecessary as he felt like Judas must have felt receiving the thirty pieces of silver. But it was a lot of money and so, feeling the weight of it, he placed it carefully in his shoulder bag without looking at it.

'I should go,' he said in a gruff voice. 'I am not needed any more. I've done my work and I suppose you can dismiss me now, like a common servant.' His resentment was rising to the surface.

Jane looked at him in dismay. She had not wanted to part on bad terms. She thought he was madly attractive.

'Oh, please sit down, Marcello.' She gave him her warmest look and put her hand out to take his. She held it and fingered the wooden beads. 'Are they to bring you luck?' she enquired.

He did not reply, but sat down beside her, pulling his chair close.

Finally, he said, 'I wish you hadn't asked me to do this job for you, Jane. But now that I have, what happens next?'

Jane demurred slightly but could sense that he needed to know what was going to happen to these horribly pornographic photographs he had taken of a woman whom he obviously felt did not deserve to be humiliated. She could see he felt bad and she felt a need to shift some of the blame from her own shoulders and transfer it onto Olivia's.

'As you know, I think she's a gold-digger, and now I'm sure she is having some sort of relationship with my husband, the conte,' she began. 'This is not typical behaviour on his part. I have never doubted his fidelity before, but I have seen from the very beginning that he is completely smitten by this little tart.'

'But she's not a tart!' he started. 'And if you look at the photos of her with the conte, well, I mean it was Acqua Alta and he had been carrying her through the water. Perhaps it was entirely innocent.' He was confused and flustered, and it showed.

'Lying in my husband's arms, Acqua Alta or no Acqua Alta, is extremely suspicious behaviour to my mind. And as for her not being a tart, well, excuse me, but these photos' — she patted her bag — 'in the gondola and in her bed, show differently. I mean, just how drugged was she anyway? She looks as though she's enjoying herself, as far as I can see. I mean, just look at all that squirming on the bed! She was having a ball.' She threw back her head and laughed, catching the eye of the barman and signalling her wish for another glass of Prosecco. She was beginning to feel the effects of the tranquilliser as it damped down the feeling of acute pain, she had experienced on seeing the photo of Olivia in the arms of her husband.

'She had no clue what was going on,' he exclaimed. 'It was terrible. She was completely zoned out; but yes, it does look as if the experience was causing her pleasure, and perhaps it was. If she ever sees these photos…' He trailed off. 'She trusted me. Perhaps this was a really bad idea. Please tell me exactly what you have planned.' He was sounding anxious now.

'The Conte is in Ireland at the moment, staying with his dreary sister for Christmas,' she began. 'I'm not sure when he is due back, but in the meantime, I intend for him to receive a set of these photographs by courier within the next few days.' She laughed her cold brittle laugh. 'Let's see how much he enjoys his Christmas this year.'

Marcello could not hold back his feelings any more. 'But, Jane, Contessa, if you love your husband like you say you do, how can you put him through such torture? I don't understand.'

Jane thought about it for a moment.

'Call it insurance,' she answered. 'I have to fight for my husband, and this is the only thing that's left to me. I want to be here for him when he comes back to Venice, crushed and disillusioned by his little Irish tart.'

He sat there on the chair next to hers, looking abjectly miserable. Where was the cocky gondolier, she had seen just the other day? Where did this conscience suddenly come from? She wondered how to handle this new situation.

'You know, don't you, that your name will never be mentioned by me ever. You do know that?'

Other than her verbal reassurance, in her opinion, there was only one way she knew about how to get a man's immediate attention. She placed her hand on his upper thigh. He started as though she had stuck a knife in him and looked directly at her. His blue eyes were enormous, she thought. She slid her hand up further, then withdrew it and stood up.

'Walk me back?' It was a question laden with innuendo, and she looked at him under her long pale lashes. He got up, paid the bill and followed her out into the chilly alleyway.

As they passed the same dark doorway where they had kissed a few days previously, Jane pulled him into the darkness once more. This time he was less responsive to her passionate, needy embrace at first. She could see he was uncomfortable.

'A bad idea?' she breathed against his neck. They were quite invisible, and the alleyway itself was quiet now, too. She ran her hands up and down the length of his muscular back.

Suddenly, as though he had made a difficult decision, he came to life and brought his lips down on hers in a hard embrace. His fingers found the buttons of her coat and he slid his hand inside its warmth to cup her breast. She pulled him close. Then, just as abruptly, he pulled back and straightened up.

'No, Contessa. I want you badly, but tonight just doesn't seem like the right time for me.' Then he added, perhaps slightly maliciously, 'Anyway, I have a date later on this evening and need to keep my strength up.' He uttered a forced laugh and Jane wondered if it were true or if he was just trying to make her feel bad. Well, he had certainly succeeded. She felt cheap.

She buttoned her coat and stood back, trying to regain her dignity while drawing herself up to her full height.

'I must go, too,' she said coldly. 'I have things to do.'

With that, she was gone.

OLIVIA

Taking the conte's advice, Olivia went online to have a look at the hotel that he had suggested as their rendezvous for the New Year in Puglia.

First of all, she looked up the town of Ostuni and she thought that the photographs and videos she found of it were stunning. It was a white town perched high on a hill overlooking the Adriatic Sea in the very south of Italy. She thought it looked more Greek than Italian, with all those white buildings outlined against the bluest sky imaginable. She was excited by the thought of a romantic week in this beautiful place with Niccolo.

She looked at the photos of the hotel. The Romantic Rooms had fabric drapes over the beds and looked right out over the White City. It all looked perfect. She could not wait.

That night, she slept soundly in the four-poster bed in Casa Antica, thinking sensual thoughts of her lover.

She thought no more about the previous night, though the torn panties niggled at the edges of her consciousness. Could she remember? Not knowing what else to do at that time, she firmly put it out of her mind.

She would talk to Marcello tomorrow. He would explain.

CHAPTER THIRTY-ONE
JANE

Jane sat up late that evening, poring over the photos of Olivia. First of all, in a close embrace with her husband Steve, then in Niccolo's arms, framed clearly in the doorway of Casa Antica. She could see the desire written on Nico's face and she gulped back a sob. She then studied the photos of Olivia lying on the fleece blanket at the bottom of the gondola, and finally, against the snowy pillows of her little house in Dorsodoro. She scrutinised the photos. It was important that the fact that they had been taken on a gondola was completely obscured. It was obvious that Marcello had been extremely careful to edit out any tell-tale signs. The only sign of him anywhere was in a few shots of his hand on the most intimate parts of Olivia's body.

"It could be anyone's hand," she thought to herself. "But these are the best shots. They show that she was taking pleasure in intimacy with another man. And they are dated, too, so Nico will know that they were taken while he was away."

Parcelling them up with a stiff card backing to keep them from bending, she placed the full-colour, glossy A4-sized photographs into a brown padded package she had purchased especially with this in mind. She kept back the photographs of Niccolo with Olivia at Casa Antica, glaring at them accusingly as she put them back in the group of photographs, she was keeping for herself.

"Now, where to keep the copies?" She mulled this over. Obviously, it had to be someplace where Nico would never look. "What a disaster if he found them!"

213

Looking around her bedroom thoughtfully, she finally decided to tape them to the back of her underwear drawer. Even opening this drawer and checking carefully, the envelope they were in was invisible. She realised that this could only be a temporary solution as, when they moved back to Venice after the work was completed, she would have to remove them and find a new hiding place in the palazzo.

She knew she should destroy them, but they had cost her a lot of money, and — she had to admit — she rather enjoyed looking at them. It gave her a sense of power to imagine Olivia brought so low. After checking that the envelope was completely invisible once more, she closed the drawer and got out her mobile phone.

OLIVIA

Mid-morning on Monday, and Olivia could wait no longer.

The floors were being carefully renovated, and it was difficult to walk about the palazzo. She decided to take an hour or two off; she needed to speak to Marcello.

This was to be the last day of work before breaking for the holidays. Everyone else was already on their Christmas break, but Giuseppe had requested permission to work after everyone else had departed in order to get the floors restored while there was nobody else on the premises. The men had laid the white cement already and sprinkled it with tiny chips of marble in colours that perfectly matched the original flooring. As Olivia watched, one of the craftsmen, wearing a type of giant, flat-soled sandal, appeared to be ice-skating on the new surface to press it into shape. Next would come the polishing and the machines were standing by for this, the final stage in the process. Olivia fully expected to return that evening to a beautifully restored terrazzo floor.

'Giuseppe!' she called to the dapper little man, who was carefully watching the team of artisans working under his supervision. He turned and greeted her. They had become firm friends ever since she had met him that morning a few weeks ago and realised he was a long-term friend of Niccolo. 'That all seems to be going well. Are you happy with the work so far?'

'Olivia, it's all looking perfect. What a lovely job you're doing!'

She loved his enthusiasm and bade him farewell, telling him she would see him later, as she headed for the tiny elevator. She was feeling anxious as she hurried over the Accademia Bridge and pushed through the Christmas shoppers, heading for Marcello's gondola stand near Santa Maria del Giglio.

Looking over the parapet at the final bridge, she peered down at Marcello's gondola. Seeing a group of gondoliers sitting in the sun, she easily spotted his blond head among all the dark ones and saw him look up and catch her eye. She waved. Was she imagining it, or did he look embarrassed to see her? Perhaps she had made a complete fool of herself the last evening together and the embarrassment was for her.

She approached him with trepidation. He rose to greet her, seemingly reluctant to leave the safe haven provided by his friends and colleagues.

'Coffee?' She tried to keep her voice from sounding anxious.

'Sure,' he agreed, and they both walked into the little bar beside where the gondolas were moored. 'I can't stay long. A group has a reservation in just about ten minutes' time.' He glanced at his watch as though for confirmation.

Carrying their tiny cups of espresso to a table in the far corner, they sat and looked at one another.

'Okay, Marcello. What exactly happened on Saturday night? I need to know.'

He stared into the cup and then threw back the coffee in one swallow. 'Nothing happened,' he told her firmly. 'You got a bit out of it after a lot of Prosecco and then you insisted on having a few brandies.' He paused. Olivia jumped in.

'But, Marcello!' she exclaimed. 'I woke up in bed yesterday morning, completely naked, and my panties are torn. Something happened. I really need to know, now.' She glared at him and he glared back at her with ferocity.

'Olivia.' He was obviously struggling, she thought. 'I found the evening difficult enough without this accusatory interrogation.' He sounded angry now. Responding to an accusation with a counter-attack. How male, she thought.

'I'm not accusing you of anything, Marcello,' she insisted. 'I just want you to tell me exactly what happened. All of it.' She sat back in her chair and waited.

'Okay. You had too much to drink. We went to a couple of bars and then I took you home. You were completely out of it and I had to put you to bed. You removed your own clothes and it's hardly my fault if you tore your underwear!' He paused for effect. 'As I said, you were out of it, completely.'

Olivia felt chastened and lost for words. Marcello saw this and jumped in with a further defence.

'Look. I think you wanted me to come to bed with you, to be honest.'

Her jaw dropped with incredulity.

He continued, 'But we're friends and I didn't want to take advantage of you.' He was looking pleased with himself, Olivia noticed. Male vanity, she thought angrily. He fiddled with the beads on his wrist and she noticed his tattoo once more: his zodiac sign of Sagittarius, with an elongated arrow that went almost to his wrist.

She wondered idly if his birthday had just gone by, but he had mentioned nothing about a celebration.

'As long as nothing happened between us,' she confirmed, thinking anxiously about her brand-new love affair with Niccolo. She cringed inwardly and felt something akin to panic.

'Relax, Olivia.' He sounded reassuring and covered her hand with his, squeezing it gently. 'I would never take advantage of a lady. Don't worry. Everything is fine.'

He looked at her keenly. Then he said, 'Sorry. I've got to go. Clients will be waiting.'

At that, Olivia noticed three very perfect-looking American girls in their twenties outside the bar, looking excited. He stood up, said a formal goodbye and left. He was immediately surrounded by this bevy of blondeness and she saw him take their hands one by one and guide them chivalrously onto his gondola.

She left the bar and went for a walk. She needed to clear her head and set off for her favourite walk to San Pietro di Castello at a brisk pace.

Thinking about Niccolo, she wondered how on earth he would react if he knew about this. He must never find out. It would be her secret, and she had to trust Marcello never to utter it to anyone.

And how had this happened? She could still barely remember having just one glass of Prosecco on Marcello's gondola. How did it happen that they went on to other places to drink and that she had been drinking brandy? She disliked spirits and had never blacked out from alcohol in her life before. Not being suspicious by nature, she put any thoughts of a spiked drink to the back of her mind as she headed towards the peace of the furthest reaches of Castello. Marcello was her friend, after all.

JANE

Christmas Day dawned cold and sunny in the Euganean Hills, just an hour's drive from Venice. Jane opened the shutters and stepped out onto her small terrace, admiring the view of the hills, a deep shade of green even in the middle of winter. The gardens looked neat and she was reminded of Niccolo. She wondered how he would react to the arrival of the photographs tomorrow.

She had asked the courier company to deliver them in the late afternoon of St Stephen's Day, when Nico would certainly be relaxing by the fire with Paul and Francesca in Dublin. The Christmas tree lights would be on, twinkling in the firelight, and the curtains would be drawn. Probably the most relaxing time during the holiday period. She wanted this to be his own personal earthquake. He deserved to suffer a bit, after all she had gone through without her husband by her side. "Let's see how you deal with this, Nico," she thought maliciously. She could not wait to hear about his reaction.

Sliding her hand along the smooth curved handrail, she descended the main staircase at Villa di Falco. She could smell bacon and immediately felt hungry. Max was here with his girlfriend Cressida and had insisted on bringing along "rashers, sausages and pudding" from London, in case it should not prove possible to eat these delights in Italy. Jane had to admit that the aroma of cooked bacon brought her back to growing up in the

English countryside. She had enjoyed her childhood and breakfast around the long table at her father's luxurious Palladian-style mansion in Gloucestershire. Her life of privilege had prepared for life as a contessa in Venice, but little else, she thought ruefully, though she knew how to walk, sit and generally behave impeccably in polite society.

She entered the dining room, which looked festive with fairy lights draped over the table, courtesy of Cressida, who believed in celebrating absolutely everything, thought Jane with irritation. Her mind was not exactly on Christmas this year. There was too much to preoccupy her. But she was delighted to have her darling son here, who rose to greet her as she entered.

'Mum!' He hugged her. 'Happy Christmas.' She looked up at his handsome face and felt a warm glow of love and pride.

'Happy Christmas, Jane,' purred Cressida, a large cuddly girl who always purred, as far as Jane could see. Purring was her default setting, it appeared.

They air-kissed and Cressida sped back to her "Full English Breakfast", downing a forkful of baked beans with gusto. "She's going to go to fat," thought Jane maliciously. "Let's see how much purring she does then."

Sitting down at the head of the table, in Niccolo's usual place, Jane surveyed the scene. Her beautiful home, her son and his girlfriend; to any outsider, this looked like a perfect life. But her husband was absent. Granted, he and Max had a fractious relationship. Last Christmas had been a disaster, as they rowed about politics over dinner, ruining everything. Max was fairly right-wing, whereas Niccolo, though not exactly left-wing, took a more relaxed view on most things and disapproved of extremism in anything.

Paola bustled in with a pot of Earl Grey tea for Jane, who had begun to nibble a piece of toast.

'Happy Christmas, Contessa.' Paola was warm in her greeting, and Jane smiled back at her.

'Happy Christmas to you, too, Paola. I hope you and Antonio have a lovely day with your family.'

Actually, Jane was less than happy that her staff would be going out for a few hours for lunch. It meant that she, Max and Cressida could not eat until after they returned. So, Christmas dinner would be at about 6pm. But what could she do? Niccolo had always run the house along these lines, whereas Maria and Marco, who stayed in the palazzo in Venice, always stayed there for Christmas and saw their families the following day, which suited her much better.

She wondered if Niccolo was enjoying his Christmas in Dublin. Let him enjoy his day. Tomorrow would see an end to his smutty little affair, if she had anything to do with it.

OLIVIA

Bells were ringing all over Venice as Christmas morning dawned. Blue skies and sunshine heralded in a chilly winter's day, which passed quietly for Olivia. She had declined an invitation from Maria and Gianni to dine with her family on the island of Giudecca. Maria had Christmas free this year for the first time in many years, as the family was out of town. She was making the most of her freedom, and Olivia was touched to have been invited. She was tempted to be part of a Venetian family Christmas, but she wanted to take the time to be by herself before going to Puglia. She was also reluctant to intrude on Maria's family time, which was precious.

It was strange to be spending the holiday season alone. She knew that Christmas was a time for family, and her parents were in Dublin, expecting various aunts, uncles and cousins to join them for dinner. Having phoned them the previous evening, she told them how much she looked forward to seeing them soon, but wanted to experience this day on her own, just to see how it felt.

In previous years, Christmas for her had been a week with Steve in sunny Lanzarote in the Canary Islands, where she had topped up her tan by the pool and read a few good books. She had never been sentimental about spending the holiday season away from her family, nor of being childless at this festive and child-friendly time of year. However, last year had been stressful. She had spent the holiday season with her parents in Dublin, where conversation had been stilted, punctured every so often by her father making critical remarks about her past lifestyle, which he had considered louche and pampered. Perhaps he was correct in some of his criticism, but she had not enjoyed being baited and had no intention of going home to Dublin to relive the experience.

On the morning of Christmas Day, she decided to go to Mass out on the island of San Giorgio Maggiore, in the wonderful church built by the great architect Andrea Palladio, almost five hundred years before. Olivia counted herself a great admirer of Palladio and was looking forward to Mass under the perfect dome of San Giorgio.

Walking through the narrow streets, quiet in the early morning, she was lost in thought. She realised she had reached a particular point in her life that would decide her future. This year heralded the end of one life and, hopefully, the beginning of another, better one. She was losing Steve, her husband, to cancer, and beginning, she hoped, a new relationship with Niccolo. These few days alone were exactly what she needed.

Arriving at St Mark's Square, where she caught the water bus to the tiny island, she entered the church and, as per Maria's instructions, walked down a side corridor, ignoring a sign barring tourists from entering. Then she ascended some marble stairs and entered a small side-chapel. The semi-circular rows of seating held well-dressed Venetians, many of the older ladies wearing luxurious fur coats.

Sitting, standing and kneeling, Olivia remembered the rites of the Catholic Mass from her childhood and teen years, when, attending a convent school in Dublin, she had been obliged to attend regularly. In the intervening decades, her interest in religion of any form had fallen away. Now she found herself, head bowed, saying a prayer for Steve.

'Please God, don't let him suffer too much.'

And for Niccolo.

'You're a married man. In your eyes, we have probably sinned. But how can something so wonderful be a sin?'

CHAPTER THIRTY-TWO
JANE

Waking on the day after Christmas, Jane stretched and lay there in her bed. Her eyes were open, and she pondered the day ahead.

"What will happen when Niccolo gets the photographs this afternoon?" She could feel her heart rate rise as she contemplated the future.

Of course, Nico would come straight home. He would want to confront Olivia. Or would he? Would he stay with Francesca for a few days and pour his heart out, or would he arrive here in Galzignano and beg her forgiveness for his foolishness? She knew that one thing was certain: he would never forgive Olivia. As Jane had finally realised, she would stoop to nothing to get him back. She would even destroy him and his trust in others in order to achieve her goal. She felt empowered.

Getting out of bed, she quietly opened her lingerie drawer and, sliding her hand to the space behind it, removed the photographs. She wanted another look. She wanted to imagine Nico's face as he saw them for the first time.

Spreading them out on her dressing table, she threw on her dressing gown and sat down to examine them once more. There was Olivia in Steve's arms. Clearly holding him tightly.

"Doesn't look as though that marriage is dead at all."

Then Niccolo, his face suffused by desire, standing with Olivia in his arms in the doorway of Casa Antica, caused a painful sensation in her breast. She examined his facial expression carefully. He had looked at her like that, too, a long time ago. Lust and raw desire, mingled with a strange tenderness, were written large on his fine features. She felt rage.

Jane needed to see this photograph to remind herself that her suspicions about her husband and Olivia were not a figment of her imagination. She was going to lose her husband, and this dramatic solution was the only way she knew how to fight. What else could she do?

She then examined the photos taken in the gondola and in the four-poster bed in Casa Antica. Olivia looked like a woman in the throes of passion, seemingly taking great pleasure from the experience, and Jane wondered what Marcello had been doing to her to arouse such obvious pleasure. She experienced a frisson of excitement as she looked at the many photographs of his long fingers splayed over different parts of Olivia's naked body. Olivia was clearly squirming with pleasure. Then blind anger returned, and Jane took satisfaction in the thought that these photographs would surely put paid to the Irishwoman's budding relationship with Niccolo.

Returning the photographs to their hiding place, Jane decided to include the two cash slips of her withdrawals for Marcello. Where else would they be safe? She padded across her huge bedroom and into the bathroom, where she showered, applied body cream and spritzed herself with perfume. Selecting a blue cashmere twinset, a fine wool skirt and low pumps, she combed her fine blonde hair, fastening it into a neat braid at the back of her neck. Looking suitably aristocratic, she descended the large curved staircase and joined Max and Cressida for breakfast.

Today, feeling quite stressed in anticipation of a call from Niccolo, telling her he was coming home, she found the smell of the bacon and sausages nauseating. Sipping Earl Grey tea from her bone china cup, she ate nothing. Paola fussed around her, trying to persuade her to have some toast, at the very least.

'No, thank you, Paola.' She waved her away. 'I had more than enough to eat yesterday. Max, are you enjoying your Christmas break?'

'Yes, Mum. Cressie and I are having some great walks here. She's very impressed with the gardens.'

"Cressie!" she thought. "Pet names. I wonder what she calls him." Though she thought the name Maxwell, having already been shortened to Max, was quite short enough.

Cressida looked up from her breakfast and swallowed a piece of sausage, smiling at Max. 'It's just beautiful here, Jane. I'm sure you'll be sorry to return to the palazzo. When do you think that will happen?'

'I don't exactly know. But if all happens on schedule, we will be back in residence in early March. Maybe sooner.'

'Your interior designer sounds amazing. Really efficient. The lady we used for our family's London flat was horrendous. Her schedule was completely bonkers, and the whole thing wasn't really to my taste.'

'Really? Whose taste was it supposed to suit?' Jane was in the mood for a row. She loathed this girl, who hung onto her son's every word, and she needed any diversion possible to try not to think about what would happen this afternoon. 'Who briefed her?'

'Oh, my stepmother.' Cressida's face stiffened. 'She has absolutely no taste whatsoever. Daddy should never have allowed her to have her head and make the place over the way she wanted to.' She looked angry and upset.

'Well, it's her home, after all. She probably doesn't mind what you think. Why would she care? Or are you a member of the Taste Police?' Jane laughed mockingly.

Cressida's face turned red at this put-down and she turned towards Max for support. Something she saw on his face caused her to stop in her tracks and she fell silent, though she looked mutinous.

'I'm going for a walk in about half an hour. Anyone like to come. Max? It would be wonderful to have a walk together and a chat. After tomorrow, I won't see you for a couple of months.'

'Of course, Mother. I'd love to walk with you.' He immediately got to his feet.

Cressida sat in silence. She knew her days with Max were numbered. To get to Max, she needed the approval of his adored mother, and it was quite obvious she had not succeeded in that particular goal.

As Jane and Max strolled around the immaculately manicured gardens, stopping at the little lake to admire the two black swans and passing over an old stone bridge onto another set of well-maintained paths, Max enquired after Niccolo.

'He's okay, but he's still grieving badly for Sofia. Since she died, to be honest, things have not been great between us.'

'I thought that things weren't going well before Sofia's death. Or am I mistaken? The great Conte seemed to be spending more and more time away from you.' There was a bitter edge to his voice. His dislike of Niccolo was obvious.

'That's true. We were going through a slightly difficult patch when Sofia died, but I never lost hope. Let's see how things go. I'm hanging in there. I think he'll be back from Dublin sooner rather than later, and I am sure we'll manage to sort things out.' She sounded more confident than she felt.

As they returned to the villa, Jane spotted a police car driving up the avenue. The blue car, with 'Polizia' written on its sides, drew to a stop in front of the house, and Jane's heart began to race.

'Max! It's the police!' she gasped. 'What do they want?'

Max crossed the gravel ahead of her and approached the car just as its two front doors flew open and two plainclothes policemen emerged. Jane recognised one of them as the detective who had interviewed her several times after Sofia's death. Their faces were solemn.

Were they going to arrest her? She was terrified.

OLIVIA

Early on the morning after Christmas, Olivia got the water bus to Santa Maria Lucia, the railway station in Venice. There, she boarded the train for Ostuni. It was a long journey via Bologna, and she expected to arrive in the early evening. She had packed a good book and picked up a few magazines at the newsagent on the station platform to keep her entertained during the day-long train ride. She planned to return by air in ten days. With Niccolo.

She could have flown. There was a speedy flight to Brindisi from Treviso every day. But she preferred the idea of taking the train and spending the day enjoying the journey through the Italian countryside.

She was feeling relaxed and happy, as Niccolo had telephoned her the previous evening and they had talked for a long time. Tender words had been exchanged, and he had told her about his happy family Christmas in Dublin with his sister Francesca and brother-in-law Paul. He was staying in The Mews behind the house and was, once more, full of praise for the work she had done there.

Finally, he admitted that The Mews had been created for him and for him alone. He had been planning to treat it as a bolt-hole away from his marriage to Jane and had been planning to divorce her when the time was right. Then Sofia had been killed and he had realised that Jane was far too vulnerable to be able to cope with a divorce at that point and had put his long-term plans on hold until now.

Now. She thought about his words. He wanted to be with her. He had not yet told her he was in love with her, and she knew it was too soon to expect such a declaration from him, but she knew that he had deep feelings for her and had been attracted to her since the days when she had designed and project-managed Hotel Orologio in Dublin.

'I recommended you to Paul and Francesca when The Mews project came up,' he confessed. 'I had seen you many times at Orologio, but you never even noticed me!' he exclaimed in mock horror. 'I thought you were the most gorgeous, clever woman I had ever come across, but you were married and so was I, though I knew my marriage was coming to a tricky end.'

Olivia was stunned. 'You were there?'

'I was anxious to see you again, under any conditions. So, when Francesca and I discussed the interior design of The Mews, I suggested you to her. She had already met you several times at the Italian Institute but had no clue that you were an interior designer.'

She digested this, then asked him spiritedly, 'Don't you remember how you made me crash my lovely Merc into a flower pot? Do you remember ignoring me? I was incredibly angry!'

'Oh, yes,' he admitted. 'I felt bad about that, but I had just been informed about Sofia's death and had driven straight to Francesca to tell her. I was out of my mind with grief and shock at the time.'

'Oh, Niccolo! I'm so sorry. I had no clue who you were. Even when we worked alongside one another on The Mews, I didn't know you were Francesca's brother who had lost his daughter.'

'I know that now,' he admitted. 'When I saw the shock and recognition on your face when we met at the villa, I knew you had had no idea who I was before. I should have realised it, but I never thought.' He trailed off.

They chatted on and on about their past. Olivia told him a bit about Steve and promised Niccolo that she would tell him everything when they met in Ostuni. She did not want to sound as though she were bringing her own sadness and humiliation into the conversation when he had told her so much. It could wait.

She would see him in two days from now, she thought, as she boarded the high-speed train known as the Frecce Argento, or Silver Arrow in English, found her seat and began to look forward to the coming week.

JANE

'Commissario Scallone.' Jane walked bravely towards the detective with apparent self-confidence and shook his outstretched hand. Inside, she was quaking, but it would not do to show any weakness at this point, she thought.

'Contessa.' He was formal in his greeting. 'I am sorry to disturb your holiday, but we need to talk.' He eyed Max. 'Privately,' he added.

Max took the hint and indicated that he would continue his walk, and Jane led the inspector to the villa, opening the front door and escorting him upstairs. Paola came forward and helped her to remove her coat and scarf, offering coffee to the policeman, who declined politely. Paola looked worriedly over her shoulder as Jane led the way to the arrangement of sofas and armchairs at the front of the *piano nobile*, looking out over the gardens.

'What a beautiful home you have here.' The inspector was appreciative of his surroundings. He had told her previously how much he enjoyed coming here with his wife and children to walk in the gardens on Sundays during the summer months. She remembered this and referred to it, asking after his family politely. Inwardly, she was terrified.

'What can I do for you, Commissario?' she asked. 'I'm assuming something must have happened to bring you down to the Hills during the holiday season.'

'Yes, Contessa. Indeed. There have been some developments in your case.' He coughed politely. 'The death of your daughter, Sofia, has been under investigation for some time, but we have finally made a breakthrough.'

Now she was really terrified. Her blood tests! They must finally have shown that she had taken a tranquilliser that very morning and maybe even shown that she had had too much to drink the night before. Not to mention the broken remains of the bottle of grappa they found in her handbag.

Her nervousness must have shown on her face, as the inspector suddenly smiled gently at her.

'Contessa. I have come to tell you that all possible charges against you have been dropped. The truck driver is being charged with dangerous driving. His log book had been altered, but we now have evidence that he had been driving for several hours longer than is permitted by law. So, you are in the clear. The investigation is at an end.'

Jane felt faint. She needed Niccolo. She wanted to tell him her news. She sat back in her armchair and burst into tears that were a mixture of grief and relief. The pent-up dam of emotion and fear that she had felt since Sofia had died burst forth, and the Commissario sat there helplessly while she sobbed her heart out.

CHAPTER THIRTY-THREE
OLIVIA

The high-speed express train from Bologna, this time called the Frecce Bianca, or White Arrow, pulled into the little station at Ostuni. It was just after six o'clock in the evening and, being winter, it was already dark. She alighted onto the platform and pulled her suitcase off the train behind her.

Immediately, a dapper gentleman stepped forward.

'Are you Ms Farrell-Lynskey?' he enquired politely.

She agreed that yes, indeed, that was who she was, and he introduced himself as Francesco from the hotel and informed her that he had come to meet her train. The Conte was, apparently, a friend of his and he had been asked personally to collect her from the station and drive her to the hotel. She was charmed and happily handed over her suitcase.

Francesco carried it down the long flight of steps to the passageway underneath the platform, mounting another set of steps to take them up the other side. He wheeled her suitcase out of the station to the car park, where he opened the passenger door of a large white Audi, placing her bag carefully in the boot.

As they drove up the hill from the station to the town of Ostuni, Olivia marvelled at the sight of the lights sprinkled over the hills. She was looking forward to seeing it in daylight.

Having checked into her room on the first floor, she arranged to go to the dining room for dinner shortly and looked excitedly around the room. She looked at the big bed, hung with drapes, and imagined herself in Niccolo's arms. She could hardly wait to see him.

Freshly showered and spritzed with her floral Gucci scent, she descended the stairs and, being early, decided to have an aperitivo in the bar. She had brought a book and was looking forward to sitting quietly in a corner with a chilled glass of Pugliese rosato. She expected to hear from Niccolo soon, as she had texted him to let him know she had arrived and was now having a pre-dinner drink. She checked her phone. Nothing yet. He must be out walking with Paul, as they liked to take a pre-dinner stroll around the pleasant suburb of Foxrock in Dublin. Maybe they had stopped off for a drink together in a local pub.

Sipping her delicious rosato and nibbling a couple of *tarelli*, those small round biscuits that are so popular in Italy, especially in Puglia, she checked her watch. Time for dinner. She idly noticed that Niccolo had not phoned yet. After their wonderfully intimate talk the previous evening, she had no fears that he would not be in contact. He had booked the hotel and had told her he could not wait to hold her, so she was relaxed. She would see him in two days.

After a tasty fish dinner and more wine, Olivia felt ready to head for bed. It had been a long day, journeying by train all the way from Venice. Now the wine had made her sleepy. She texted Niccolo, "Going to bed now. Exhausted. Talk tomorrow. xx" Fully expecting an answering text before she turned out her light shortly afterwards, she was mildly disappointed that the screen of her telephone remained puzzlingly blank.

JANE

She had a perfect excuse to phone Niccolo. Her name had been cleared and she was no longer under investigation for the death of Sofia. She also wanted to hear his voice as he would definitely have received the photos of Olivia by now. She could not wait to speak to him. She bubbled with excitement.

Lying back on her bed, propped up by fluffy goose-down pillows encased in the very best Egyptian cotton imaginable, she picked up the phone.

'Hi, Francesca,' she greeted her sister-in-law. 'How was Christmas?'

'Oh, hi, Jane! Yes, all well here. We've been having a lovely time. It's so lovely to see Niccolo in such good form. He and Paul have gone out for a walk and probably a drink in the pub on the way home. I'm assuming you want to speak to him?'

'Oh, yes, Francesca. I wanted to have a quick chat. I'm glad he seems happier,' she added, thinking to herself, "Not for long."

'If you ring him on his mobile, tell him a courier company came while he was out and left a package for him. I see it's from Italy.'

Jane swallowed. So, he had not seen the photos yet. She would try his mobile anyway.

'Thanks, Francesca. Happy New Year, by the way. I hope we'll see you in Venice soon. We'll be back in the palazzo in a couple of months.'

'Ah, yes. The palazzo. How is Olivia getting on?'

'Fine. She's getting along fine. The work is progressing well.'

'I was thinking of going over after the New Year festivities to see her and check on the work. Perhaps I could stay with you and Nick in Galzignano for a few days?'

'Of course, Francesca. You're always welcome.' She crossed her fingers here, as she was less than keen on Francesca and her possessiveness towards Nico and everything to do with the di Falco family. 'Just let me know when and we'll meet you at Venice airport.'

'Okay, then. I'll let you know. But I think I'll visit in a couple of weeks. Early January would suit me well.'

They exchanged a few more pleasantries and each hung up. Jane did not know whether to be glad or sorry that Nico had not received the photos yet. Perhaps her wonderful news and if she was extra loving, just maybe she could sow a few seeds of the idea of a reconciliation. She would be as wifely on the phone as she knew how to be.

She dialled his mobile number. He picked up on the third ring.

'Jane. How are you? I'm here in a pub with Paul, having a pint of the "black stuff".'

He sounded quite amiable and she reflected how much he enjoyed Ireland and its big best-seller, Guinness.

'Well, cheers then! I'm phoning with great news, Nico.' She launched straight into her story about the visit of Commissario Scallone from the

Venice Questura and the fact that the truck driver had been charged and she was off the hook. 'So, I've been cleared,' she finished. 'Finally. I can't begin to tell you how relieved I am. The fear of being charged with dangerous driving leading to Sofia's death was just about too much to bear for the past year and a half.'

His voice was sympathetic, and he seemed to be happy about the outcome of this long-drawn-out affair.

She plunged ahead. 'Nico.' She tried to keep the wheedling sound out of her voice, as she knew it irritated him profoundly. 'I miss you, darling. When are you coming home? I'd like to celebrate with you. Just us. Quietly.' She tried to inject a slightly sultry and suggestive timbre into her voice. It was difficult, as she was completely out of practice.

'Well. I'm not returning to Galzignano for a couple of weeks. I have a lot on right now. I'm pretty busy. We'll celebrate when I get back. I'm very happy for you, my dear.'

'Oh, okay, Nico.' She did her best not to sound disappointed, but she was. That new negligee would have to wait. But she would greet him with love and passion when he returned. He would need comforting. Her heart beat faster as she thought about what was about to transpire when he got back to Paul and Francesca's home. He would need more than a Guinness to get past this. She smiled maliciously and relaxed back into her pillows.

OLIVIA

Olivia pulled back the curtains and peered out of the hotel window, just as the sun was rising over the Adriatic Sea on the stiletto heel of Italy's boot. The old town of Ostuni looked extraordinary, and its white buildings glowed in the early-morning light. She could see the cathedral at the top of the hill, surveying all below it. She promised herself she would be exploring the streets of this quaint town this very morning.

Picking up her mobile phone, she lay back in bed for a few minutes, expecting to read a loving text from Nick. Nothing. She felt a frisson of alarm. Perhaps there was a problem. Perhaps she should phone him. She mulled this over.

"I've never chased after a man before," she thought, "and I'm not starting now," she spoke firmly to herself. She was not exactly worried, but she could not help feeling a bit anxious. Perhaps he was arriving early to surprise her and had been travelling last night. She felt anticipation. He was not the sort of man to be fickle. Had he not told her just two days ago how much he had always desired her? She needed to relax. There would be a perfectly reasonable explanation for his lack of communication.

Just because she could not help herself, she fired off a quick text: "Good morning from Ostuni! So, looking forward to seeing you tomorrow. Now for breakfast and then a walk. It looks glorious here. xx"

Returning to the dining room and finding it all set up for breakfast, she looked at the array of delicious-looking food. Tempted by a croissant filled with apricot jam, she nevertheless decided to have some cooked ham, a slice of cheese and a few tiny datterino tomatoes with a little white roll. The friendly waitress asked her how she liked her coffee and in just a few minutes had brought her two white jugs, one with strong-smelling black coffee and the other with hot milk, foaming beautifully on top.

She enjoyed her breakfast, returned to her room and had another look at her phone. Nothing. A small spasm of panic gripped her heart. "I hope everything is okay," she said to herself. "In the meantime, I am going to enjoy this day in what appears to be an absolutely beautiful town."

Wrapping up against the winter chill, though it was far milder than in Venice, she set off in the direction of the old town. The views of the White City of Ostuni overlooking the Adriatic Sea were magnificent and she found herself taking photo after photo as she walked, finally arriving in a large piazza paved with shiny tiles that appeared to be travertine, or *"chianche"*, according to her guidebook.

The piazza was lined with restaurants and coffee shops, with a tall statue in the middle. Winding upwards were the narrow streets leading to the cathedral on top. Every so often she checked her mobile, and still nothing. Though she enjoyed her morning, she could not quite suppress her anxiety.

"I'll stop for lunch," she thought finally, spying a cosy-looking eatery. Many people were sitting outside, enjoying the winter sunshine. Rugs had been provided for those who wanted to eat al fresco, but Olivia decided to eat inside, where she chatted with the friendly owners.

Eating bruschetta with fresh tomatoes and *"capocollo"*, a delicious, locally produced salami, and a glass of chilled rosato, she began to feel relaxed again. Niccolo had broken no law by not phoning her or returning her texts. She had to trust him; and, anyway, she would see him tomorrow. She raised her glass of wine to absent friends.

Being keyed up as she was, she decided to stay at the hotel that evening and have a quiet dinner there. Then she would have an early night and be well rested for her week with Niccolo the following day.

She would need to be rested for the difficult days ahead, but she slept peacefully, unaware that, once more, her fortunes were about to change drastically.

Descending the stairs to the reception area the following morning, still glowing from her shower and having left her blonde hair loose around her shoulders, she knew she was looking good.

Francesco was at the desk and looked at her appreciatively.

'Signora Olivia,' he greeted her warmly. She was about to pass by on her way to the dining room when he called to her, 'I have a message for you.' He handed her an envelope with a folded piece of paper inside, which she took out quickly, fumbling slightly in her haste. It had to be from Niccolo, telling her when he would arrive. Nobody else knew she was there.

She read it and went over to one of the sofas in the foyer to sit down. She felt weak as she re-read the note.

"My dear Olivia. I am sorry but I will not be joining you in Ostuni. I can see that this was all a dreadful mistake and I will not be seeing you again. I have paid for the hotel for the next week and for your New Year dinner at the Masseria as promised. Niccolo."

Francesco dashed over to her side. 'Are you okay?' he enquired solicitously. 'Can I get you a glass of water? Anything?'

'No, thank you.' Olivia stood and tried to muster some dignity. After all, Francesco must have seen this curt note and was probably wondering at her sudden fall from grace. It was only the other day when the conte had phoned him personally to ensure that this lovely lady would be well looked after until he arrived. Now he was not coming and had given no explanation. She could see sympathy in his warm brown eyes.

She fled upstairs to her room and threw herself on the bed. She needed to think. What on earth had happened? What was going on? A mistake? What did it all mean?

Taking the bull by the horns, she picked up her mobile phone and dialled his number. She could hear her heart pounding in her ears. It rang out. She tried again, with the same result. She felt completely shell-shocked. What was she supposed to do?

She thought of emailing him but dismissed the thought as soon as it entered her head. What could she say that wouldn't sound needy? She would remain quiet and composed and deal with it when she returned to Venice.

Spending the entire morning on the bed, only going for a stroll when she knew that the cleaning ladies needed access, she wandered through the town feeling completely lost. She needed to talk to someone about her predicament. She instinctively wanted to speak to her mother, needed to hear her words of comfort, but she had already caused her more than enough worry over the past couple of years. She felt very alone as she suddenly realised that she had nobody in whom she could confide with confidence.

What had she done over these past years that she had ended up friendless? Too ambitious, and her dazzling career came first. And always taking her luxury breaks with only Steve for company. She knew very well that many people she had thought of as her friends had disappeared into the woodwork as soon as Steve absconded with Diana and her business was seen to be in trouble. Nobody wanted to be around a woman who exuded an air of such bad luck. Also, she realised to her chagrin that many of her women acquaintances would not invite her to their homes because they were worried about what thoughts their husbands might have about a newly single, beautiful woman like Olivia.

She would have liked to phone Francesca, but she really did not think it would be appropriate. After all, it was highly unlikely she knew about her relationship with her brother. He was a married man, and Francesca might not have approved. But perhaps something had happened over Christmas to bring this about.

She returned to the cosy little restaurant in the centre of Ostuni and had lunch once more, this time a wonderfully colourful salad with fresh ricotta cheese. She chatted once more with the young couple who owned the restaurant.

They seemed to sense that she was upset, and they were solicitous, pouring another glass of rosato for her, "on the house".

She told them that she would be here alone for a week and asked them what she should do in order to spend her time here to its best advantage. They suggested that she explore the surrounding countryside and visit some of the beautiful little towns that dotted the area.

'You know, you will have to hire a car,' they advised. 'We have the number of a good car-hire company, if you would like to call them.'

Olivia spent her week driving the length and breadth of the Salento peninsula, visiting seaside towns, tasting olive oil and wine and generally trying to get her head to stop spinning. It was the first real holiday she had had in a couple of years and she was going to make the very most of it. Niccolo or no Niccolo, she decided firmly. She would deal with whatever problem had arisen between them when she returned to Venice.

She rang in the New Year feeling self-conscious at her table for one in the masseria that Niccolo had booked in advance. The staff were friendly and the visitors at the next table toasted her health when the countdown to midnight was announced and everyone cheered, went outside and watched fireworks lighting up the starry sky. She wished she had not come and was unhappily aware that she was now living a fly-on-the-wall existence, watching couples and entire families hug and kiss one another, obviously secure and happy in their lives. She was acutely aware that she had never felt so alone in her entire life.

CHAPTER THIRTY-FOUR
JANE

Pacing up and down her bedroom in Galzignano in early January, Jane wondered when Niccolo would return. She had heard nothing from him since he had phoned her briefly the previous week to wish her a Happy New Year. She had asked him if he was coming home soon and he had been non-committal. The hoped-for reunion did not appear to be happening as she had planned, but there was still time.

Breakfast was a lonely affair at the head of the long table. Max and Cressida were long gone, and it was just her in this enormous villa with Paola and Antonio for company.

Paola came into the dining room with a small rack of freshly made toast.

'You must be pleased,' she said, placing the toast on the table and checking that the butter, marmalade and pot of tea were all within reach.

'Why?' Olivia was mystified. Paola was looking positively gleeful.

'Well, the conte will be home shortly. Antonio has gone to Venice airport to collect him. They should be home within the hour.' She bustled out to the kitchen, leaving Olivia stunned into silence.

Nico was coming home! She rose from the table, leaving her breakfast untouched, and rushed upstairs. Changing into a pale pink cashmere sweater — she had decided to look extra feminine for Nico — and a soft grey skirt, she brushed her blonde hair around her shoulders, applied a little light make-up, gave herself a quick spritz of perfume and descended the stairs.

As she reached the hall, she heard a car crunch to a halt on the gravel outside and froze. She knew it had to be Nico. Why had he not told her he was coming? She walked to the door and pulled it open. There he was, tall and handsome in a pair of jeans and a navy sweater, his tweed jacket thrown over one shoulder. His black hair was tousled, and his eyes looked tired. He looked at her for a long moment. She knew she looked well.

Niccolo approached her across the short space of gravel and kissed her on both cheeks.

'Jane,' he said. 'You look well. It's good to be home.'

OLIVIA

Work had resumed on the palazzo and Olivia was, once more, deeply involved in the project and had buried herself in work. She tried not to think about Niccolo. It was far too painful and, not understanding what had happened, she decided to bury herself in work. Honestly, she thought, the sooner I finish the interior of this palazzo and get home to Dublin the better.

She was seated at her usual spot at the long kitchen table when she heard Maria greeting someone at the door. It sounded like a woman's voice.

She looked up in time to see Francesca framed in the kitchen doorway. She leapt to her feet.

'Francesca!' She was overjoyed to see this lovely woman after all this time. 'How wonderful to see you!' Her pleasure in greeting her friend and employer was obvious.

'Olivia!' Francesca appeared to be just as happy to see her, and they sat together at the table chatting, then wandered around the palazzo for the next couple of hours. Francesca was overjoyed at the results of Olivia's work and praised the work of the craftsmen, too.

'Almost finished,' said Francesca. 'Maybe another month or six weeks, I'm guessing.'

Olivia agreed. 'Latest end of March, but I think we'll be finished a week or so before then.'

They sat and chatted companionably for a long time. Francesca finally asked her, 'What are your plans when this project ends? Will you go back to Ireland?'

'Oh, yes. I have no choice, Francesca. There's nothing to keep me here once I'm finished. My roots are in Dublin. At least, they used to be. Actually, I feel very adrift from the world in general right now.'

'I have an idea, Olivia.' Francesca moved closer and adopted a confidential tone. 'Do you remember I told you we were doing up The Mews for a family member?'

Olivia agreed that she did. She knew it was Niccolo but did not intimate that she had been told.

'Well, that has changed. I don't really like to say too much, but that particular family member is not planning to use The Mews for some time. Maybe never. It has been suggested that I rent it out to a suitable tenant. I was going to offer it to you for a nominal rent. It would almost be like being a caretaker. You can rent it indefinitely, or at least until your life is back on track.'

Olivia was stunned. She sat back, her heart beating fast. So Niccolo was not going to live there after all. What did it mean?

'My goodness, Francesca! That would be fabulous.' She could not think of any other way to react. This was a wonderful offer. It would remove her from her parents' house, and she loved The Mews. It would be perfect for her needs for the foreseeable future. 'I don't know what to say.'

'Just say yes.' Francesca looked at her with her soft violet eyes, so like her brother's. She patted Olivia's hand. 'My dear, I know you have had a dreadful couple of years and need to establish yourself again. There would be no pressure living at The Mews. And, to be perfectly honest, I would love to have you close by. I can't think of another person I would prefer to have living there.'

Olivia was deeply touched by this wonderful offer and decided, there and then, to accept.

'Then yes, Francesca. I would love to live there. Thank you so very much. I really don't know what to say. This is like a dream come true.'

And so, it was decided. Olivia would move into The Mews on her return to Ireland in March. At last, she had something to look forward to: a beautiful home from which she could, hopefully, reorganise her future. She felt a warm glow of affection for this woman. They would be good friends; of that she was sure.

JANE

Darkness fell over the Euganean Hills on a cold, quiet January night. Jane was wide awake, waiting for the clock to show three o'clock. She wanted to be sure that Nico was deeply asleep. She had heard him go to his room at about one o'clock, so she could be pretty sure he would be deeply asleep by now.

She slipped out of bed and prepared herself for a night of love-making the best way she could. She smoothed a fragrant body lotion all over her body, loosened her hair about her shoulders and donned her silkiest negligee. This had been a carefully chosen item, guaranteed, she thought, to seduce Niccolo. Short, black, see-through and pricy. Throwing her robe over the top, she quietly opened her door and slipped out into the darkened corridor. A scent of a gentle floral perfume trailed behind her like a cloud.

She reached her husband's bedroom and, twisting the handle gently, slipped inside. It was dark, quiet. All she could hear was the sound of Nico's breathing. The curtains were not fully drawn, and faint moonlight illuminated his dark head on the pillow. She dropped her gown and slipped into bed beside him.

Gently touching his waist with her hand, she nestled behind him and slid her arm around him. He groaned slightly and turned over to face her, sliding his hand over her silken negligee. Her body buzzed with desire as she guided his hands to her breasts.

'Olivia,' he moaned, as he pressed hard against her. Jane froze. Niccolo must have sensed that something was wrong, as he suddenly pulled away from her and leaned over to turn on the bedside lamp.

'Jane!' He looked at her in astonishment and alarm. 'What are you doing?'

'Trying to make love to my husband,' she snapped. 'What do you think? And all you can think of is that Irish tart.'

She climbed out of bed and was aware of Niccolo looking in amazement at her as she stood there in her flimsy negligee.

An amused expression had appeared in his eyes. 'You look quite ridiculous,' he said, laughing affectionately.

Furious, she snatched up her dressing gown from where it had fallen, threw it on and stormed out of the room. She did not go back to her bedroom, however, but descended the stairs to the sitting room, where she sought solace in a bottle of brandy which had been left over from Max's visit at Christmas. It had escaped Niccolo's eagle eye, as she had hidden it at the back of the cupboard behind some decanters. Bringing it and a glass back to bed with her, she knew there was nothing for her to do except get completely and madly drunk.

Her last thought, before passing out, was that someone was going to pay for this. I am still desirable, just wait and see.

OLIVIA

Suddenly, everything was going to be all right. For the first time since Christmas, Olivia was in a good mood when she headed to the palazzo the next morning. Renting The Mews! She could hardly believe her luck. Francesca would be a wonderful friend to have close by, too. She would not feel so isolated.

Entering the palazzo and greeting the electricians, who were rewiring the entire property, she took up her space at the table and opened her laptop. She was engrossed in her work when she heard Maria going to the lift to welcome someone. She heard female voices.

It was Jane. Olivia's heart sank.

'Good morning, Contessa' she greeted Jane formally and politely. 'What brings you to Venice?'

Jane assumed her haughtiest expression.

'I am here on behalf of my husband, the conte, to inspect the work to date.' She looked around pointedly. 'It doesn't look nearly finished to me. Are you sure you're on schedule?'

'Oh, don't mind how things look now. It's still infrastructural work. The real visual change will come when we do the painting and wallpapering. And, of course, hang the curtains and light fittings. In fact,' she added, 'we're actually ahead of schedule.'

'Oh, excellent!' Jane purred. 'The Conte and I are dying to move back into our home. We want it to be perfect.' She looked slyly at Olivia. 'How was your holiday? I think you went away for the New Year. How did it go?'

'I had a lovely Christmas and New Year, thank you for asking. Very peaceful, in fact.' Olivia would not allow Jane to goad her and kept her voice quiet and calm.

'I'd like to take you to lunch today,' announced Jane suddenly. 'I know I was very difficult the last time, but I thought that Nico fancied you.' She laughed. 'But I know now that I was wrong.'

Olivia stayed silent. She really did not want to have to undergo another painful lunch with this woman, but she could not think how she could refuse. She was her employer, after all. But on top of that, she wondered if, by having lunch with Jane, she would be able to figure out what had happened to change Niccolo's mind about their relationship. She still felt a sharp pang whenever she thought about him, which was most of the time. She was hurting badly.

The two women walked to the same fish restaurant that they had lunched in previously. As they strolled towards San Barnaba, both were unaware of the admiring glances thrown their way by most people they passed. Two beautiful blonde women, who turned heads wherever they went. Jane, tall and elegant; Olivia, smaller and with a more voluptuous figure. They were both thinking their own thoughts.

Jane was thinking about how she could ensure that Olivia would keep away permanently from Nico. She had plotted her next move carefully and knew that she was about to drop a bombshell on her rival's head, if all went well. She felt smug. How could she fail? She had already pretty well destroyed her rival by having the photographs sent to her husband, but she needed to be sure of killing this relationship stone dead.

Olivia was deeply uneasy about finding herself about to have lunch with Jane, to sit across the table from this woman who so obviously loathed her. Her anxiety threatened to destroy her composure if Jane was in any way nasty. She vowed to remain calm, no matter what Jane said. She had a strong impression that this lunch was not going to be enjoyable. Jane was up to something. And it was not going to be pretty.

She was right, but even worse than she could have predicted.

CHAPTER THIRTY-FIVE
OLIVIA

Sitting down in the same corner as before, Jane ordered the *fritta mista* and a half-litre of the house white wine, which promptly arrived. The restaurant was quiet today, as after 6th January many businesses closed until just before *Carnivale* at the end of February. It was definitely off season in Venice.

'I do so enjoy the mixed fish platter here.' Jane reached for the carafe and poured generous glasses for both of them. She helped herself to some of the deep-fried fish and enthusiastically picked up a large prawn.

Olivia was not hungry but speared a mussel from its shell and ate it. She sipped from her glass of wine and tried to dispel the feeling of uneasiness that would not go away.

'I apologise for our last lunch engagement,' began Jane, 'but my marriage to Nico has been difficult since we lost Sofia. I suppose we were briefly estranged, but now that has all changed and I am ready to admit I made a mistake in accusing you of getting too close to my husband. I'm really dreadfully sorry, Olivia. What must you have thought of me?'

Olivia stayed silent. She could not think of a single thing to say. What comment could she make, after all?

Jane continued, adopting a confidential tone. She leaned forward and looked Olivia straight in the eyes. Olivia noticed that her pupils were dilated and that her voice was slightly slurred. Had she taken something? 'I think we could be good friends.'

Olivia recoiled in surprise. That was the last thing she could imagine. 'And, seeing we're now friends, I'm going to share a secret with you.' Jane sat back again, knowing that she had a captive audience. She could see that Olivia was curious. It was written all over the tart's face, she thought. 'Nico and I are trying for another baby!'

Olivia thought she could actually faint, so great was her shock. 'Seriously?' she whispered. 'Another baby?'

'I know I'm perhaps a little bit past normal child-bearing years, but I'm still in good working order.' She laughed merrily, the sound giving Olivia a chill. Without a doubt, she thought, this woman is unstable. Can this be true? But Jane was warming to her theme. 'When Nico came home from Dublin, he told me he had decided to try to revive our marriage. He realised that he had been distant for the past couple of years and promised to change.'

So Niccolo had had a change of heart while he was away, thought Olivia miserably. She wondered why. It seemed unbelievable. Especially this last piece of news.

'When he came home, he swept me off my feet.' Jane was clearly enjoying herself. 'It was like we were on honeymoon.' She nibbled another piece of fish and swallowed some more wine, clicking for the waitress to bring another carafe. 'He was insatiable,' she added for good measure.

Olivia felt emotionally battered and bruised by this encounter and thought that perhaps she had heard enough. It was torture. She ached inside. "Niccolo," she groaned inwardly, "why have you done this to me?"

Her phone rang and she fished it out of her handbag. It was Steve.

'Can you come?' he whispered.

JANE

Fortified by more than half a litre of vino della casa, Jane marched to Giglio, where Marcello was sitting in his usual spot outside the bar, chatting to Gino and trying to catch the eye of various ladies to come for a ride in his gondola. The sun was beginning to set as she approached him.

'Are you free to take me for a gondola ride?'

He stood up and approached her. 'Of course.' His eyes held a question and hers held the answer.

'Do you still have that fleece rug on board?'

'I certainly do,' he breathed.

He held out his hand to her and they boarded his gondola, gliding into the gloom.

Gino could hear Marcello begin to sing his favourite song, "*La Biondina in Gondoleta*", in his lilting tenor voice, and smiled to himself. Marcello was quite the lad, he thought.

'The other evening, I went rowing with a blonde in a gondola.

The poor girl was so happy that she fell sound asleep immediately.

As she slept in my arms, each time I woke her

The rocking of the boat sent her back to sleep again.'

OLIVIA

Olivia landed at Dublin Airport the following morning and got a taxi to her parents' house. Paying the driver, she turned to face her old family home. So many memories, good and bad, flashed through her mind. The tidily kept front garden of the fifties house with its red-brick and white pebble-dash was an old friend; after all, this was where she had grown up, played in this street as a child. Its familiarity brought an ache to her chest. She felt like weeping.

Before she reached the front steps, the door opened, and her mother was wrapping her arms around her.

'Olivia! Carissima!' Her mother clung to her and Olivia hugged her warmly, suddenly aware of how frail and tiny she had become.

Her mother already knew about Steve's illness and that he had collapsed a few days previously. She knew that he had been taken to hospital by ambulance and that the prognosis was bad.

'Oh, Mamma! I felt I had to come. No choice, really.'

'Of course, you had a choice, darling. You really shouldn't waste one moment feeling sorry for him. Look at how he treated you. You should just forget about him completely.' Her mother had never been particularly fond of Steve, and now hated to see her lovely daughter being summoned to his bedside in a peremptory fashion, or that's how she perceived it.

'It's okay, Mamma,' she tried to placate her agitated mother. 'I'm fine. And anyway, it's a great excuse to see you both for a few days.' She tried to smile. But her mother was in full flight.

'But you can't just arrive at the hospital!' she exclaimed. 'What if Diana is there at his bedside?'

'I'm going to give Penelope Finn a buzz first. Find out what's the general lie of the land.'

She had not spoken to Penelope since that fateful dinner party in County Meath almost two years previously. And she was not looking forward to it. Penelope knew everybody and, what's more, she figured that she also knew everything about everybody. She made it her business to know what was going on and was endlessly curious. She would be delighted to hear from Olivia, as she would be eager to hear how she had been doing since she left for Venice.

So, it was with some trepidation that Olivia dialled her number and recoiled inwardly when she heard Penelope's fluting tones at the end of the line.

'Finn residence. Penelope speaking.'

Olivia braced herself.

'Hi, Penelope. It's Olivia here. Olivia Lynskey. How are you?'

'Oh my God, Olivia!' It was almost a shout. 'Where are you?'

'In Dublin. I had a call from Steve two days ago and he told me he's in hospital. Do you know what's going on right now? I'm about to go to see him, but I was wondering if you had any information about his condition and, umm, whether he is on his own or is Diana around?'

Penelope could hardly keep the glee from her voice, or at least that's how it sounded to Olivia.

'Well, yes. Diana is with him fairly constantly. Also, his two sisters and his brother were expected to visit today. I saw him yesterday and he appears to be fine. He was sitting out on a chair beside his bed. If I were you, I'd leave it until tomorrow, when the family have had their visit. If you go in the early morning, he'll probably be on his own,' she added 'You don't really want to run the gauntlet of that ghastly family, do you?'

Olivia agreed that indeed she did not want to face Steve's family. They all thought she was stuck up and, perhaps, in their eyes they were right. She must certainly have appeared like that to them. They were part of the background that Steve had never been keen to embrace. Their father had been a poorly educated truck driver and Steve had clawed his way out of the straitened circumstances of his childhood by sheer hard work and a brilliant mind. She had asked him once to drive past the house where he grew up and he had refused point blank. There was no looking back, he insisted. He rarely saw his brother and sisters and considered himself, frankly, to be on a different planet.

'Thanks, Penelope. I'll go in early tomorrow morning and see him. What's his mood? Is he in much pain? Tell me some more about what's going on.'

'Well, his pain is under control now, though he was in a terrible state until about a month ago when they brought him in to organise his meds. Before that he couldn't even sleep; just sat up watching television all night. They let him go home a couple of weeks ago, but he collapsed last Friday and was rushed back to hospital.' She paused for effect. 'Goodness, Olivia! He looks ghastly; gaunt and grey and terribly thin. He even needs to be helped to the bathroom!' This was uttered with an air of incredulity, as if this were the ultimate humiliation, which, for Steve, it probably was.

'Okay. I'll talk to you soon. And really, thanks. Say hi to everyone for me.'

Up early the next morning, Olivia prepared to leave for the hospital. She swallowed a cup of tea and was just climbing into her mother's car, ready to leave for the hospital, when her phone rang. It was Penelope.

'Olivia. I'm so sorry. I just got word. Steve died during the night.'

***

Steve's funeral and the lead-in to the event were torture for Olivia. What should she do? Should she go to the removal, where the family of the deceased stood around the open coffin and received commiserations from all who had known him? Should she just go to the funeral? She decided to do the latter and put the removal out of her mind. Though she had been Steve's wife, she did not want, or need, to shake the hands of Diana and Steve's annoying siblings. She would pay her last respects to Steve by standing at the back of the church during the funeral Mass and leave it at that.

Then she would return to work in Venice. She longed to return to that beautiful city and to leave the wasps' nest that Dublin had become for her, with all the gossip and scandal she wanted to avoid. She was not ready to resume even a semblance of her old life yet. She needed time to regain some of her old self-confidence first.

Standing at the back of the church in the leafy suburbs of south Dublin, she saw Steve's coffin in front of the altar and tried to find a prayer for him to wish him well. But her mind was empty. After the Mass, she stood as the coffin was carried back down the long, never-ending aisle by six of his relatives and friends. She felt a deep sadness.

Steve's brother, Joe, had stood up towards the end of the ceremony and invited everybody back to a reception at a local hotel. Olivia decided that she would leave directly and stood in her place in the church, waiting for the funeral cortege to file past before she took her leave.

Suddenly, she realised she was eye-to-eye with Diana, walking slowly, her tall, dark beauty striking in her slim-fitting black woollen coat. Diana's eyes were sweeping over the congregation, searching. Finally, they alighted on Olivia. A small smile of recognition flitted across her face. Olivia froze. Rage and indignation threatened to envelop her. She stared back angrily at this woman who, not just content to take her place in Steve's bed, had taken her place at his funeral, too. She was boiling with animosity and longed to march over to slap this brazen woman's face.

Waiting for the rest of the congregation to file out, Olivia left the church and slipped through the crowd, carefully making no eye contact with anyone. She hurried down the street to the car and jumped in, almost slamming the door on Penelope's fingers. She had obviously followed her from the church. Her eyes were red.

'Olivia! Are you okay?'

'How could I be okay?' she snapped. 'This has been an ordeal, and I just want to leave now. Sorry, Penelope, nothing personal, but I can't wait to get back to Venice and a semblance of sanity. You've been very kind, but I'm going now.'

She made to shut the door. Penelope stood on the footpath. Strewn brown leaves were soggy underfoot and the sky was grey, threatening rain.

Penelope pulled her coat tight around her.

'Come and see us, darling, when you return from Venice. You know you're always welcome.'

Olivia thought she almost meant it, as she crunched the car into first gear, and it leaped into the traffic

CHAPTER THIRTY-SIX
OLIVIA

Coming in to land over the Venice Lagoon, Olivia was thrilled with some sort of excitement. She loved this city, visitors and all. Of course, she had been living here in the off-season. What would it be like in summer? She had heard many horror stories of tourists wandering the streets in their swimsuits and diving off bridges to swim in the canals in July and August, even trying to enter churches with almost nothing to cover them and sitting to eat their slices of pizza on the steps of the bridges, causing congestion. She was aware that many people saw Venice as some sort of holiday resort, not a fully operational, working city, which it was. Their lack of respect towards the Venetians themselves, who had to live with the huge downside of daily life among literally millions of tourists, left her speechless.

Marco was waiting for her at the airport dock and she climbed gratefully aboard the di Falco motor launch. Gliding across the lagoon on this late January morning, she felt a sense of well-being. She was newly widowed, and she felt no real pain about this. When she examined her conscience, she knew it was because she had experienced all the hurt when Steve had left her, which had turned to indignation. Now she had no real feelings about him or his untimely death any more. A chapter in her life was now completely closed.

She thought about Niccolo. That wonderful man who had turned his back on her, just when she had thought they might have found love together. She ached still when she thought about him, but she forced herself to put these feelings aside, as she considered them now to be a waste of time, if

Jane were to be believed and they were actually trying for another child. She needed to move on with her life.

Marcello came into her mind as they passed the many gondoliers who were rowing tourists, with flashing I-phones, cameras and excited faces, out into the lagoon. She did not think that she would be seeing him again and, if that was the case, it was fine with her. She was also deeply embarrassed to think that he had helped to undress her and put her to bed. The memory of the torn underwear flashed briefly into her mind, stirring a memory. She tried to put her finger on it but could not.

Casa Antica was waiting for her. She walked from room to room, opening shutters and letting in fresh air and light. She loved this little house and knew she would be sorry to leave it in just a couple of months. It had become home to her by now. She felt safe and secure at night in her four-poster bed, surrounded by big, goose-down pillows encased in the finest cotton. It was perfect.

Next morning, she packed her briefcase with her laptop and all current notes and schedules. Walking past the haunted house and the Peggy Guggenheim Collection, she fronted the Accademia Bridge and was soon at the palazzo and entering the *piano nobile*. Maria greeted her like a long-lost friend, despite the fact that she had only seen her a few days previously.

Taking a coffee to her usual spot at the kitchen table, she took up residence once more and prepared to meet with the man who would be doing the wallpapering. She was checking her notes when she heard a sound from the hallway. Maria had returned upstairs, and the contractors had not yet arrived. She rose and, walking briskly across the *piano nobile*, entered the narrow corridor running between the bedrooms. The door to Sofia's room was slightly ajar. She approached with caution and pushed the door open gently.

There, sitting at the little dressing table was Niccolo. She had not seen him since before Christmas and the sight of him made her start. He looked terrible. Dishevelled and exhausted, he looked as though he had not slept for days. He turned around, startled.

'Olivia! I thought you were in Dublin.' He stood abruptly and made to walk past her. She barred his way.

'Niccolo.' She was calm. Almost cold when she spoke, though she was quaking inside. 'What happened?'

He pushed her hand aside and left the room, hurrying down the corridor like an animal that has just escaped from its cage, such was his urgency to get away. She rushed after him.

'Talk to me, Niccolo,' she demanded. 'You owe me an explanation. You stood me up over the New Year and I spent a week in Ostuni alone. My husband just died, as you obviously know. I am weary, exhausted and have no clue why you are behaving as though I have the plague.' She felt her voice breaking and tears springing to her eyes. She looked away.

'Olivia. You know as well as I do that, as soon as I left Venice, you fell straight into bed with another man.'

Olivia took a step backwards and her mouth fell open.

'What? What are you talking about? That's complete nonsense.'

'You know what I'm talking about. Tell me you didn't go out with another man when I was in Dublin. Go on! Let's hear the truth.' His face was ashen, and he was trembling with emotion.

'I went out with my gondolier friend, Marcello, to have a farewell drink. That's all. Just a drink.' The memory of waking naked in bed and of her torn panties tickled the edges of her memory and she shrank inwardly. What had happened? Had he found out about it? If so, how?

'Just a drink?' Now he was shouting. 'That's not what it looked like to me. You tramp. Jane was right.'

And with that, storming out of the palazzo, he turned on his heel and left.

JANE

Humiliation threatened to engulf Jane as she struggled with the fact that Niccolo did not want her in his bed. She had imagined that if he knew she still desired him, he would return to her, but the memory of the word 'Olivia', uttered with a passionate groan when she had pressed herself to him in her tiny silken negligee rankled still. It felt like a constant irritation which she wanted to scratch but could not quite manage to.

That she hated Olivia was not in doubt. But her rival seemed to have the upper hand in Nico's affections. However, she would be returning to Dublin in just a few short weeks as the work on the palazzo was nearing completion. Once she was out of the way, all would be well. Or at least there was a better chance of things going her way.

Niccolo had told her that he would not be returning to Dublin in the foreseeable future. She quite understood this, as he obviously wanted to stay out of Olivia's way, and that would be a lot easier if he were to stay in Italy after she left. Francesca had agreed to rent out The Mews to someone suitable, who would look after it for now.

Jane realised fully how important it was to keep Nico and Olivia from meeting, so she undertook to make a weekly inspection of the palazzo, and he acquiesced on that point, with apparent relief. She had no idea that they had met briefly on that one occasion when Olivia had returned from Dublin. She had no idea that Nico had challenged Olivia about her fidelity.

Her plan appeared to be working out fine. She just needed to find a way to lure him into her bed and, after that, all would be perfect.

Thank goodness she had had her evening of passion with Marcello. What a lover! She felt hot just thinking about how his hands had roamed over her body, touching her most fragile places, stimulating every nerve, every bone, every fibre of her being. She had needed him. It had been far, far too long since she had been touched intimately and told she was beautiful and dangerous.

She was tense. A couple of tranquillisers here, a shot or two of grappa there, and she began to slide once more as she tried to capture her husband's attention and to regain his love. But all her efforts seemed to be in vain. He appeared lost to her. She would have to avail herself of Marcello's attentions more frequently to get her through this trying time. He would keep her calm.

OLIVIA

As the weeks ticked by, the painting was completed, and the wallpaper and curtains were installed in the palazzo. It looked magnificent. Olivia stood back and admired her handiwork. Nobody could ever criticise this. She took some photographs for her files and took a last look around. Her work was complete. Just a couple of days until she would return to Dublin, having completed this challenging and difficult project.

Jane arrived to do a final inspection in a flurry of expensive perfume and designer clothes. Olivia noticed the deep shadows around her eyes. No beauty salon could repair the obvious ravages of drugs and alcohol. She looked haggard and older than her years. When she leaned in to give Olivia the obligatory two air-kisses, she smelled alcohol on her breath. So, she had not been imagining it, then. Jane was back on the booze big time and looking at Olivia with intense dislike.

Jane was wondering viciously how on earth Olivia could look so perfect when, surely, she must be exhausted. After all, she had been up until all hours of the night for the past few weeks, finishing up the palazzo with the last of the sub-contractors.

Jane had to admit that the work was perfect. She would have loved to have been able to find fault, but could not, no matter how hard she tried. She noticed Olivia scrutinising her, probably wondering if she was pregnant yet. She smiled to herself. Her plan had worked perfectly, without a hitch. Niccolo was home to stay, she was sure of it. He would soon recover from his infatuation with the Irish tart. He just needed time.

JANE

Arriving home in Galzignano, she found Paola beginning to pack up their belongings prior to their move back to the palazzo.

As it was mainly clothing and everyday bits and pieces that needed to go, Jane did not worry about it too much. She was happy to know that Olivia would be leaving in a couple of days and that, as she imagined, was that. But she would not be able to let down her guard until she knew that Olivia's plane had lifted off from Venice airport and she was worried sick that Niccolo would go to see her before she left.

Sitting down with Niccolo for dinner, she was feeling her usual insecure self. Her neurotic behaviour was something she was aware was instrumental in driving her husband away and killing her marriage, but she was unable to control herself after a few glasses of wine.

Wine was poured. She could see Niccolo watching her with unease.

'Are you packed?' he enquired. 'I asked Paola to leave a couple of suitcases in your bedroom. Antonio will take everything to Venice tomorrow and Maria can put your things away at the palazzo. Paola would pack for you, but only you yourself know what stays here and what goes to Venice.'

"How reasonable he sounds," she thought, helping herself to another glass of wine, not waiting for him to pour for her. He looked at her disapprovingly. But she needed to get through two more days. Just two more days, please goodness. Then she would give up alcohol and pills and concentrate on her marriage. She felt utterly vulnerable and threatened. Niccolo had absolutely no idea how much turmoil she was in. How could he, after all?

Thank goodness for her refuge in the hard embrace of Marcello, she thought. Without his desire for her, she would feel like nothing.

'Please make sure you leave the suitcases ready before you go to bed.' These days, Nico sounded tired and preoccupied, she thought, and wondered if he thought of Olivia. Of her perfect features and voluptuous body. She poured another glass of wine. 'Please, Jane. That's enough wine. What's wrong with you?'

'You had an affair with Olivia, didn't you?' she blurted, instantly regretting her outburst.

Niccolo paled and looked at her in surprise.

'What makes you think such a thing?'

'I just know.' Now she was really sorry she had spoken out of turn. She evaded his questioning gaze.

'I don't want to discuss Olivia. What's done is done, and there's nothing going on now. Please, Jane, drop it. This is a conversation that will go nowhere and will only cause further problems for both of us. Let's move on with our marriage. Please.'

Did he ever wonder where the photographs had come from, that fateful day after Christmas? Jane was curious. Surely, he must have his suspicions. Now she was leading this possible line of questioning to her very door.

She swallowed nervously, taking another gulp of wine to calm her nerves.

Dinner was over and Jane could not wait to get back to her room. Niccolo was looking pensive, as though he were trying to think something through and not making much headway. He looked confused.

He helped her out of her chair, and she staggered slightly. Her head was spinning. "How much wine did I have anyway?" she asked herself.

Niccolo held her by the elbow and guided her up the stairs to her room. Paola watched them go. She would have loved to see them united once more, but obviously knew that they shared separate rooms and never saw evidence to suggest that they ever shared a bed. She felt sad for them. Such a beautiful couple. What a great pity about the contessa's drinking and the fact that they had lost their much-loved daughter. She shook her head and returned to the kitchen. Her crossword was only half-finished, and she had figured out the answer to one particularly cryptic clue while she had been serving the roast meat. She was anxious to fill in the letters.

Jane's two empty suitcases were parked just inside her bedroom door. Niccolo helped Jane to her bed. He was now feeling angry. He was puzzled by Jane's outburst about Olivia over dinner. What was going on?

Looking at Jane, he could see that she was going to be in no condition to pack for herself tonight. Antonio was bringing the suitcases to Venice at six o'clock in the morning. Jane's cases would never be ready. He opened them and placed them on the floor in front of the bureau. Opening the top drawer, he pulled it out completely and emptied a floating sea of lingerie into the case, placing the drawer on the floor when he had finished. Progressing to the second drawer, he noticed something stuck to the back of the top drawer. A brown envelope.

CHAPTER THIRTY-SEVEN
OLIVIA

She was sad to be leaving. Olivia began to pack her suitcases in preparation for her departure from Venice. Would she ever return, she wondered? And Niccolo. What about him? Her feelings for him now consumed her. Why did he accuse her of seeing another man? What had happened? Did he know about her disastrous evening with Marcello? And if so, then how? Her head was in a constant whirl.

She was still shaking inwardly about her run-in that morning and wondered constantly about his accusation. She just could not think about it and thought a few minutes with Marcello at this point, before she left Venice, would, at the very least, have him confirm that nothing had happened between them. She couldn't imagine what Niccolo was referring to. She puzzled constantly.

Had Marcello told someone about their evening when she had, apparently, got drunk?

She wondered if she should say goodbye to the gondolier. She had not seen him since the day after their evening out. He had not contacted her, and she had been too embarrassed to drop by his gondola berth in Giglio.

As he had been kind and patient, as far as she could tell, since she had arrived in Venice, she decided that she would pay him a visit first thing in the morning, before she did her last patrol of the palazzo, ensuring that everything was completely ready for the return of the Di Falco family.

She had telephoned Francesca and told her that she would be arriving in two days. The Mews would be ready for her, and she knew that this was to be her consolation for all the stresses and strains of the last couple of years. Francesca would be there, her new friend, who would make sure that she was all right. It was a comforting thought.

Her second to last time to sleep in the comfortable four-poster bed in Casa Antica was a poignant one. How she would miss this house and this wonderful bed! Thank goodness she had The Mews waiting for her. She did not think she could have coped if she had had to return to her parents' home, with her hyper-critical father giving her a hard time whenever they had a conversation.

OLIVIA

'Marcello!' She waved, and he turned his blond head in her direction. He was polishing his already gleaming gondola in the early-morning sunshine with concentration. She admired his golden good looks as he downed his chamois and came to greet her.

'Olivia!' he exclaimed. 'It's been so long since I've seen you. Where have you been, my darling?'

He kissed her softly on both cheeks and she remembered his warm kisses.

'Oh, this and that,' she responded airily. 'But I leave Venice tomorrow morning and I wanted to say goodbye. I couldn't go without seeing you one more time.'

He hugged her to him, this incredibly sexy woman who seemed oblivious to her voluptuous beauty. He often dreamed about her and awoke hot and aroused at night. Taking those photographs had been incredibly difficult and he still thought about her constantly. He had stayed away as he was too frightened of Jane and the leverage, she had over him.

Suddenly, Olivia froze. Niccolo was standing on the bridge that crossed the canal overhead. He was looking at her with curiosity and had an inscrutable look on his face. He disappeared almost immediately, melting into a crowd of Asian tourists laden with cameras and selfie sticks. Olivia disengaged herself from Marcello's warm hugs, feeling decidedly rattled; but she decided to ignore this interruption as she sat in the spring sunshine with Marcello for about half an hour, enjoying his company like in the old days, she thought, before things became complicated. Her heart ached when she thought of Niccolo and of how he had looked at her from the bridge with that unfathomable expression on his face.

Waving goodbye to Marcello as she walked over that same bridge on her way to the palazzo, Olivia wondered if she would ever see him again; and, indeed, if she would ever see Niccolo or return to Venice in this lifetime.

JANE

Sunshine peeped from behind the curtains as Jane awoke. Her head ached and her mouth felt dry. She reached for a bottle of water from her bedside locker and a couple of paracetamol to try to dull her throbbing skull. How much had she had to drink anyway?

She looked at her clock. It was already ten o'clock. She had certainly overslept.

Getting out of bed, she slipped her feet into a pair of furry mules and made her way to her en suite bathroom on unsteady legs. Brushing her teeth and splashing her face to make herself feel more human, she emerged once more into the bedroom. Pulling back the curtains, she opened the French doors and stepped out onto her little terrace overlooking the front of the villa. Spring sunlight, complete with early blossoms, had created a pastoral scene worthy of a painting. Jane was oblivious to all this beauty as she blinked her eyes and felt the chill morning air on her bare shoulders.

Returning inside, she noticed that the suitcases were gone. Oh, yes, she remembered. Antonio was supposed to be picking them up at 6am. She wondered if she had packed them without remembering. Wandering over to her bureau, she opened the drawers one by one. They were empty.

Showered, dressed, perfumed and perfectly coiffed, make-up applied with plenty of concealer under her eyes to try to disguise the dark rings, she descended the stairs for a welcome coffee.

Paola bustled to the table with a pot of coffee and a jug of hot milk, topped with an inviting froth.

'The Conte asked me to tell you that he will be out today and not to wait up for him tonight.' She poured a cup of coffee for Jane, who appeared to be in a trance. She was just sitting there as if she were trying to think about something but could not quite figure out what it was.

'Was it you who packed up my lingerie for Antonio to take to Venice?'

'No, Contessa. Everything was already packed, and the suitcases were standing outside your room when Antonio went upstairs this morning. Why? Is there a problem?' Paola was standing nervously beside the table, waiting to be excused.

'I'm not sure.' Jane suddenly stood up, almost knocking over the pot of coffee, and fled from the room. She dashed upstairs and opened the bureau, throwing the empty top drawer onto the floor. It was gone. Her heart sank. The envelope containing the incriminating photographs and cash slips had been removed. Had Nico found them? If so, it was a disaster.

OLIVIA

All her bags were packed, and Olivia was ready to catch the morning flight to Dublin. Her life in Venice was over and she felt a deep regret, as she had loved it here. Marco would be picking her up in an hour to take her and her luggage to the airport.

She padded around her little house in Dorsodoro, touching everything for the last time. This green gas stove had become her friend, as had the enormous brass taps in the bathroom. Furnishings she had thought she disliked on her first day here had become endearing and she was heartbroken to leave them.

She had spent almost five months in this quaint house tucked into an alleyway near Accademia, and it had rapidly become her refuge. Now she had to leave. Her work in Venice was over.

She thought about Niccolo. Really, she did not blame him for ending their fledgling relationship. She, too, would have struggled to put a love interest before a spouse. She admired him for having had the resolve to save his marriage, no matter how much it had upset her. He was a good and decent man and she wished him happiness. She swallowed the ache in her heart when she thought about him. The wounds inflicted went deep and it would take more than a few months for her heart to heal, if ever.

It was unbelievable that he thought she had been unfaithful to him. This was the strangest thing of all. She could not help but wonder if Jane had poisoned his mind in some way. Jane, she thought, was capable of just about anything.

Marcello. That lively, handsome gondolier of whom she had become so fond. She wished she had been able to maintain a platonic relationship with him and to just be his friend. But he had made that impossible. He obviously desired her, and that made life difficult.

Jane was mad and dangerous, she thought. Yes, she was Niccolo's wife and he had a cross to bear being married to her, as she was indeed a difficult woman. She hoped that Jane would be able to make Niccolo happy. She wanted the best for him in the end. Perhaps Jane would actually have another child, if that was what she and Niccolo wanted. She hoped for the best for him. For them.

She was sitting at the breakfast bar, enjoying her final cup of tea, when the buzzer rang for the intercom.

"Marco isn't due for almost an hour," she thought. "Who can that be?"

Looking into the intercom screen, she saw it was Niccolo.

"Oh, no!" she thought. "Niccolo is the last person I want to have to speak to right now. I don't want to have a painful goodbye. This has all been difficult enough."

She ignored the buzzer, which sounded a second time. She watched Niccolo move away, then pause as if undecided about something. Suddenly, he turned, came back and dropped an envelope into her mailbox, finally walking along the alleyway and out of sight.

She descended the stairs cautiously and opened the front door an inch or two to make sure he was gone. There was nobody to see. She inserted her key into the mailbox and withdrew a large envelope, quickly running upstairs to see what was inside.

Opening the envelope at the breakfast bar, she almost fainted with shock when she saw the photographs in full colour and detail.

There she was with Steve. Poor Steve, she thought. She was hugging him goodbye, the last time they met before he died.

Her breath caught in her throat when she saw herself lying on a fleece rug, completely naked, with a hand cupping her breast.

'Oh! Oh! What's going on?' She felt hot and cold at the same time, as she looked at the photographs, all of them showing her naked and in various sexual poses, leaving nothing to the imagination. The same hand was in many of the photographs, on her most intimate parts. She shivered in shock. She had no clue how to react or what to do. She should have let Niccolo in, she thought agitatedly. Perhaps he could have explained.

Realisation dawned on her.

"Marcello took them!" Her mind was clear now. She studied the pictures once more, trying to overcome her horror at the degrading photographs. That was the fleece from the boat and that was Marcello's hand on her breast and placed strategically on other intimate parts of her body. She could see clearly the distinctive wooden bracelet that he always wore and most of his zodiacal tattoo of the Sagittarian symbol of which he was so proud. He had set her up. But why? And how did Niccolo get these? Suspicion began to flood her mind.

She threw on her coat and dashed from the house. She needed to see Marcello once more. He had questions to answer.

As she walked briskly towards his mooring place near Santa Maria del' Giglio, she thought about what had happened. What good would talking to Marcello do? Niccolo obviously thought she had had an affair. There was nothing she could do to alter that fact; no protestations of innocence would be enough. But why did he take them? Helplessness overwhelmed her.

She felt a weight on her heart. She knew deep down that nothing she could ever say or do would persuade the man she loved that there had been nobody else. Nothing else mattered. She stopped in her tracks.

Why would Marcello have done this? Who would gain from her downfall in Niccolo's eyes? The answer was painfully clear. It was Jane.

It was all over; Niccolo and Venice were nothing more than a magical dream. She felt more broken than ever before, and it was all too much for her to bear. Yet another betrayal. Too many difficulties and rejections to cope with, she thought. Drained of energy, overwhelmed, she felt her knees begin to give way and she leaned on a parapet, gazing down at the water below.

"I can't take any more." It was like a whisper in her ear. "My life is broken."

CHAPTER THIRTY-EIGHT
JANE

Jane was desperate to see Niccolo. Had he discovered the photographs? Had she been so drunk and drugged that she could not remember removing them and putting them elsewhere? She was utterly confused. Where had he gone this morning? Had he gone to Venice?

She needed to quiz him carefully. But how do you enquire if someone has an envelope of pornographic photos without revealing some involvement? She had no idea what to do.

She decided to go to Venice and speak to Marcello. At the very least, the appreciative company of this lovely blond man would make her feel better. This handsome gondolier who, according to what he had said and done on that heady night when he had lain her gently on the fleece on the floor of his gondola, found her beautiful and desirable. That time he knew he was with a woman who urgently wanted him in a way he could understand and, as far as she was concerned, he was a welcome change from her moody, difficult husband, as that was how she viewed Nico, much as she loved him.

Arriving at the train station in Venice once more, she hailed a water taxi to take her to the palazzo. She urgently needed to check if the envelope might still be among her lingerie, though instinctively she knew it was with Niccolo. Her stomach clenched at the thought. She had to be sure. It was an idyllic morning in March and spring was in the air. Soon, the mauve wisteria blossoms would be appearing, hanging down over the red-brick walls of the mysterious gardens of Venice. Jane's frantic frame of mind blotted out all the beauty surrounding her as she anxiously entered her Venetian home.

'Contessa! I was expecting you tomorrow. Is everything all right?' Maria emerged from the kitchen, wiping her hands on a towel, a dab of flour on her otherwise immaculate uniform.

'I'm here to do an inspection.' Jane sounded imperious as she walked through the freshly renovated rooms. 'The Conte and I will return tomorrow.'

Anxious to rush to her bedroom to check her suitcases, Jane made a show of appearing to stroll through the palazzo, with Maria fussing and clucking at her heels, panicked by the thought that the contessa had arrived a day early, and hoping she could find nothing to criticise. But, no matter how much Jane wanted to find fault, everything appeared to be perfect.

'What time will you be here? I want to prepare a special lunch or dinner for you and the conte to welcome you home.' Maria obviously longed to resume the old order and see a semblance of normality returning to the palazzo.

'Dinner will be fine, Maria,' she answered shortly. She was anxious to be away. 'I just want to pop into my bedroom. I'll see you before I leave.'

'Oh, Contessa,' exclaimed Maria. 'I haven't unpacked your bags yet. I was going to do that later today.'

Barely managing not to break into a run and having reassured Maria that she understood, Jane entered her bedroom and closed the door behind her. Her heart raced. What if the photos were missing? She hoped to find them among her lingerie; otherwise she definitely had a problem. All she could hope and pray was that Niccolo had not seen them. Otherwise, the game was up. Her treachery was discovered. Life could never return to the way she wanted it to be.

Her suitcases were standing in the middle of the floor. She got down on her knees and opened them hurriedly, throwing her silken underwear everywhere. Frantically searching the side pockets, even under the lining, it was obvious. No photos. Nothing. Feeling cold, she reached for her handbag and withdrew her ever-ready packet of pills and her small flask of grappa. Knocking back two pills with a mouthful of the burning liquor immediately brought a sense of unreality to the situation.

"It's just a bad dream. There must be an explanation. Perhaps I missed them at the villa. I need to go back." Jane knew well that the effects of the sedation would not last long, but at least they brought temporary relief to the terror of the moment.

Leaving her bedroom looking as though there had been an explosion of lace and silk, she dashed out of the palazzo, leaving a puzzled Maria in her wake as she threw on her coat and hurried to Giglio to see Marcello. She needed to talk to him urgently. She needed his reassurance that all would be well. Maybe he would hold her in his arms. "I need to be comforted. I can't cope with this on my own."

As she crossed over the little bridge, she looked down. His gondola was missing he was obviously taking visitors out for a tour of the canals that criss-crossed the area. But there was his friend Gino. She waved and descended to greet him. He took both her hands in his and looked into her face.

'Contessa. How are you? Are you looking for Marcello?'

Resisting the urge to tell Gino that she was completely panicked and needed to see Marcello urgently, she agreed to wait in the little bar for Marcello to arrive back with the usual bevy of blondes. Ordering a brandy to calm her nerves, she was feeling utterly frazzled when there was still no sign of him forty-five minutes later, and she had begun to contemplate a second drink. Instead, she went to find Gino again, but he was also out with clients.

She sat on the parapet at the bottom of the bridge. Where was Marcello? Had his clients decided they wanted a double tour? This was not unheard of, so she bided her time. He had to return soon. Her head felt fuzzy in the sunshine, probably the effects of the pills and too much alcohol, she thought.

She saw the prow of a gondola and stepped forward hopefully. It was Gino.

'Any sign of Marcello?' she asked him, as a troupe of Asian tourists, chatting animatedly together, alighted from his shiny craft. 'He's been ages.'

'Did he not return?' He looked surprised. 'It was just one lone gentleman who wanted to go out.'

'Really?' she laughed. 'Poor Marcello. Not the usual young American girls that he loves, then?'

'No, Contessa. It was just a man. A tall, dark man. He looked Italian and wasn't dressed like a tourist,' he added, musing at this oddity. 'Marcello seemed shocked to see him and they seemed to recognise one another.'

There was something about this statement that hit a nerve with Jane. No, it couldn't have been Niccolo. She was becoming paranoid. He knew nothing about Marcello. Nothing at all. Or had he seen something in those photos that had not been disguised properly? Had he recognised the gondola? No, it was impossible.

***

Jane got into bed that night in the villa in Galzignano full of trepidation. There was no sign of Niccolo. Nobody knew where he was.

The phone rang. It was her husband.

'I know what you did.' His voice was icy as he hung up.

It was all over. Her marriage. Her life. She reached for her pills and put them in her bag. She must speak to Niccolo face to face.

Dressed once more in a dark coat, she descended the stairs and walked through to the kitchen.

Paola was just finishing up her crossword and looked up in puzzlement at the sight of Jane, so obviously agitated.

'I want Antonio to take me to Venice,' she demanded.

'You want to go back again, Contessa? At this time of night? Surely you're going there tomorrow.'

'Don't question me.' Despite her anguish, Jane imperiously instructed her. 'Just tell him to bring the car around to the front door.'

She turned on her heel and disappeared before Paola could say another word.

Putting her seat slightly in the recline position, Jane thought the one-hour drive to Venice would never end. Where was Niccolo? Was he at the palazzo? The fact that he now knew about her hand in Olivia's downfall was devastating to her. She had to find him and talk to him. This was unbearable. She slipped another tranquilliser between her lips, feeling the reassuring shape of her flask of grappa in her handbag. She would save that for when she got to the palazzo.

Climbing out of the Range Rover at Piazzale Roma and boarding a water taxi, she gave the address to the driver and bent forward as she entered the little cabin for the journey down the Grand Canal.

'Pull in here,' she demanded, and the motor launch glided to a stop at the dock beneath the palazzo. She alighted, tipping him generously on top of the hefty amount he already charged.

Exiting the lift into the *piano nobile*, she was approached by an anxious Maria. She had obviously been talking to Paola.

'What brings you here so late, Contessa? I wasn't expecting you until tomorrow afternoon. Your bed is not yet made up; there is still some unpacking to do…' She trailed off when she saw Jane's face. 'Can I help?' She looked at Jane helplessly.

'No, Maria. Just go to bed. I won't be staying.' She paused. 'Is the conte here? Have you seen him?'

'He was here earlier today, Contessa, but I haven't seen him since. He hasn't been back this evening, as far as I know.'

'Good night then, Maria. And…' She looked at her faithful housekeeper, who had attended to her every need for the past sixteen years and who had loved Sofia like her own child. 'Thank you for everything.' Her eyes glistened and Maria was deeply uneasy.

Alone on the long terrace which overlooked the Grand Canal, Jane looked down at the dark waters below. It was late and the usual traffic had thinned out. There was only one solution to her problems.

THE LAGOON

At first, the old fisherman thought it was seaweed. The swirling tendrils just below the surface of the Venetian Lagoon appeared to be different somehow, and he shuffled his arthritic frame over to the other side of his boat to take a closer look. The sun had barely risen, and he needed to pull in the nets to get his fish to the Rialto Market in time for the early risers and restaurateurs who flocked there to ensure that they got the best of the day's catch.

"Looks like hair," he thought, craning his neck further over the side.

The shock of what he saw made him fall backwards into the boat, hurting his shoulder. He pulled himself upright again with difficulty and peered carefully over the side. He had not been mistaken. Long blond hair was floating on the dark waters of the lagoon and he could clearly see that a dead body was visible just below the surface.

CHAPTER THIRTY-NINE
OLIVIA

Francesca sat with Olivia, who shook all over.

'It seems that there was some trouble between Nick and a gondolier in Venice. The gondolier ended up dead.'

Olivia knew already that it was Marcello. It was all over the Internet, on Twitter and the various newsfeeds. 'GONDOLIER DROWNED IN VENICE!' 'BODY OF GONDOLIER RECOVERED IN VENICE LAGOON!' There was no escaping the news. She kept shaking. Perhaps, she thought idly, I'm in shock.

'You're in shock, Olivia,' confirmed Francesca, topping up her cup of tea solicitously. 'We all are. Paul has just headed off to the airport to find a flight, or two flights if necessary, to take him to Venice immediately. Nick will want a family member there.'

Olivia was silent, except for the chattering of her teeth.

'Of course, they won't keep Nick overnight at the Questura. He'll be allowed home, but they'll take his passport and he won't be permitted to leave Venice. They'll soon realise, if they haven't by now, that Niccolo is no killer. He is insisting it was an unfortunate accident and I am sure that's true. The question they're asking is why he was on the gondola in the first place. That's the strangest part of the story.'

Olivia could easily imagine why Niccolo wanted to speak to Marcello but said little.

'Sorry, Francesca. But I think I need to have a lie down. I'm exhausted and pretty freaked out about this. It must have happened around the time I was leaving.'

She stood and went over to The Mews, where her, as yet, unpacked suitcases awaited her. Unpacking just the things she needed immediately, she went upstairs and lay on the bed fully clothed. Before she knew it, she awoke, and everything was dark and silent.

She had become accustomed to the constant sound of water lapping at the side of the fondamenta when she was in Venice, so this deep silence was strange and unfamiliar.

Staring into the darkness, she thought about Niccolo and Marcello. What had happened? There were so many things she did not understand. She somehow knew that the photographs of her were the key to the mystery. Jane's jealousy. She must have hired Marcello to do her dirty work. She remembered the torn underwear and the fact that she had awoken naked in her bed at Casa Antica.

But Niccolo! Had he actually killed Marcello in a fit of rage? It seemed highly unlikely that such a gentle person as Niccolo would do such a thing. He was the least likely person on the planet to raise his hand to anyone, she thought.

JANE

Nothing in this life would ever erase Jane's feelings of guilt. She was a murderer. Not deliberately, but she had certainly been involved in the deaths of two people.

First of all, her beloved daughter Sofia. If she had not had those pills that morning. If she had not been drinking the night before the accident, perhaps her reflexes would have been quicker. So, what if the lorry driver was over the limit of the hours he was allowed to drive a commercial vehicle? She knew deep down that if she had been more alert, the accident could have been avoided.

Secondly, there was Marcello. Poor Marcello, whom she had manipulated for her own ends. His attraction to Olivia, coupled with his desire for a get-rich-quick scheme had made it easy for her to lure him into her web. Now he was dead. She thought about his beautiful body, now bloated and lying in a morgue in Venice, and felt completely broken.

Then she thought about Nico. Her handsome husband who had never really loved her. She knew that he had married her because she was expecting Sofia and had loved their precious daughter with all his heart and soul. He was broken after she died and, quite rightly, blamed Jane for this turn of events. Now he stood possibly about to be charged with murder because of her mad scheme to keep him.

She could never go back. Life had to begin again if she were to rescue herself. "I can make amends to Nick when I'm better," she told herself, as she downed the contents of a plastic tumbler of warmish white wine.

Heathrow airport was a seething mass of people as Jane dragged her suitcase through the Arrivals hall. Two men waited for her: one old, supporting himself on a cane, the other young and vigorous.

'Daddy! Max!' she cried. Then threw herself into her father's arms, sobbing brokenly.

'Let's go home, darling,' her father's voice consoled her, and they left the terminal together, with Jane leaning on both of them, Max's arm protectively around her hunched shoulders.

NICCOLO

It had been a terrifying experience. He just wanted to talk to the gondolier, and how could he do that other than to hire him for a trip on the canals of Venice, his own home town? Now he was in police custody. How had this happened?

It all began with the phone call.

'I would like to book a trip on your gondola today, please. I got your number from a friend.'

'Certainly,' agreed Marcello, arranging a time.

When Niccolo arrived at Giglio, he was gratified to see the naked shock on Marcello's face when he recognised his prospective customer. Giving him no time to change his mind, Niccolo clambered across Gino's boat and settled himself on the red velvet seats of Marcello's gondola, which was tied up alongside. He placed his briefcase on the seat beside him.

Marcello felt queasy. 'I know you,' he stated, picking up his oar and positioning himself at the back of the gondola. Then he noticed the conte staring at his tattoo and bracelet and knew he had been found out.

'I want to talk to you.' Niccolo unfastened his briefcase and brought out a couple of the photographs that he had held back for this purpose. 'Just one question: why? What is between you and Olivia? I need clarity. Why would you take these photographs and send them to me?' His stomach tightened as he visualised Marcello's hands on Olivia's voluptuous body.

Marcello looked away, keeping a steady pace with his oar along the narrow canal. Niccolo could see that he was struggling with words.

'I don't want to get anyone into trouble.' He ducked his head for a moment while he navigated his way underneath a low bridge.

'You need to tell me. Otherwise, I am going to go to the licensing authority to lodge a complaint and get your licence revoked. I may even go to the police.' He proffered one of the photos. 'You see, it's your tattoo and wooden beaded bracelet. It's obviously you who took these.' He paused. 'I need to know why.'

'Ask your wife.' The words were spat with venom. Marcello had had enough of this charade. He was angry. 'She knew you were unfaithful to her.' He adopted a self-righteous tone. 'You treated her badly. She was unhappy and was afraid of losing you.' Now he had said it.

'Our marriage was over long ago.' Now it was Niccolo's turn to feel outrage. 'But why the photos of Olivia? Were you having an affair with her?'

'No, unfortunately.' He ran his hand through his hair and tweaked the elastic band holding his ponytail in place. 'Those were Jane's idea. She was desperate, you need to understand. She needed Olivia out of your life and felt that these photos would do the trick. And it worked,' he gloated.

'But the photos look consensual… wait a moment. Are you saying that Olivia was set up? Was she drugged? Did you drug her?' His voice was loud and pedestrians along the canal-side looked at them curiously. 'Did Jane pay you?' He brought out the two bank receipts and waved them at the gondolier.

Marcello was silent. Niccolo stood up to face him, causing the gondola to tilt dangerously. 'You low life. How could you try to ruin a woman like

Olivia?' He stepped menacingly towards the gondolier, who swung the oar in his direction to try to fend him off.

Niccolo grabbed the oar just in time to prevent himself from falling into the murky water and they struggled to keep upright. Spectators gathered on the canal-side, watching the spectacle with amazement. A few photos were taken by tourists, agog at the drama unfolding before their eyes.

Just then, a heavy barge carrying building materials swept past, creating a large wave that made the gondola wobble just enough to tip Marcello, who was grappling with the oar, into the murky water, where he was sucked under the barge and promptly disappeared beneath its bulk.

A police launch and ambulance arrived within minutes, obviously alerted by a bystander or two. Marcello had disappeared without trace and the conte was taken to the Questura for questioning. Luckily, there were plenty of witnesses to vouch for the fact that the gondolier had been the one to swing his oar in Niccolo's direction, although the Polizia were obviously sceptical, as it is highly unusual for a gondolier to drown; in fact, it is virtually unheard of.

Later that evening, Niccolo was escorted home in a police launch, to be greeted by Maria, who told him that Jane had packed a suitcase and asked Marco to take her to the airport. She had left him.

He sat at the kitchen table, a large glass of wine and a small dish of Maria's creamy *baccala mantacata* in front of him, just thinking. Thinking about Jane and Olivia and what a mess he had made of everything. His lack of love for Jane and their emotionally draining marriage. His doubting Olivia, his mistrust. How would he ever make it up to these women that he had treated so badly and whose lives he had turned upside down? He realised that Jane must have been at her wits' end to have resorted to such a sordid plan, and that Olivia must hate him for disbelieving her.

He thought about the fact that Jane had returned to England to be with her father and son. They would look after her, and he fully intended to keep in touch and to tell her that he forgave her for everything and that he hoped her life would be better, now that she was with family who obviously loved her. He recognised that his marriage was over. There was no going back

273

now. He hoped that she would find happiness elsewhere, but first she needed to mend.

Niccolo needed a strong, stable woman in his life. Olivia. Would she forgive him? He stumbled to bed, in his newly refurbished bedroom, which made him think even more about the woman he had lost. He did not sleep.

Next morning, early, Marcello's bloated remains were discovered by a local fisherman, far out in the Lagoon where the tide had taken him. His mother was waiting at the morgue when he was wheeled in for identification. Her beautiful son. She screamed with sorrow at her loss.

OLIVIA

One week later, and Olivia was getting back into the swing of being in Dublin once more. She kept her head down and concentrated on a burst of creative social media to announce her return to the business world and began to draw up a plan of action for her future.

She tried not to think too much about Niccolo and all the problems he was facing in Venice. Francesca had told her that Jane had left him and that he was at home in the palazzo and Paul was with him for support.

'Niccolo has not been charged with anything to do with that gondolier's death.' Francesca had popped over for a cup of tea and a chat, a late afternoon visit which had become fairly routine if they were both at home. 'Thank heaven for tourists with their cameras. It was obviously an accident, so he's in the clear, but very depressed about everything.' She paused. 'I wish you could have met Sofia. What a special little girl.'

They sipped tea companionably in The Mews. The kitchen was cosy, and the Aga belched heat and comforting smells of cooking. Olivia was in a cooking frenzy these days. Ever since her sojourn in Venice, she had begun to love the art and was constantly experimenting.

'Would you like some of my biscotti with that?' she asked, bringing over a plateful of hard, almond biscuits from a side table, where they had been cooling on a wire rack.

'How could I resist?' Francesca was already reaching for one.

A crunch on the cobblestones outside prefaced the sound of a letter dropping into the slot on the front door. Olivia went to fetch it.

The postmark indicated that it was from Venice and she recognised the writing on the front as from Niccolo. She put it on the dresser to read later, not in front of Francesca, who was happily nibbling her second biscotti.

After Francesca had departed, Olivia took the letter down from the shelf and took it to the kitchen table. She sat and looked at it for a while, examining its Italian stamp. She knew it must be important, but would the news be good or bad? She opened it with dread.

Olivia.

I now know the whole story. Please try to find it in your heart to forgive
me.

I love you.
Niccolo

Olivia spent a great deal of the following day thinking about Niccolo's brief letter. So, he had found out the truth. She had been sexually assaulted by Marcello, the man she had thought of as her friend. It was a shocking betrayal.

"He should have believed me," she thought. But she knew that the photographic evidence pointed to her faithlessness and she could not really blame him for having backed away from her at that point. He was accustomed to being mistrustful of women, and she knew there was a sort of innocence about him that made her heart warm, and she felt a stab of compassion. He had been through so much.

Later that evening, Olivia prepared for bed. The luxury of a deep, foam-filled bath was something she had begun to enjoy once more after almost five months of only showering, as Casa Antica did not possess a bath. Towelling herself dry, she smoothed scented Italian body cream all over her body and slid her long, silk negligee over her head. The bed looked cosy with its white bed-linen. The bedside light was on and her book awaited her. She slid between the sheets and picked it up.

Lying back against her mound of pillows in the half-dark, she was startled to hear a car pull up outside. She put down her book and listened.

Footsteps crunched on the cobbles outside. She slipped out of bed and slid her feet into her furry mules, hurriedly donning her creamy silk robe. She slipped downstairs to see who it was arriving at her home at midnight. Her bedroom faced away from the courtyard; and anyway, she would not want to be seen at the window.

There was silence as she tried to peer out into the night.

The sudden peal of the doorbell shattered the silence.

'Who's there?' Her voice sounded anxious.

'It's Niccolo.'

She opened the door, and, for a long moment, they stood there in the doorway, just looking at one another. Words were unnecessary.

The time for talking would be tomorrow. Tonight, they would begin to heal their wounds.

Her robe slipped to the floor like a cream silken drift.

THE END